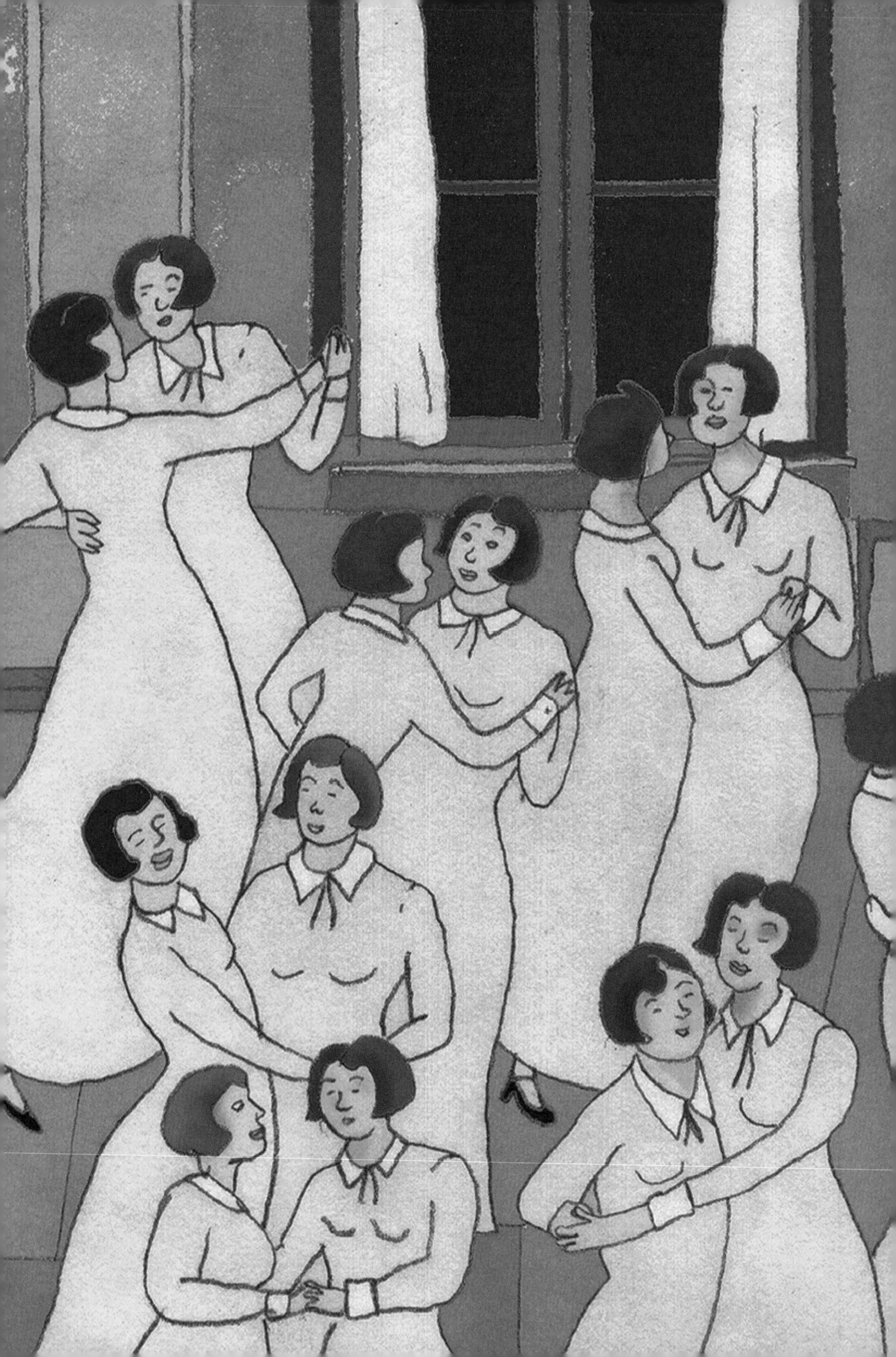

Jamilti & Other Stories

Rutu Modan

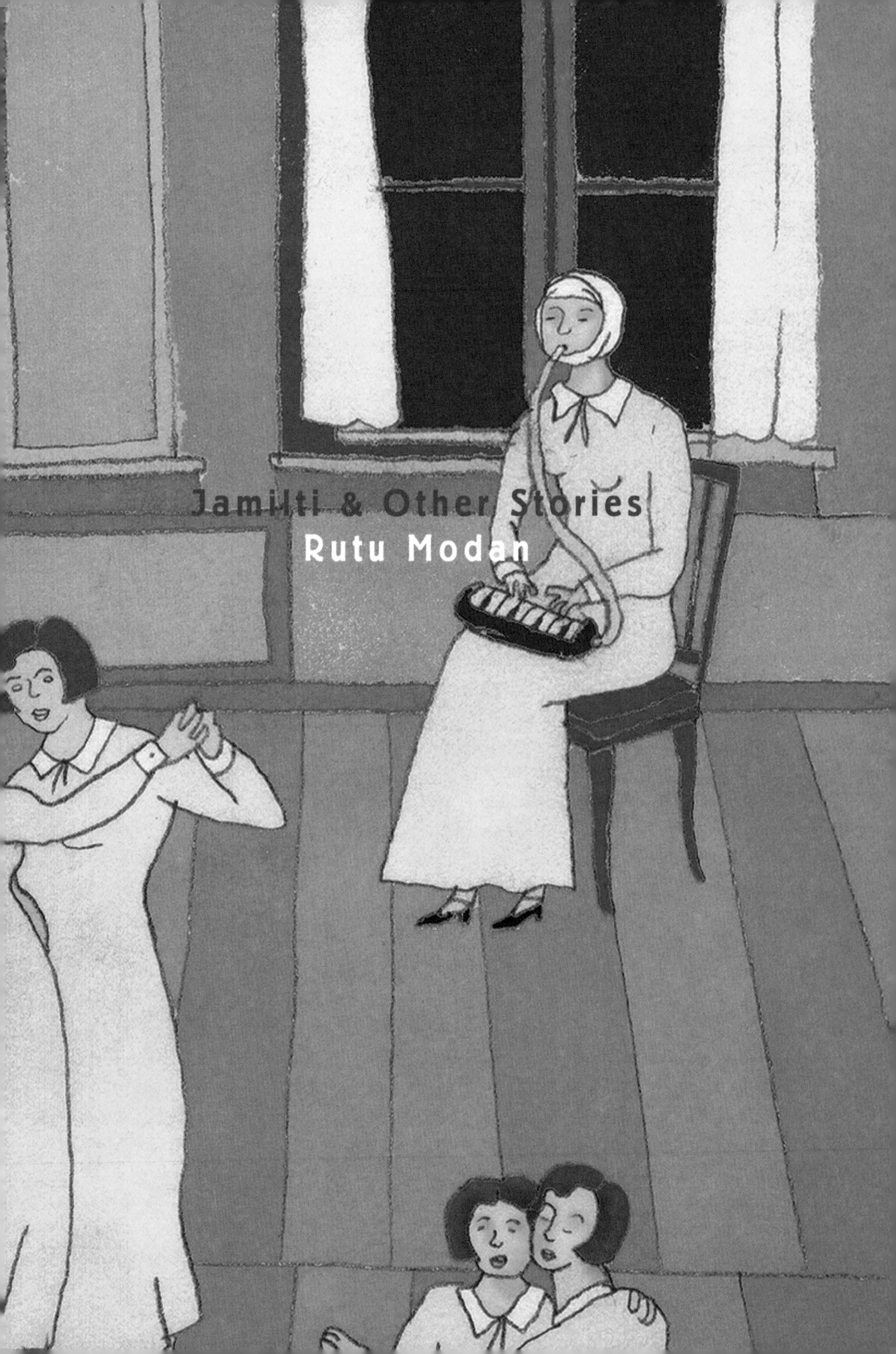

Entire contents © copyright 1998–2008 by Rutu Modan. All rights reserved. No part of this book (except small portions for review purposes) may be reproduced in any form without written permission from Rutu Modan or Drawn & Quarterly. Drawn & Quarterly; Post Office Box 48056, Montreal, Quebec, Canada H2V 4S8. www.drawnandquarterly.com; First Hardcover edition: August 2008. Printed in Singapore. 10 9 8 7 6 5 4 3 2 1; Library and Archives Canada Cataloguing in Publication; Modan, Rutu; Jamilti and other stories / Rutu Modan.; ISBN 978-1-897299-54-8; I. Title.; PN6790.I73M63 2008   741.5'95694   C2008-903102-4; Distributed in the USA and abroad by Farrar, Straus and Giroux; 18 West 18th Street, New York, NY 10011; Orders: 888.330.8477. Distributed in Canada by Raincoast Books; 9050 Shaughnessy Street, Vancouver, BC V6P 6E5; Orders: 800.663.5714; All the stories were originally published by Actus Independent Comics (actustragicus.com). Translation credits: "Energy Blockage", "The Panty Killer" and "King of the Lillies" by Noah Stollman; "Bygone, Homecoming", "Fan", and "Jamilti" by Jesse Mishori.

Jamilti & Other Stories
Rutu Modan

drawn & quarterly
montréal

To Lilian

מביתי לביתך המרחק קילומטר
מליבי לליבך אף לא מילימטר

JAMILTI

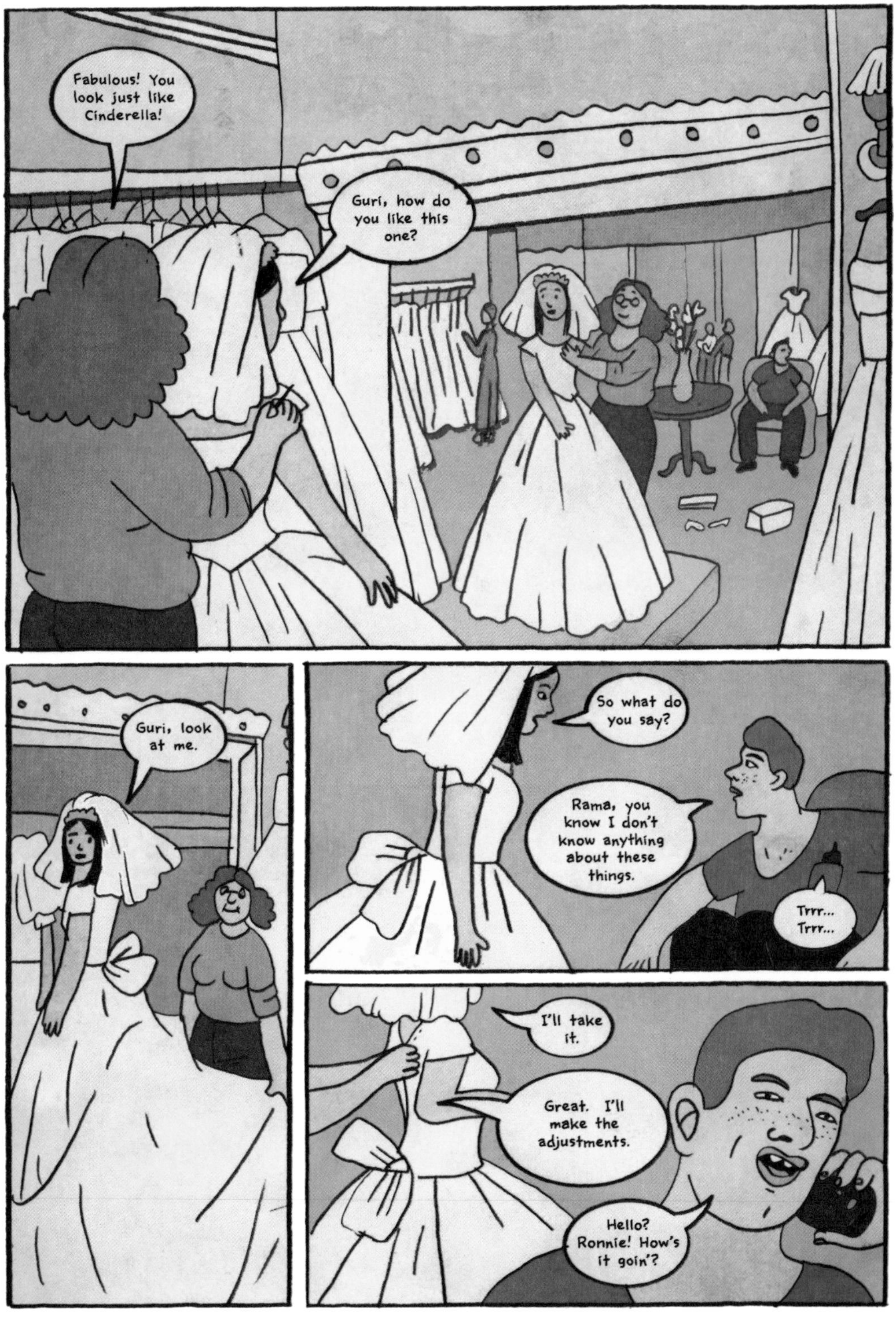
Fabulous! You look just like Cinderella!
Guri, how do you like this one?
Guri, look at me.
So what do you say?
Rama, you know I don't know anything about these things.
Trrr... Trrr...
I'll take it.
Great. I'll make the adjustments.
Hello? Ronnie! How's it goin'?

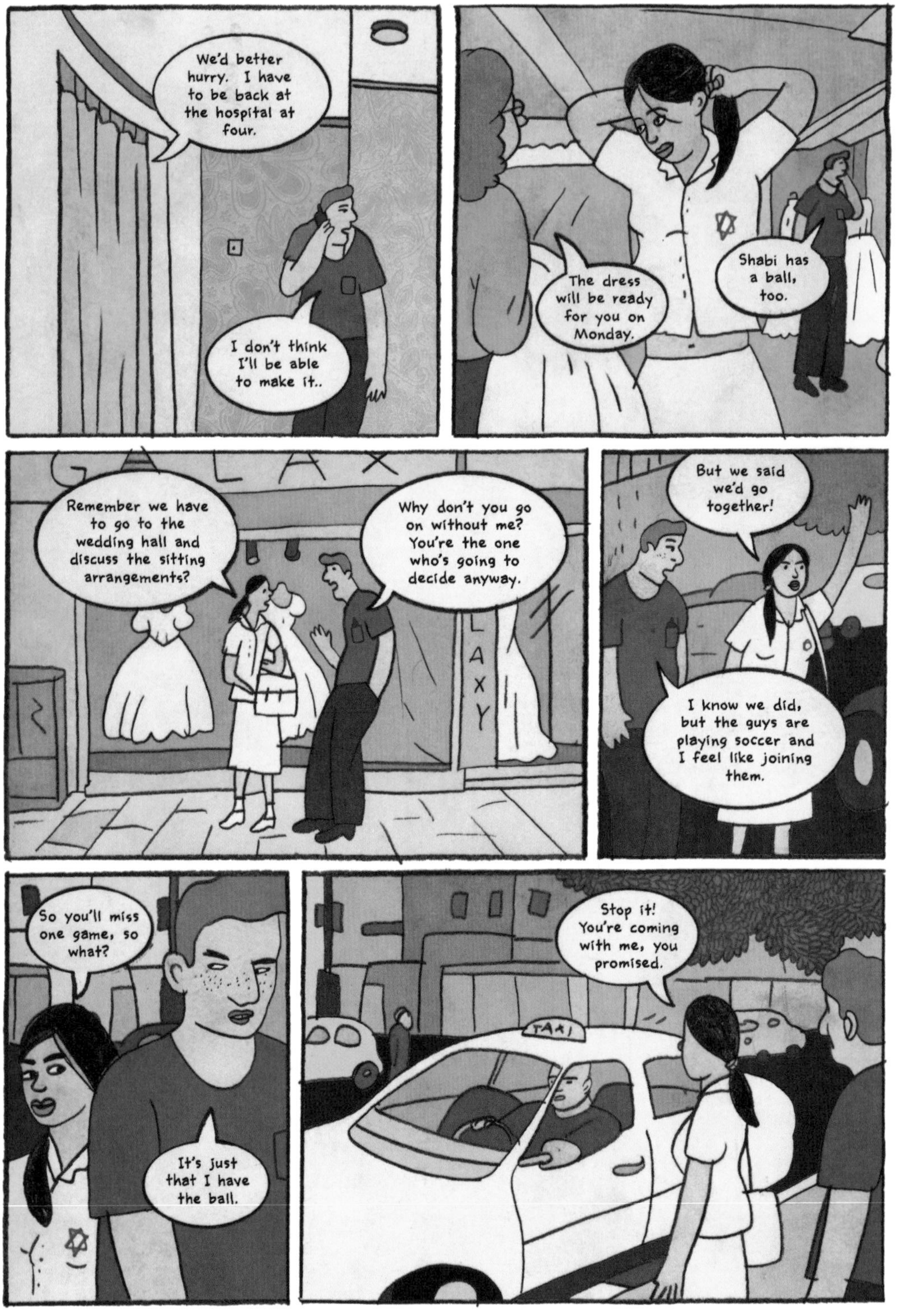
We'd better hurry. I have to be back at the hospital at four.
I don't think I'll be able to make it..
The dress will be ready for you on Monday.
Shabi has a ball, too.
Remember we have to go to the wedding hall and discuss the sitting arrangements?
Why don't you go on without me? You're the one who's going to decide anyway.
But we said we'd go together!
I know we did, but the guys are playing soccer and I feel like joining them.
So you'll miss one game, so what?
It's just that I have the ball.
Stop it! You're coming with me, you promised.

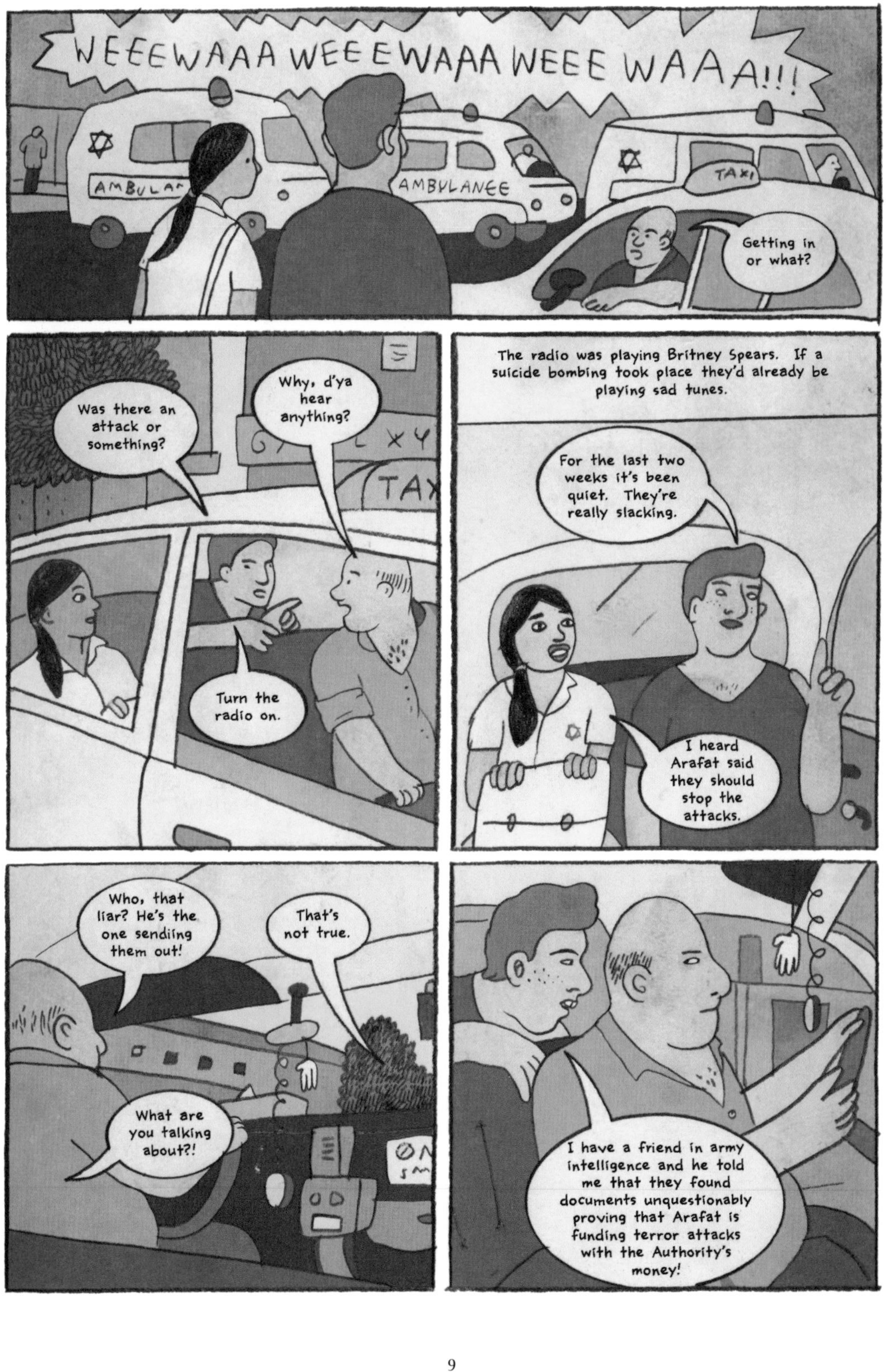
WEEEWAAA WEEEWAAA WEEE WAAA!!!
AMBULANCE
TAXI
Getting in or what?
Was there an attack or something?
Why, d'ya hear anything?
Turn the radio on.
The radio was playing Britney Spears. If a suicide bombing took place they'd already be playing sad tunes.
For the last two weeks it's been quiet. They're really slacking.
I heard Arafat said they should stop the attacks.
Who, that liar? He's the one sendiing them out!
That's not true.
What are you talking about?!
I have a friend in army intelligence and he told me that they found documents unquestionably proving that Arafat is funding terror attacks with the Authority's money!

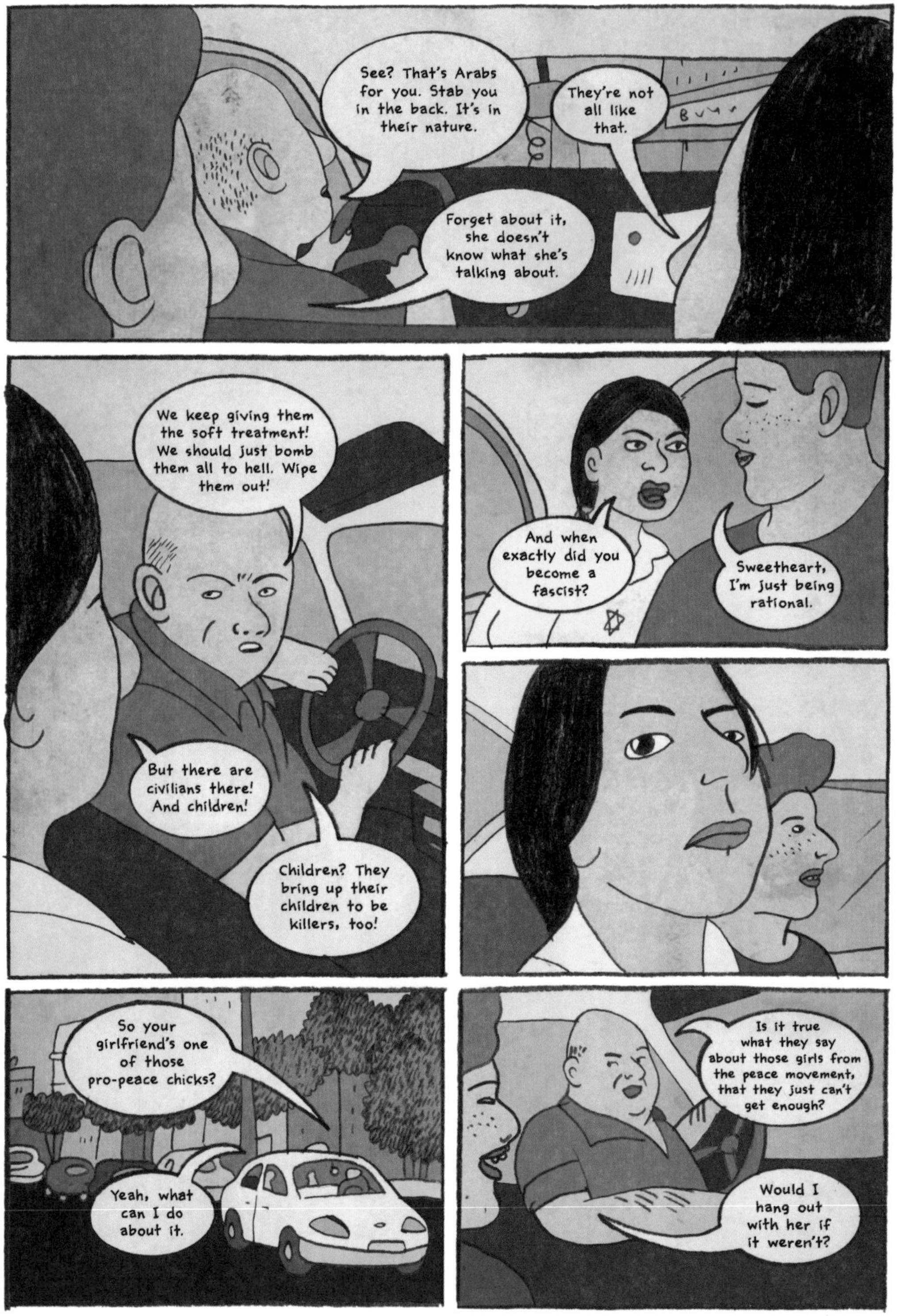
See? That's Arabs for you. Stab you in the back. It's in their nature.
They're not all like that.
Forget about it, she doesn't know what she's talking about.
We keep giving them the soft treatment! We should just bomb them all to hell. Wipe them out!
But there are civilians there! And children!
Children? They bring up their children to be killers, too!
And when exactly did you become a fascist?
Sweetheart, I'm just being rational.
So your girlfriend's one of those pro-peace chicks?
Yeah, what can I do about it.
Is it true what they say about those girls from the peace movement, that they just can't get enough?
Would I hang out with her if it weren't?

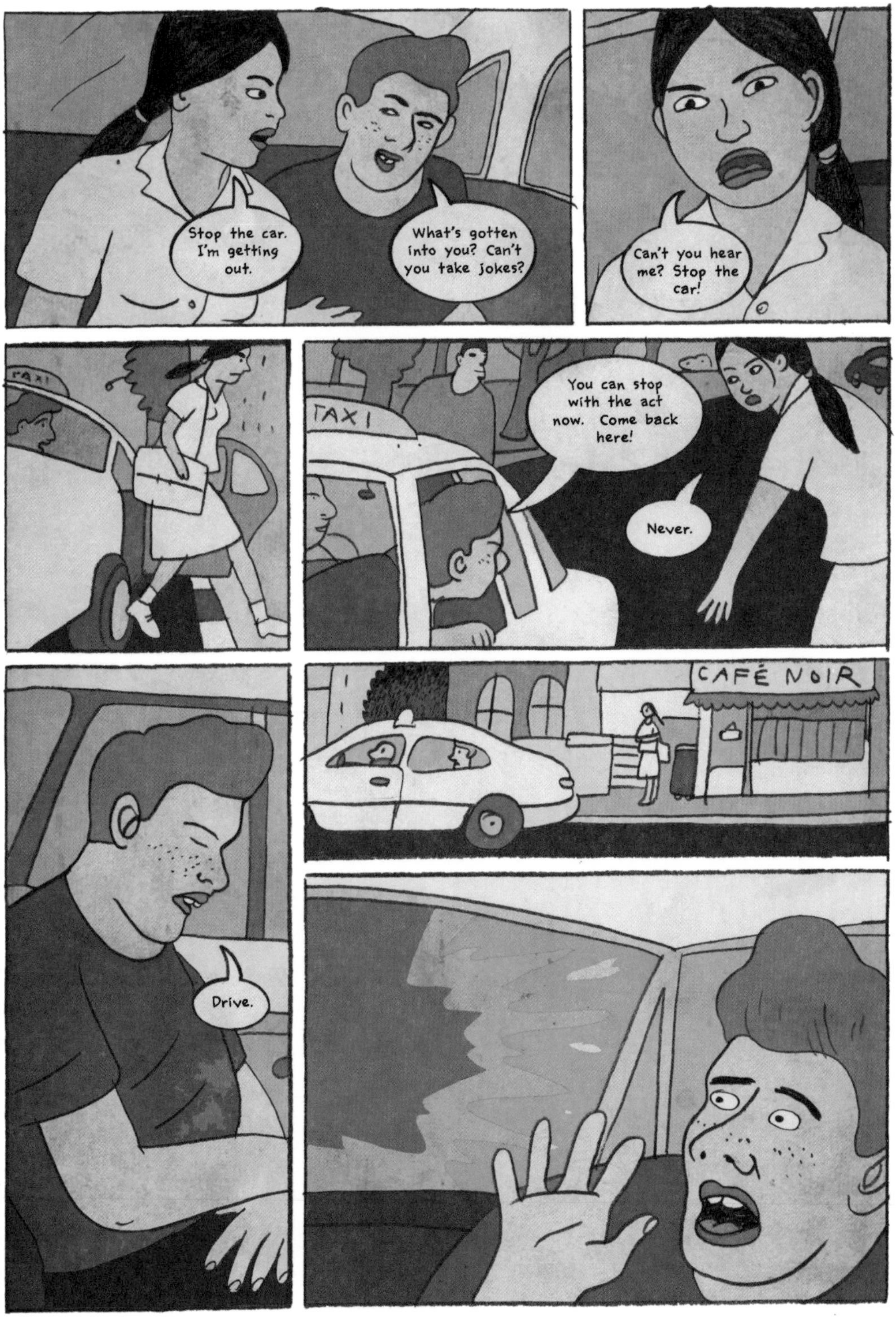
Stop the car. I'm getting out.
What's gotten into you? Can't you take jokes?
Can't you hear me? Stop the car!
TAXI
TAXI
You can stop with the act now. Come back here!
Never.
Drive.
CAFÉ NOIR

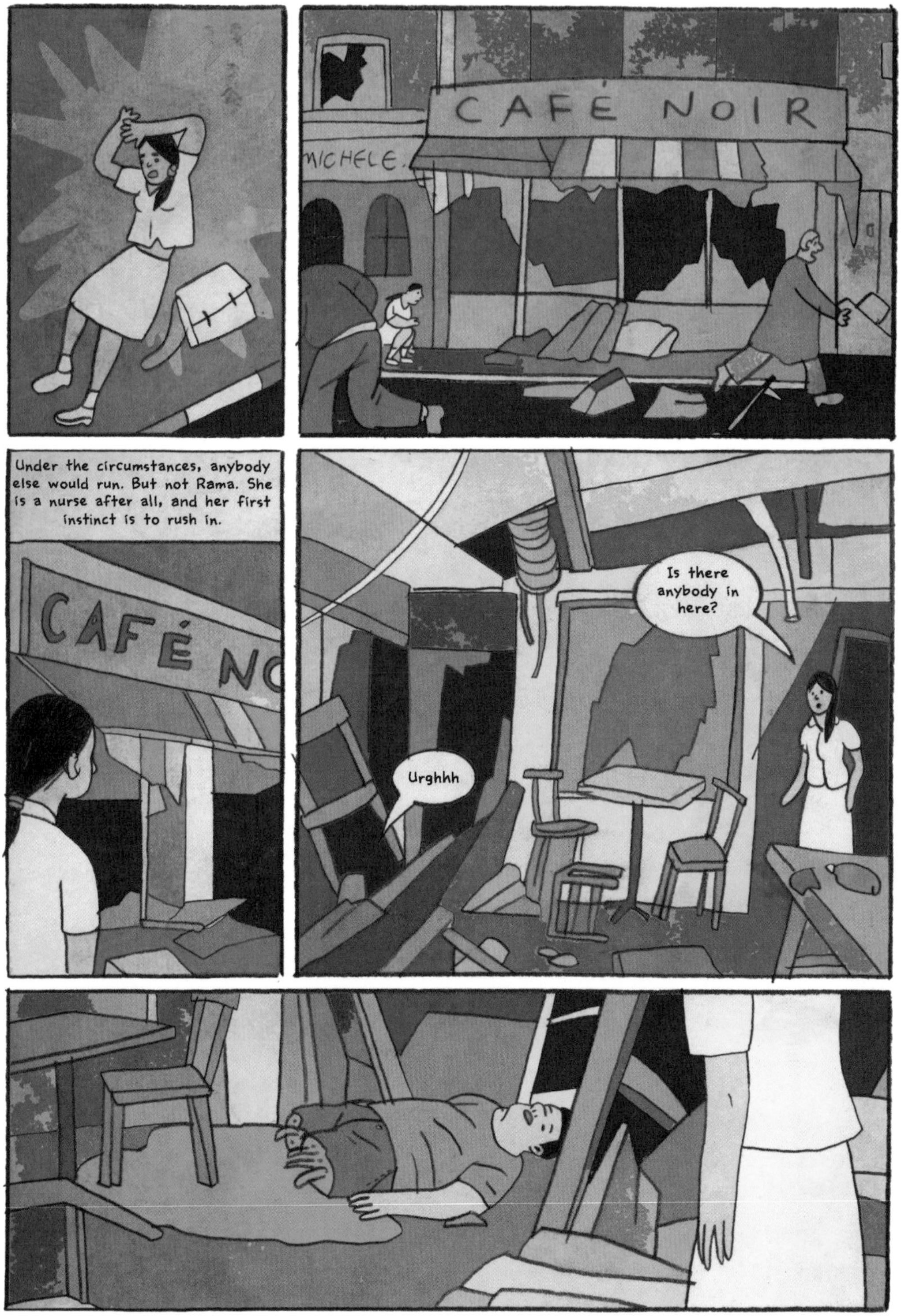
CAFÉ NOIR
MICHELE.
Under the circumstances, anybody else would run. But not Rama. She is a nurse after all, and her first instinct is to rush in.
CAFÉ NO
Is there anybody in here?
Urghhh

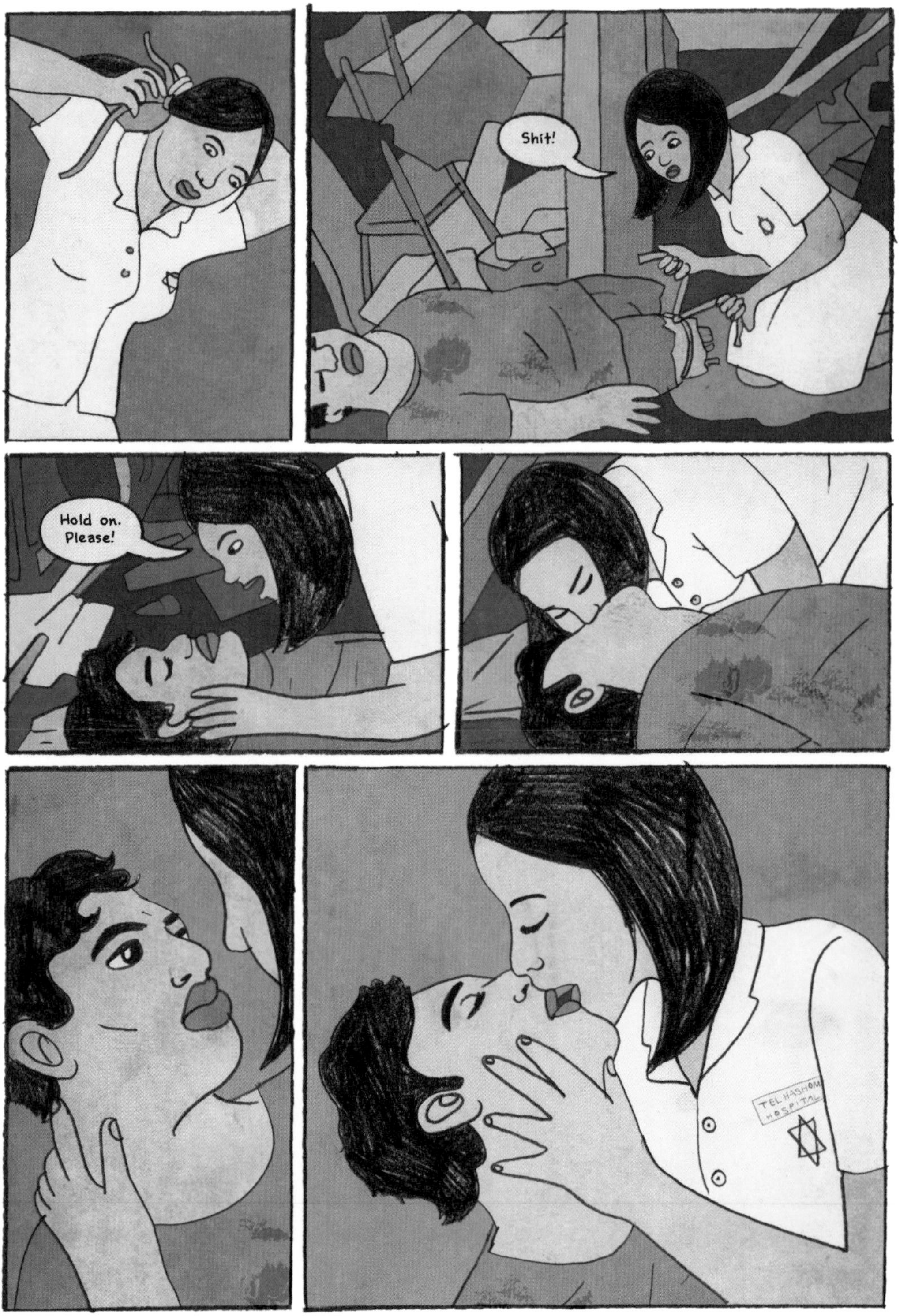
Shit!
Hold on. Please!
TEL HASHOM
HOSPITAL

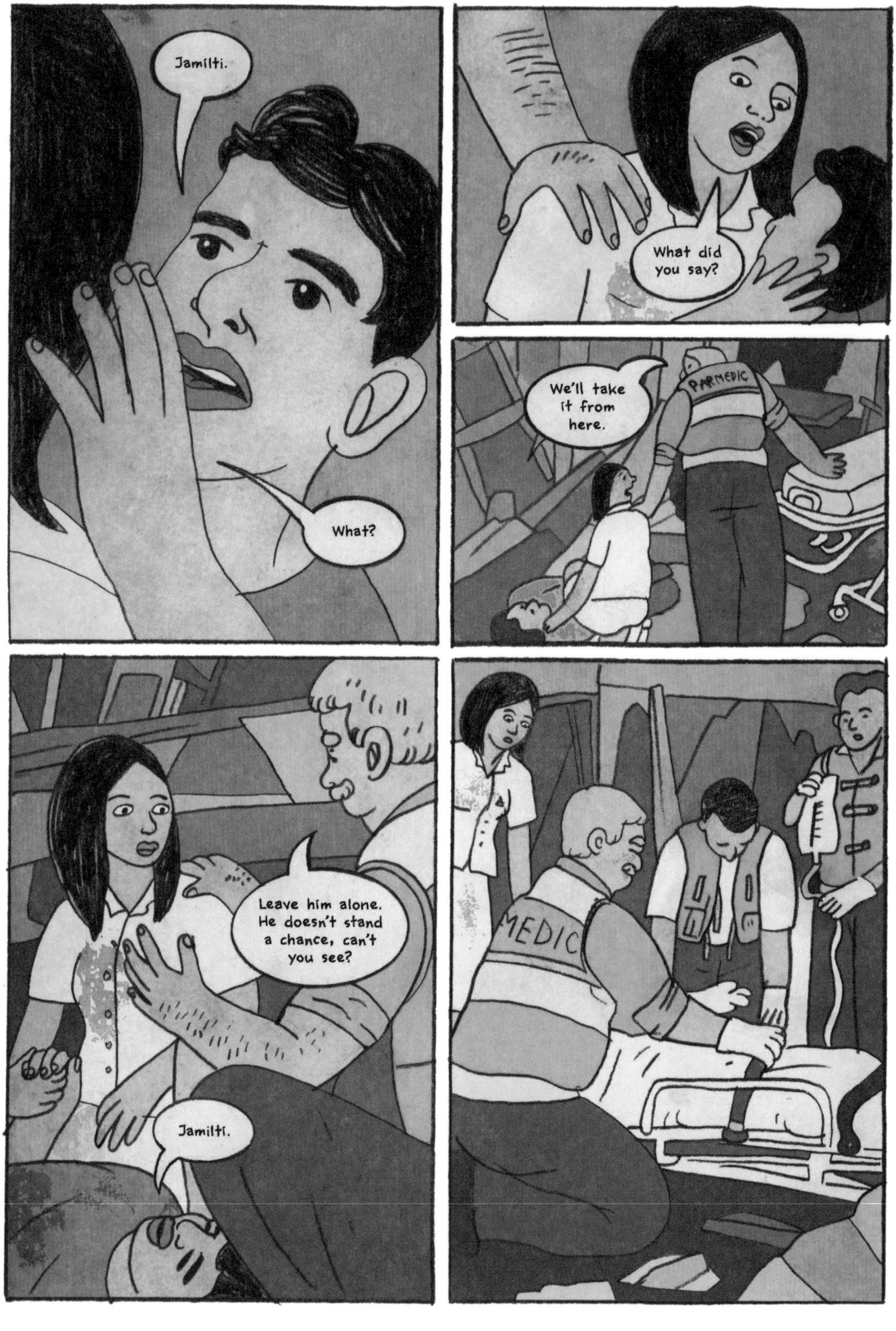
Jamilti.
What?
What did you say?
We'll take it from here.
PARMEDIC
Leave him alone. He doesn't stand a chance, can't you see?
Jamilti.
MEDIC

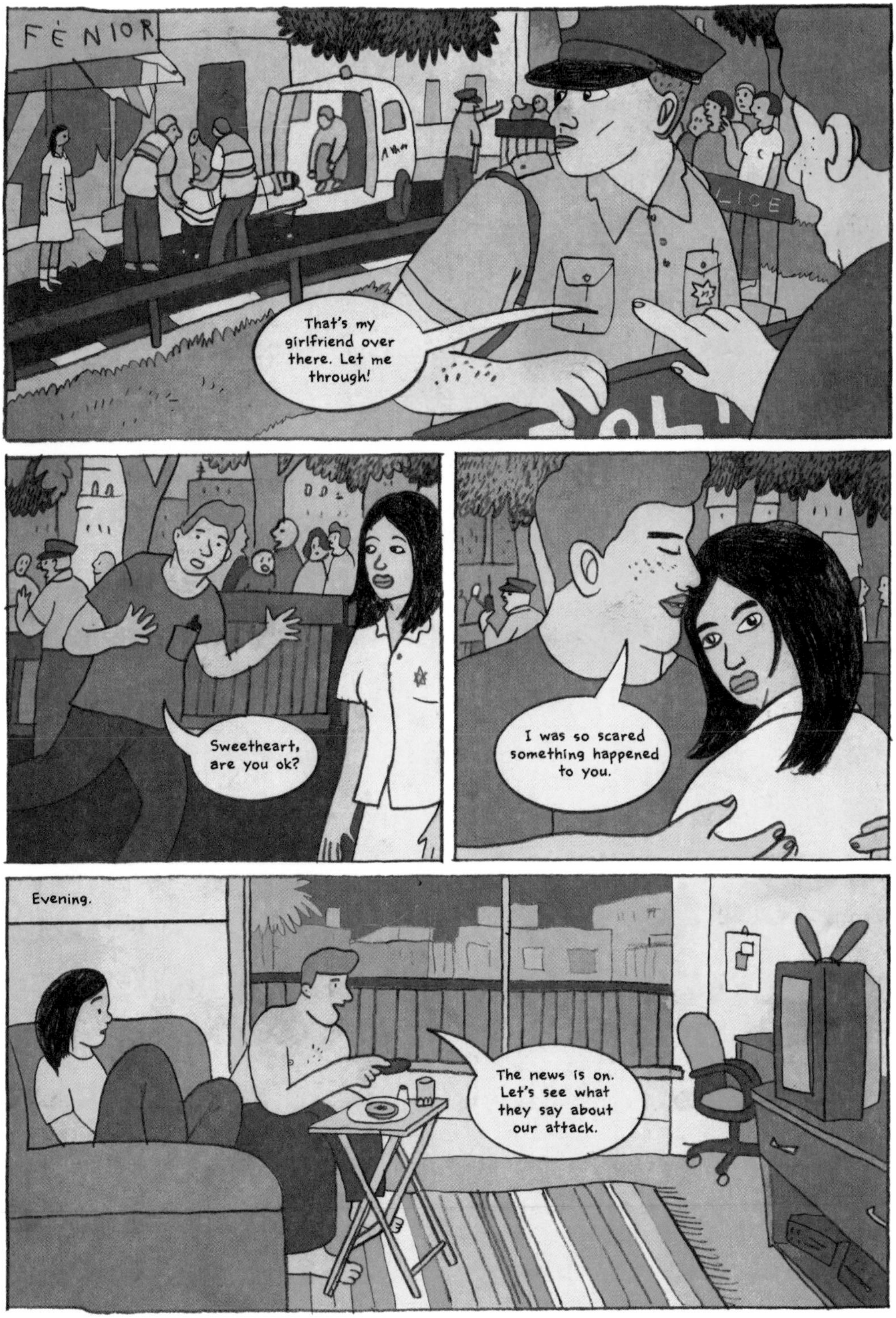

That's my girlfriend over there. Let me through!
Sweetheart, are you ok?
I was so scared something happened to you.
Evening.
The news is on. Let's see what they say about our attack.

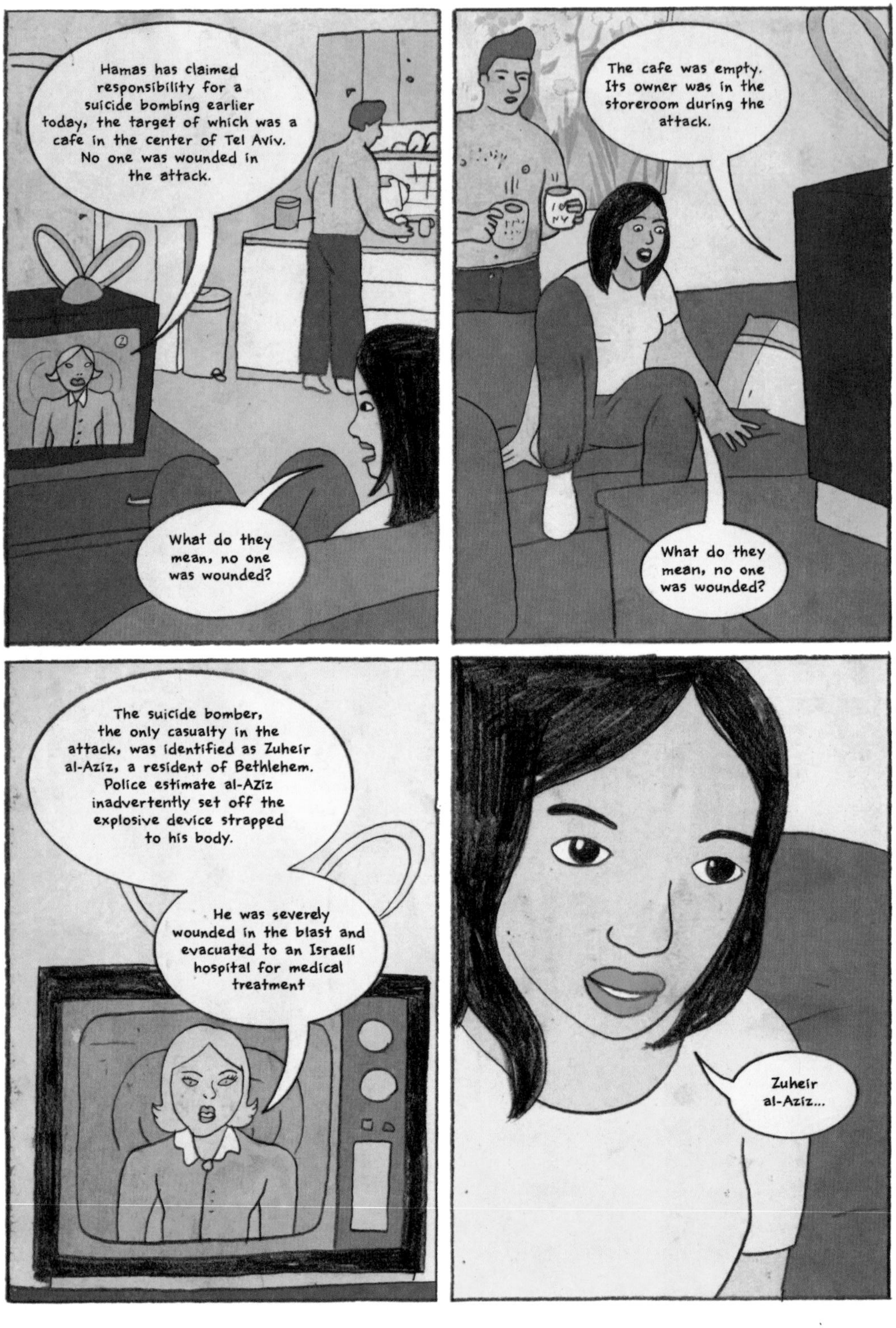
Hamas has claimed responsibility for a suicide bombing earlier today, the target of which was a cafe in the center of Tel Aviv. No one was wounded in the attack.
What do they mean, no one was wounded?
The cafe was empty. Its owner was in the storeroom during the attack.
What do they mean, no one was wounded?
The suicide bomber, the only casualty in the attack, was identified as Zuheir al-Aziz, a resident of Bethlehem. Police estimate al-AZiz inadvertently set off the explosive device strapped to his body.
He was severely wounded in the blast and evacuated to an Israeli hospital for medical treatment
Zuheir al-Aziz...

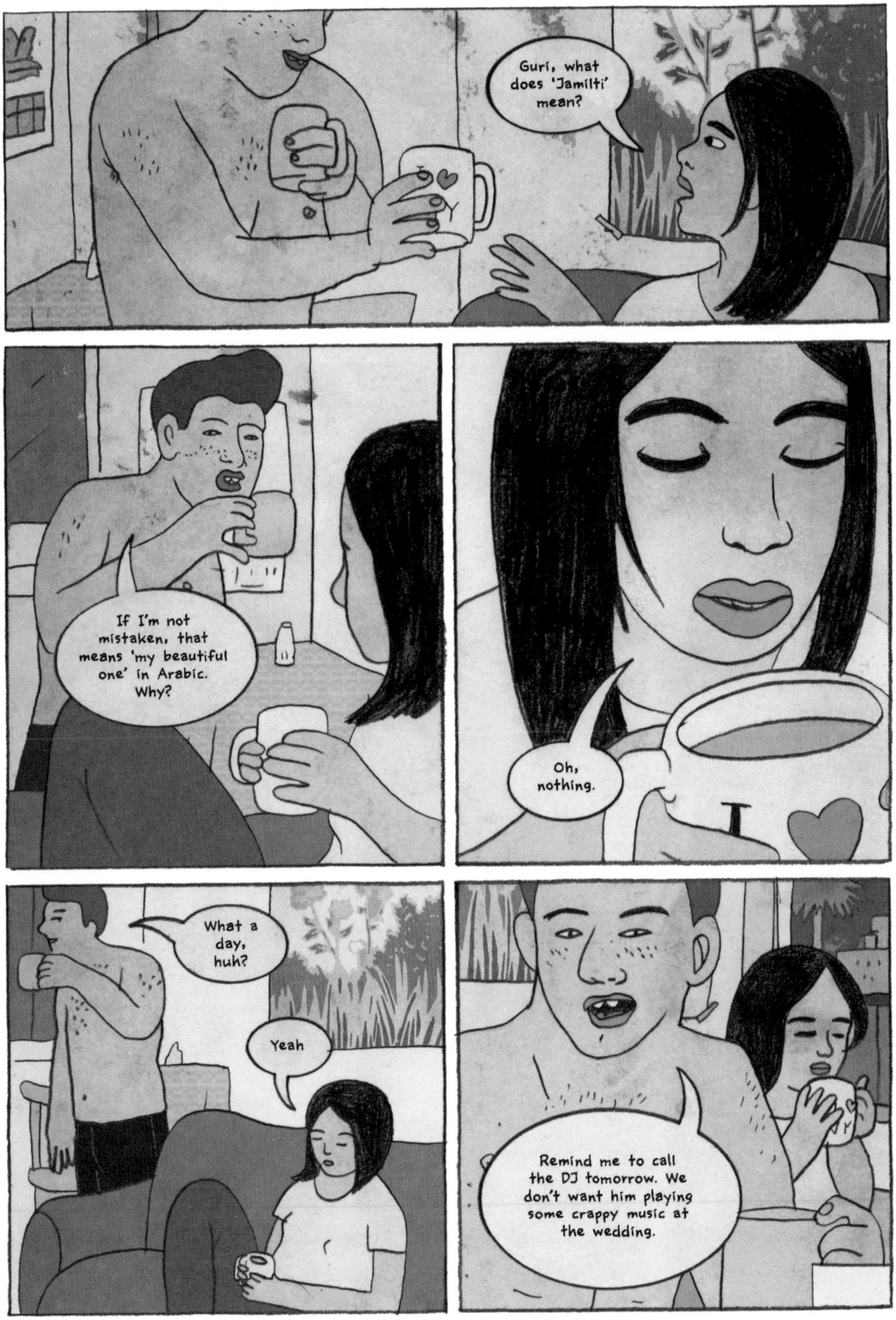
Guri, what does 'Jamilti' mean?
If I'm not mistaken, that means 'my beautiful one' in Arabic. Why?
Oh, nothing.
What a day, huh?
Yeah
Remind me to call the DJ tomorrow. We don't want him playing some crappy music at the wedding.

ENERGY BLOCKAGE

Some jerk meets a broad, she falls for him, it goes to his head and he walks out on his wife, leaves her with two little girls. They don't hear a word from him for fifteen years.

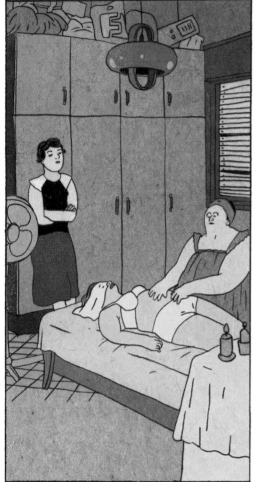

The wife swallows some pills and almost croaks.

Do you feel the current?

Yes... Oh yes!

Almost? She croaks, all right. Brain dead, then comes back to life. But it all worked out for the best.

That means she's located the problematic area with her energies...

Because while she was lying there dead she had a vision. She saw the light, encountered spectral beings from the beyond, and woke up with healing powers. Electricity in her hands that can cure any sickness.

You can get up now. The session is over.

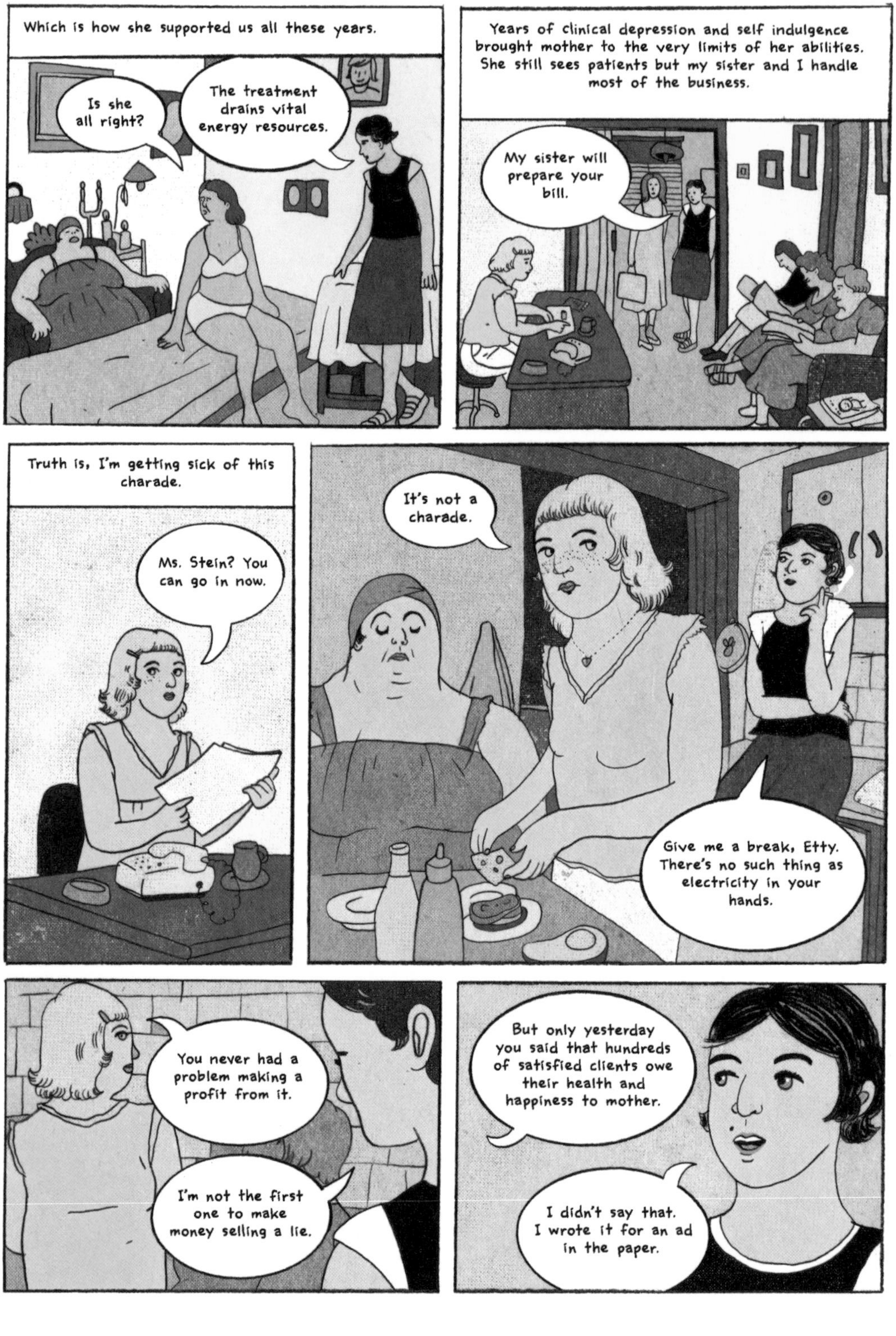

Which is how she supported us all these years.
Is she all right?
The treatment drains vital energy resources.
Years of clinical depression and self indulgence brought mother to the very limits of her abilities. She still sees patients but my sister and I handle most of the business.
My sister will prepare your bill.
Truth is, I'm getting sick of this charade.
Ms. Stein? You can go in now.
It's not a charade.
Give me a break, Etty. There's no such thing as electricity in your hands.
You never had a problem making a profit from it.
I'm not the first one to make money selling a lie.
But only yesterday you said that hundreds of satisfied clients owe their health and happiness to mother.
I didn't say that. I wrote it for an ad in the paper.

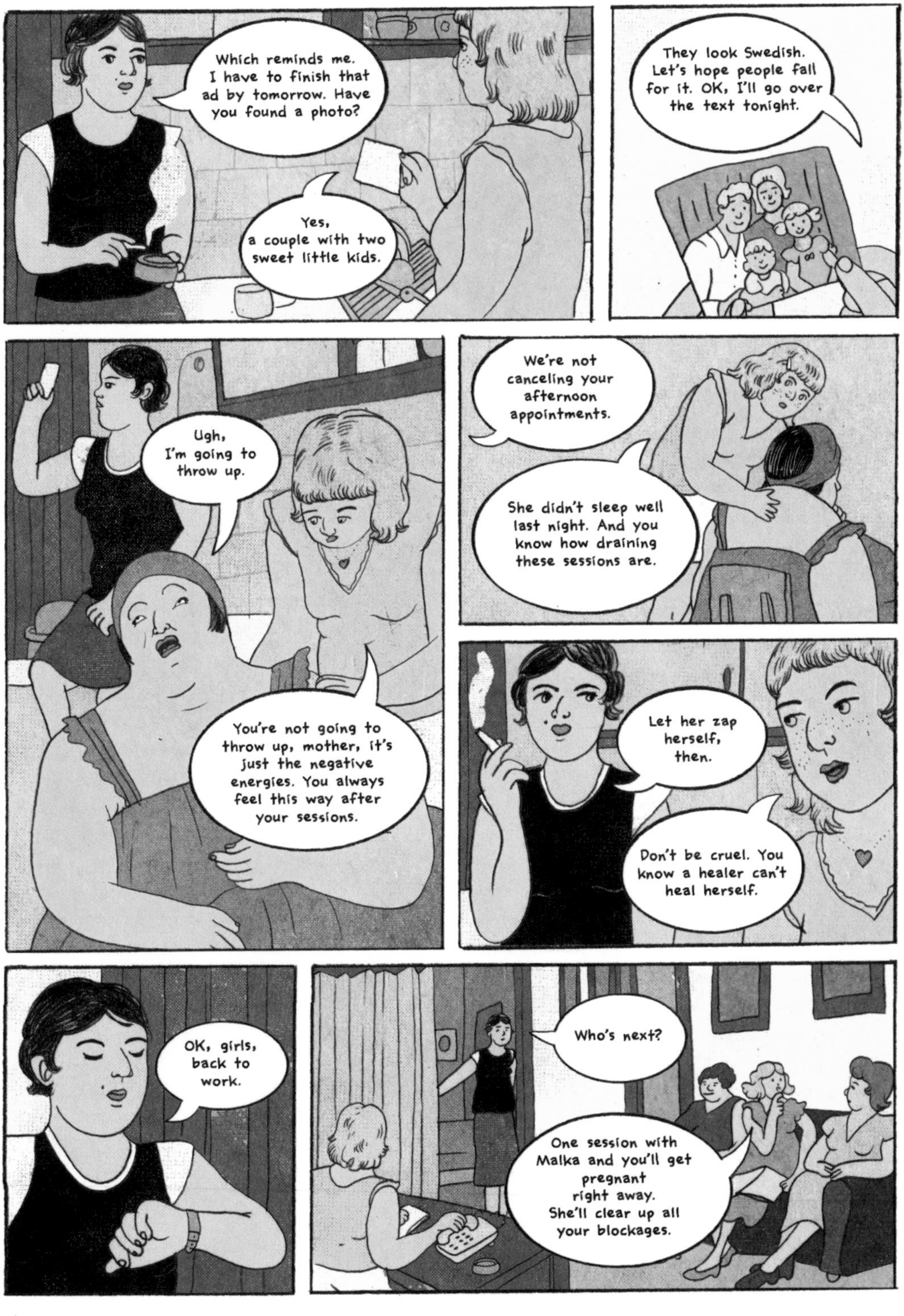
Which reminds me. I have to finish that ad by tomorrow. Have you found a photo?
Yes, a couple with two sweet little kids.
They look Swedish. Let's hope people fall for it. OK, I'll go over the text tonight.
Ugh, I'm going to throw up.
You're not going to throw up, mother, it's just the negative energies. You always feel this way after your sessions.
We're not canceling your afternoon appointments.
She didn't sleep well last night. And you know how draining these sessions are.
Let her zap herself, then.
Don't be cruel. You know a healer can't heal herself.
OK, girls, back to work.
Who's next?
One session with Malka and you'll get pregnant right away. She'll clear up all your blockages.

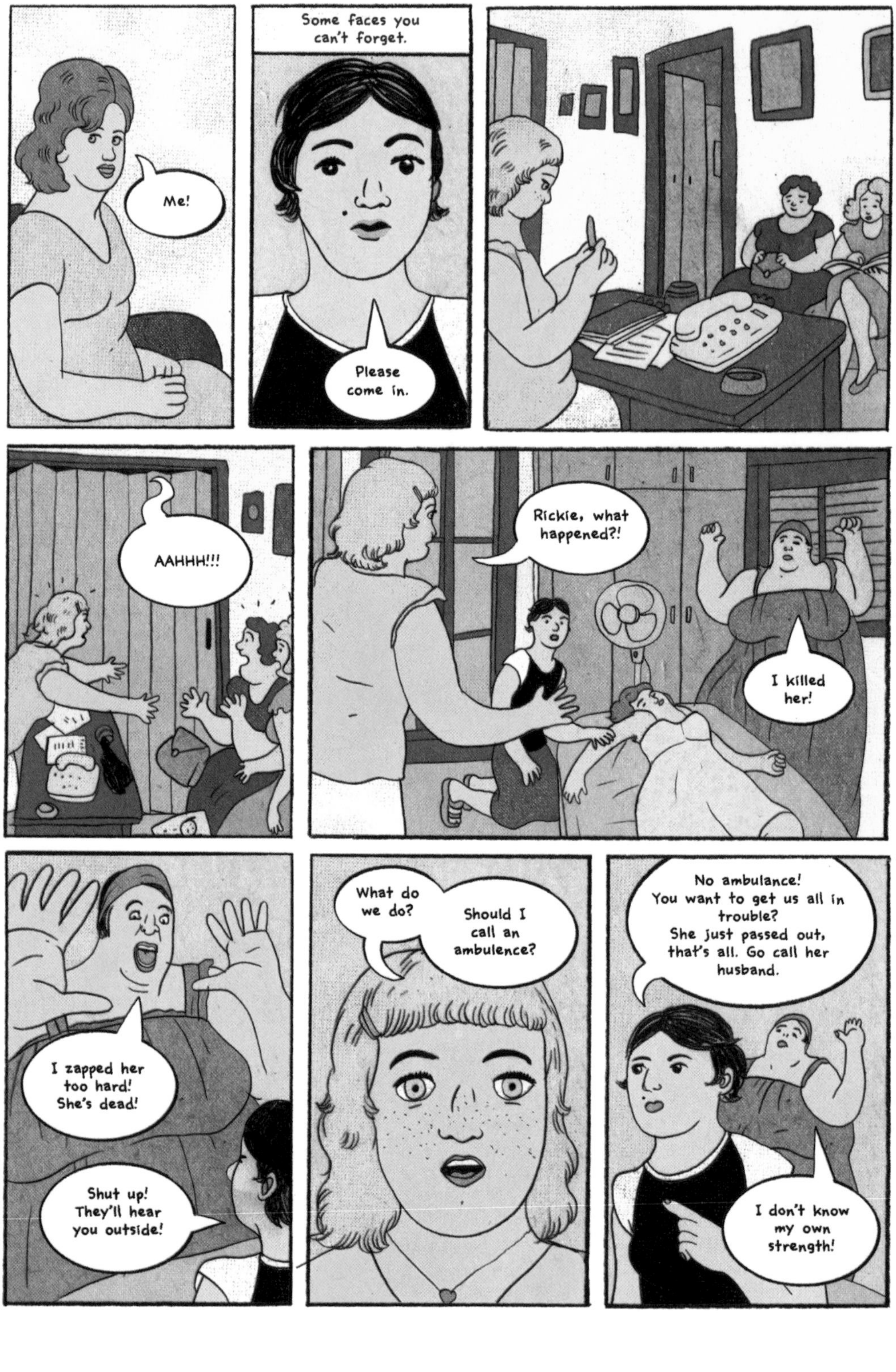
Me!
Some faces you can't forget.
Please come in.
AAHHH!!!
Rickie, what happened?!
I killed her!
I zapped her too hard! She's dead!
Shut up! They'll hear you outside!
What do we do?
Should I call an ambulence?
No ambulance! You want to get us all in trouble? She just passed out, that's all. Go call her husband.
I don't know my own strength!

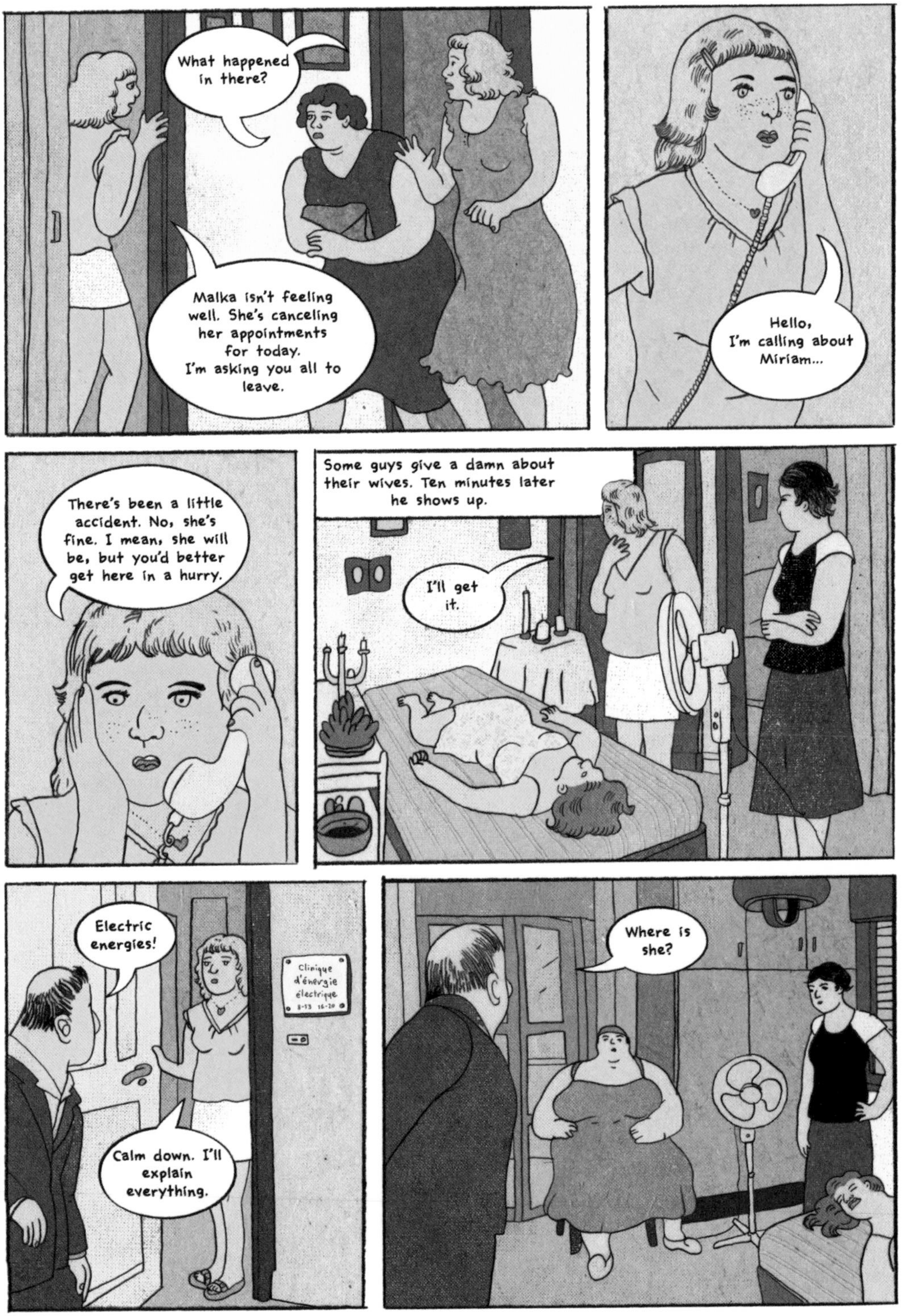

What happened in there?
Malka isn't feeling well. She's canceling her appointments for today. I'm asking you all to leave.
Hello, I'm calling about Miriam...
There's been a little accident. No, she's fine. I mean, she will be, but you'd better get here in a hurry.
Some guys give a damn about their wives. Ten minutes later he shows up.
I'll get it.
Electric energies!
Clinique d'énergie électrique 8-13 16-20
Calm down. I'll explain everything.
Where is she?

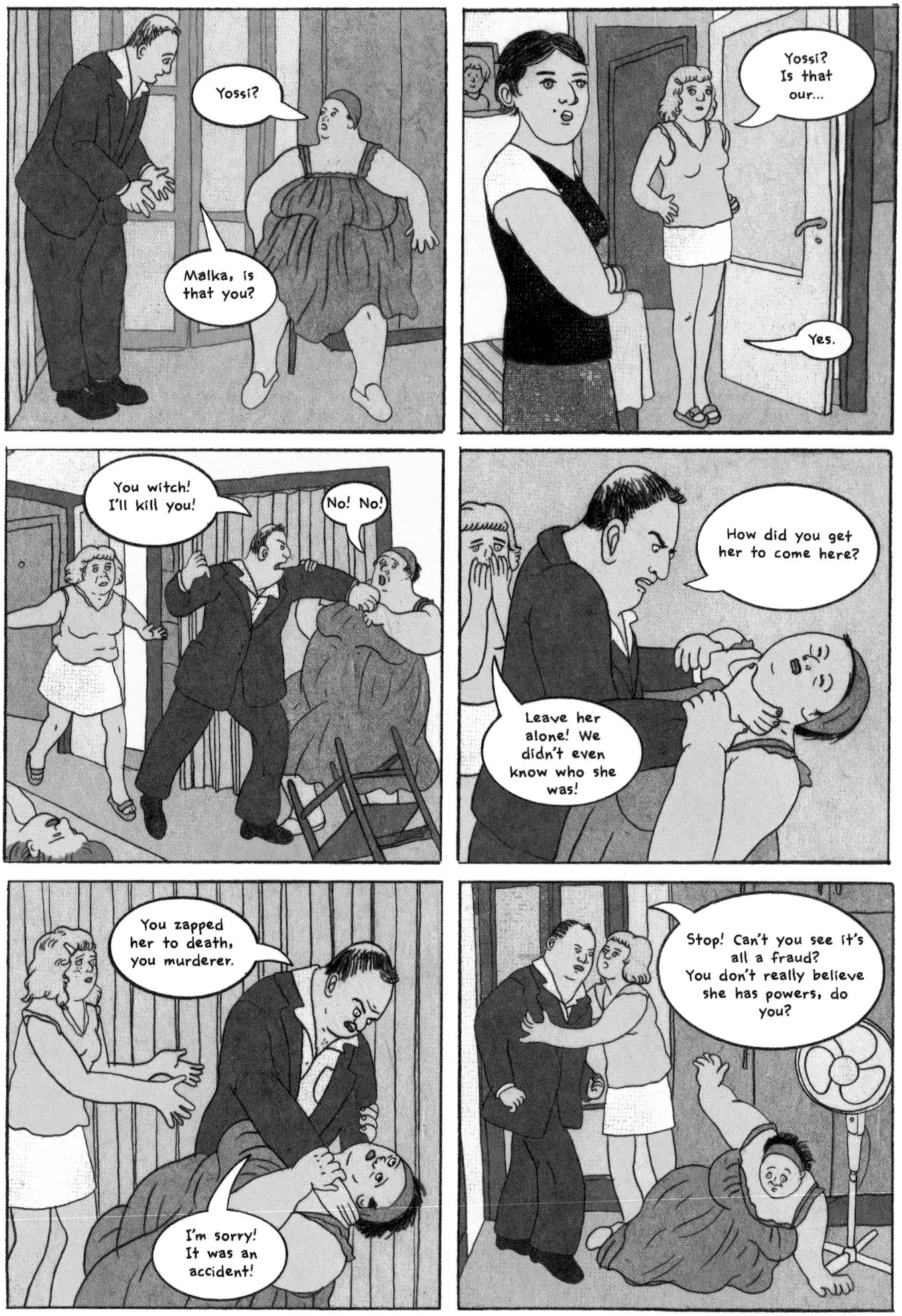
Yossi?
Malka, is that you?
Yossi? Is that our...
Yes.
You witch! I'll kill you!
No! No!
How did you get her to come here?
Leave her alone! We didn't even know who she was!
You zapped her to death, you murderer.
I'm sorry! It was an accident!
Stop! Can't you see it's all a fraud? You don't really believe she has powers, do you?

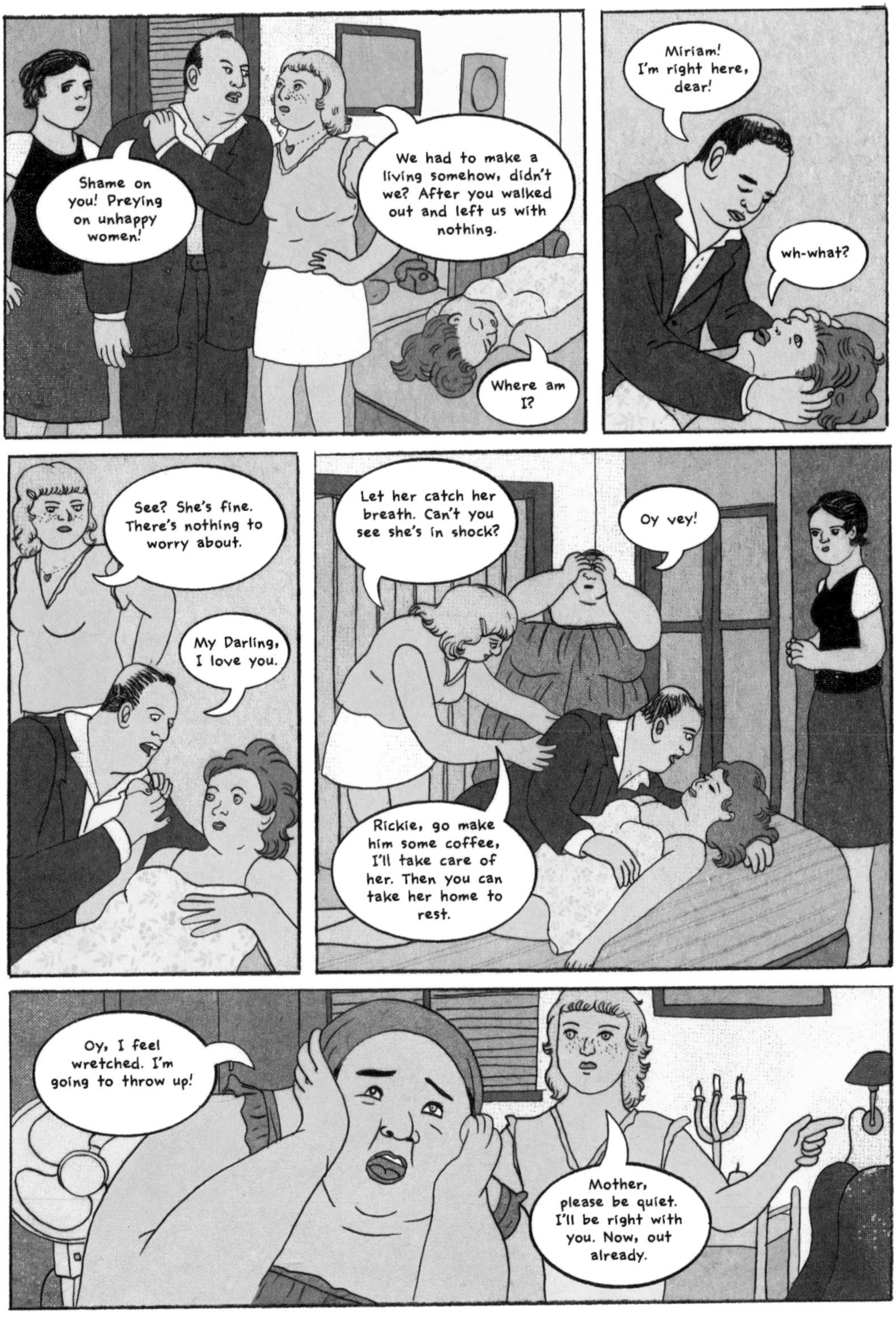
Shame on you! Preying on unhappy women!
We had to make a living somehow, didn't we? After you walked out and left us with nothing.
Where am I?
Miriam! I'm right here, dear!
wh-what?
See? She's fine. There's nothing to worry about.
My Darling, I love you.
Let her catch her breath. Can't you see she's in shock?
Oy vey!
Rickie, go make him some coffee, I'll take care of her. Then you can take her home to rest.
Oy, I feel wretched. I'm going to throw up!
Mother, please be quiet. I'll be right with you. Now, out already.

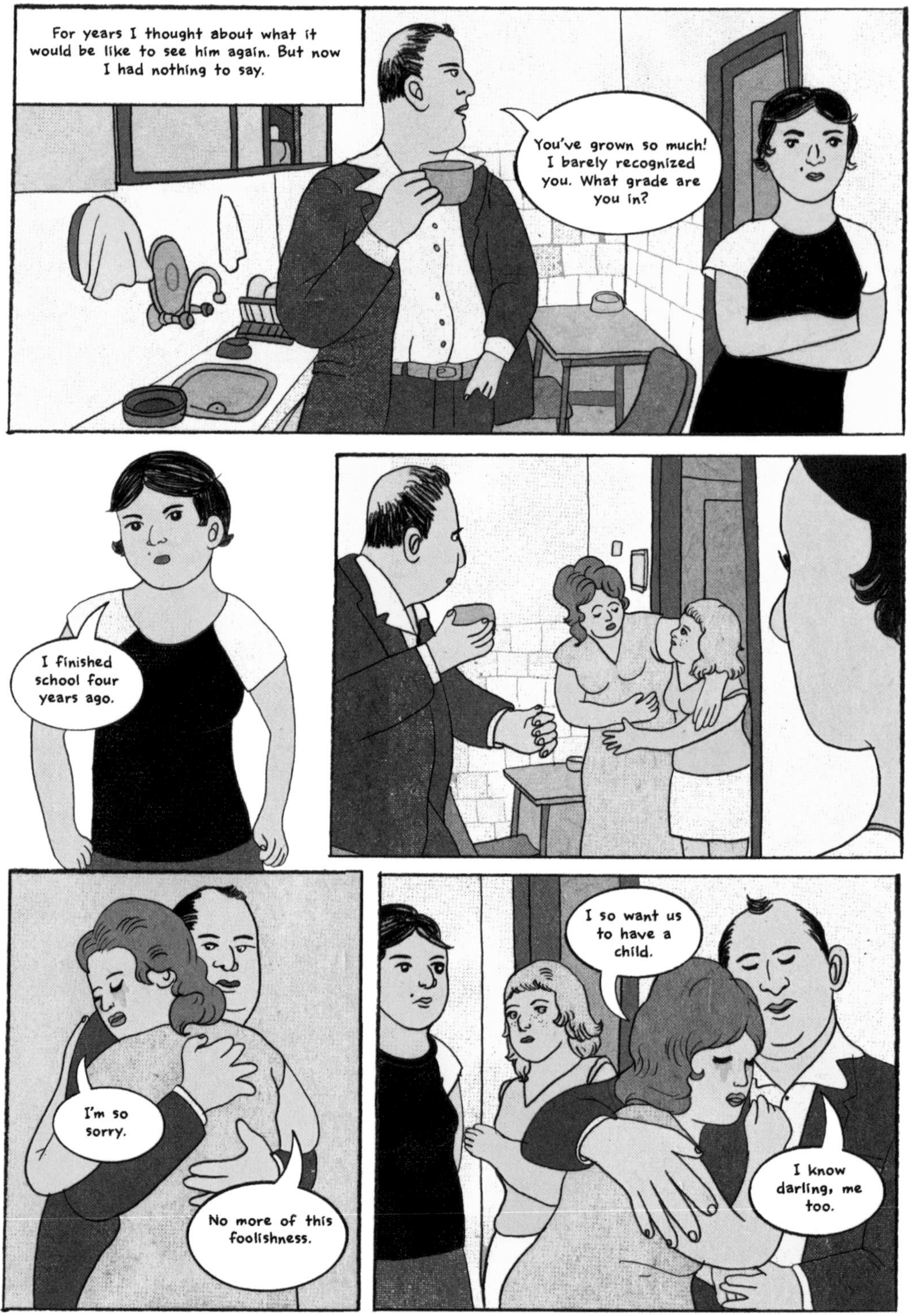
For years I thought about what it would be like to see him again. But now I had nothing to say.
You've grown so much! I barely recognized you. What grade are you in?
I finished school four years ago.
I'm so sorry.
No more of this foolishness.
I so want us to have a child.
I know darling, me too.

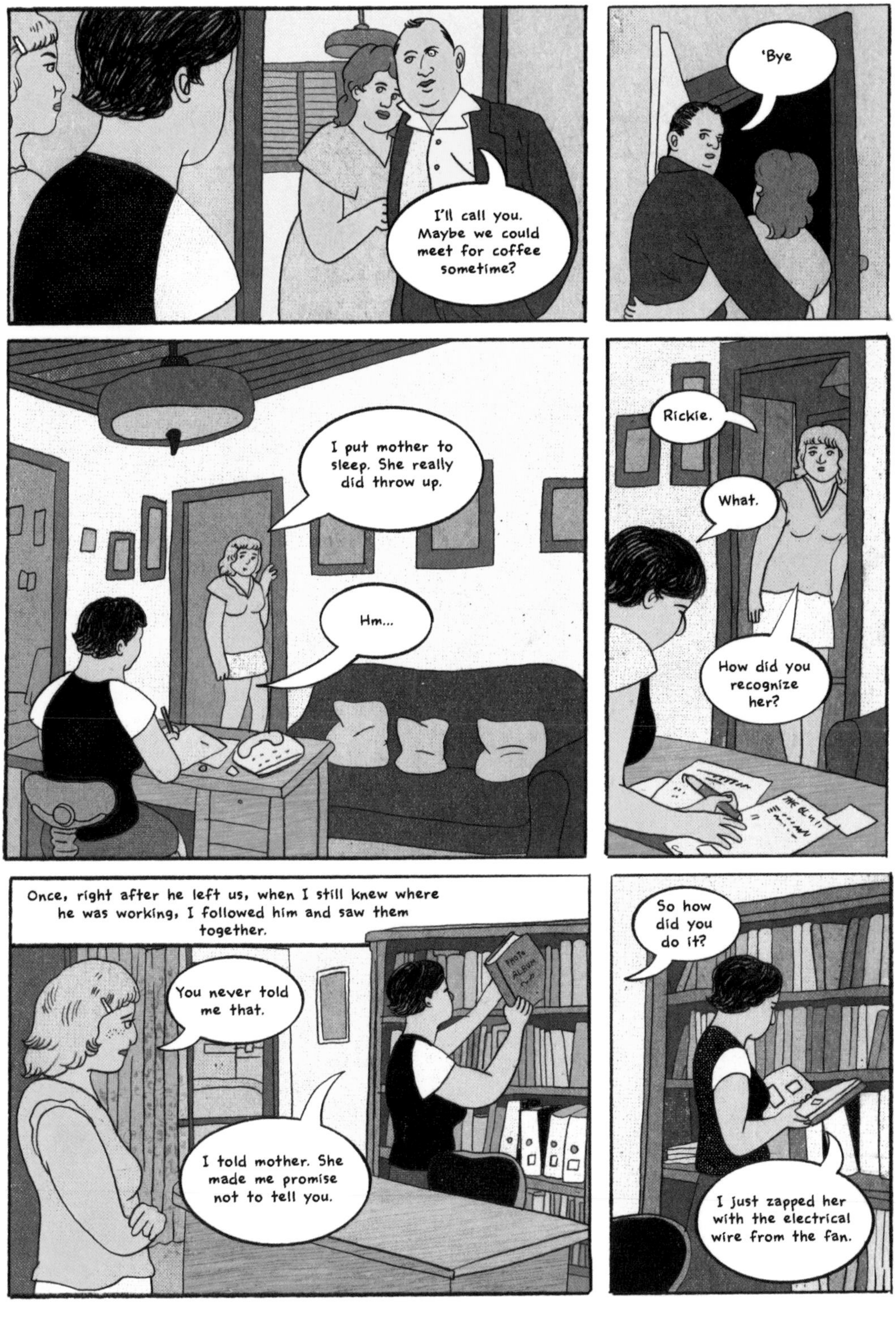
I'll call you. Maybe we could meet for coffee sometime?
'Bye
I put mother to sleep. She really did throw up.
Hm...
Rickie.
What.
How did you recognize her?
Once, right after he left us, when I still knew where he was working, I followed him and saw them together.
You never told me that.
I told mother. She made me promise not to tell you.
So how did you do it?
I just zapped her with the electrical wire from the fan.

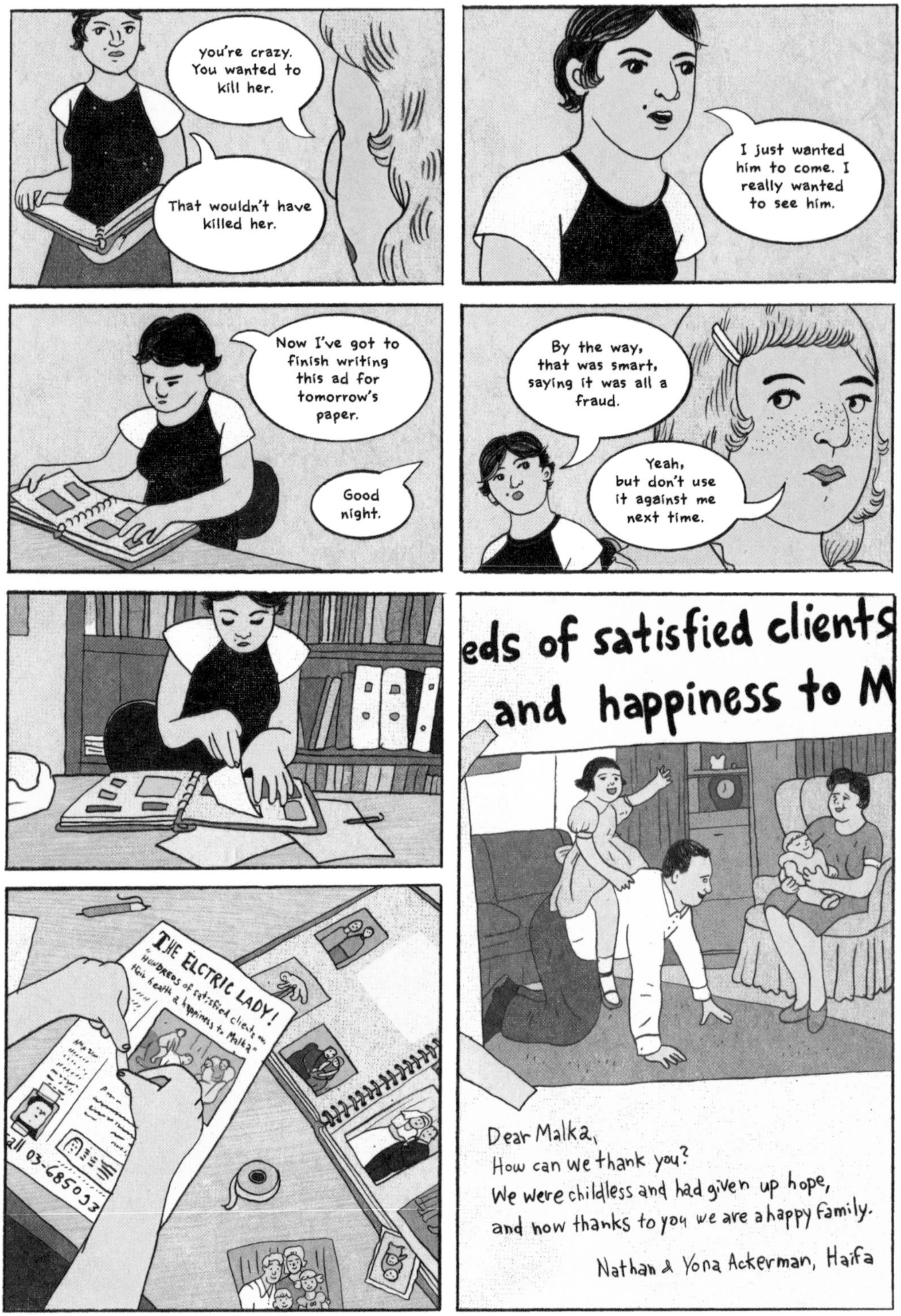
you're crazy. You wanted to kill her.
That wouldn't have killed her.
I just wanted him to come. I really wanted to see him.
Now I've got to finish writing this ad for tomorrow's paper.
Good night.
By the way, that was smart, saying it was all a fraud.
Yeah, but don't use it against me next time.
THE ELCTRIC LADY!
eds of satisfied clients
and happiness to M
Dear Malka,
How can we thank you?
We were childless and had given up hope,
and now thanks to you we are a happy family.
Nathan & Yona Ackerman, Haifa

BYGONE

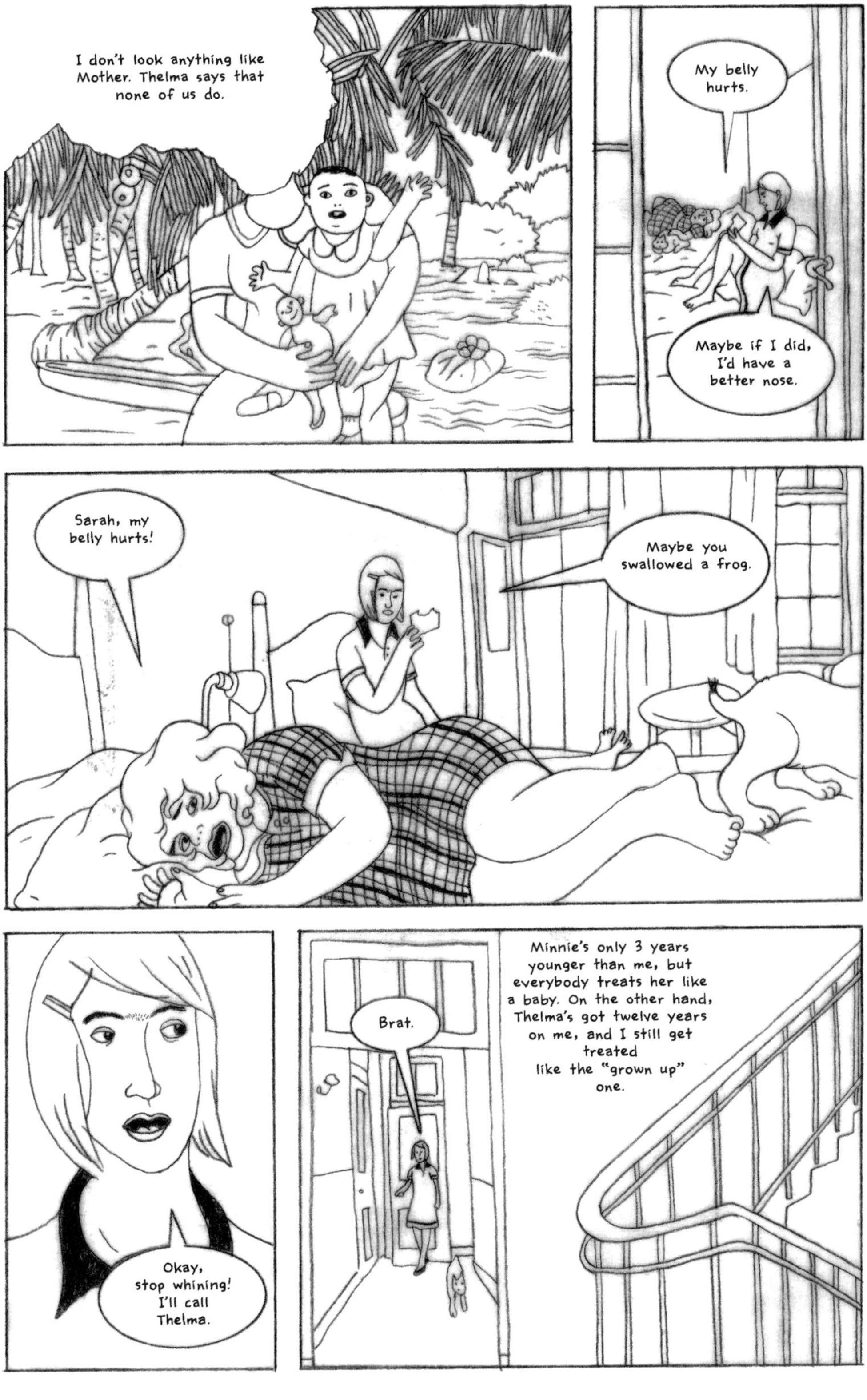
I don't look anything like Mother. Thelma says that none of us do.
My belly hurts.
Maybe if I did, I'd have a better nose.
Sarah, my belly hurts!
Maybe you swallowed a frog.
Okay, stop whining! I'll call Thelma.
Brat.
Minnie's only 3 years younger than me, but everybody treats her like a baby. On the other hand, Thelma's got twelve years on me, and I still get treated like the "grown up" one.

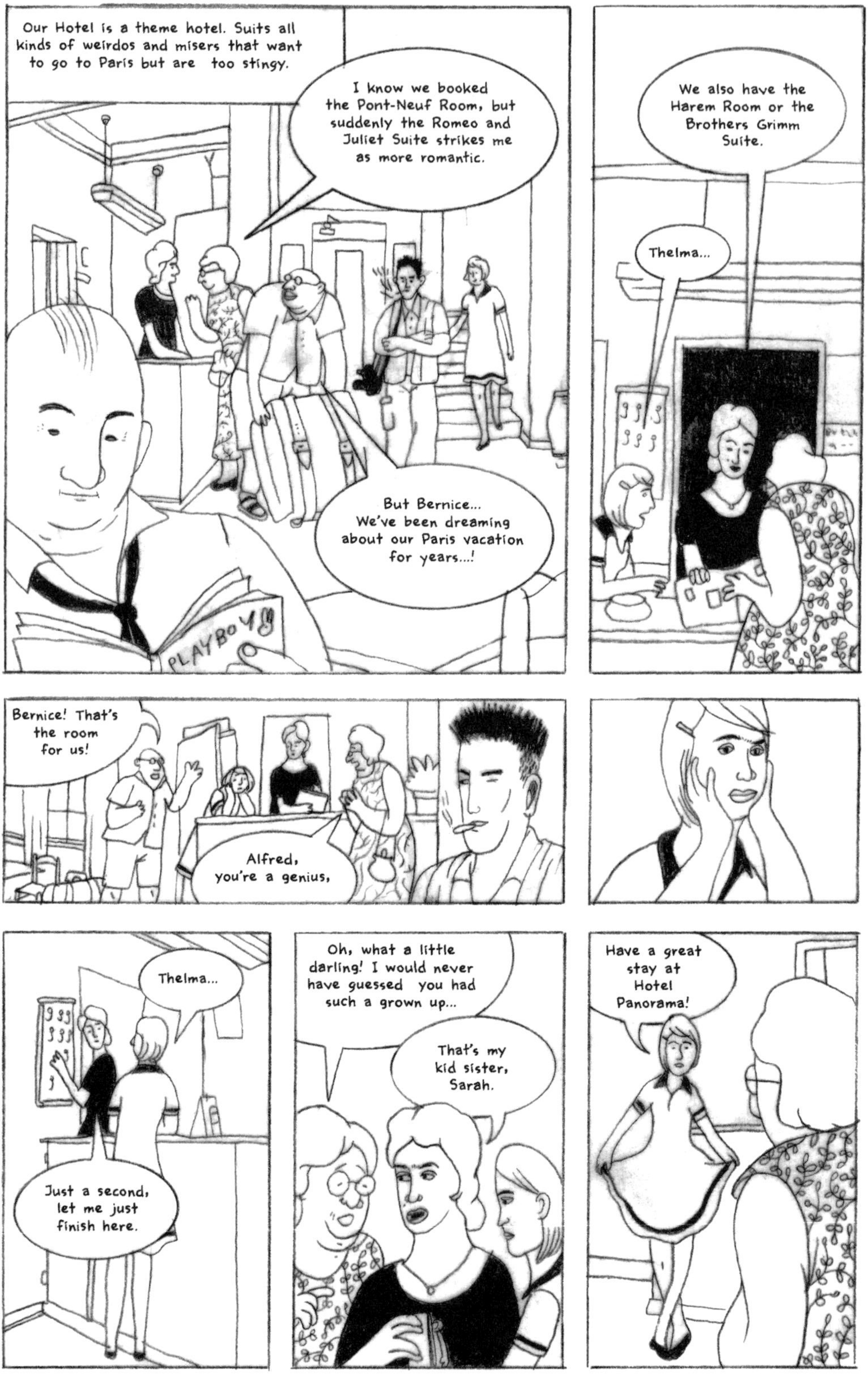

Our Hotel is a theme hotel. Suits all kinds of weirdos and misers that want to go to Paris but are too stingy.
I know we booked the Pont-Neuf Room, but suddenly the Romeo and Juliet Suite strikes me as more romantic.
But Bernice... We've been dreaming about our Paris vacation for years...!
PLAYBOY
We also have the Harem Room or the Brothers Grimm Suite.
Thelma...
Bernice! That's the room for us!
Alfred, you're a genius,
Thelma...
Just a second, let me just finish here.
Oh, what a little darling! I would never have guessed you had such a grown up...
That's my kid sister, Sarah.
Have a great stay at Hotel Panorama!

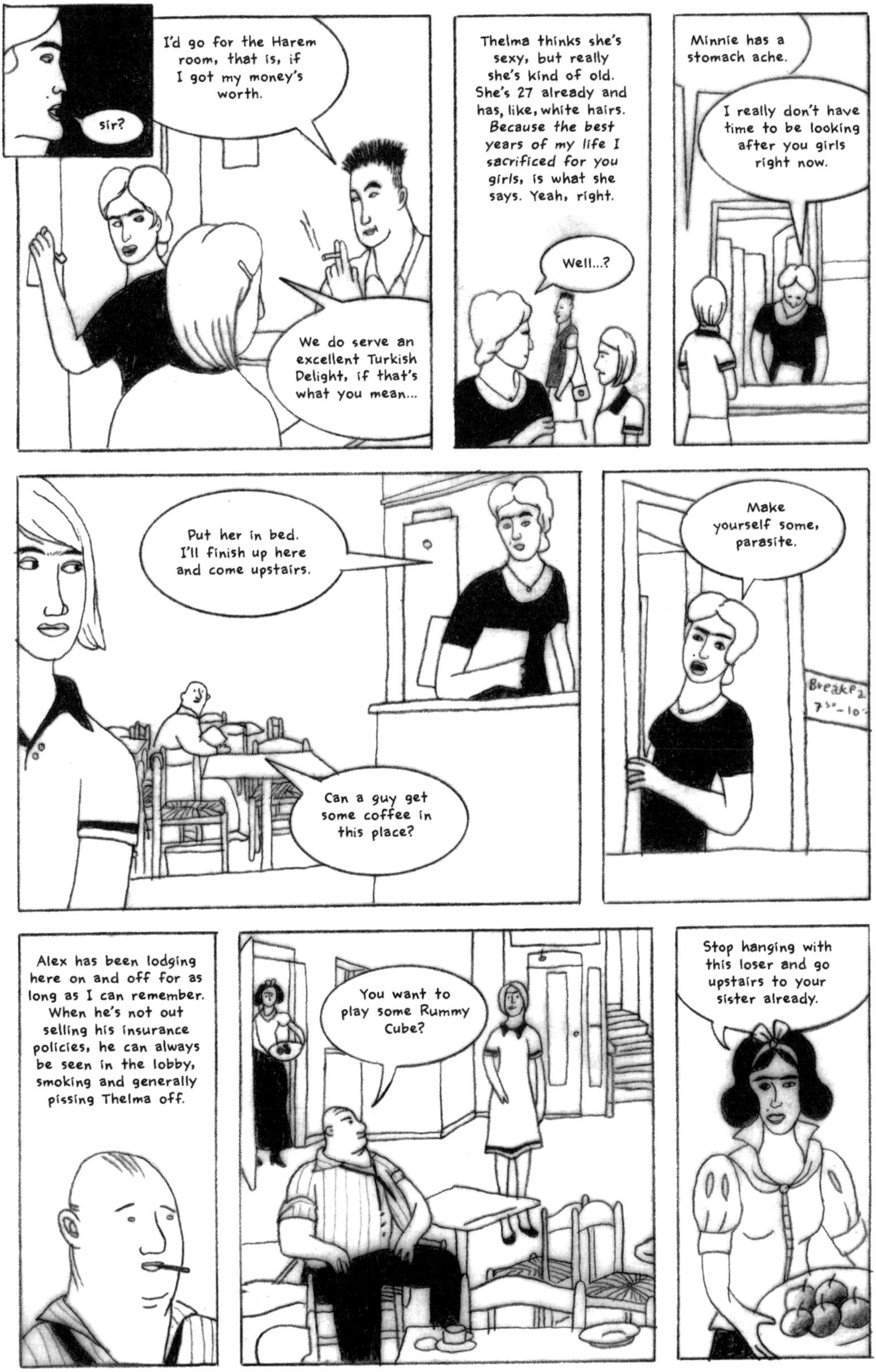
I'd go for the Harem room, that is, if I got my money's worth.
sir?
We do serve an excellent Turkish Delight, if that's what you mean...
Thelma thinks she's sexy, but really she's kind of old. She's 27 already and has, like, white hairs. *Because the best years of my life I sacrificed for you girls,* is what she says. Yeah, right.
Well...?
Minnie has a stomach ache.
I really don't have time to be looking after you girls right now.
Put her in bed. I'll finish up here and come upstairs.
Can a guy get some coffee in this place?
Make yourself some, parasite.
Alex has been lodging here on and off for as long as I can remember. When he's not out selling his insurance policies, he can always be seen in the lobby, smoking and generally pissing Thelma off.
You want to play some Rummy Cube?
Stop hanging with this loser and go upstairs to your sister already.

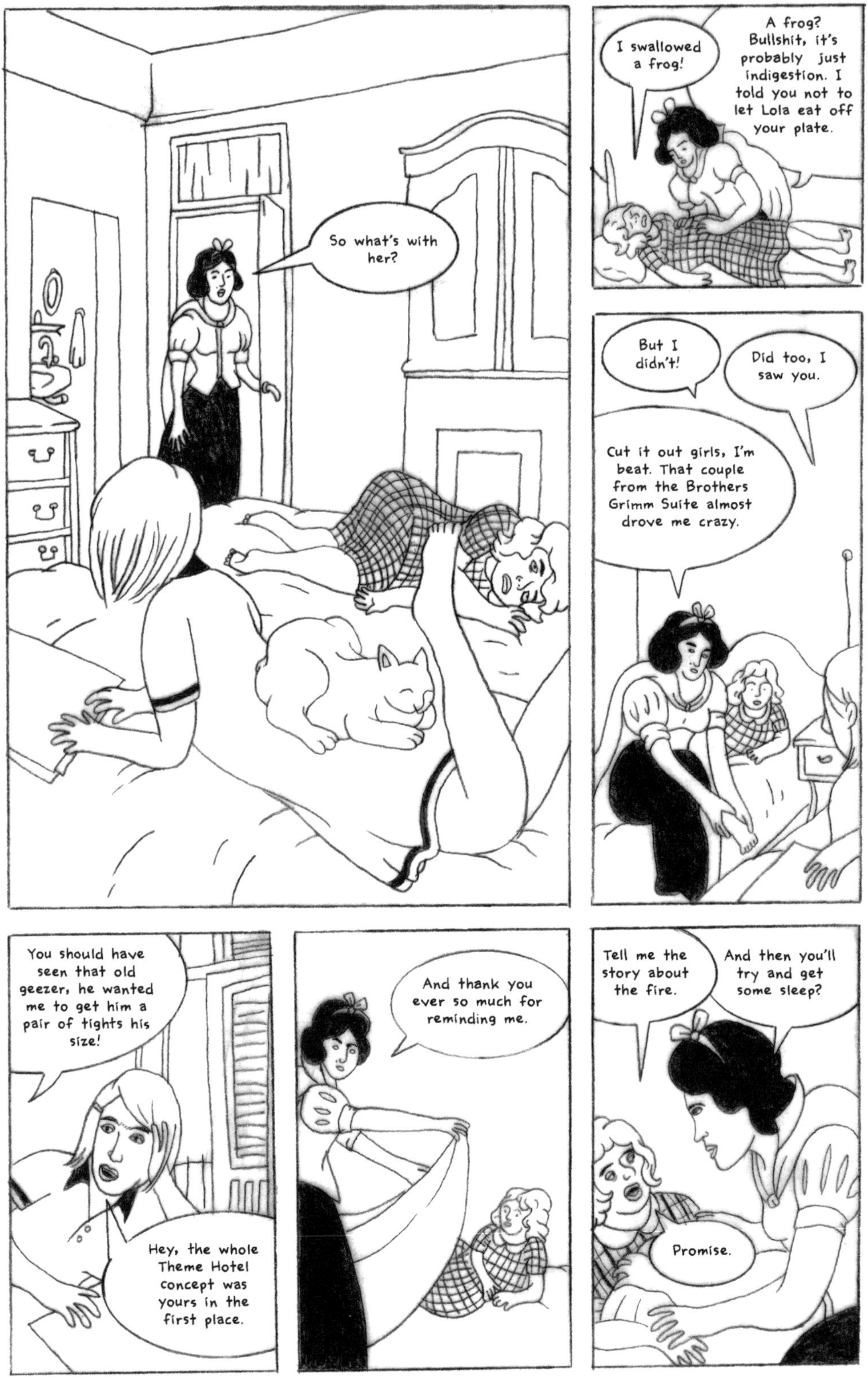
So what's with her?
I swallowed a frog!
A frog? Bullshit, it's probably just indigestion. I told you not to let Lola eat off your plate.
But I didn't!
Did too, I saw you.
Cut it out girls, I'm beat. That couple from the Brothers Grimm Suite almost drove me crazy.
You should have seen that old geezer, he wanted me to get him a pair of tights his size!
Hey, the whole Theme Hotel concept was yours in the first place.
And thank you ever so much for reminding me.
Tell me the story about the fire.
And then you'll try and get some sleep?
Promise.

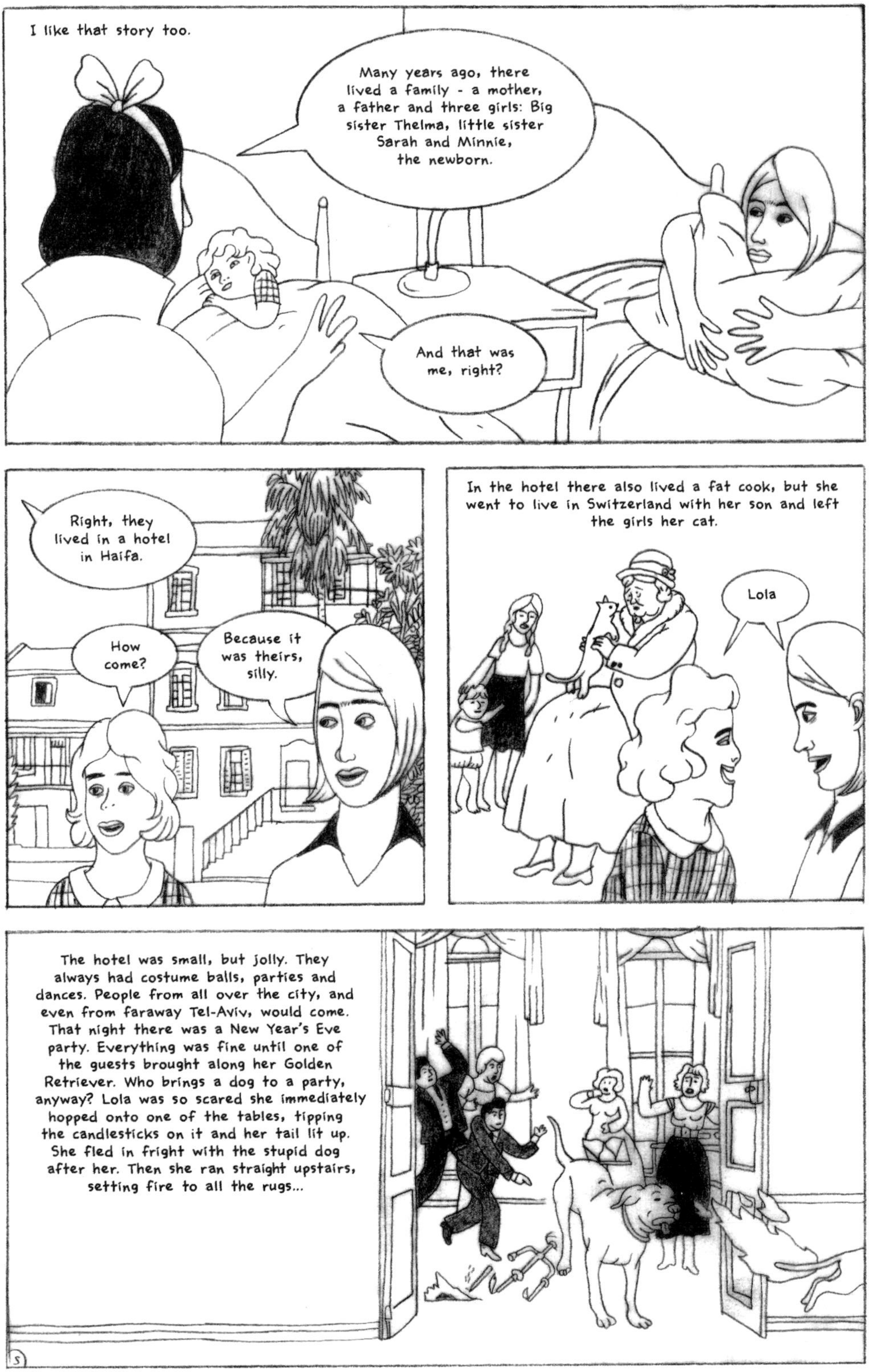

I like that story too.
Many years ago, there lived a family - a mother, a father and three girls: Big sister Thelma, little sister Sarah and Minnie, the newborn.
And that was me, right?
Right, they lived in a hotel in Haifa.
How come?
Because it was theirs, silly.
In the hotel there also lived a fat cook, but she went to live in Switzerland with her son and left the girls her cat.
Lola
The hotel was small, but jolly. They always had costume balls, parties and dances. People from all over the city, and even from faraway Tel-Aviv, would come. That night there was a New Year's Eve party. Everything was fine until one of the guests brought along her Golden Retriever. Who brings a dog to a party, anyway? Lola was so scared she immediately hopped onto one of the tables, tipping the candlesticks on it and her tail lit up. She fled in fright with the stupid dog after her. Then she ran straight upstairs, setting fire to all the rugs...
5

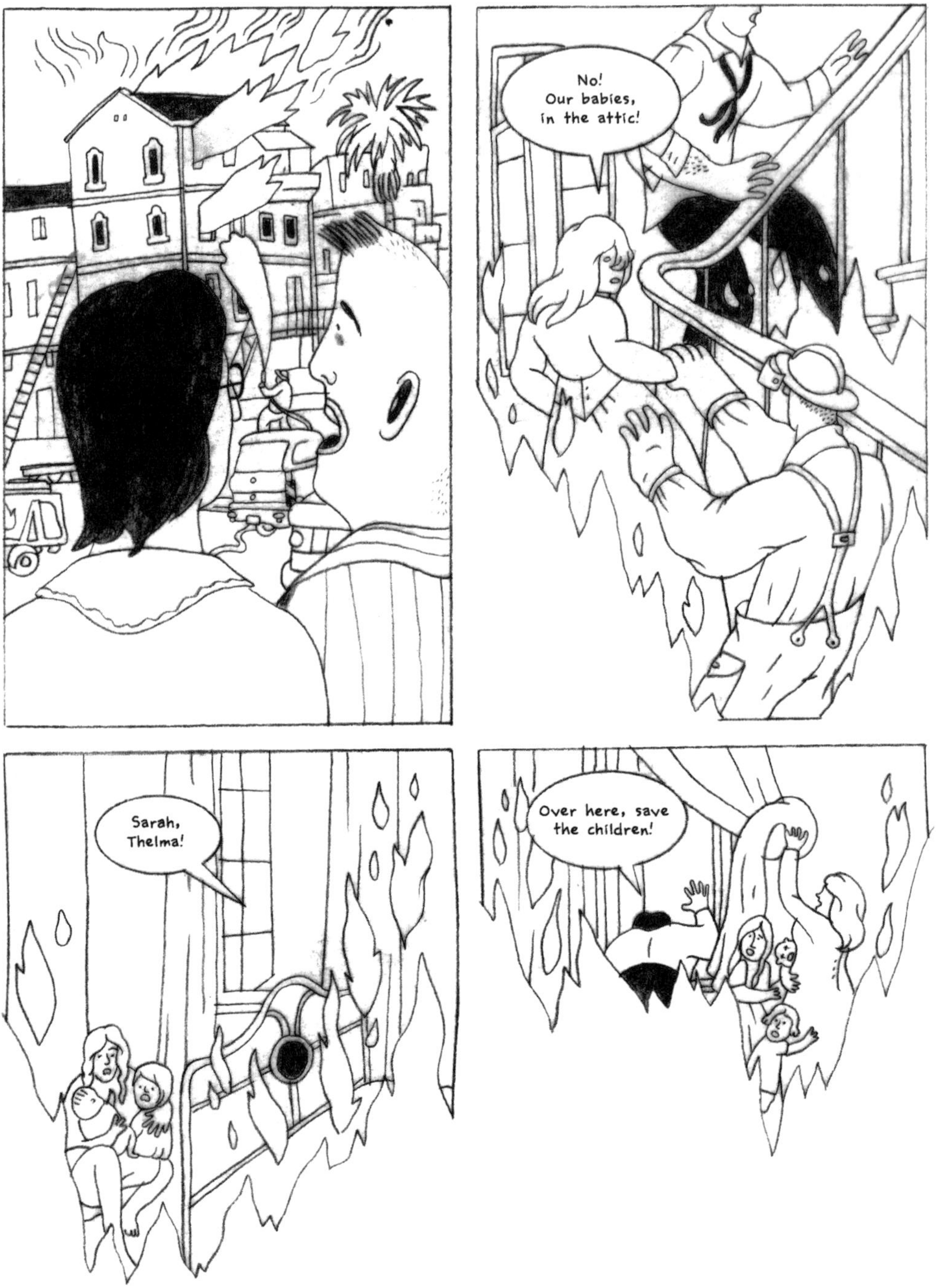
No! Our babies, in the attic!
Sarah, Thelma!
Over here, save the children!

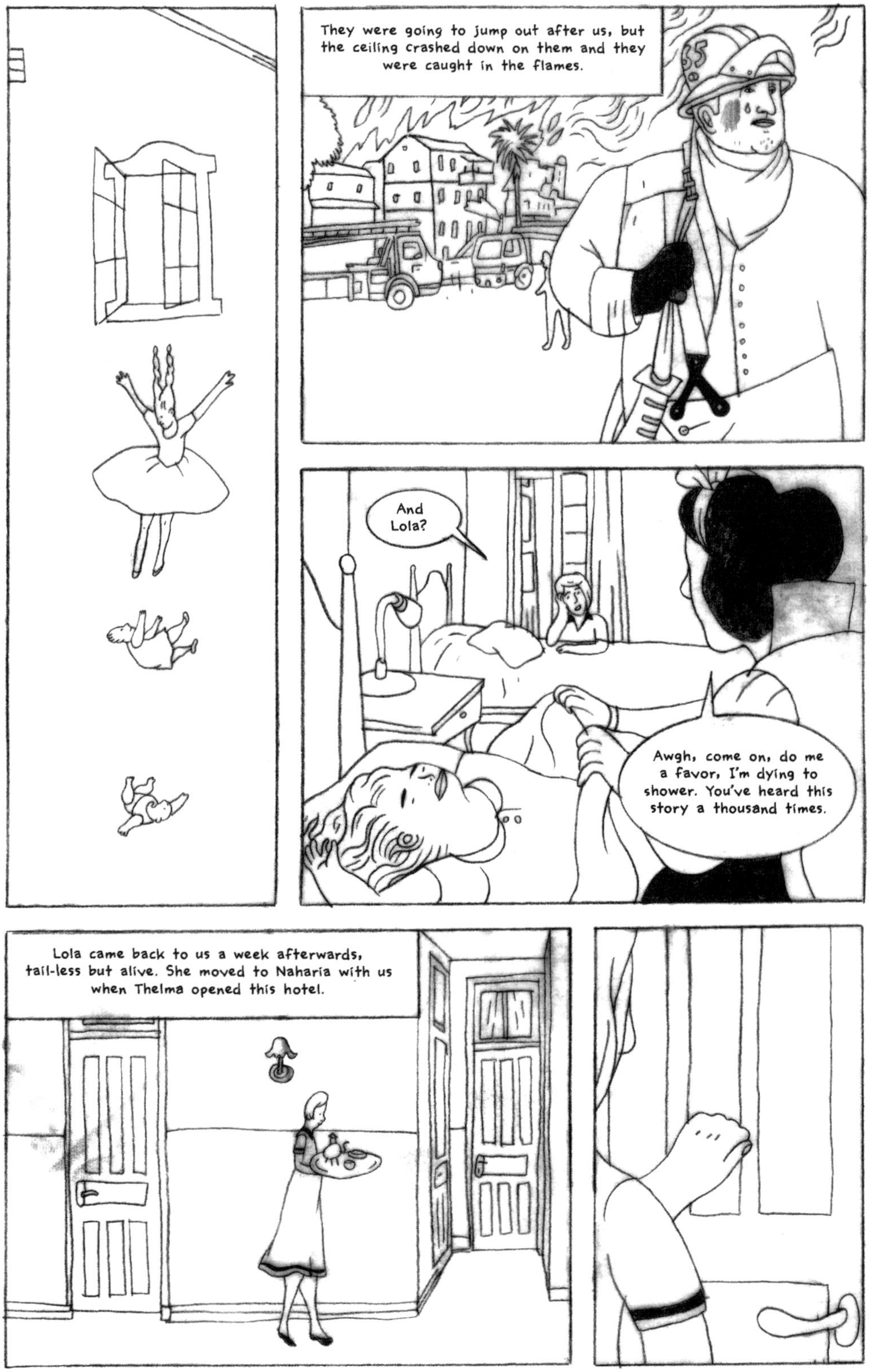

They were going to jump out after us, but the ceiling crashed down on them and they were caught in the flames.
35
And Lola?
Awgh, come on, do me a favor, I'm dying to shower. You've heard this story a thousand times.
Lola came back to us a week afterwards, tail-less but alive. She moved to Naharia with us when Thelma opened this hotel.

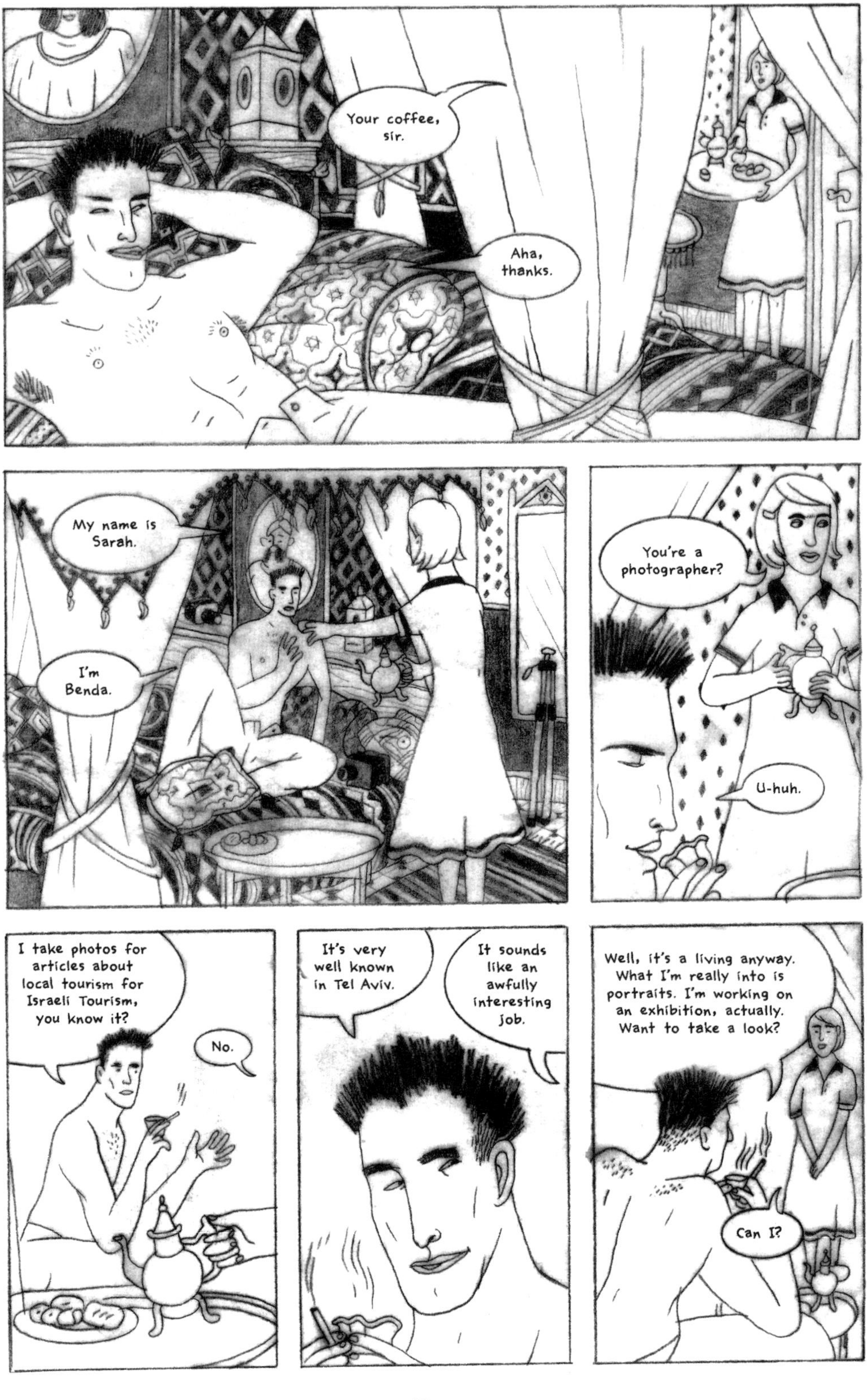
Your coffee, sir.
Aha, thanks.
My name is Sarah.
I'm Benda.
You're a photographer?
U-huh.
I take photos for articles about local tourism for Israeli Tourism, you know it?
No.
It's very well known in Tel Aviv.
It sounds like an awfully interesting job.
Well, it's a living anyway. What I'm really into is portraits. I'm working on an exhibition, actually. Want to take a look?
Can I?

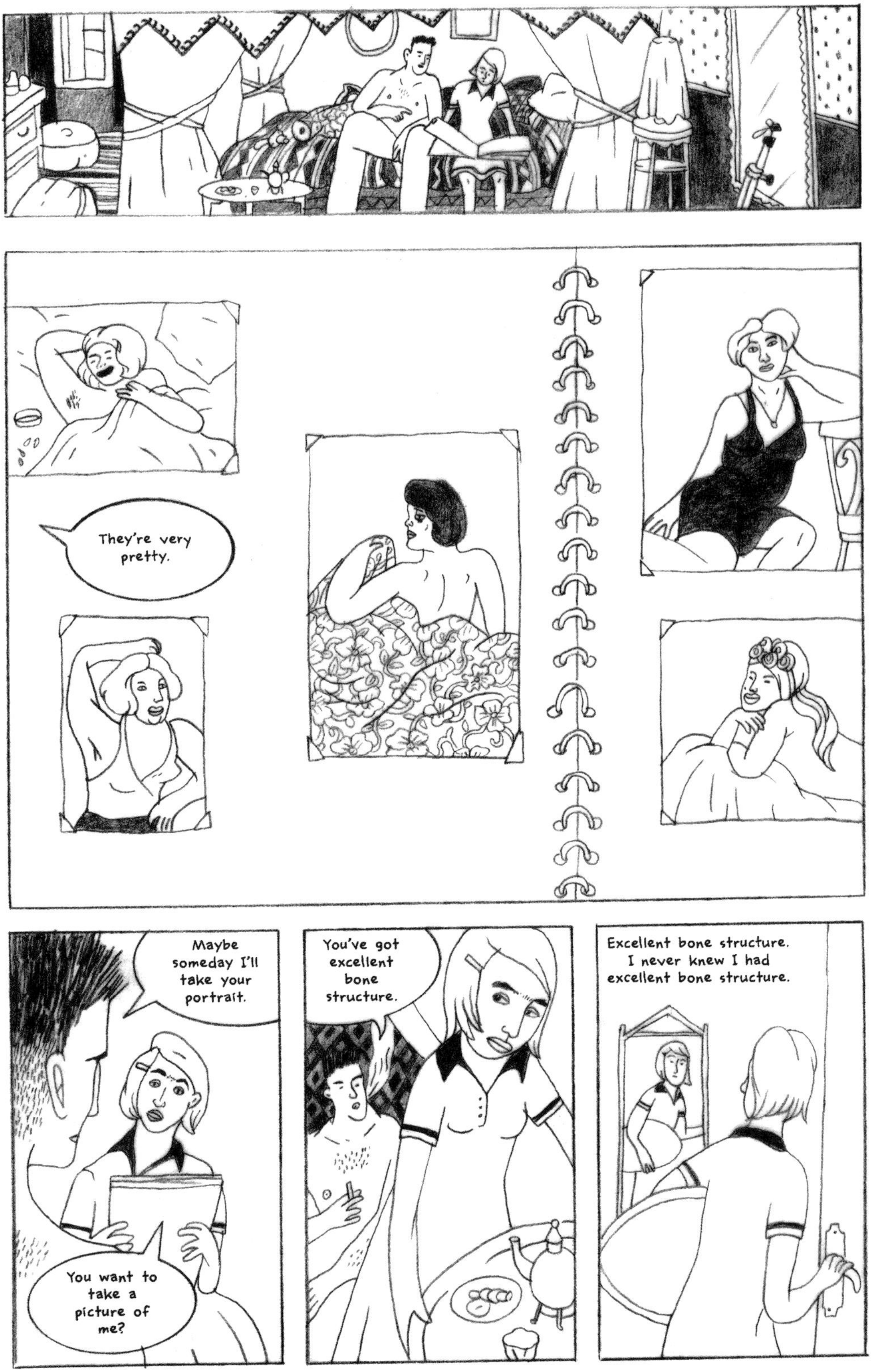
They're very pretty.
Maybe someday I'll take your portrait.
You want to take a picture of me?
You've got excellent bone structure.
Excellent bone structure. I never knew I had excellent bone structure.

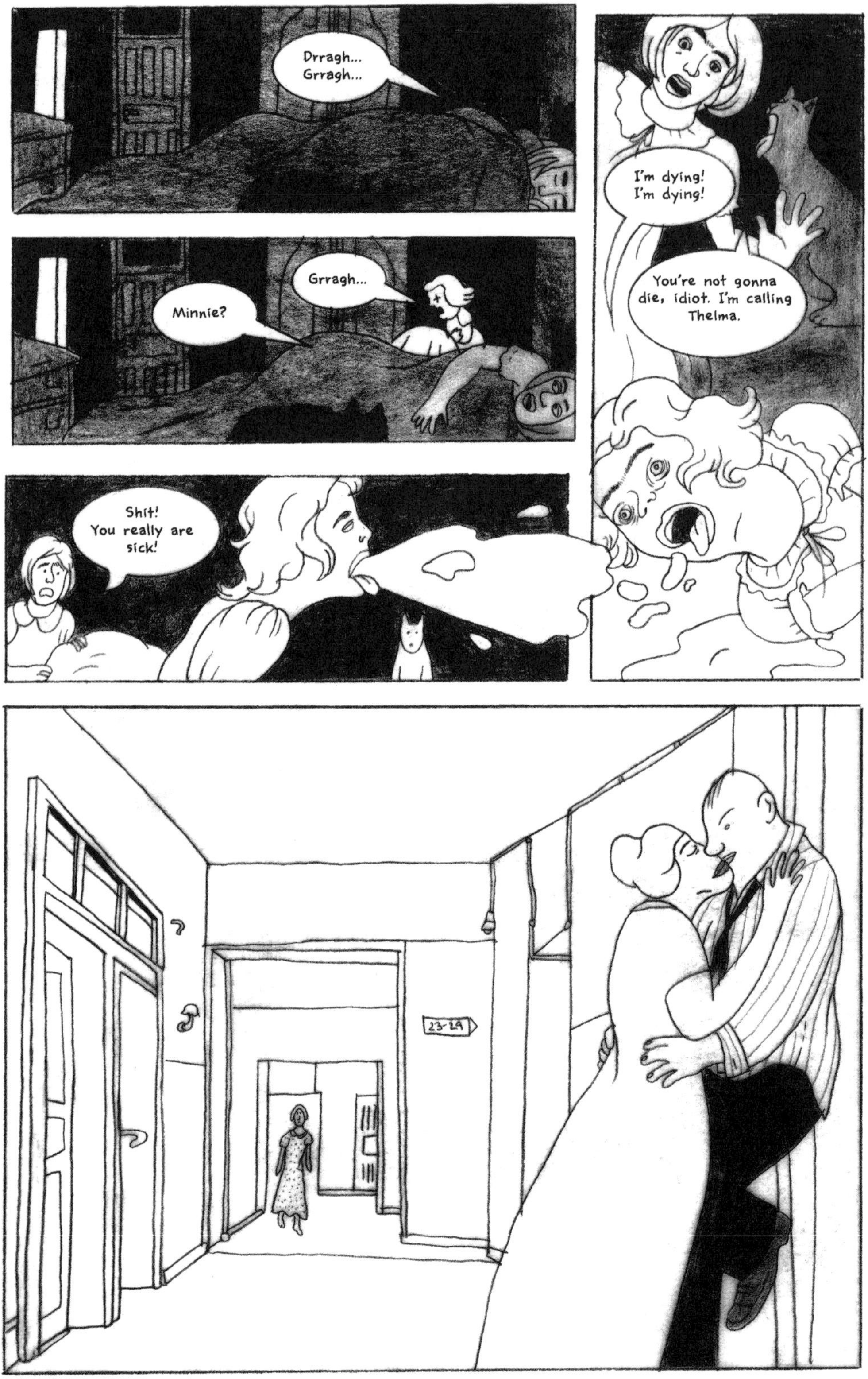
Drragh...
Grragh...
Minnie?
Grragh...
Shit!
You really are
sick!
I'm dying!
I'm dying!
You're not gonna
die, idiot. I'm calling
Thelma.
23-29

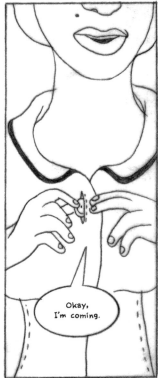

Why are you sneaking about like that?

Minnie's throwing up.

Okay, I'm coming.

How can you fool around with Alex? You don't even like him.

Well, you know, because he's there.

So that's why you let him hang around for free? That's really disgusting.

Mind your own business. You're nothing but a nosy little girl.

You wouldn't do it if mother were here.

My dear, if mother were here, I wouldn't be the one cleaning up little girls' vomit in the middle of the night.

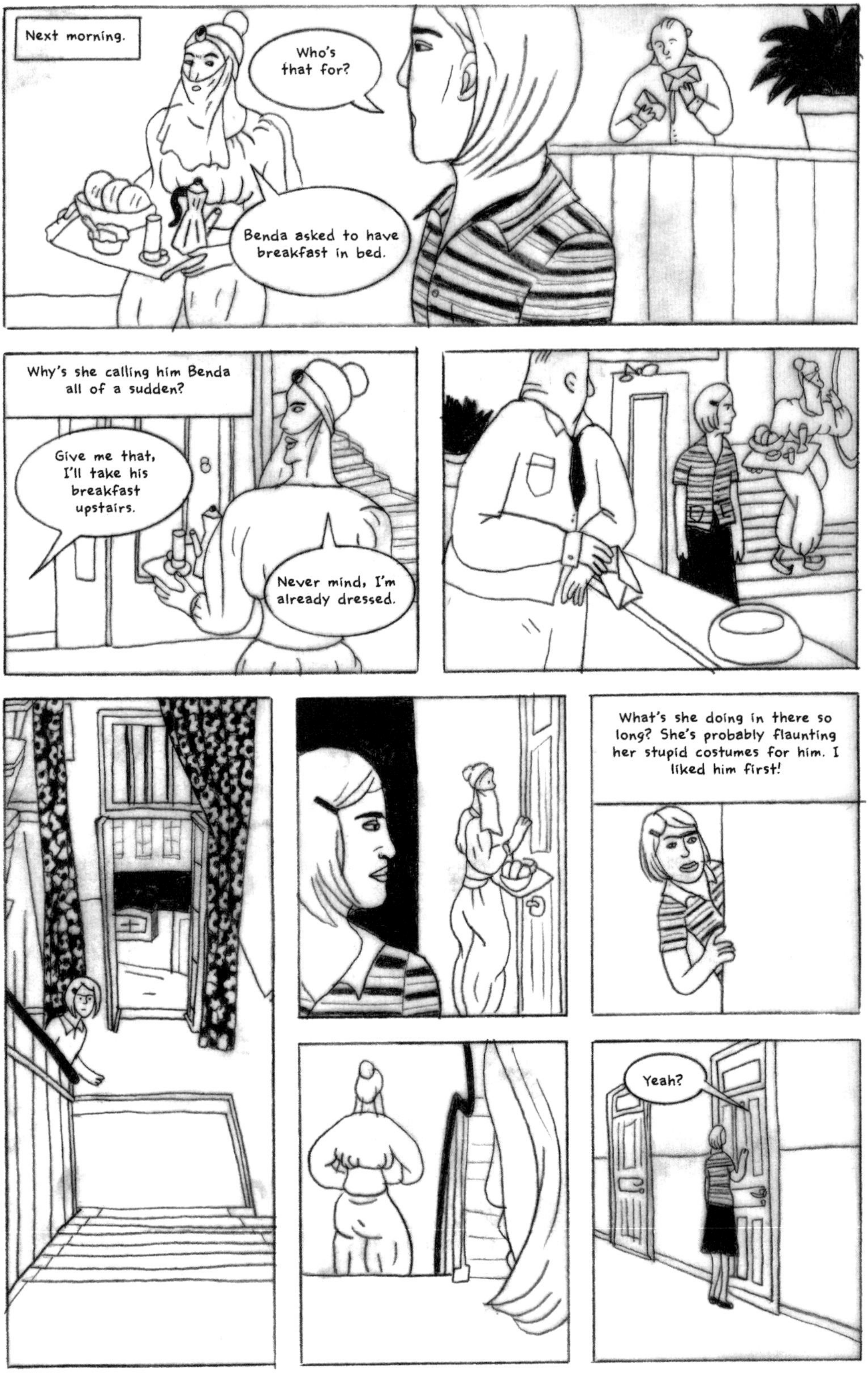
Next morning.
Who's that for?
Benda asked to have breakfast in bed.
Why's she calling him Benda all of a sudden?
Give me that, I'll take his breakfast upstairs.
Never mind, I'm already dressed.
What's she doing in there so long? She's probably flaunting her stupid costumes for him. I liked him first!
Yeah?

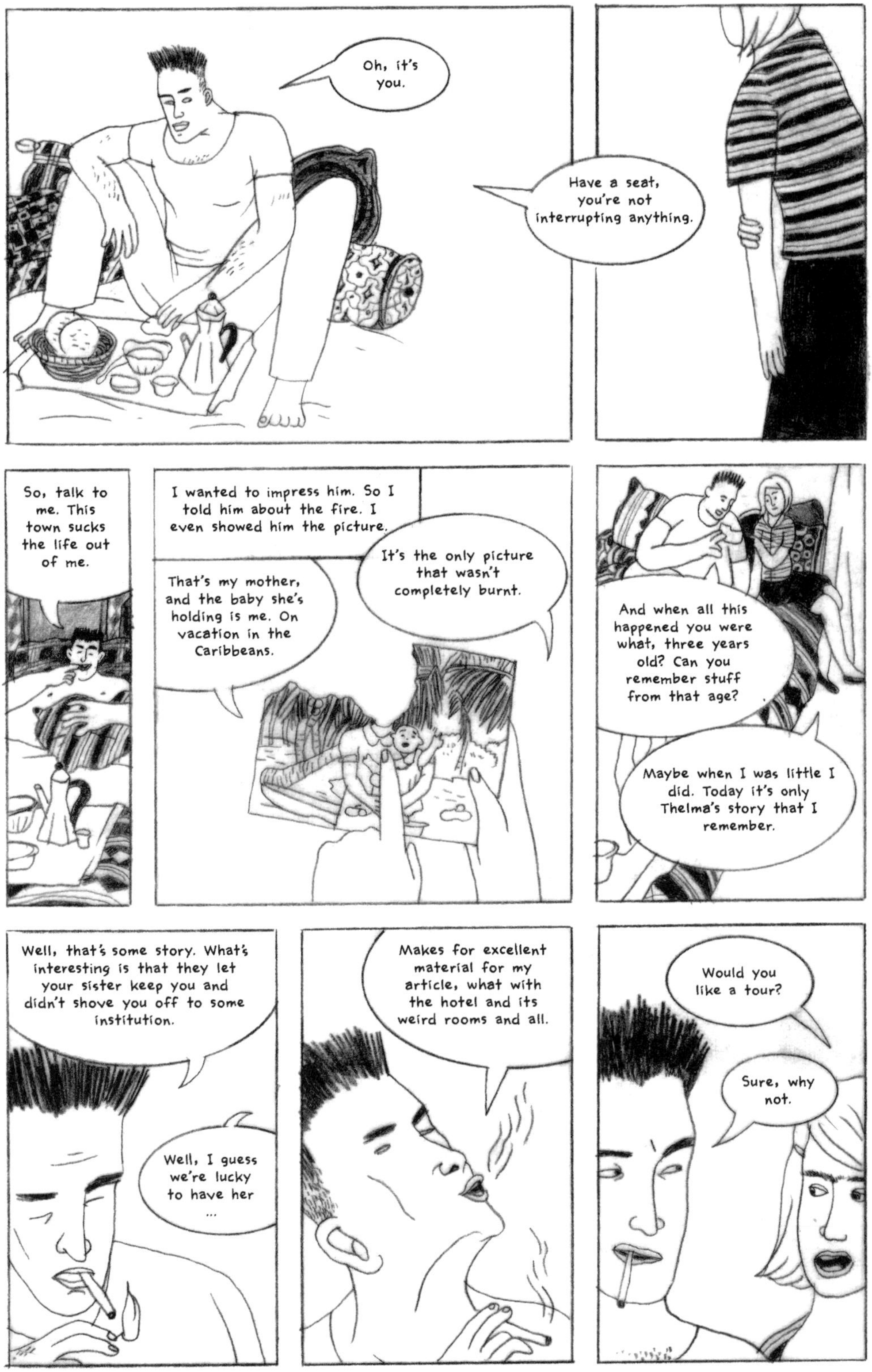
Oh, it's you.
Have a seat, you're not interrupting anything.
So, talk to me. This town sucks the life out of me.
I wanted to impress him. So I told him about the fire. I even showed him the picture.
That's my mother, and the baby she's holding is me. On vacation in the Caribbeans.
It's the only picture that wasn't completely burnt.
And when all this happened you were what, three years old? Can you remember stuff from that age?
Maybe when I was little I did. Today it's only Thelma's story that I remember.
Well, that's some story. What's interesting is that they let your sister keep you and didn't shove you off to some institution.
Well, I guess we're lucky to have her ...
Makes for excellent material for my article, what with the hotel and its weird rooms and all.
Would you like a tour?
Sure, why not.

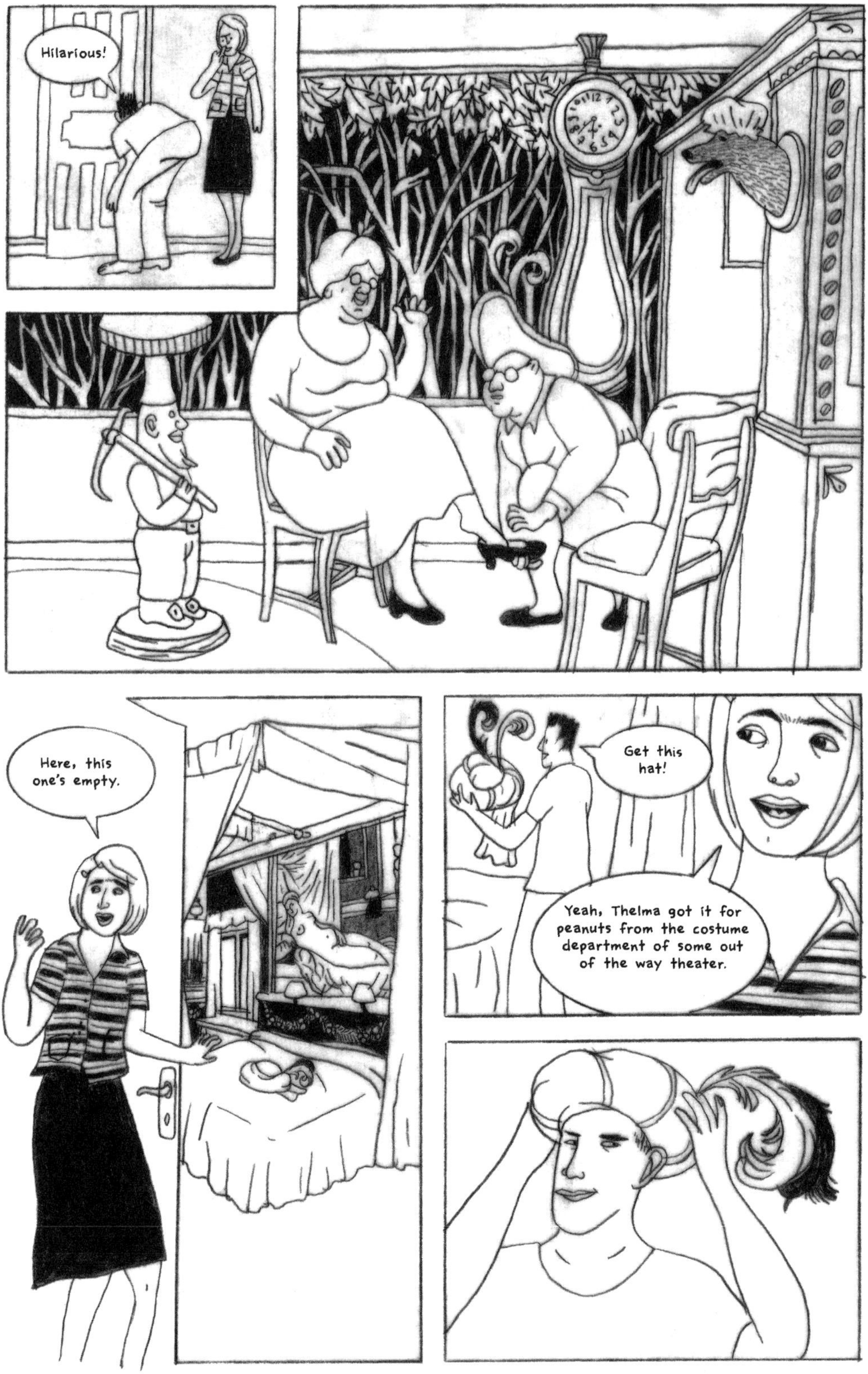
Hilarious!
Here, this one's empty.
Get this hat!
Yeah, Thelma got it for peanuts from the costume department of some out of the way theater.

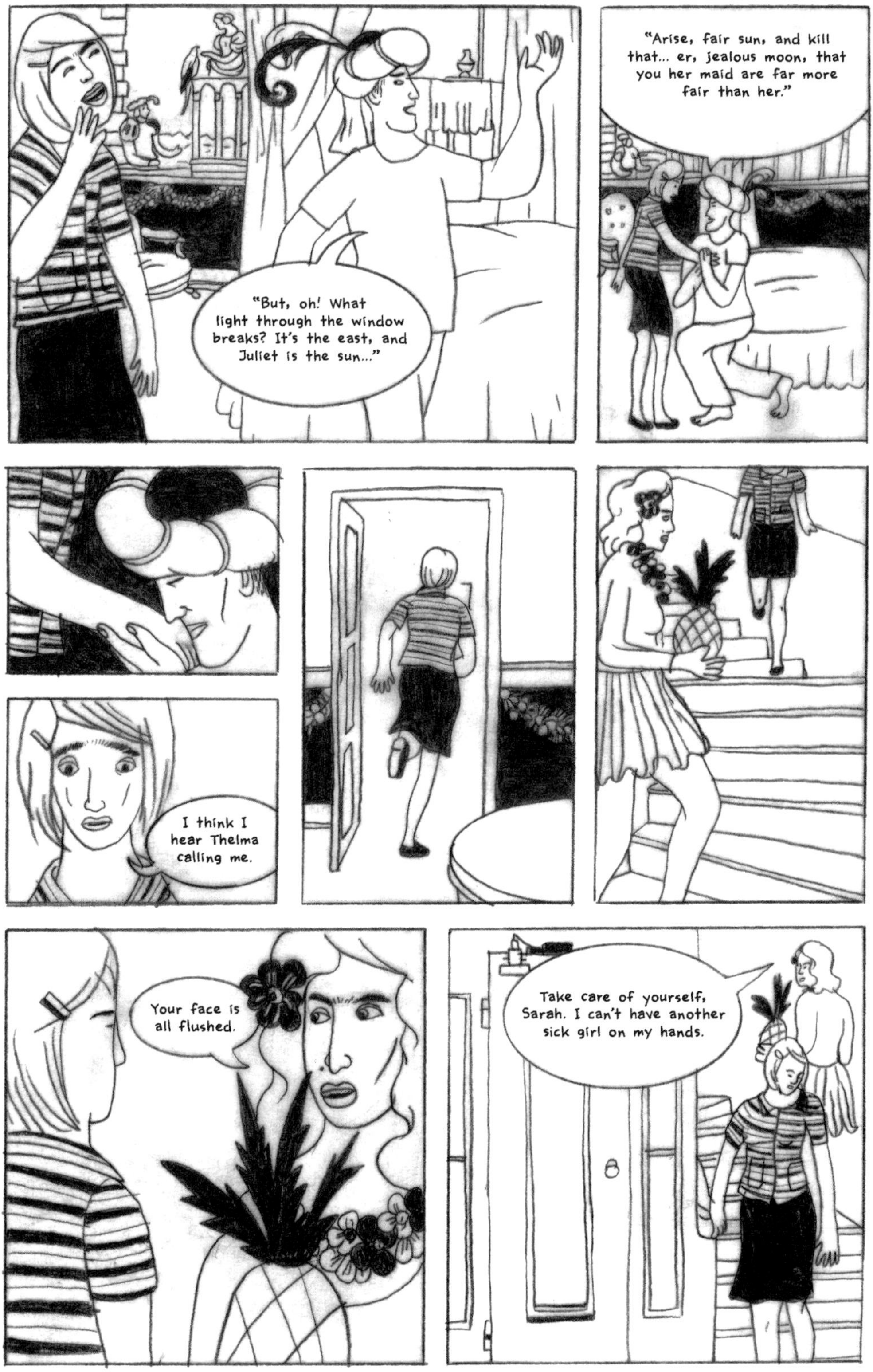
"But, oh! What light through the window breaks? It's the east, and Juliet is the sun..."
"Arise, fair sun, and kill that... er, jealous moon, that you her maid are far more fair than her."
I think I hear Thelma calling me.
Your face is all flushed.
Take care of yourself, Sarah. I can't have another sick girl on my hands.

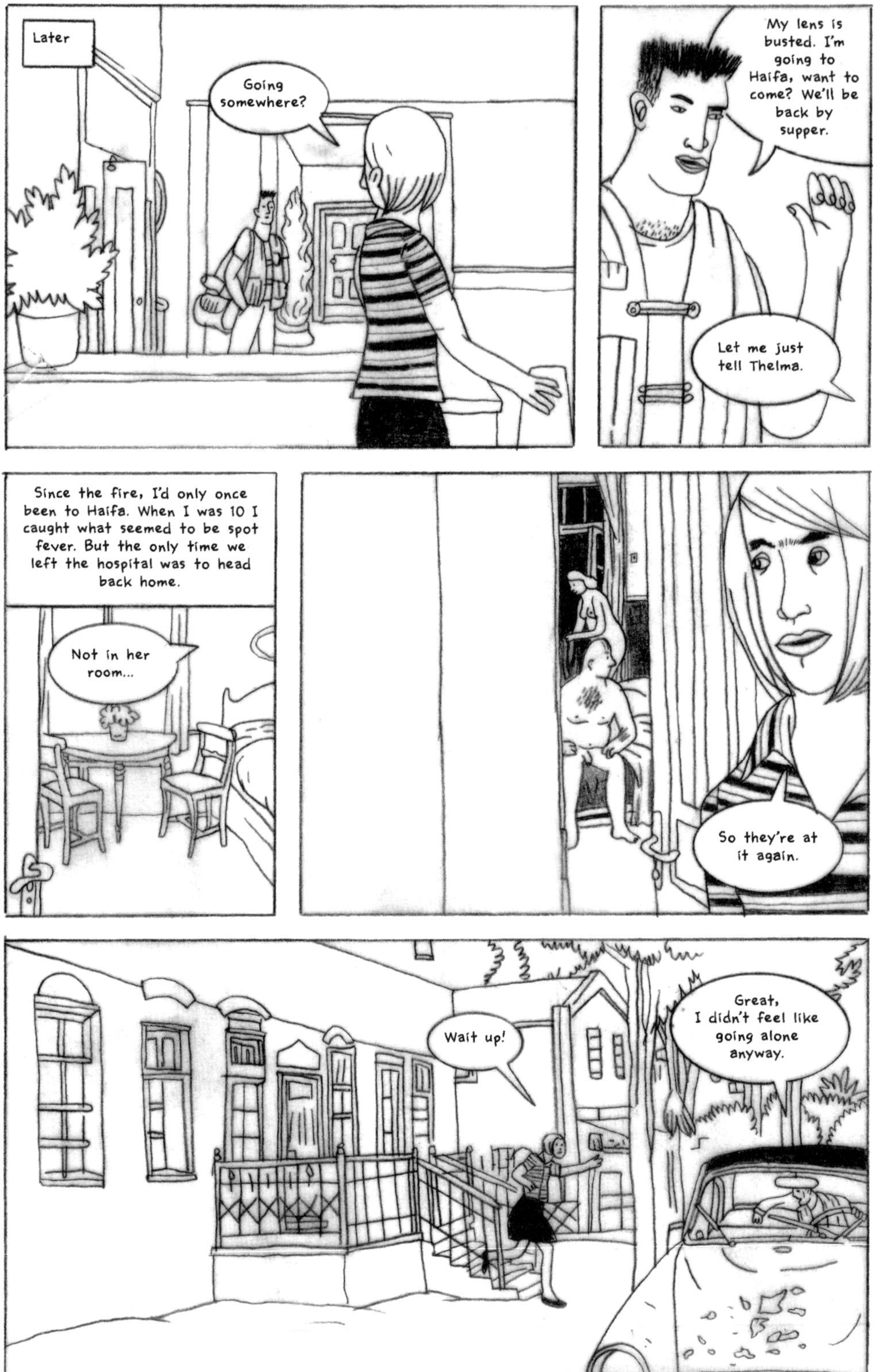
Later
Going somewhere?
My lens is busted. I'm going to Haifa, want to come? We'll be back by supper.
Let me just tell Thelma.
Since the fire, I'd only once been to Haifa. When I was 10 I caught what seemed to be spot fever. But the only time we left the hospital was to head back home.
Not in her room...
So they're at it again.
Wait up!
Great, I didn't feel like going alone anyway.

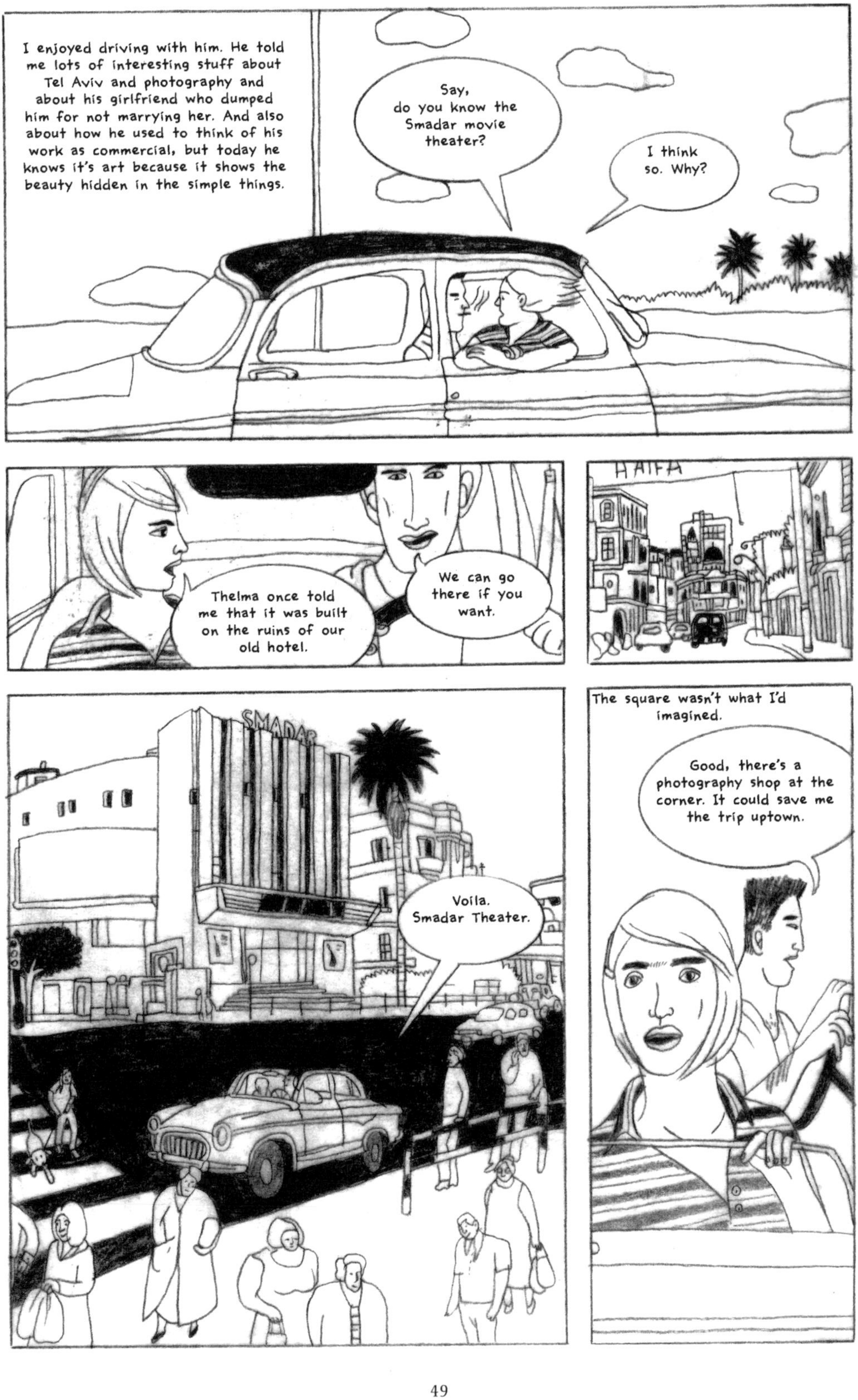

I enjoyed driving with him. He told me lots of interesting stuff about Tel Aviv and photography and about his girlfriend who dumped him for not marrying her. And also about how he used to think of his work as commercial, but today he knows it's art because it shows the beauty hidden in the simple things.
Say, do you know the Smadar movie theater?
I think so. Why?
Thelma once told me that it was built on the ruins of our old hotel.
We can go there if you want.
HAIFA
SMADAR
Voila. Smadar Theater.
The square wasn't what I'd imagined.
Good, there's a photography shop at the corner. It could save me the trip uptown.

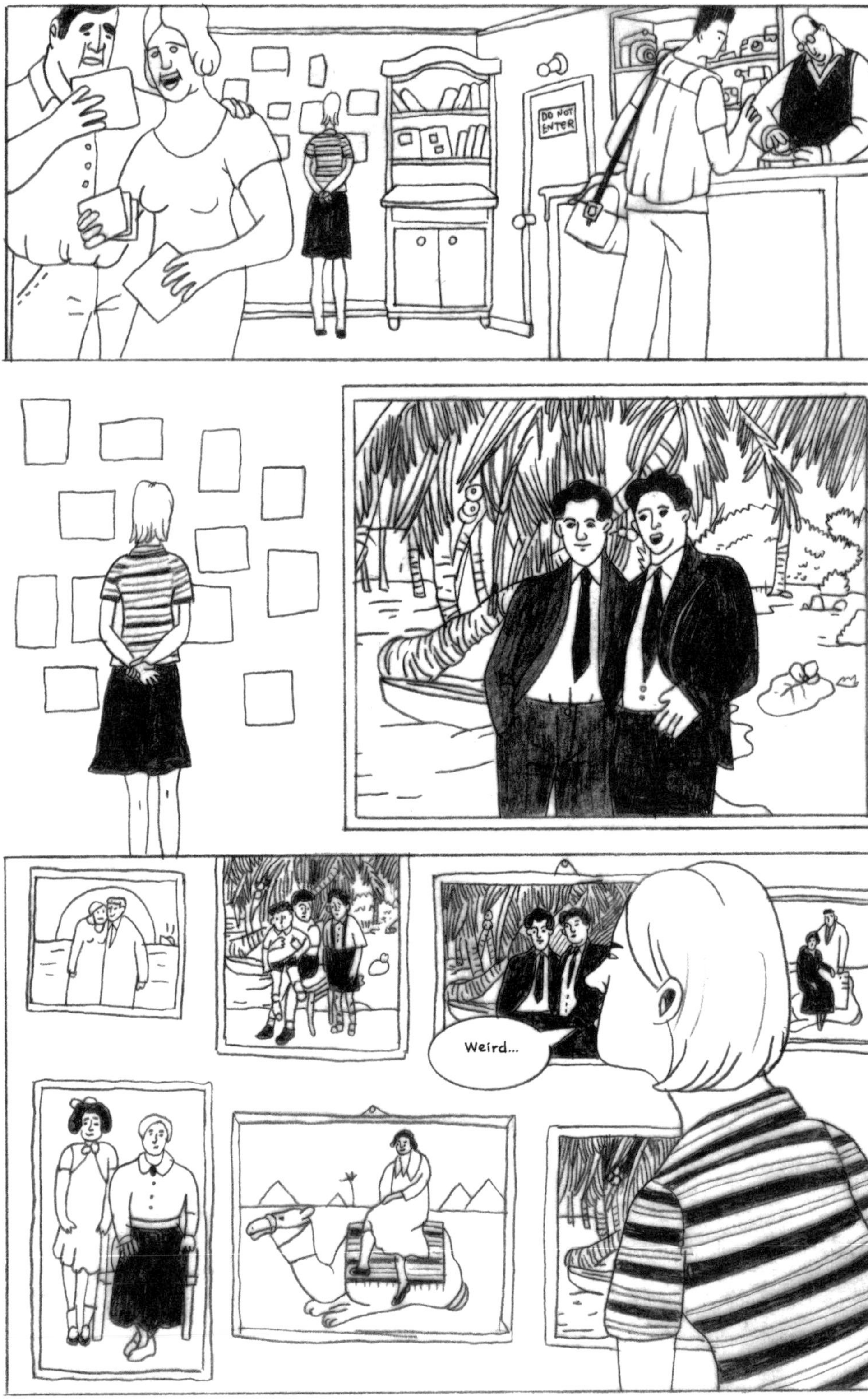
DO NOT ENTER
Weird...

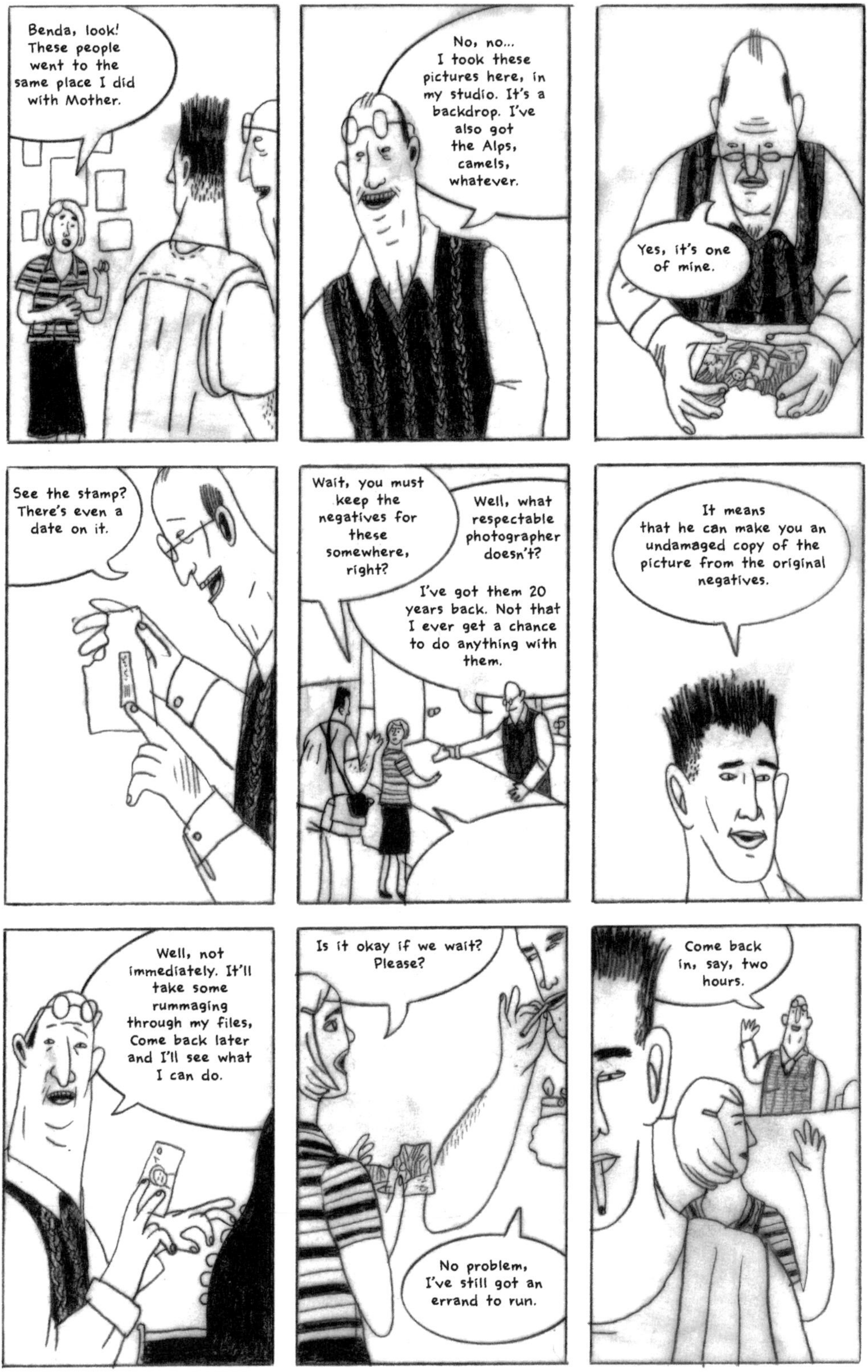
Benda, look! These people went to the same place I did with Mother.
No, no... I took these pictures here, in my studio. It's a backdrop. I've also got the Alps, camels, whatever.
Yes, it's one of mine.
See the stamp? There's even a date on it.
Wait, you must keep the negatives for these somewhere, right?
Well, what respectable photographer doesn't?
I've got them 20 years back. Not that I ever get a chance to do anything with them.
It means that he can make you an undamaged copy of the picture from the original negatives.
Well, not immediately. It'll take some rummaging through my files, Come back later and I'll see what I can do.
Is it okay if we wait? Please?
No problem, I've still got an errand to run.
Come back in, say, two hours.

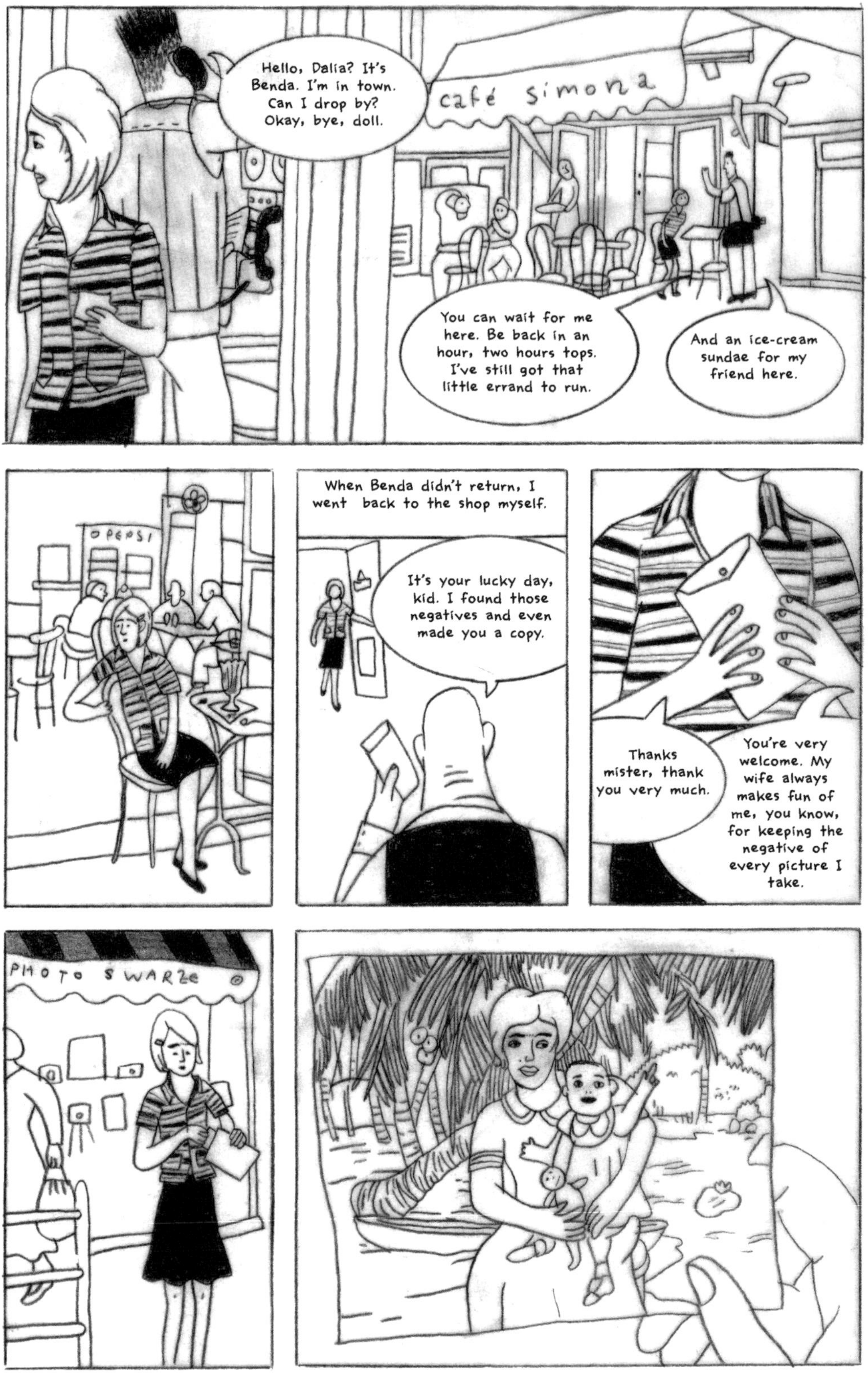
Hello, Dalia? It's Benda. I'm in town. Can I drop by? Okay, bye, doll.
café simona
You can wait for me here. Be back in an hour, two hours tops. I've still got that little errand to run.
And an ice-cream sundae for my friend here.
PEPSI
When Benda didn't return, I went back to the shop myself.
It's your lucky day, kid. I found those negatives and even made you a copy.
Thanks mister, thank you very much.
You're very welcome. My wife always makes fun of me, you know, for keeping the negative of every picture I take.
PHOTO SWARZE

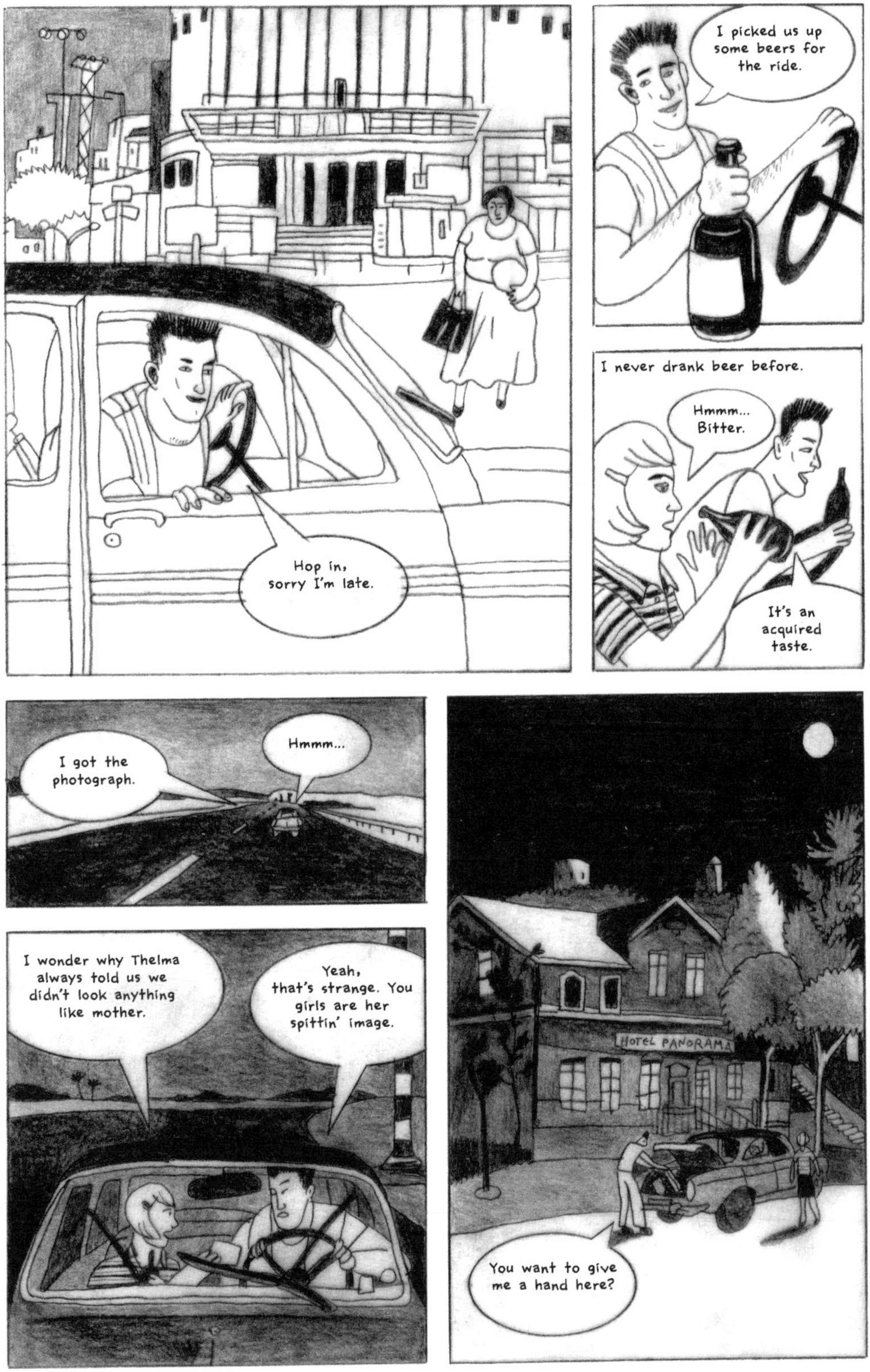

Hop in,
sorry I'm late.
I picked us up some beers for the ride.
I never drank beer before.
Hmmm... Bitter.
It's an acquired taste.
I got the photograph.
Hmmm...
I wonder why Thelma always told us we didn't look anything like mother.
Yeah, that's strange. You girls are her spittin' image.
HOTEL PANORAMA
You want to give me a hand here?

mew
Shhh... Stupid cat!
oops..
CRASH
What a day...!

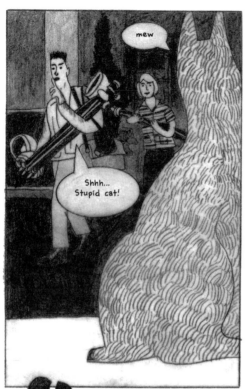

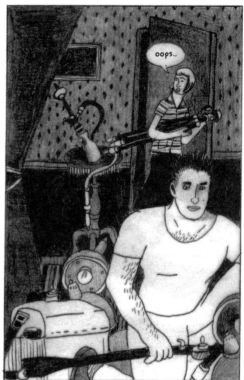

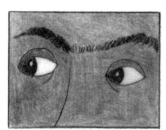

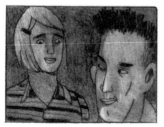

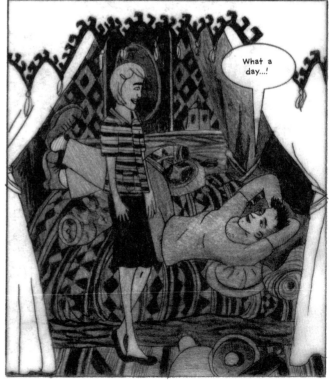

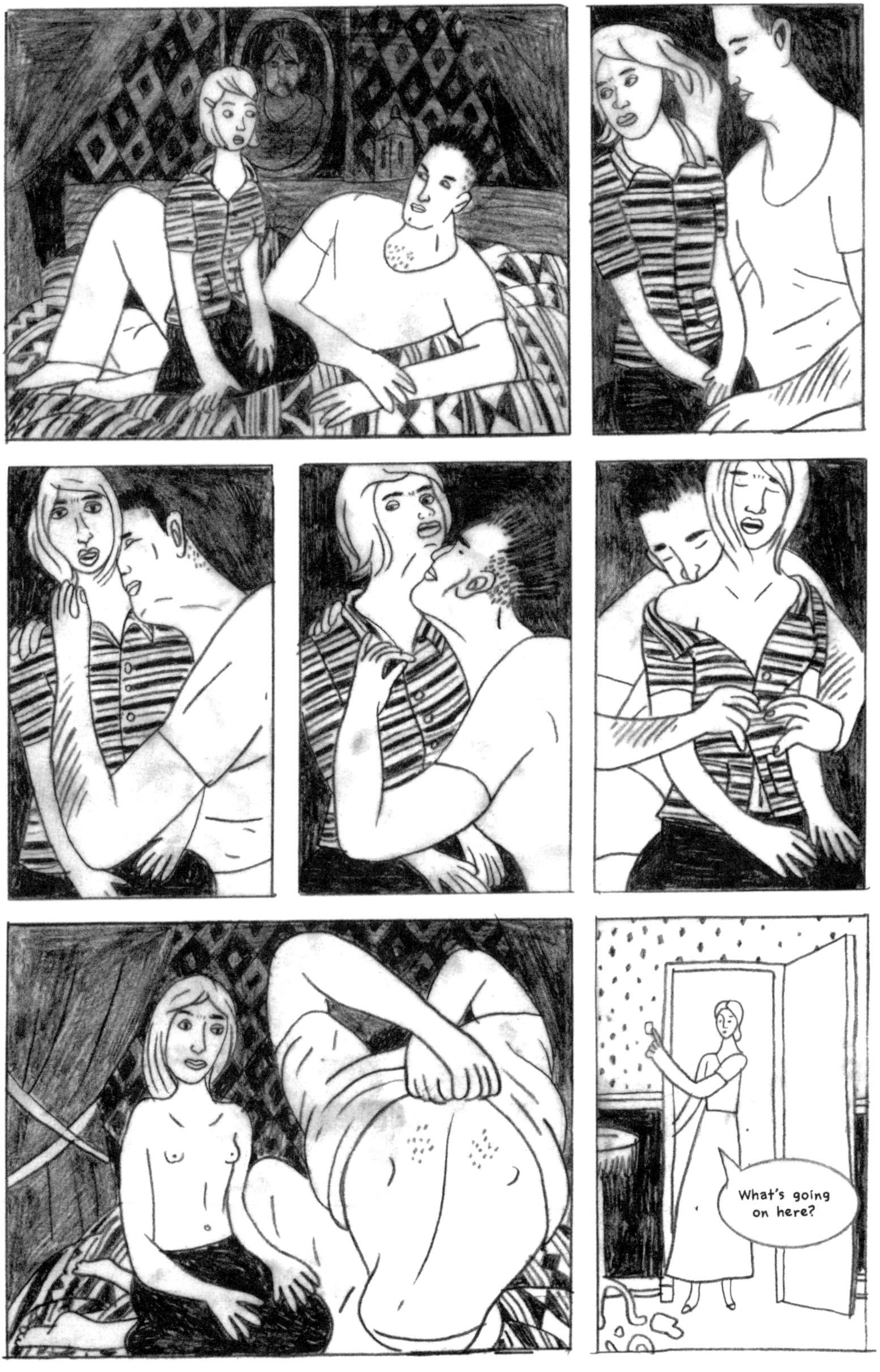
What's going on here?

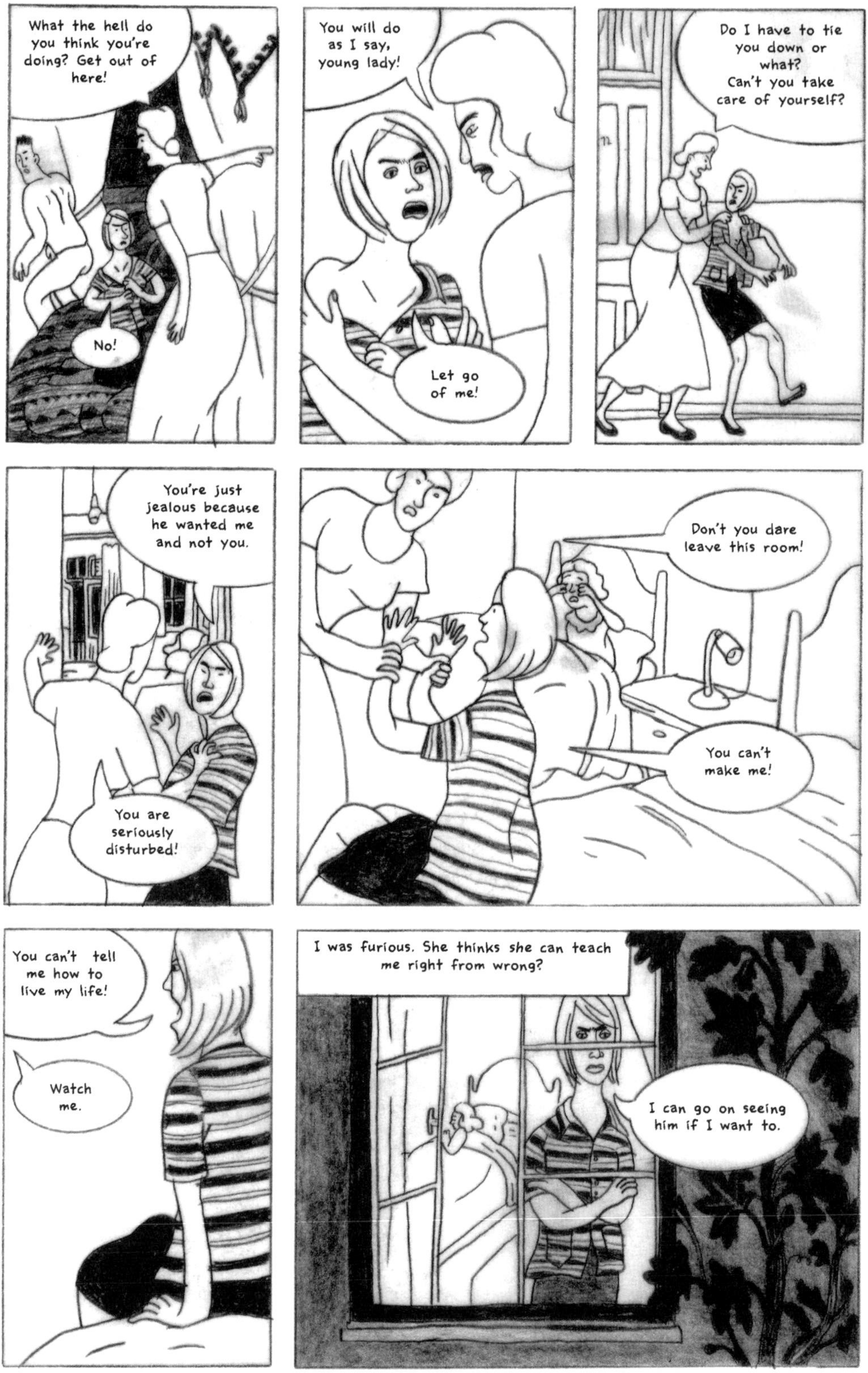
What the hell do you think you're doing? Get out of here!
No!
You will do as I say, young lady!
Let go of me!
Do I have to tie you down or what? Can't you take care of yourself?
You're just jealous because he wanted me and not you.
You are seriously disturbed!
Don't you dare leave this room!
You can't make me!
You can't tell me how to live my life!
Watch me.
I was furious. She thinks *she* can teach *me* right from wrong?
I can go on seeing him if I want to.

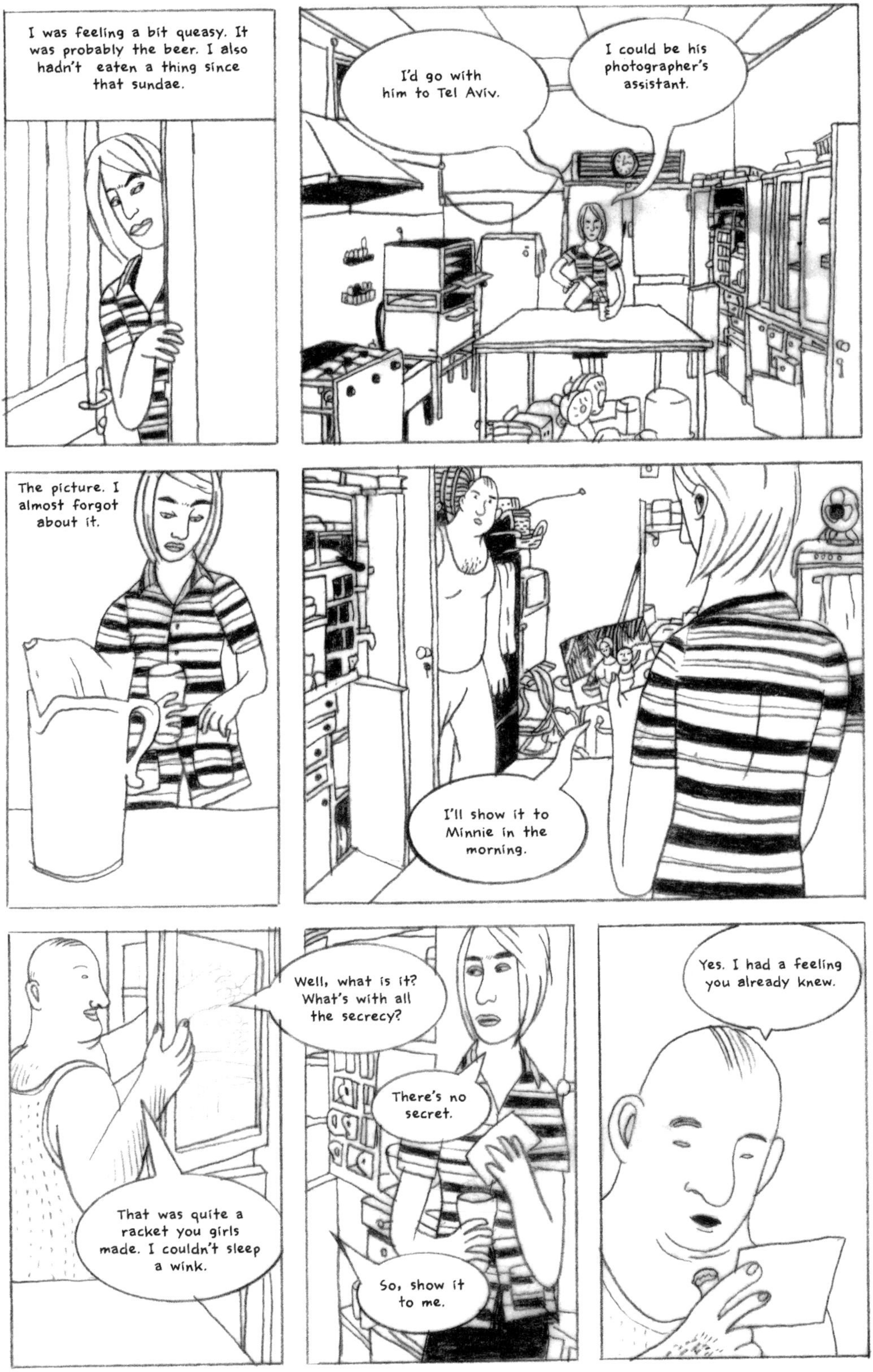
I was feeling a bit queasy. It was probably the beer. I also hadn't eaten a thing since that sundae.
I'd go with him to Tel Aviv.
I could be his photographer's assistant.
The picture. I almost forgot about it.
I'll show it to Minnie in the morning.
That was quite a racket you girls made. I couldn't sleep a wink.
Well, what is it? What's with all the secrecy?
There's no secret.
So, show it to me.
Yes. I had a feeling you already knew.

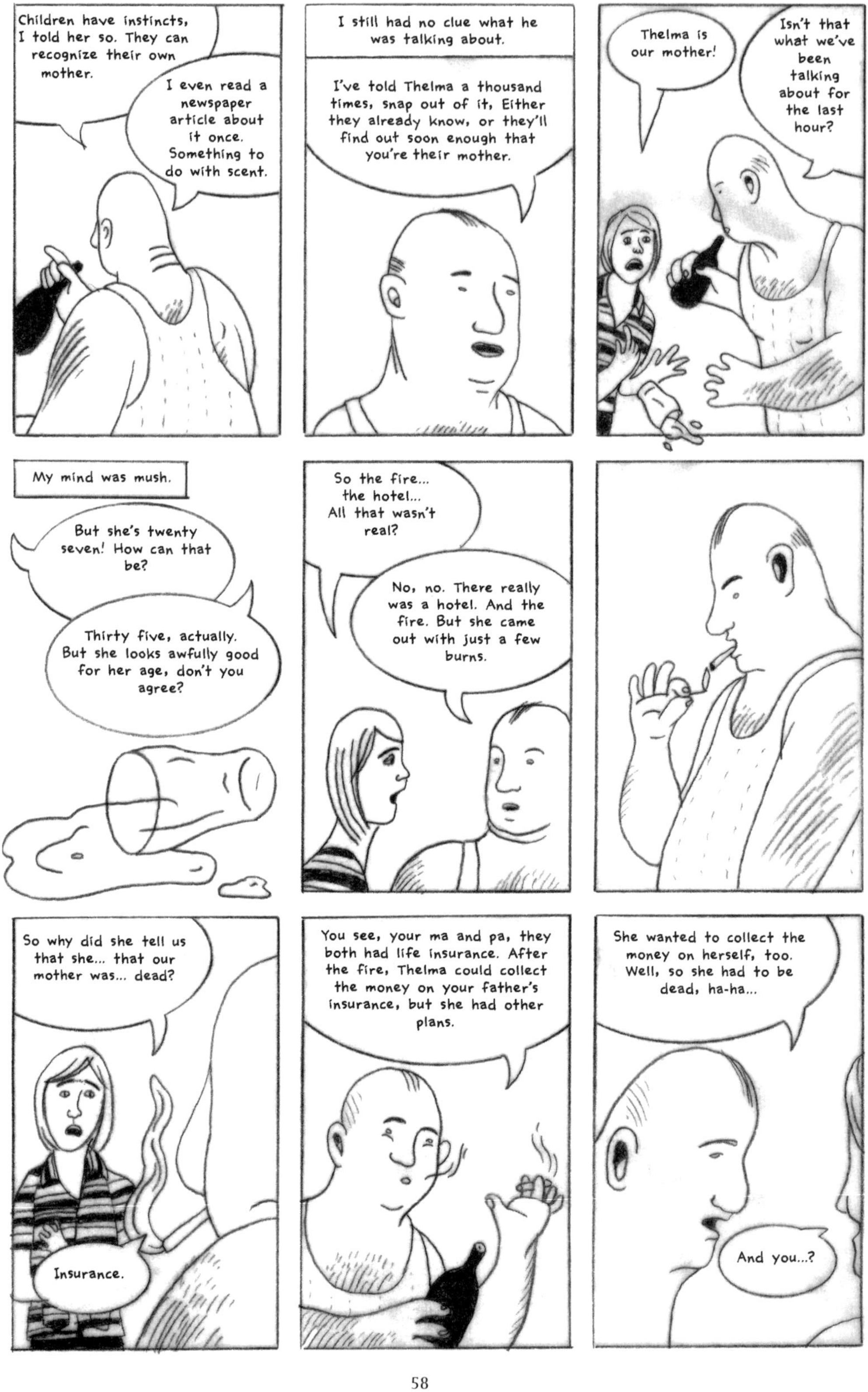
Children have instincts, I told her so. They can recognize their own mother.
I even read a newspaper article about it once. Something to do with scent.
I still had no clue what he was talking about.
I've told Thelma a thousand times, snap out of it, Either they already know, or they'll find out soon enough that you're their mother.
Thelma is our mother!
Isn't that what we've been talking about for the last hour?
My mind was mush.
But she's twenty seven! How can that be?
Thirty five, actually. But she looks awfully good for her age, don't you agree?
So the fire... the hotel... All that wasn't real?
No, no. There really was a hotel. And the fire. But she came out with just a few burns.
So why did she tell us that she... that our mother was... dead?
Insurance.
You see, your ma and pa, they both had life insurance. After the fire, Thelma could collect the money on your father's insurance, but she had other plans.
She wanted to collect the money on herself, too. Well, so she had to be dead, ha-ha...
And you...?

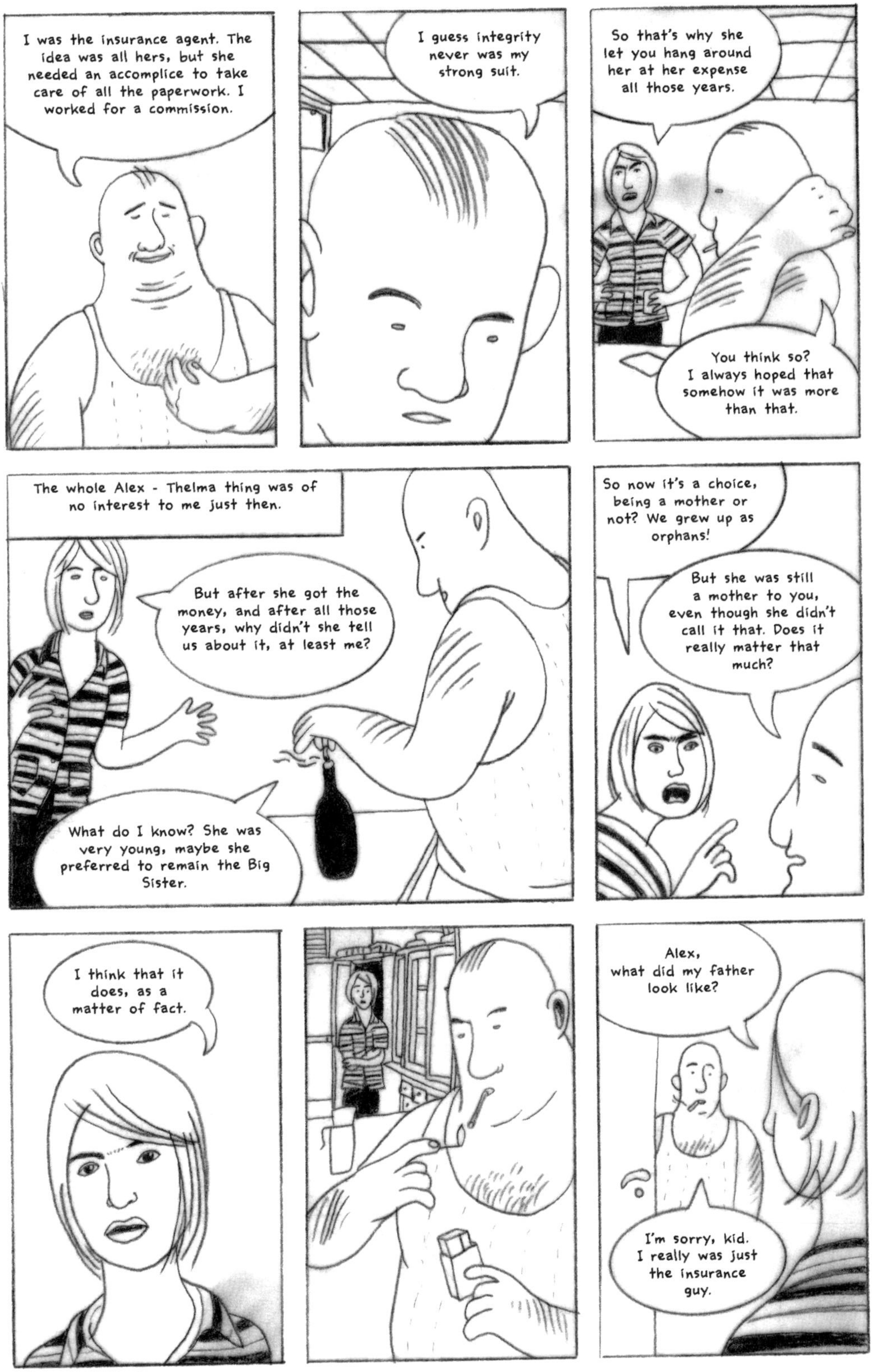
I was the insurance agent. The idea was all hers, but she needed an accomplice to take care of all the paperwork. I worked for a commission.
I guess integrity never was my strong suit.
So that's why she let you hang around her at her expense all those years.
You think so? I always hoped that somehow it was more than that.
The whole Alex - Thelma thing was of no interest to me just then.
But after she got the money, and after all those years, why didn't she tell us about it, at least me?
What do I know? She was very young, maybe she preferred to remain the Big Sister.
So now it's a choice, being a mother or not? We grew up as orphans!
But she was still a mother to you, even though she didn't call it that. Does it really matter that much?
I think that it does, as a matter of fact.
Alex, what did my father look like?
I'm sorry, kid. I really was just the insurance guy.

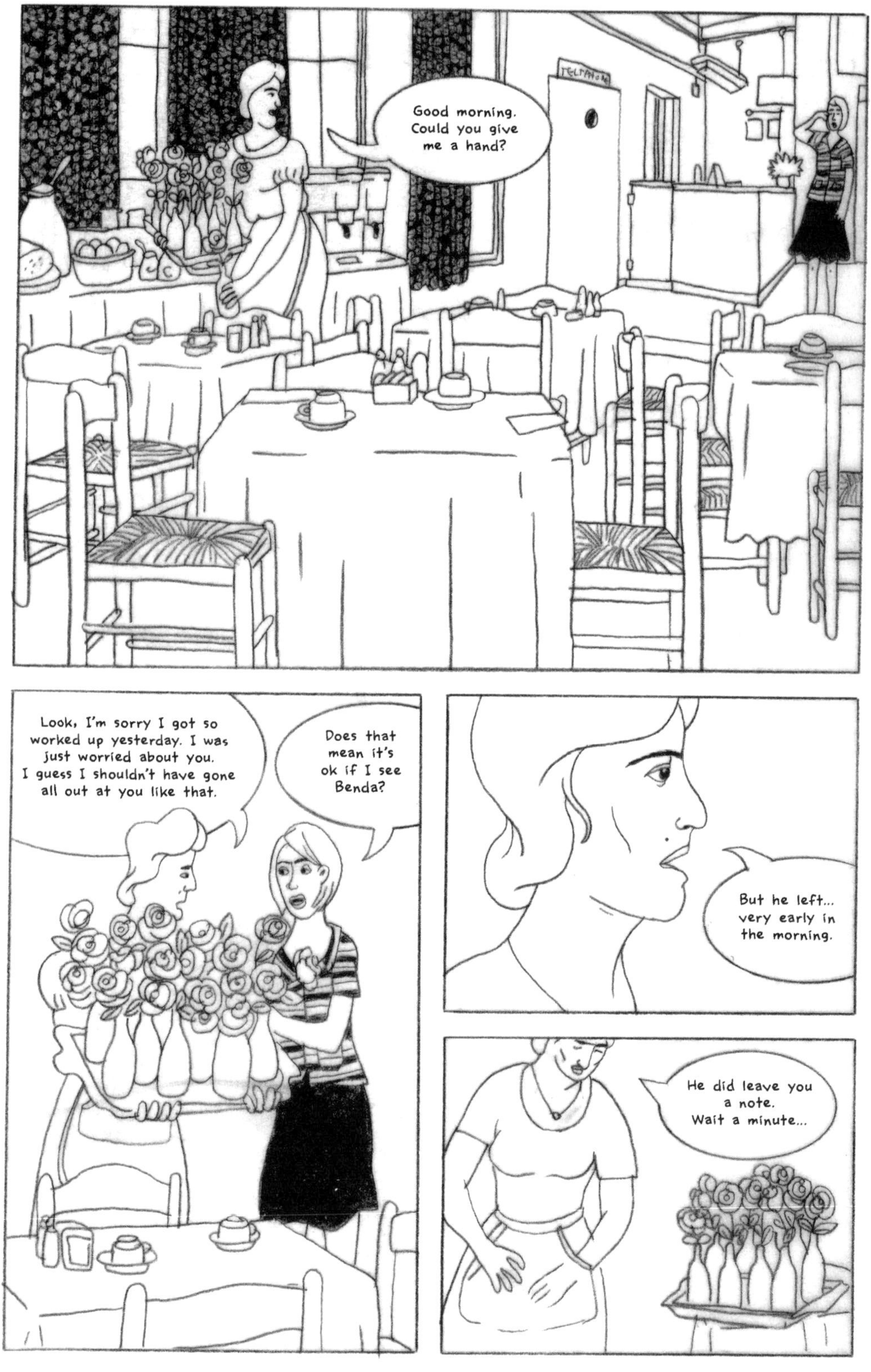
Good morning. Could you give me a hand?
Look, I'm sorry I got so worked up yesterday. I was just worried about you. I guess I shouldn't have gone all out at you like that.
Does that mean it's ok if I see Benda?
But he left... very early in the morning.
He did leave you a note. Wait a minute...

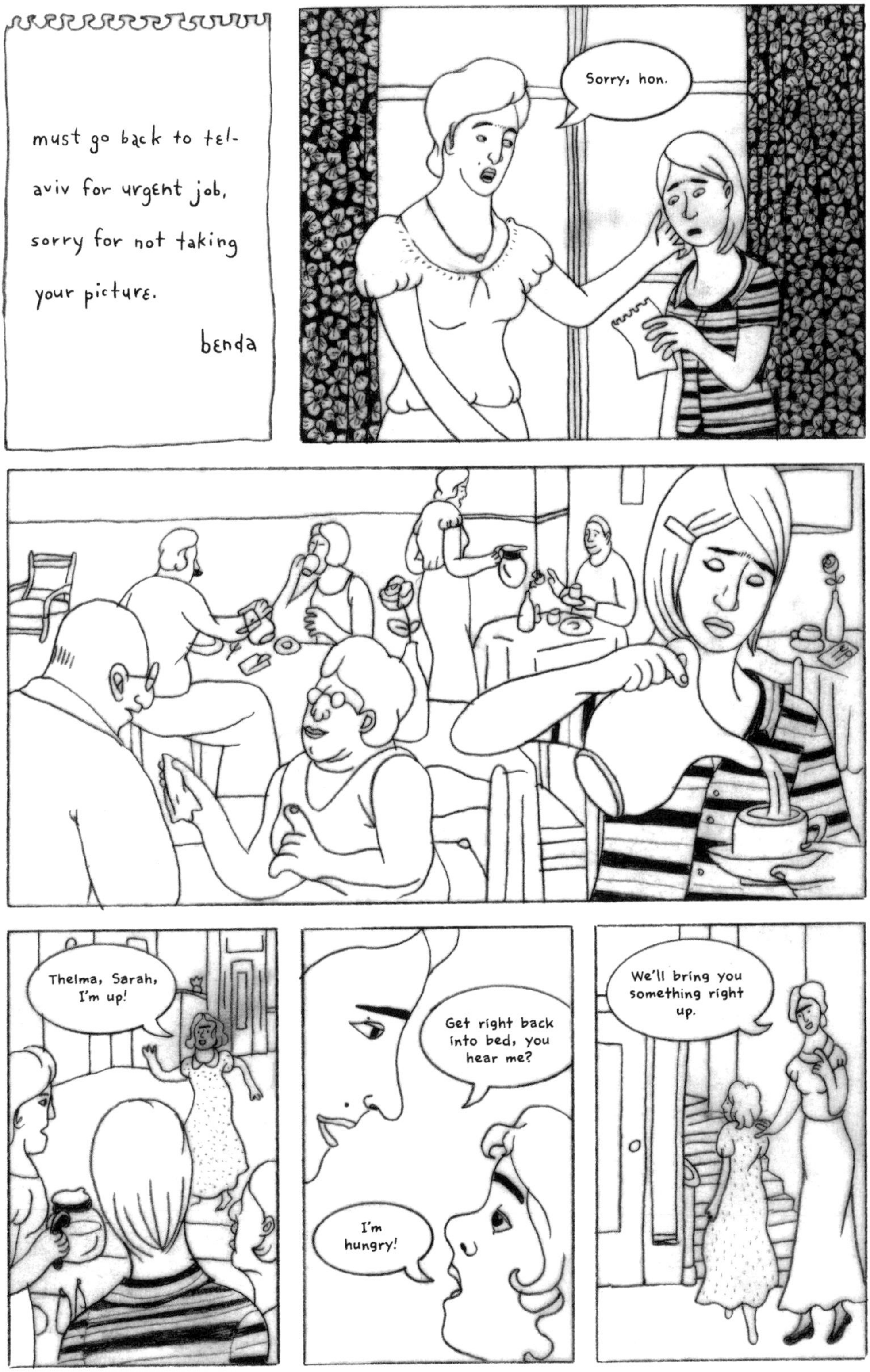
must go back to tel-aviv for urgent job, sorry for not taking your picture.
benda
Sorry, hon.
Thelma, Sarah, I'm up!
Get right back into bed, you hear me?
I'm hungry!
We'll bring you something right up.

Now tell me about the fire.

Again about the fire? It's such a sad story.

Minnie... Look... about the fire...

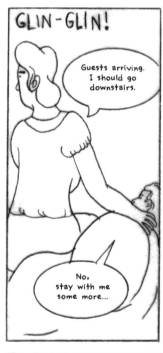
GLIN-GLIN!

Guests arriving. I should go downstairs.

No, stay with me some more...

Y...yeah, you can stay here. I'll take care of the guests.

Tell me about the fire... please...

Okay okay. Let's just take Lola off the bed.

So, many years ago, there lived a family...

THE PANTY KILLER

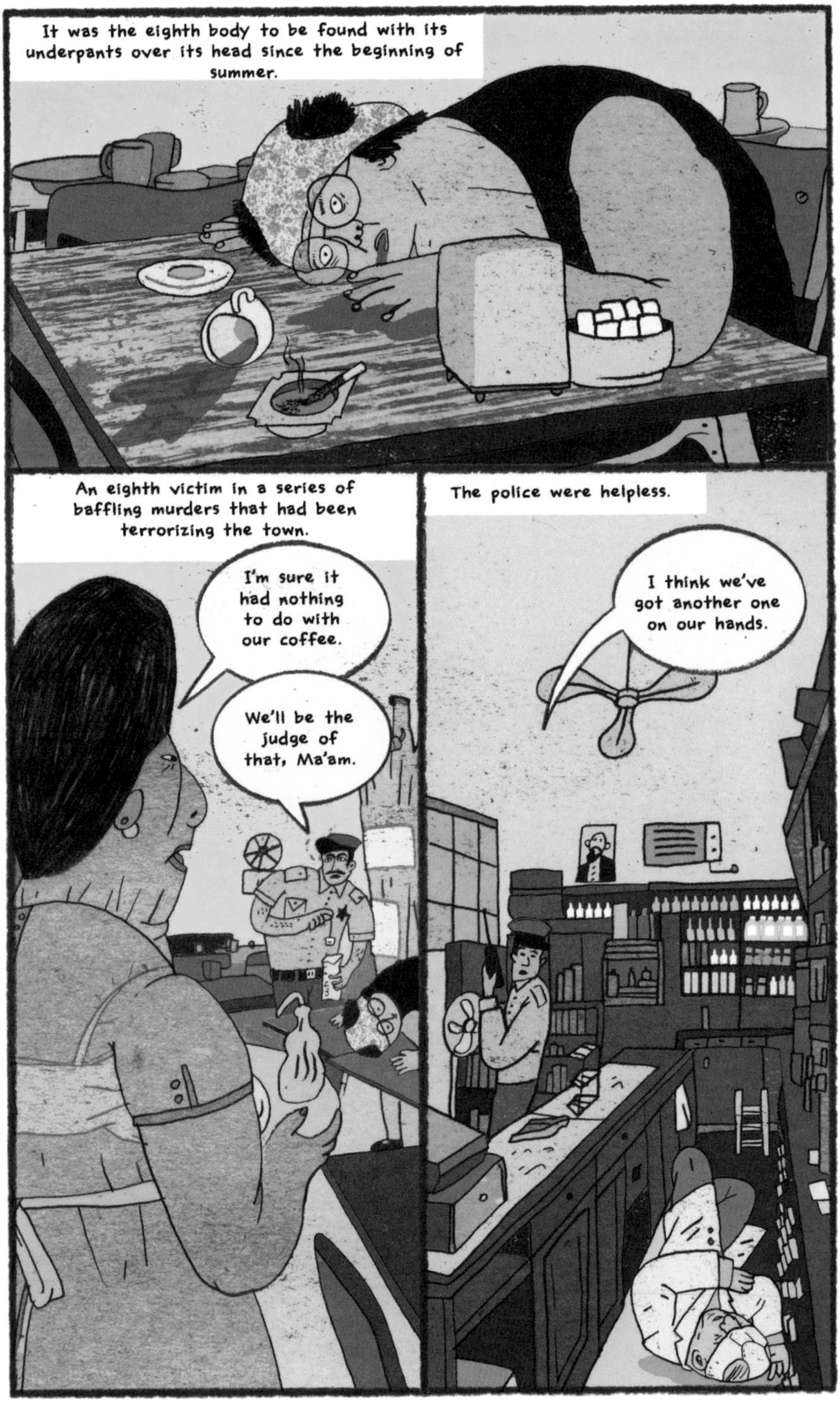
It was the eighth body to be found with its underpants over its head since the beginning of summer.
An eighth victim in a series of baffling murders that had been terrorizing the town.
I'm sure it had nothing to do with our coffee.
We'll be the judge of that, Ma'am.
The police were helpless.
I think we've got another one on our hands.

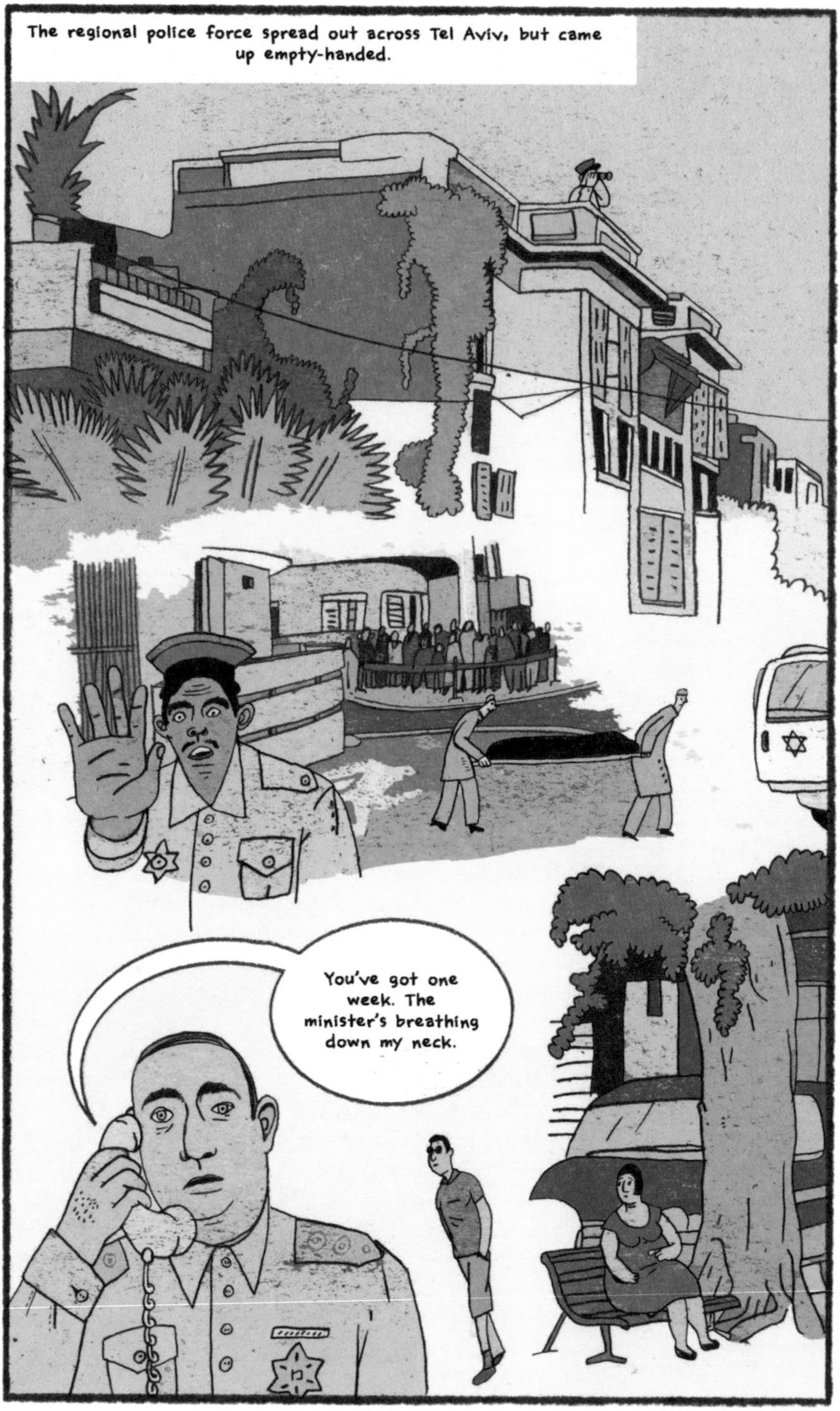
The regional police force spread out across Tel Aviv, but came up empty-handed.
You've got one week. The minister's breathing down my neck.

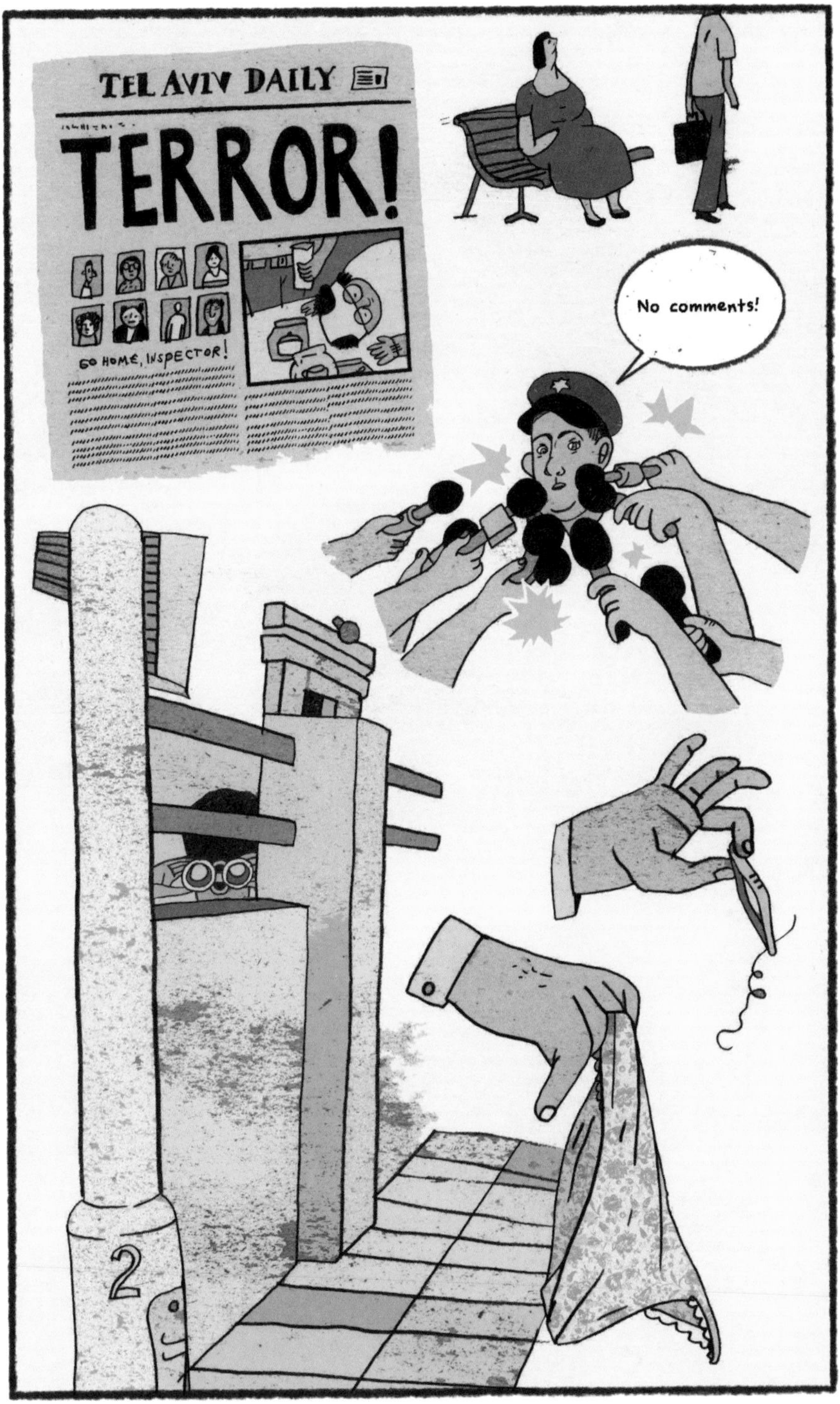
TEL AVIV DAILY
TERROR!
GO HOME, INSPECTOR!
No comments!
2

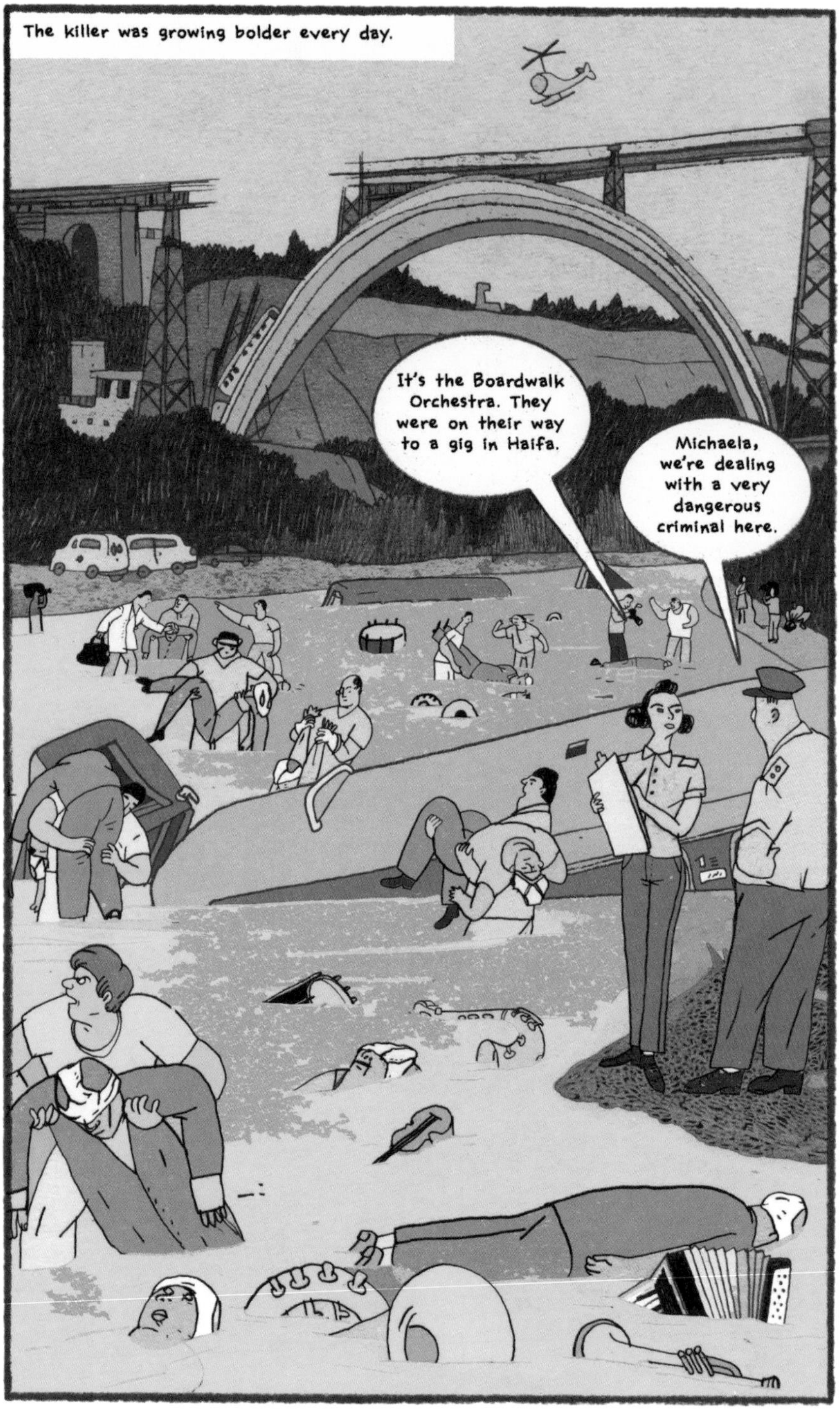
The killer was growing bolder every day.
It's the Boardwalk Orchestra. They were on their way to a gig in Haifa.
Michaela, we're dealing with a very dangerous criminal here.

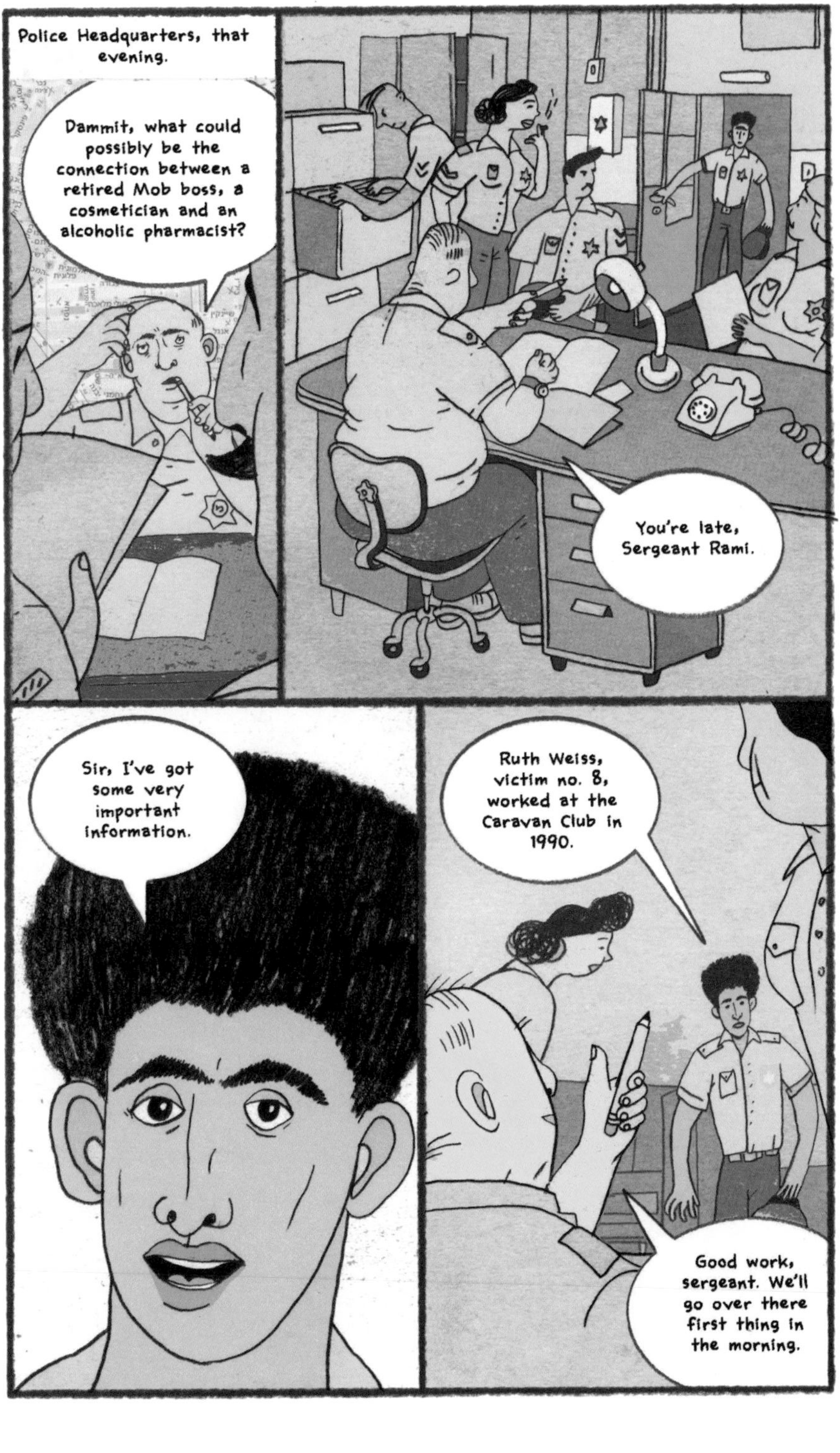
Police Headquarters, that evening.
Dammit, what could possibly be the connection between a retired Mob boss, a cosmetician and an alcoholic pharmacist?
You're late, Sergeant Rami.
Sir, I've got some very important information.
Ruth Weiss, victim no. 8, worked at the Caravan Club in 1990.
Good work, sergeant. We'll go over there first thing in the morning.

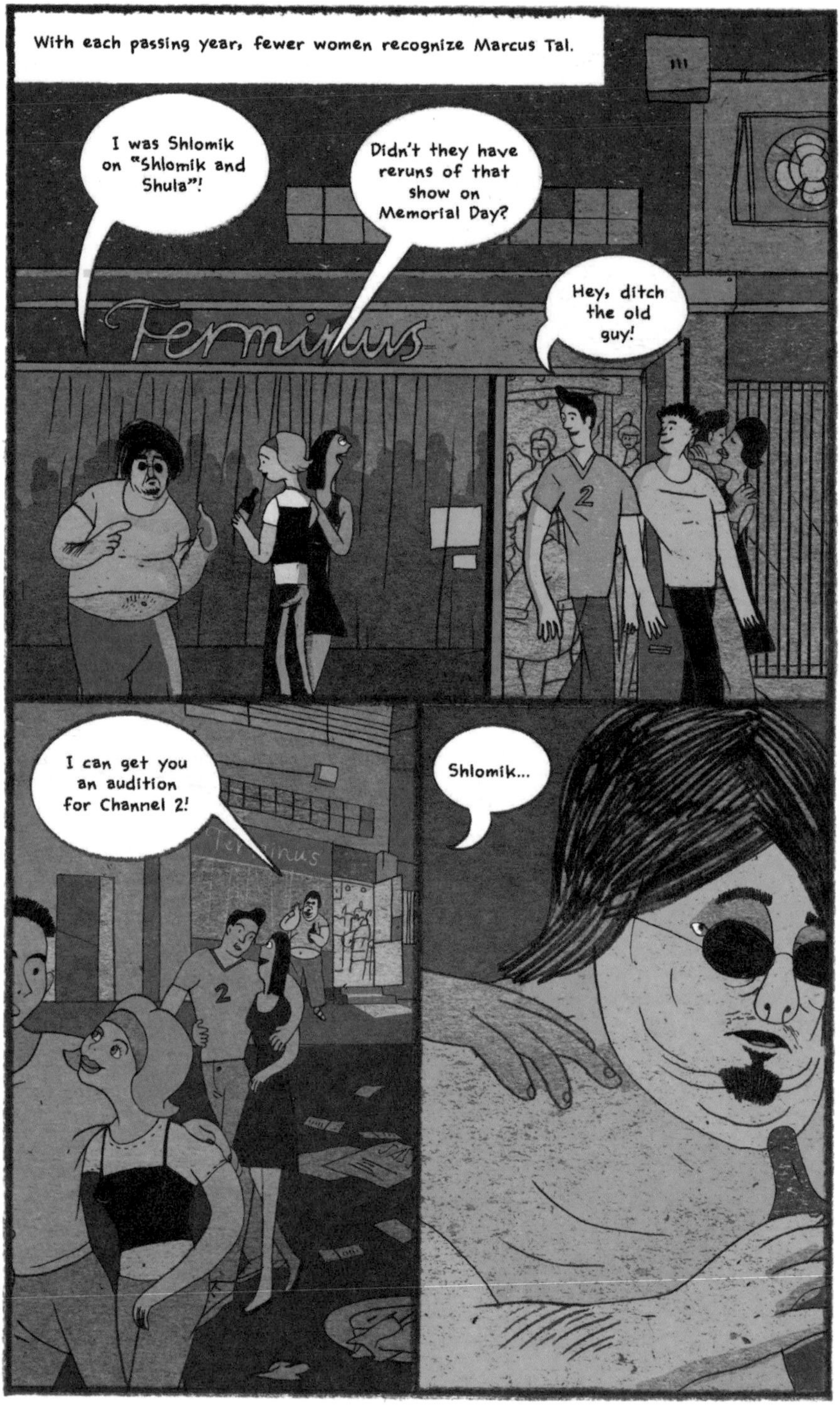
With each passing year, fewer women recognize Marcus Tal.
I was Shlomik on "Shlomik and Shula"!
Didn't they have reruns of that show on Memorial Day?
Termimus
Hey, ditch the old guy!
I can get you an audition for Channel 2!
Shlomik...

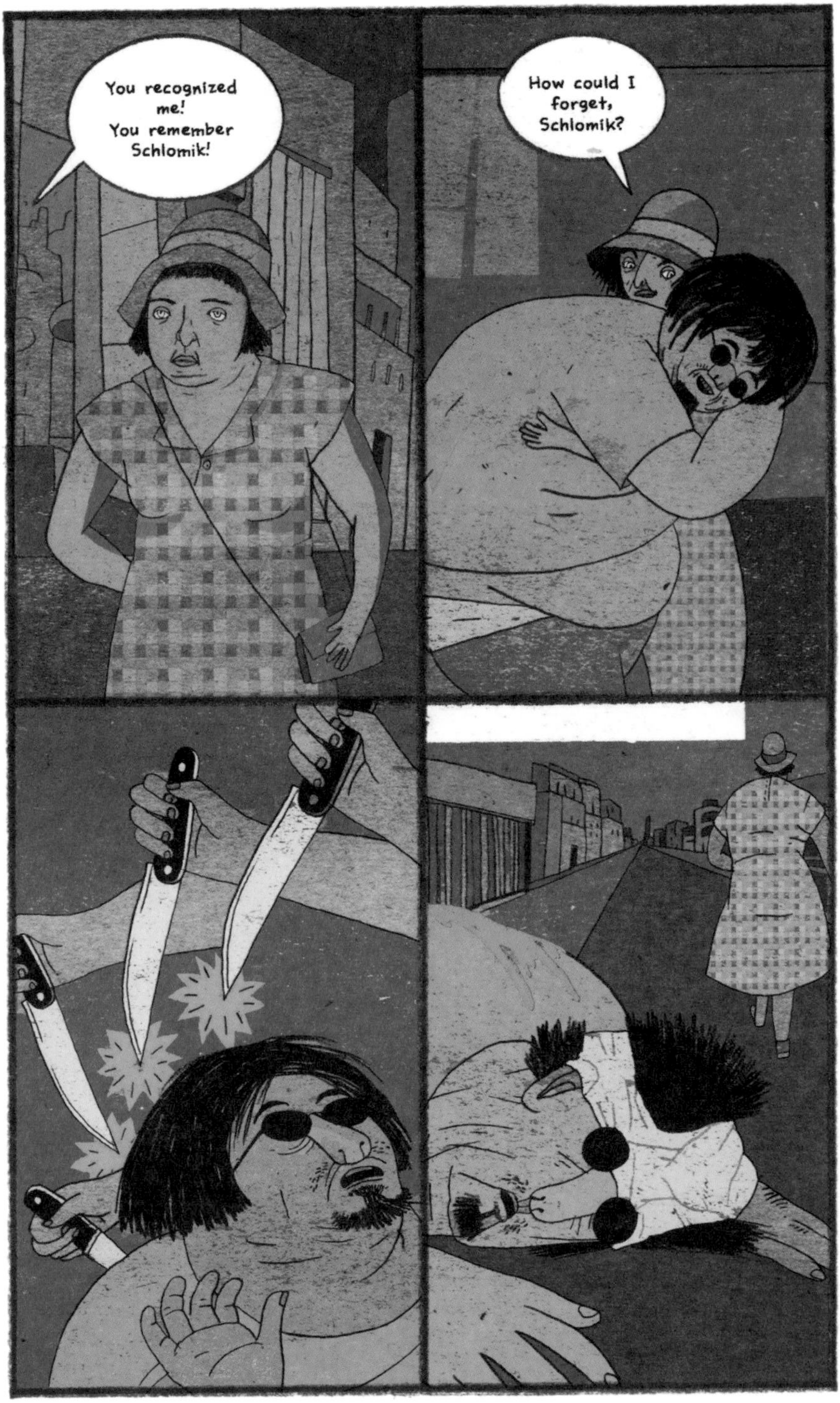
You recognized me! You remember Schlomik!
How could I forget, Schlomik?

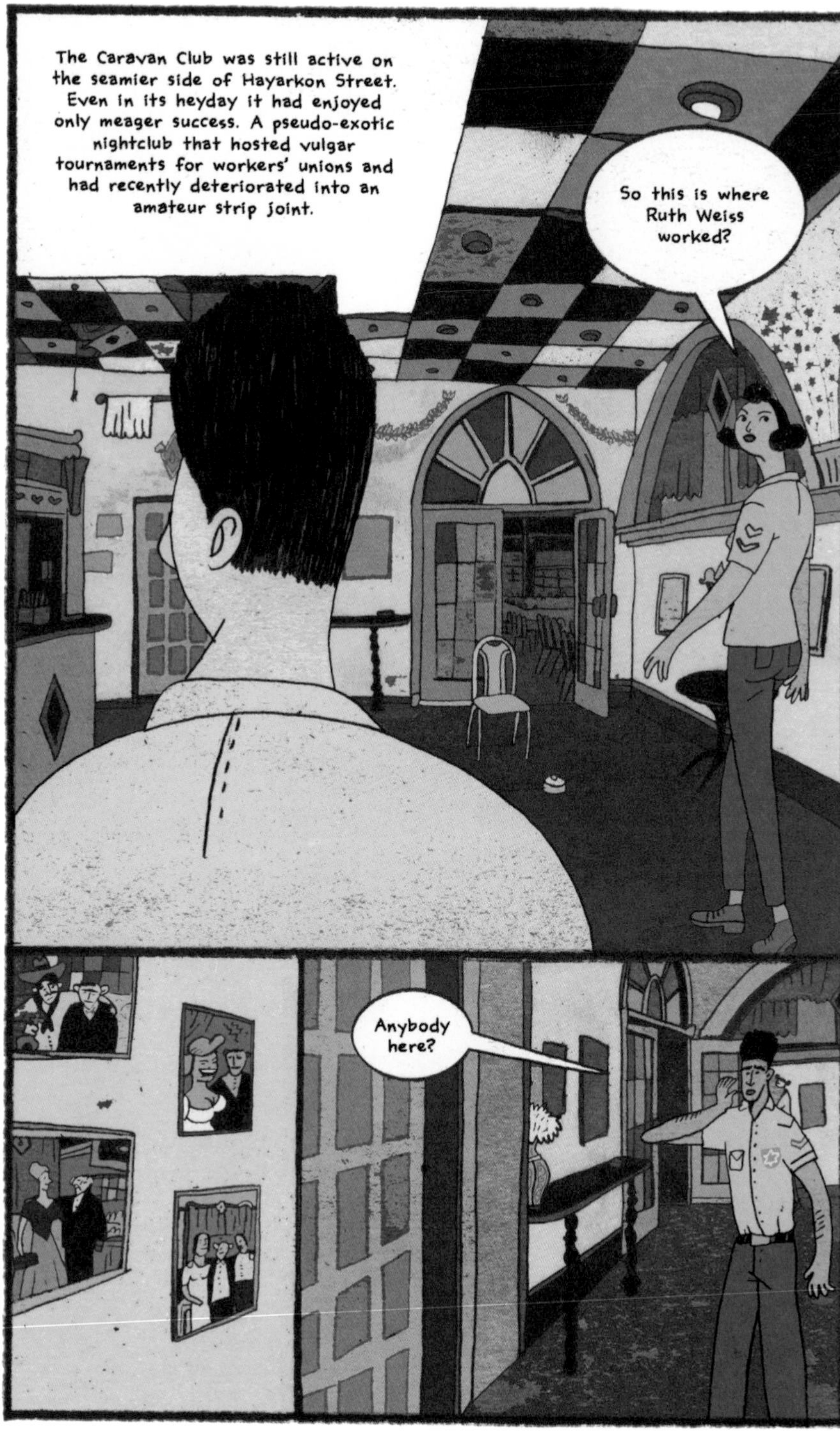
The Caravan Club was still active on the seamier side of Hayarkon Street. Even in its heyday it had enjoyed only meager success. A pseudo-exotic nightclub that hosted vulgar tournaments for workers' unions and had recently deteriorated into an amateur strip joint.
So this is where Ruth Weiss worked?
Anybody here?

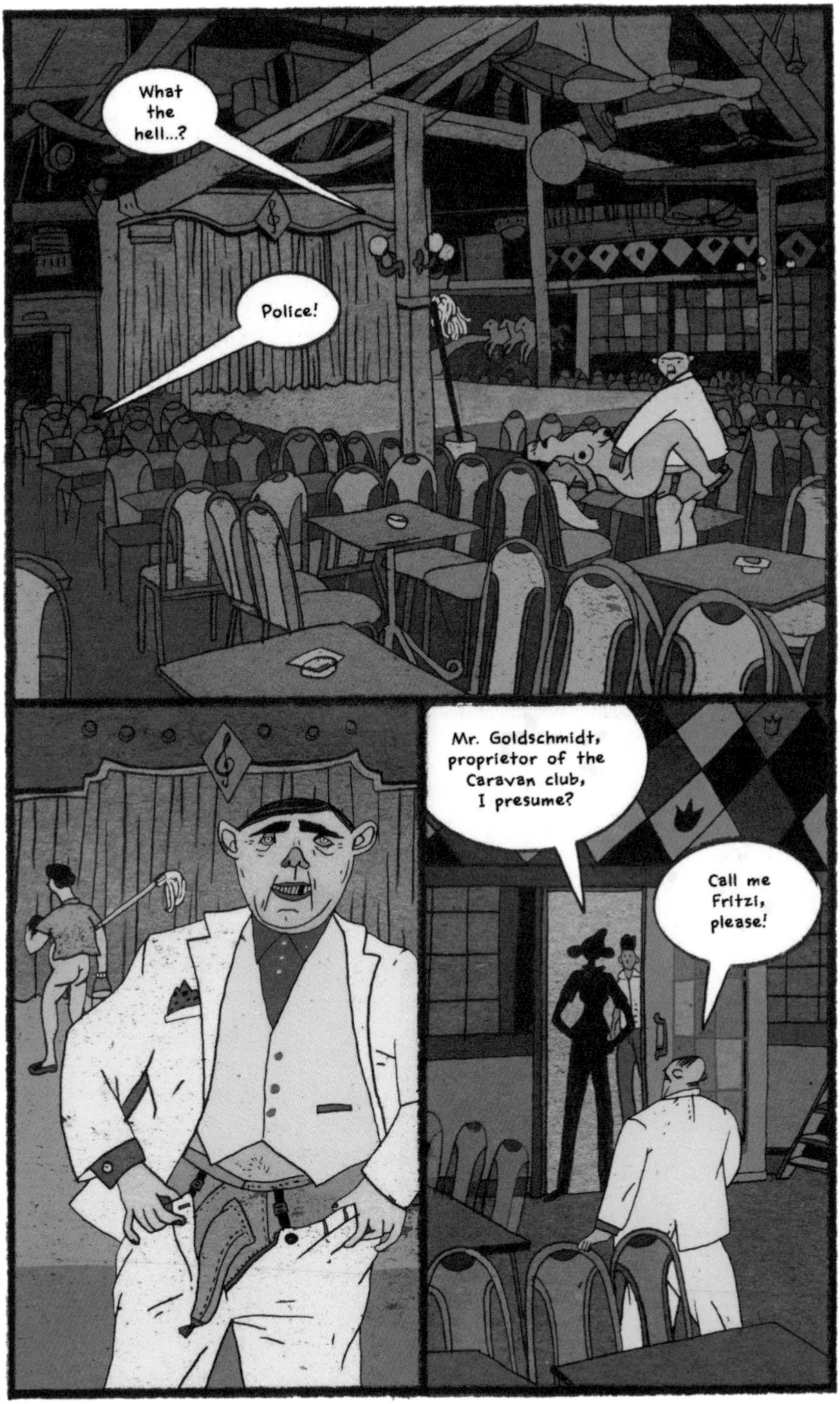
What the hell...?
Police!
Mr. Goldschmidt, proprietor of the Caravan club, I presume?
Call me Fritzi, please!

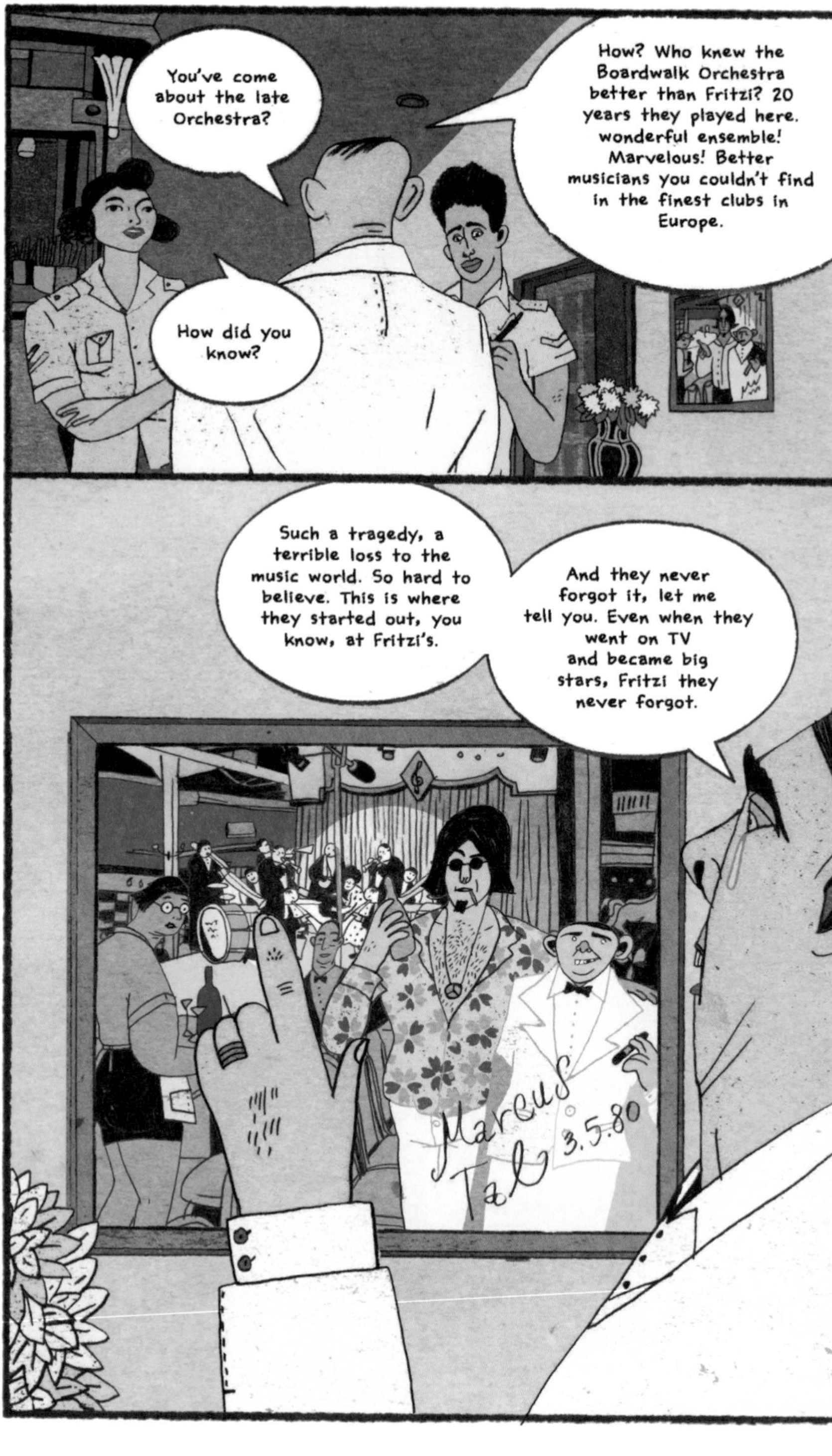
You've come about the late Orchestra?
How? Who knew the Boardwalk Orchestra better than Fritzi? 20 years they played here. wonderful ensemble! Marvelous! Better musicians you couldn't find in the finest clubs in Europe.
How did you know?
Such a tragedy, a terrible loss to the music world. So hard to believe. This is where they started out, you know, at Fritzi's.
And they never forgot it, let me tell you. Even when they went on TV and became big stars, Fritzi they never forgot.
Marcus Tal 3.5.80

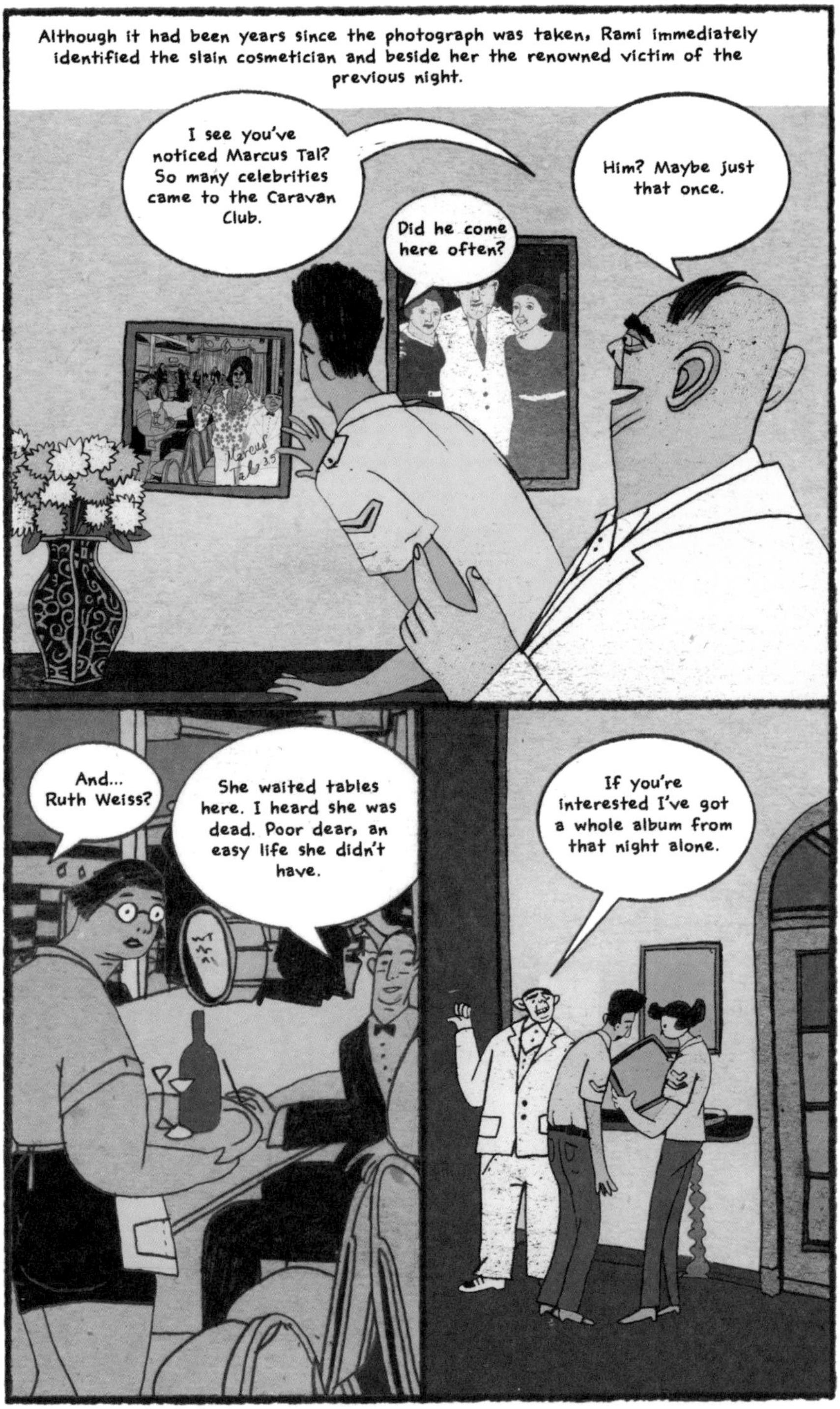
Although it had been years since the photograph was taken, Rami immediately identified the slain cosmetician and beside her the renowned victim of the previous night.
I see you've noticed Marcus Tal? So many celebrities came to the Caravan Club.
Did he come here often?
Him? Maybe just that once.
And... Ruth Weiss?
She waited tables here. I heard she was dead. Poor dear, an easy life she didn't have.
If you're interested I've got a whole album from that night alone.

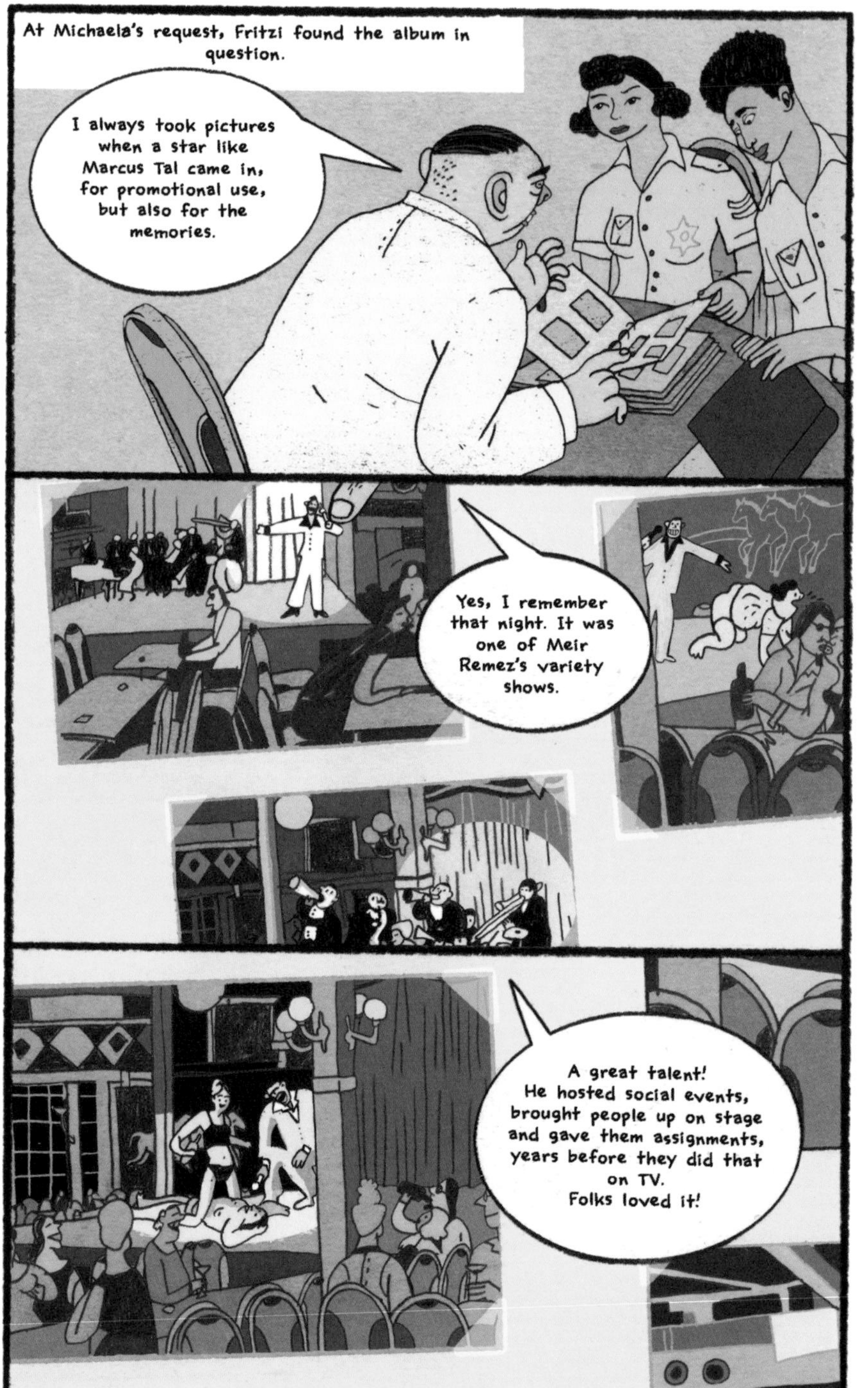
At Michaela's request, Fritzi found the album in question.
I always took pictures when a star like Marcus Tal came in, for promotional use, but also for the memories.
Yes, I remember that night. It was one of Meir Remez's variety shows.
A great talent! He hosted social events, brought people up on stage and gave them assignments, years before they did that on TV. Folks loved it!

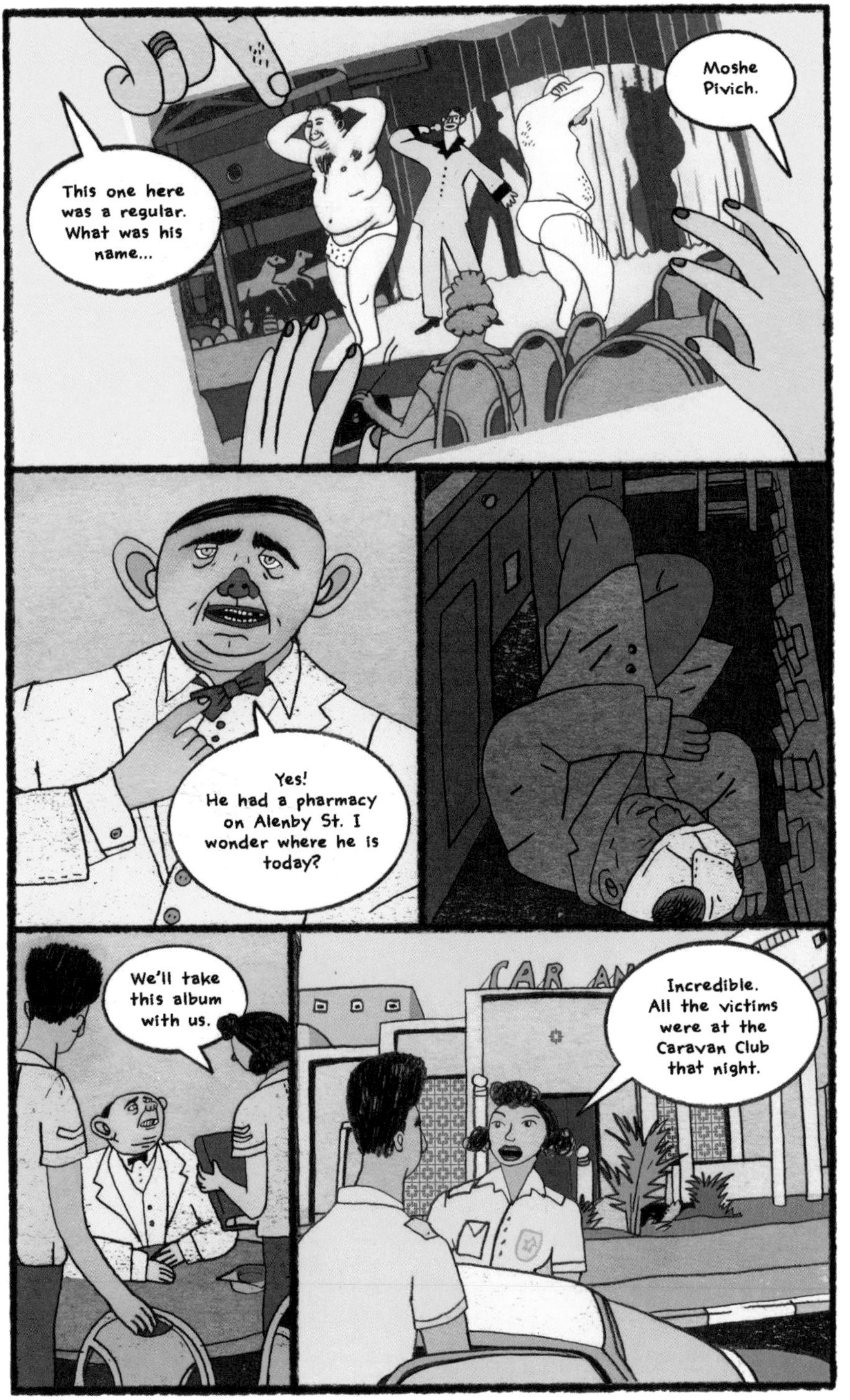
This one here was a regular. What was his name...
Moshe Pivich.
Yes! He had a pharmacy on Alenby St. I wonder where he is today?
We'll take this album with us.
Incredible. All the victims were at the Caravan Club that night.
CAR AN

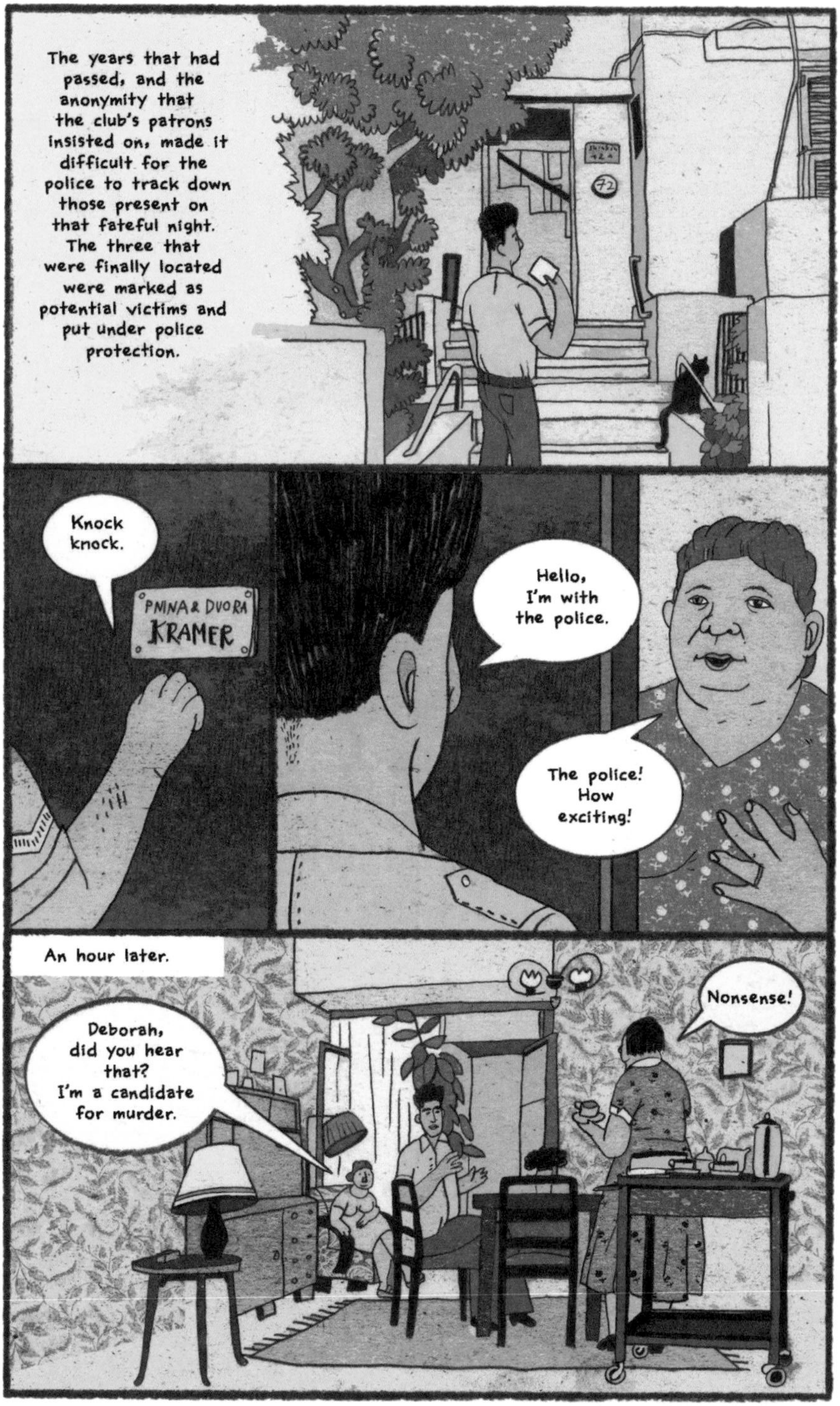

The years that had passed, and the anonymity that the club's patrons insisted on, made it difficult for the police to track down those present on that fateful night. The three that were finally located were marked as potential victims and put under police protection.
72
Knock knock.
PNINA & DVORA KRAMER
Hello, I'm with the police.
The police! How exciting!
An hour later.
Deborah, did you hear that? I'm a candidate for murder.
Nonsense!

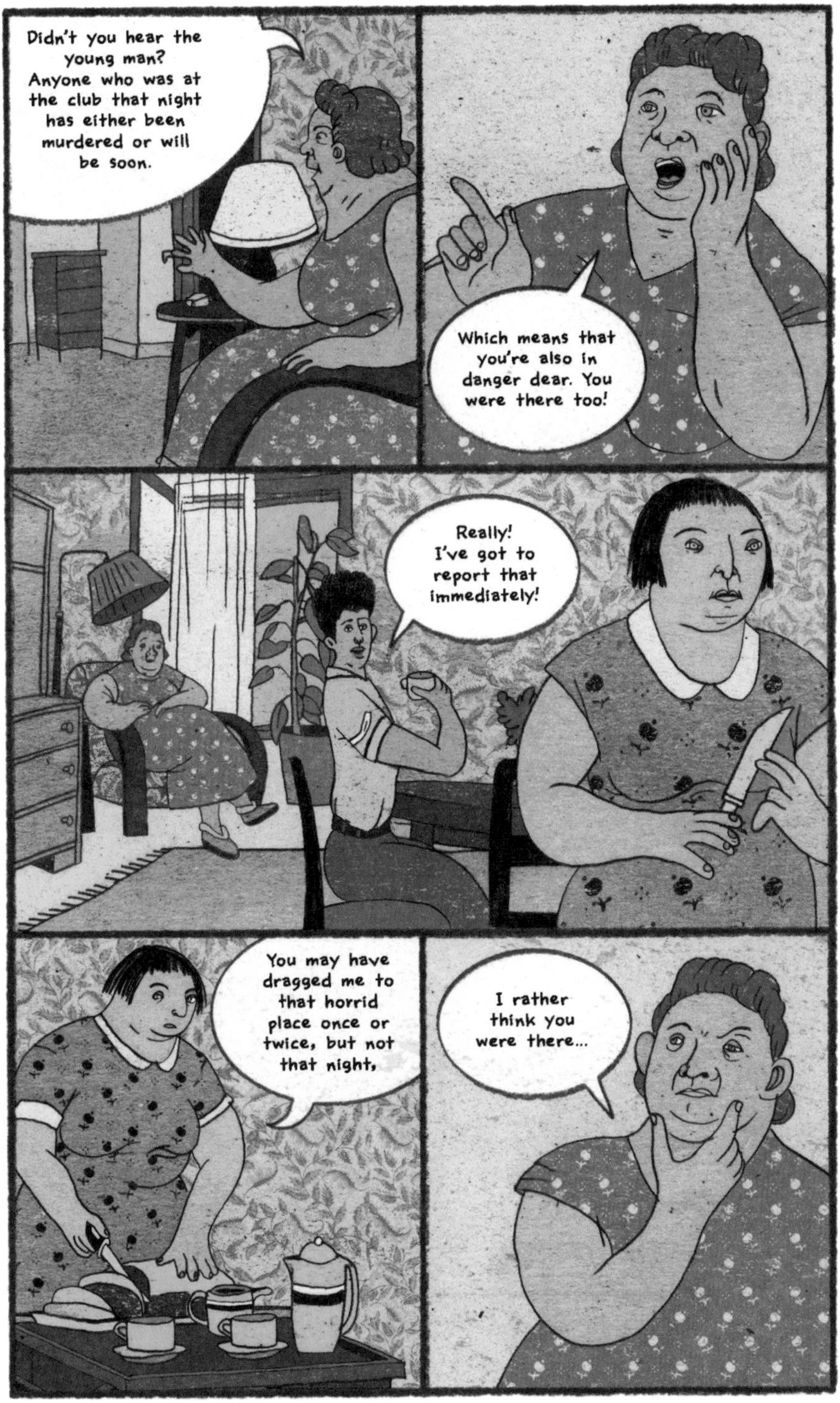
Didn't you hear the young man? Anyone who was at the club that night has either been murdered or will be soon.
Which means that you're also in danger dear. You were there too!
Really! I've got to report that immediately!
You may have dragged me to that horrid place once or twice, but not that night,
I rather think you were there...

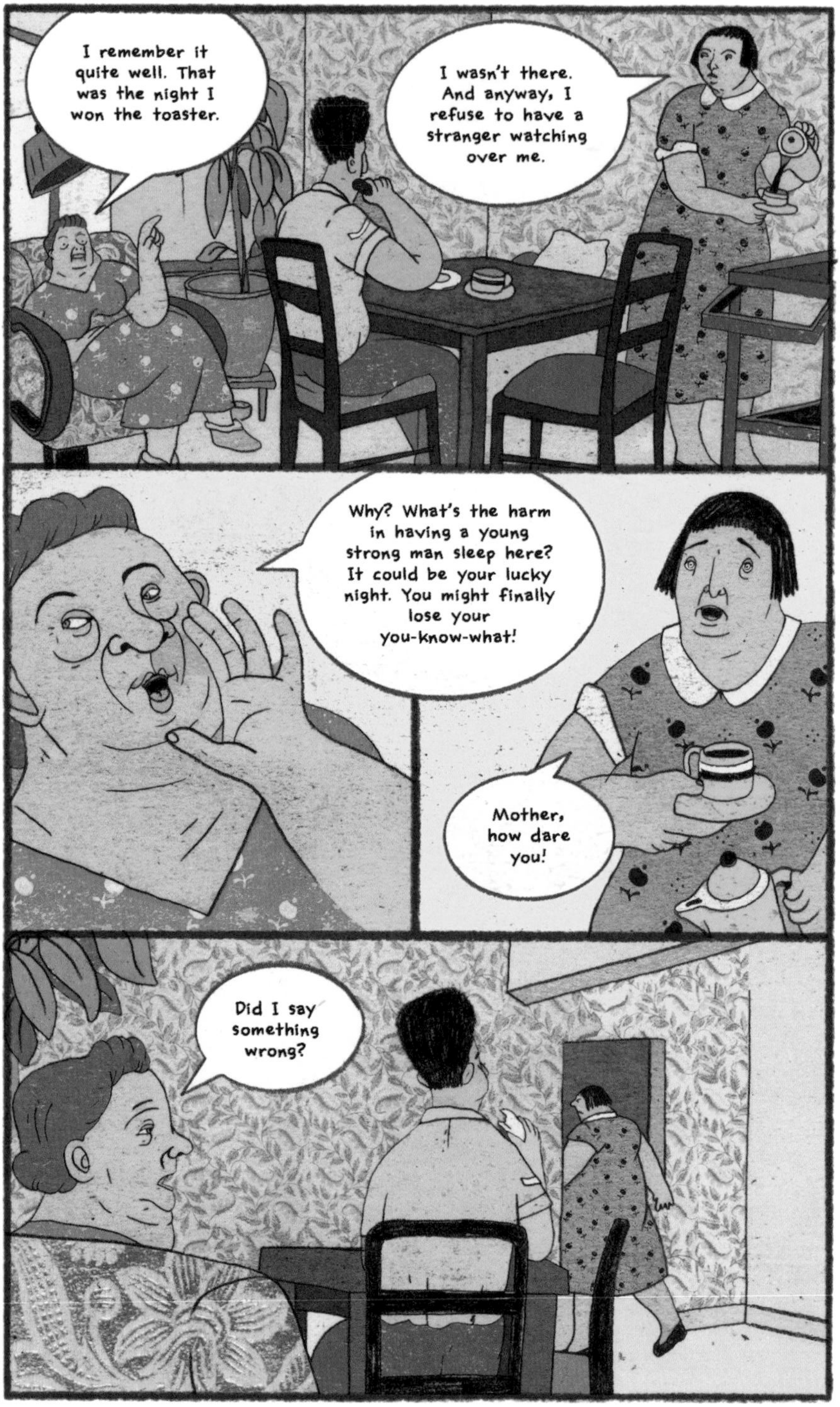
I remember it quite well. That was the night I won the toaster.
I wasn't there. And anyway, I refuse to have a stranger watching over me.
Why? What's the harm in having a young strong man sleep here? It could be your lucky night. You might finally lose your you-know-what!
Mother, how dare you!
Did I say something wrong?

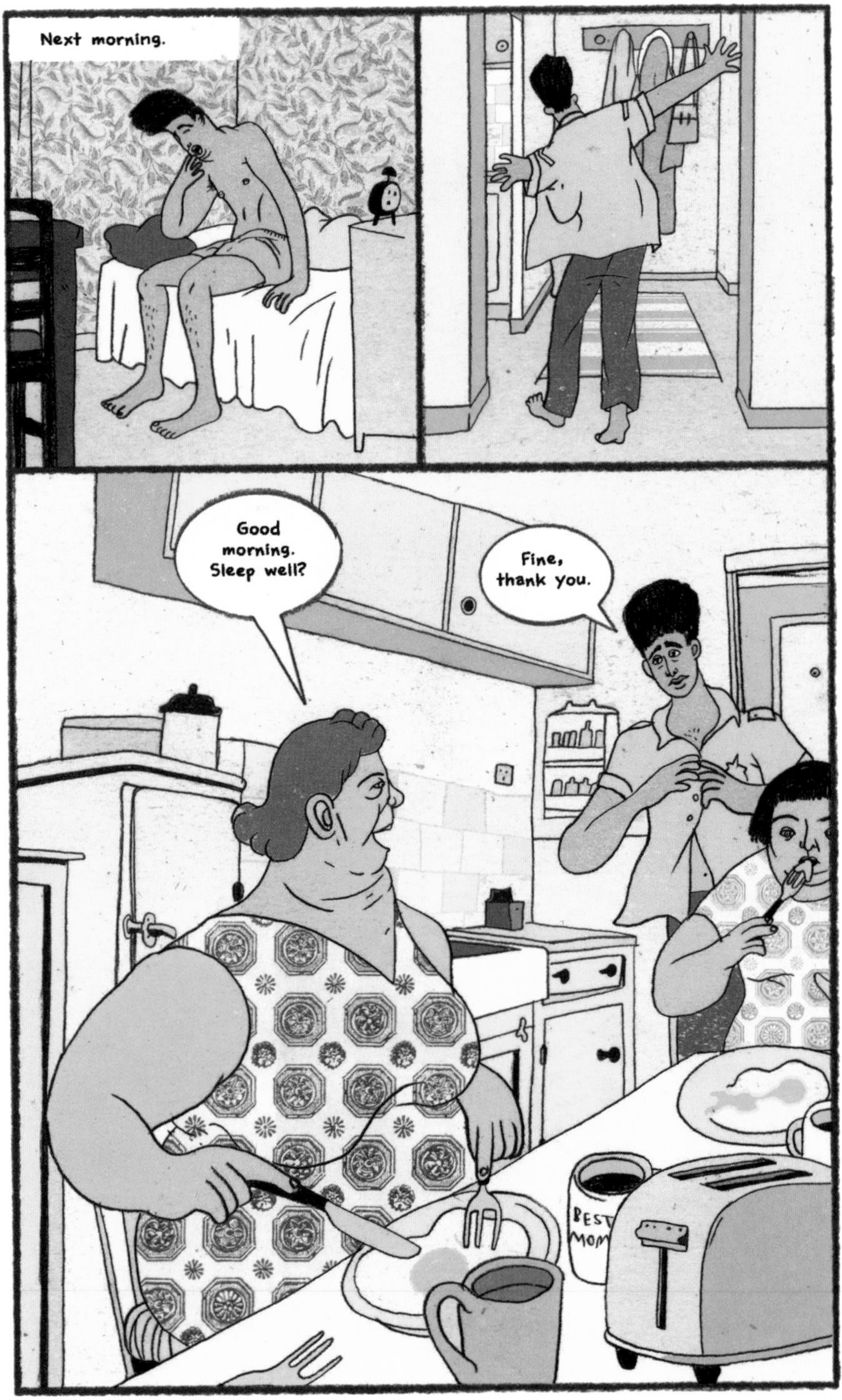
Next morning.
Good morning. Sleep well?
Fine, thank you.
BEST MOM

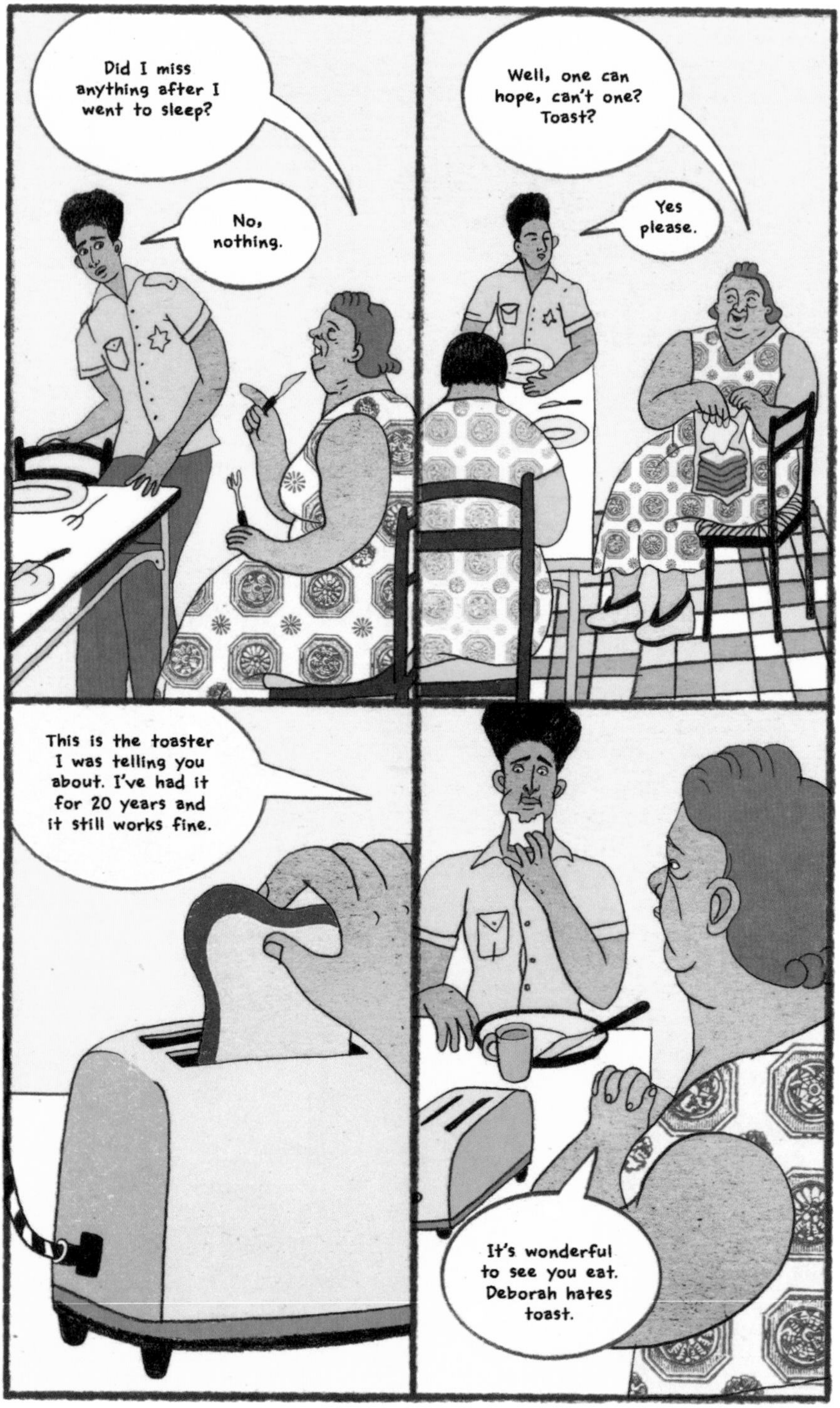
Did I miss anything after I went to sleep?
No, nothing.
Well, one can hope, can't one? Toast?
Yes please.
This is the toaster I was telling you about. I've had it for 20 years and it still works fine.
It's wonderful to see you eat. Deborah hates toast.

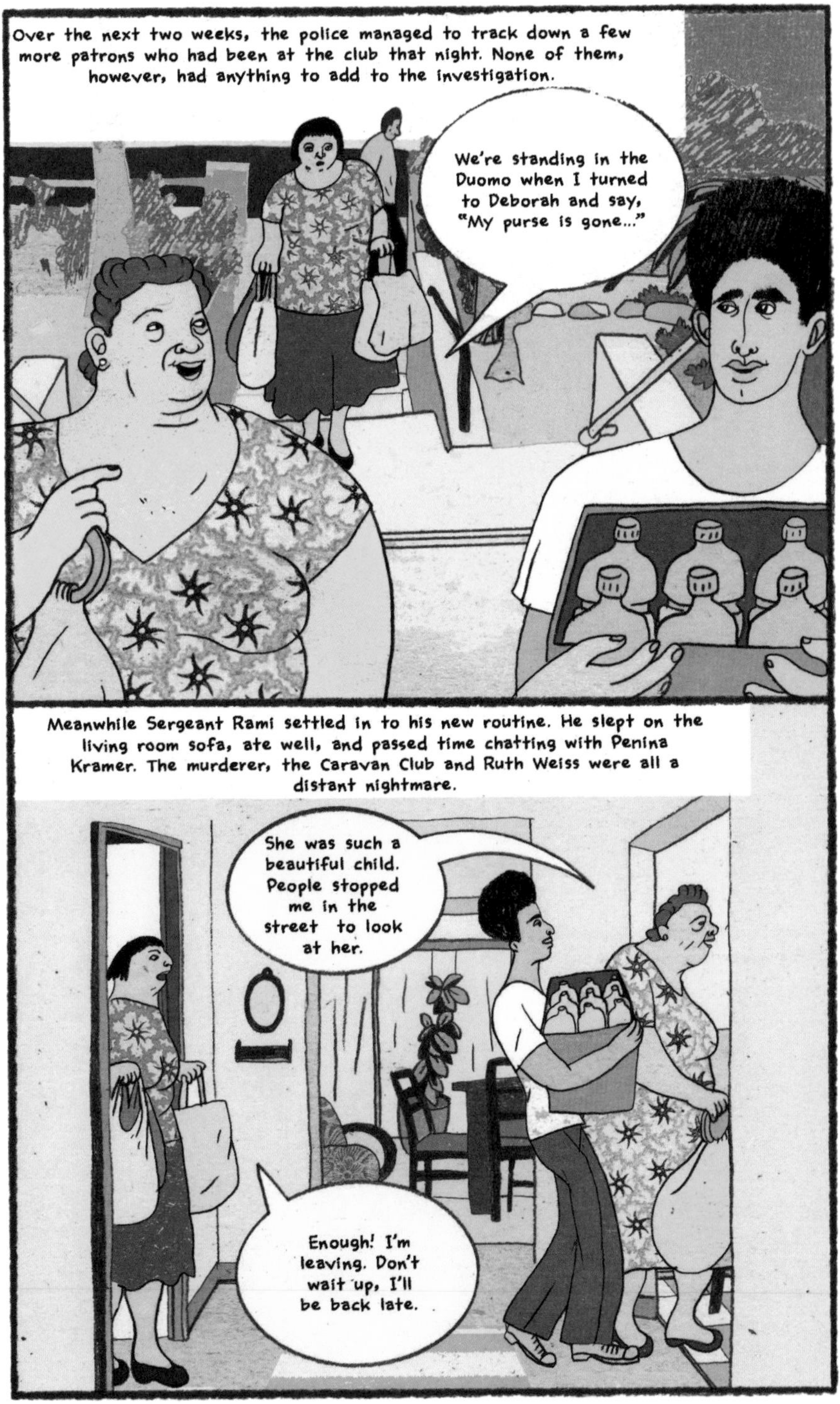
Over the next two weeks, the police managed to track down a few more patrons who had been at the club that night. None of them, however, had anything to add to the investigation.
We're standing in the Duomo when I turned to Deborah and say, "My purse is gone..."
Meanwhile Sergeant Rami settled in to his new routine. He slept on the living room sofa, ate well, and passed time chatting with Penina Kramer. The murderer, the Caravan Club and Ruth Weiss were all a distant nightmare.
She was such a beautiful child. People stopped me in the street to look at her.
Enough! I'm leaving. Don't wait up, I'll be back late.

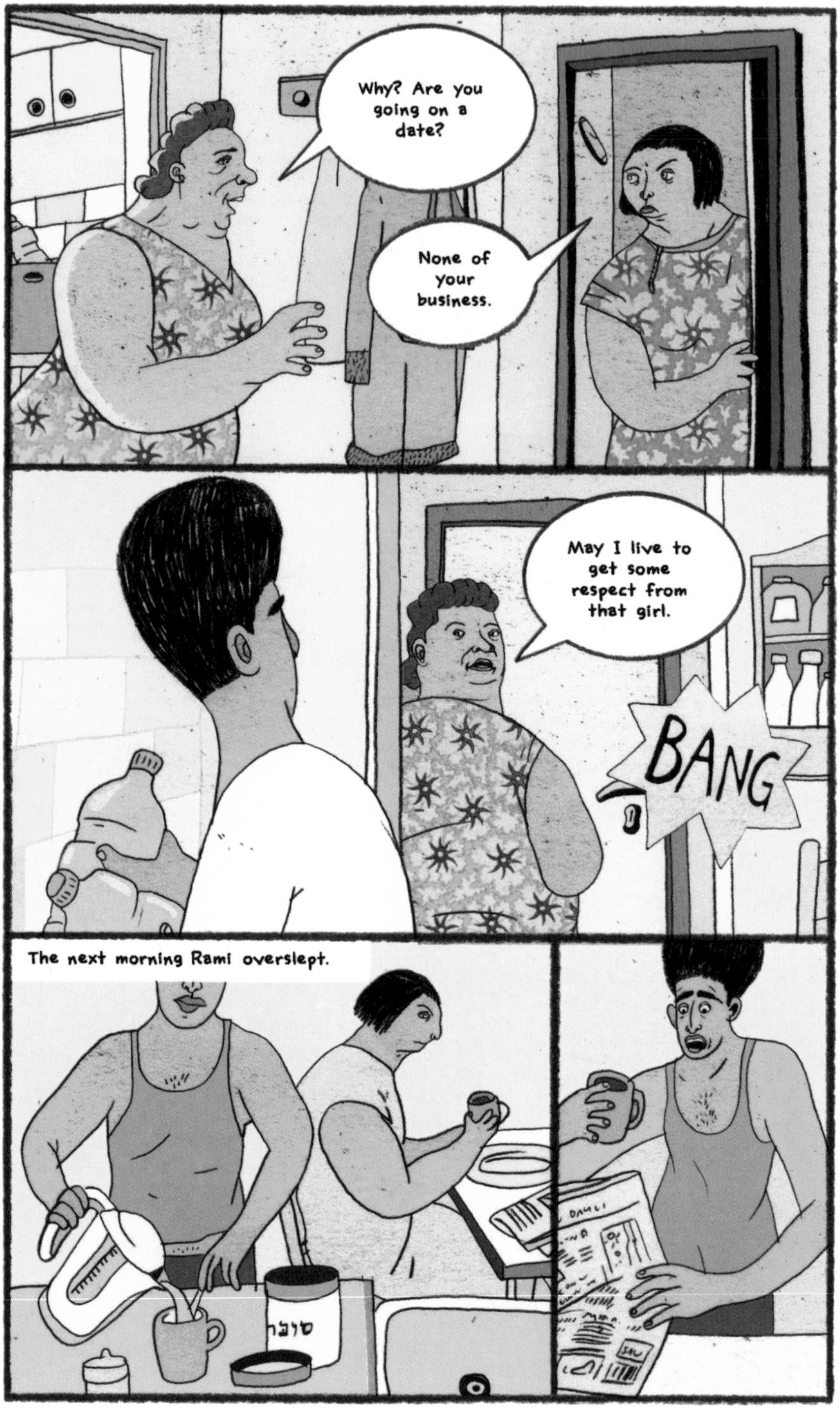
Why? Are you going on a date?
None of your business.
May I live to get some respect from that girl.
BANG
The next morning Rami overslept.

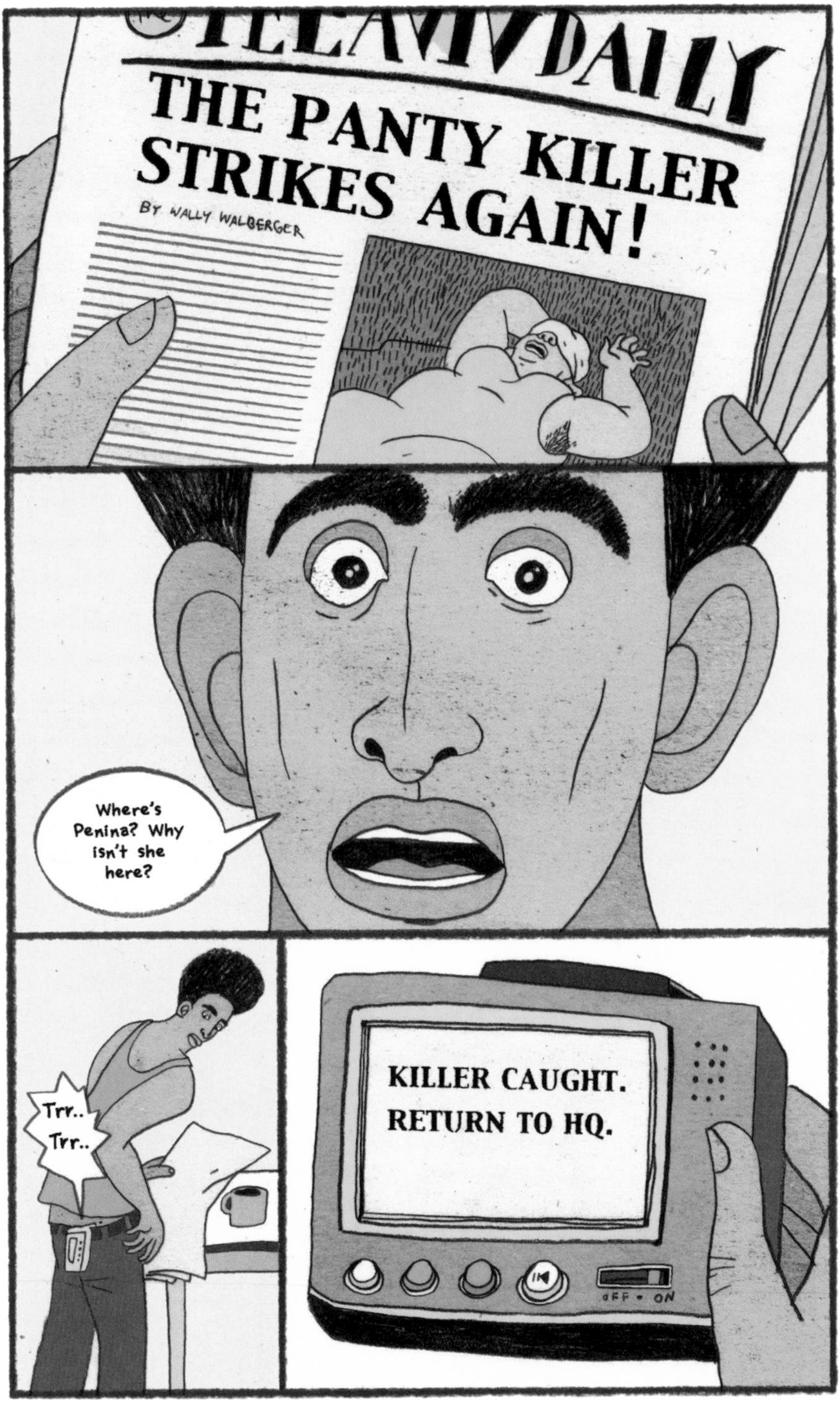
THE PANTY KILLER STRIKES AGAIN!
BY WALLY WALBERGER
Where's Penina? Why isn't she here?
Trr.. Trr..
KILLER CAUGHT. RETURN TO HQ.
OFF • ON

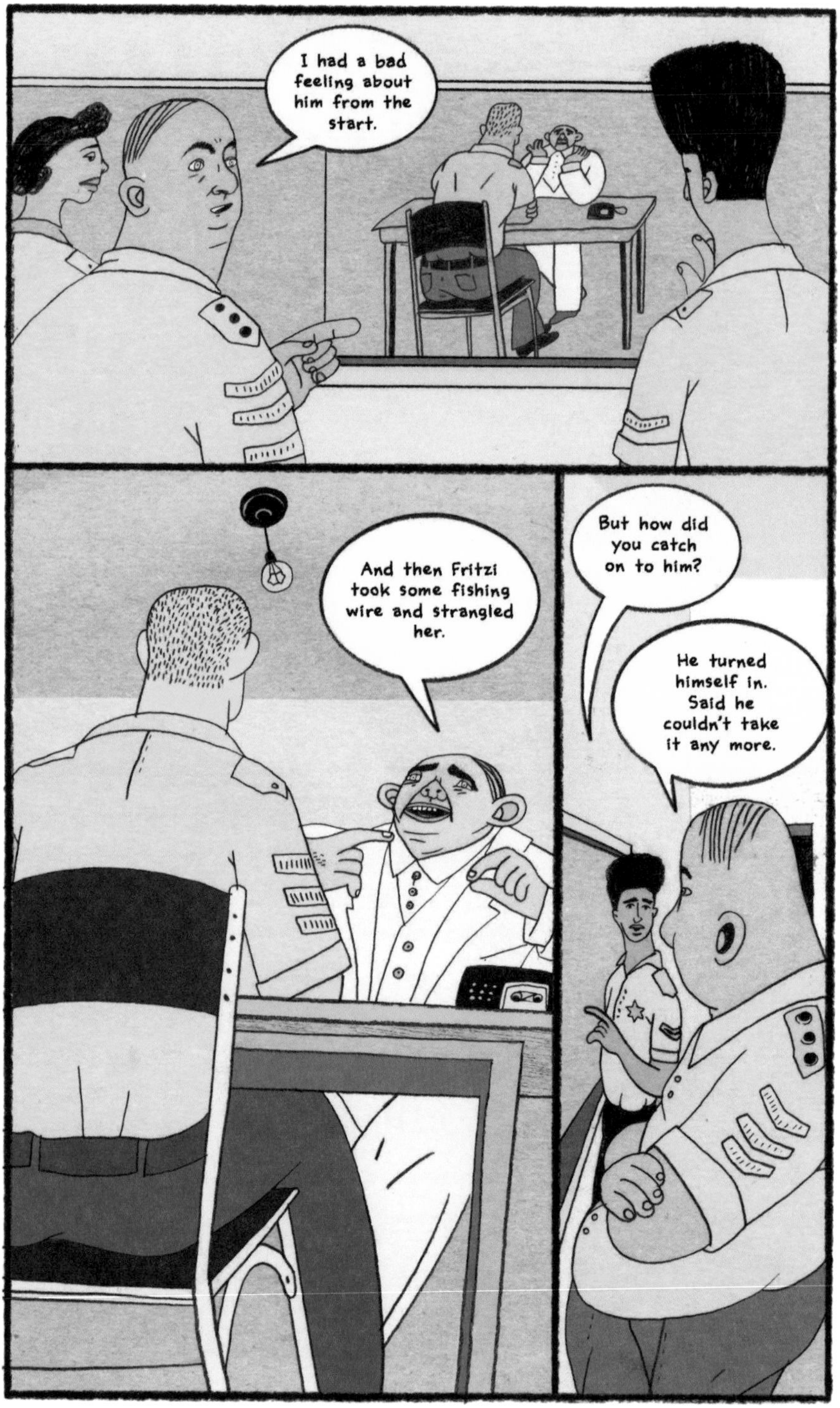
I had a bad feeling about him from the start.
And then Fritzi took some fishing wire and strangled her.
But how did you catch on to him?
He turned himself in. Said he couldn't take it any more.

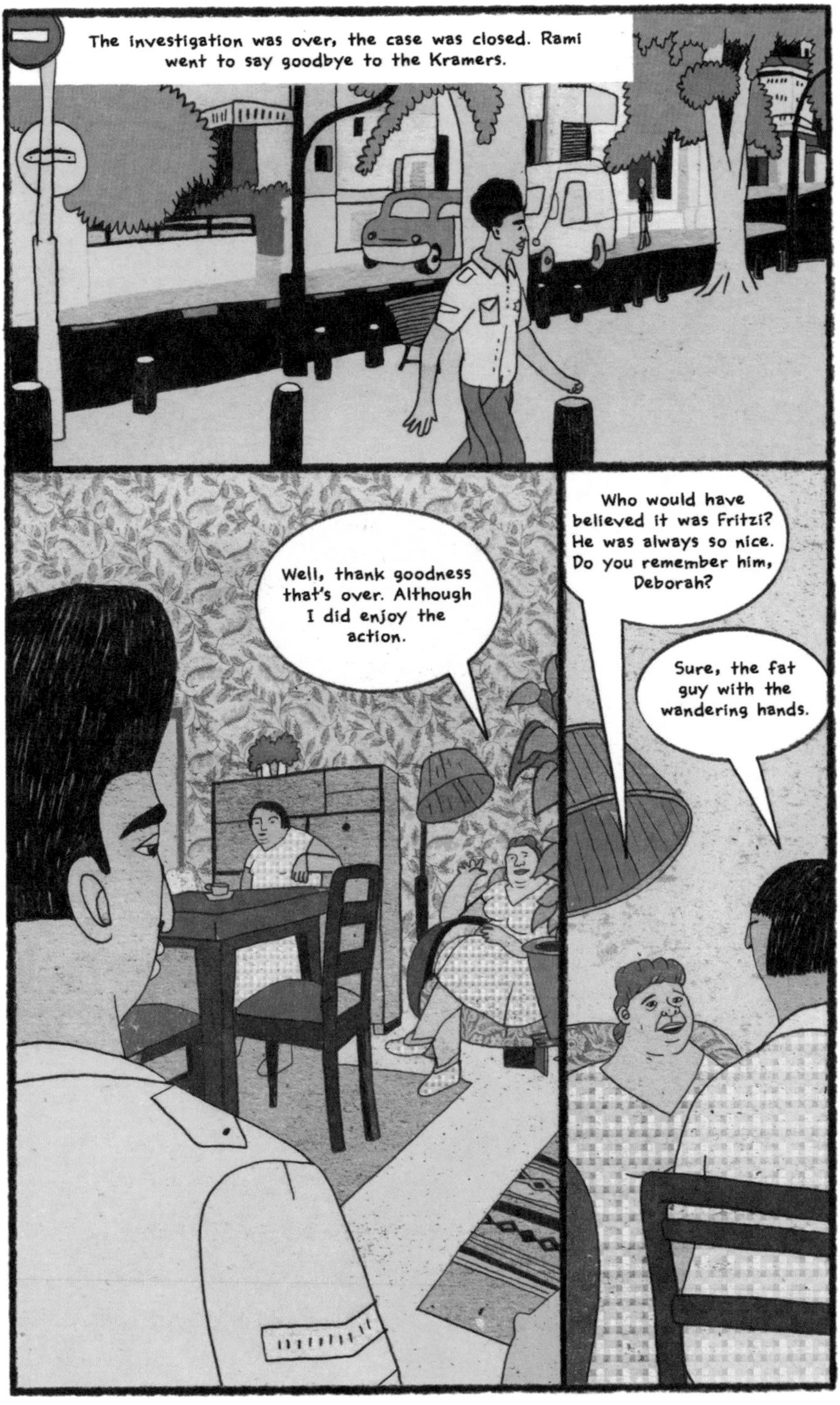
The investigation was over, the case was closed. Rami went to say goodbye to the Kramers.
Well, thank goodness that's over. Although I did enjoy the action.
Who would have believed it was Fritzi? He was always so nice. Do you remember him, Deborah?
Sure, the fat guy with the wandering hands.

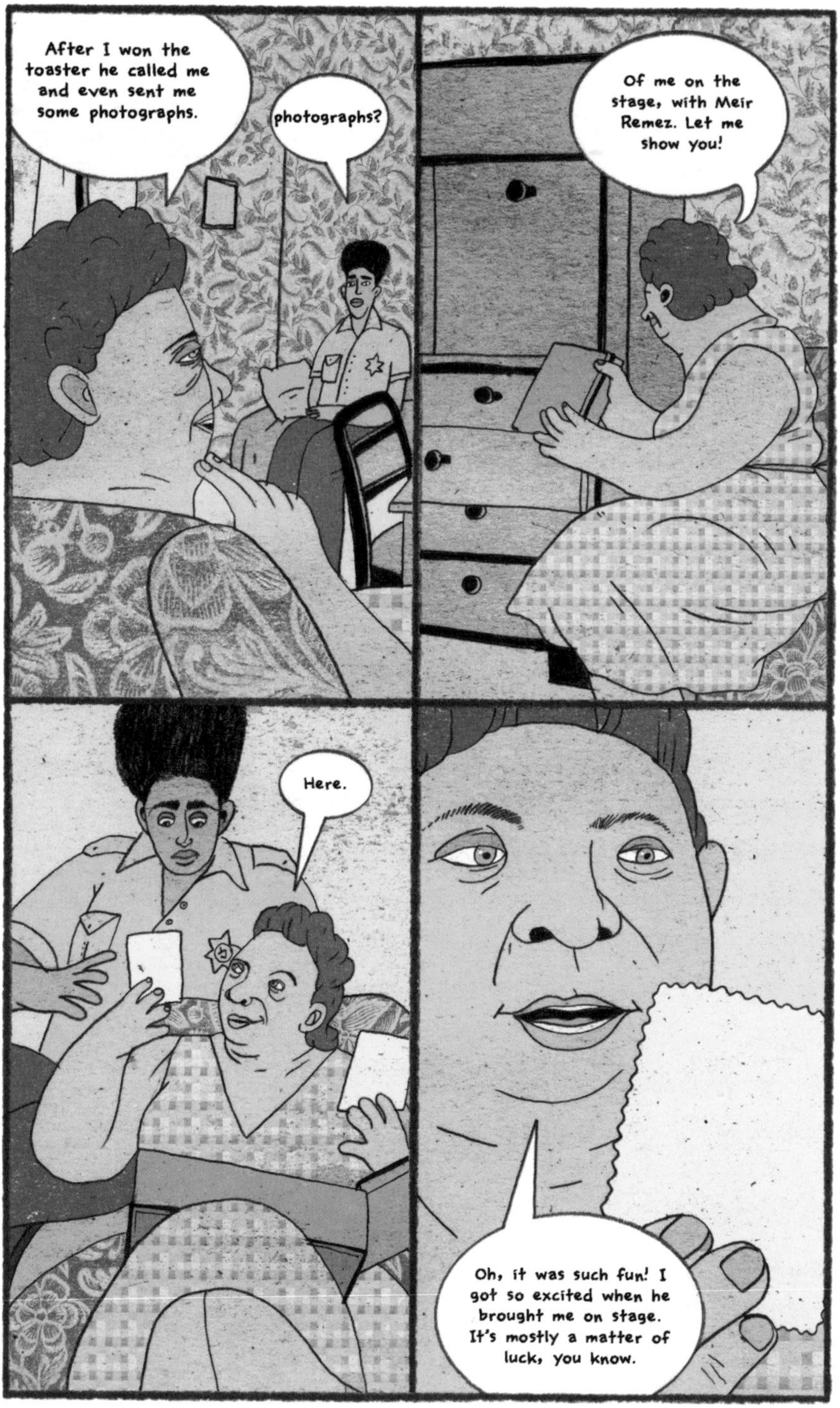
After I won the toaster he called me and even sent me some photographs.
photographs?
Of me on the stage, with Meir Remez. Let me show you!
Here.
Oh, it was such fun! I got so excited when he brought me on stage. It's mostly a matter of luck, you know.

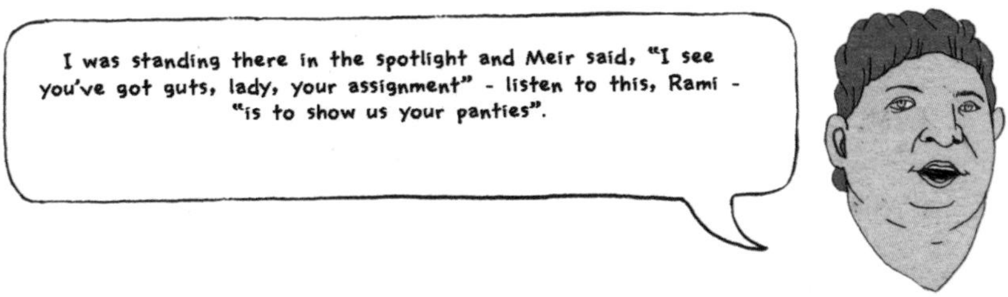
I was standing there in the spotlight and Meir said, "I see you've got guts, lady, your assignment" - listen to this, Rami - "is to show us your panties".

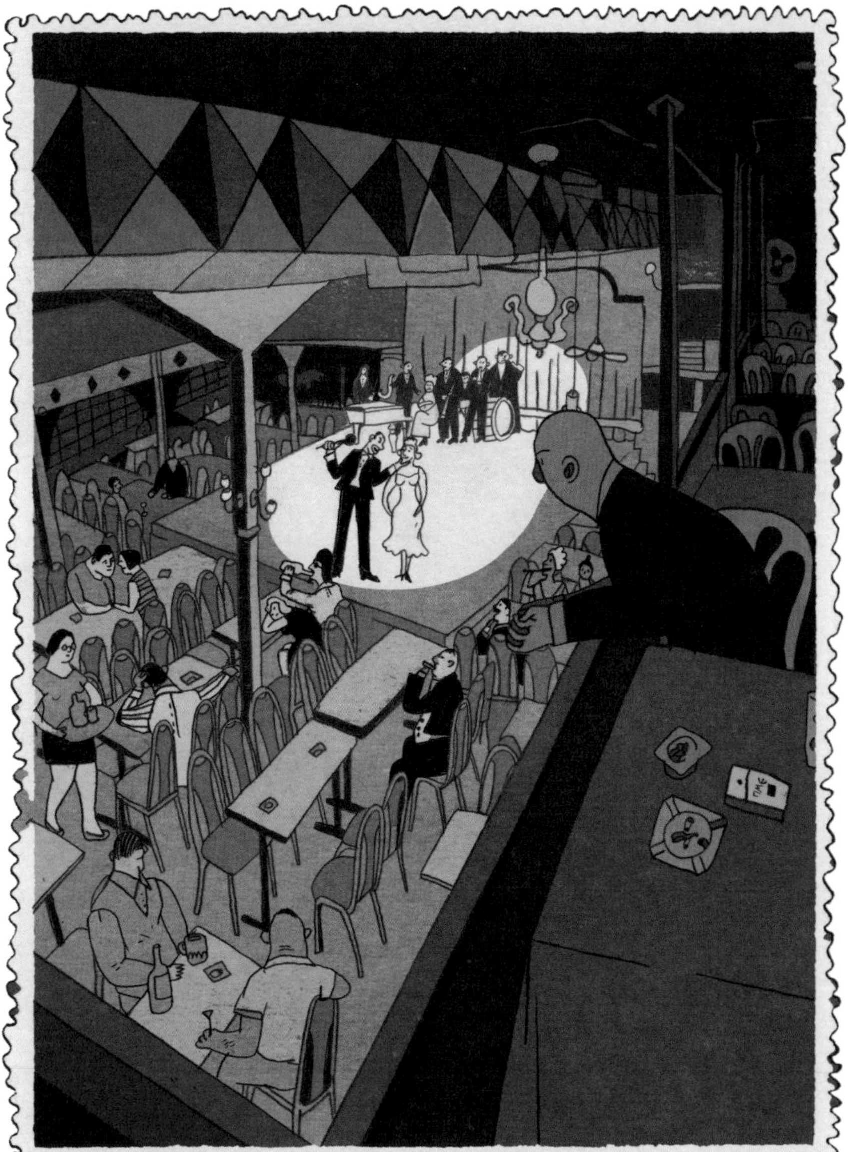

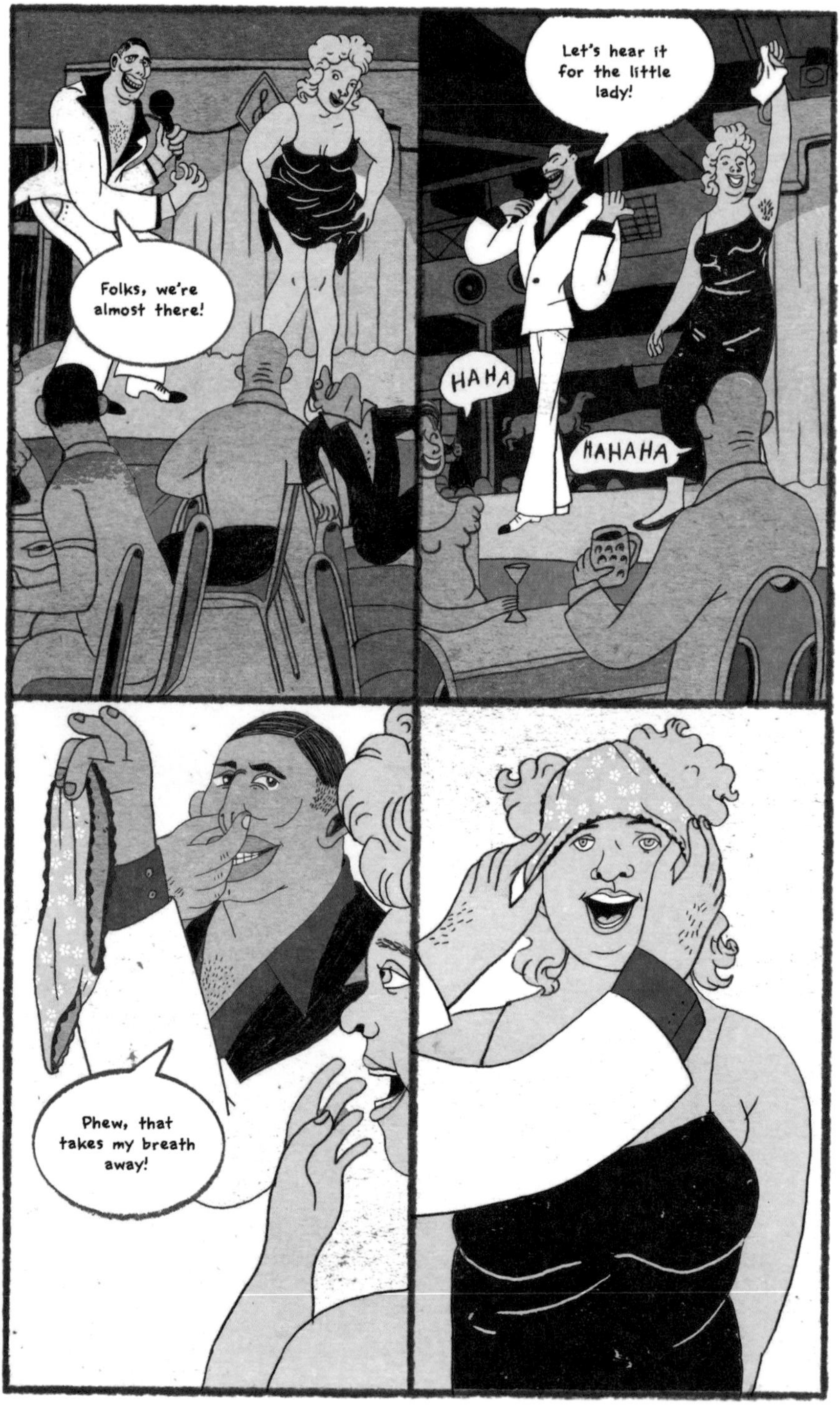
Folks, we're almost there!
Let's hear it for the little lady!
HAHA
HAHAHA
Phew, that takes my breath away!

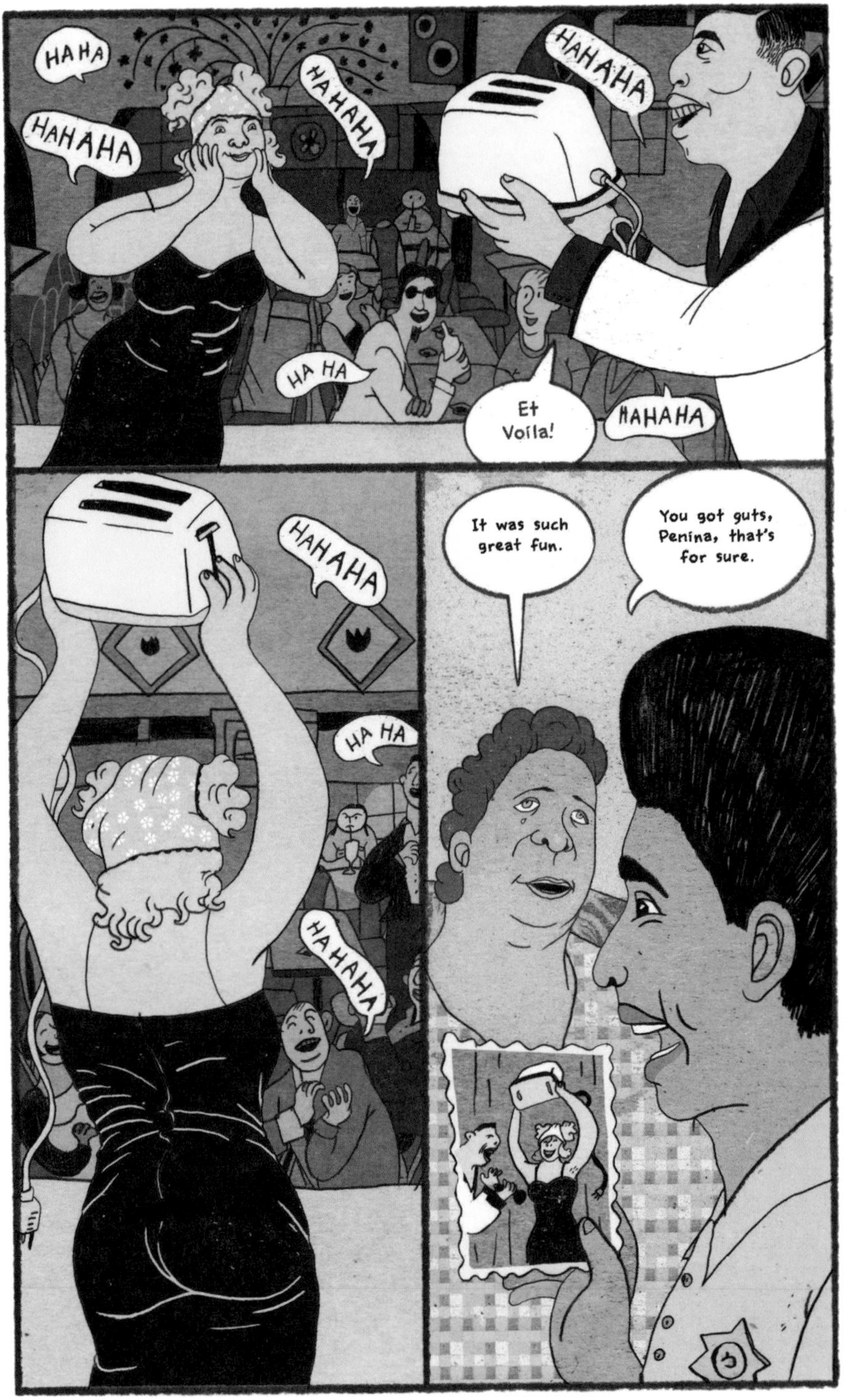
HAHA
HAHAHA
HAHAHA
HAHAHA
HA HA
Et Voíla!
HAHAHA
HAHAHA
HA HA
HAHAHA
It was such great fun.
You got guts, Penina, that's for sure.

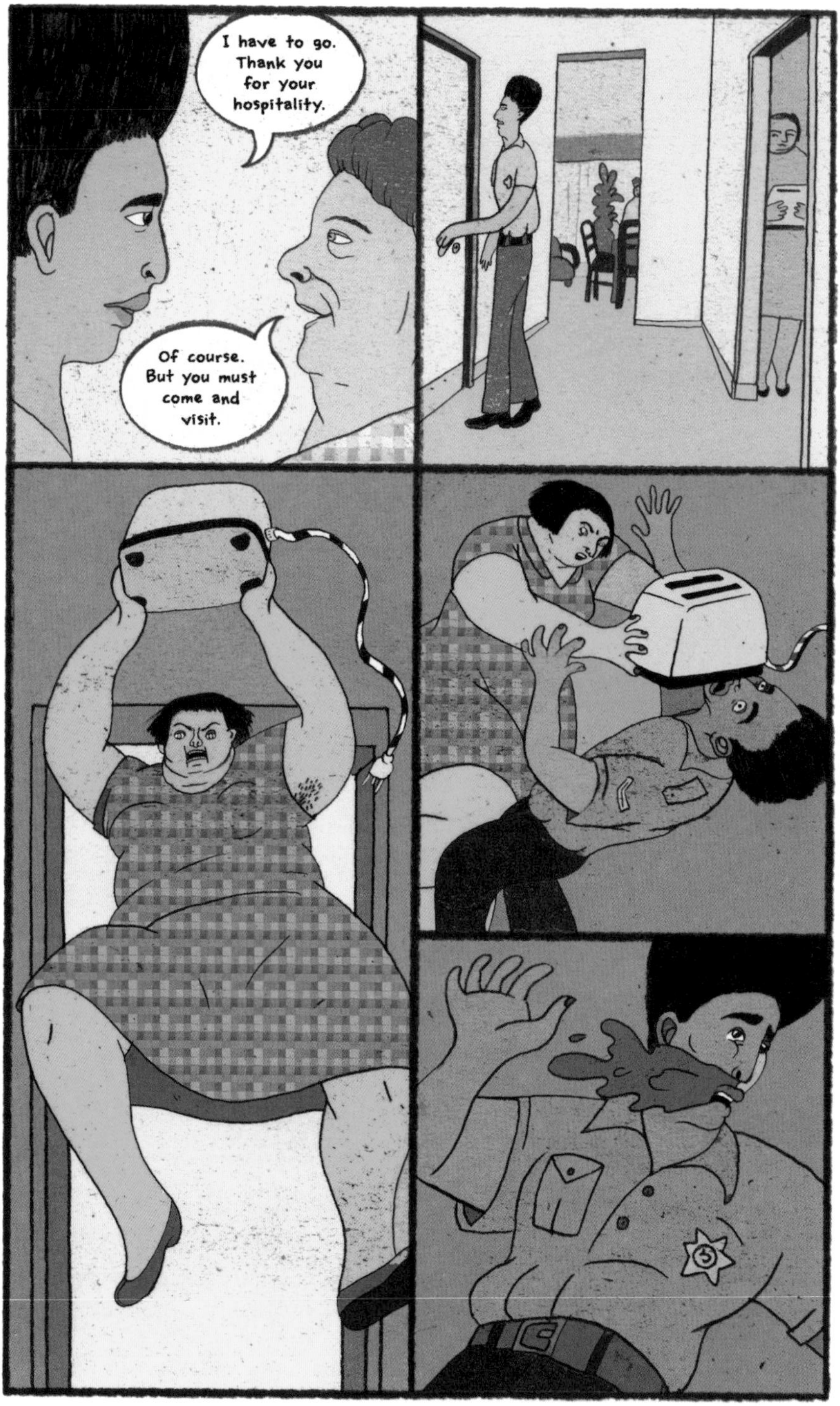
I have to go. Thank you for your hospitality.
Of course. But you must come and visit.

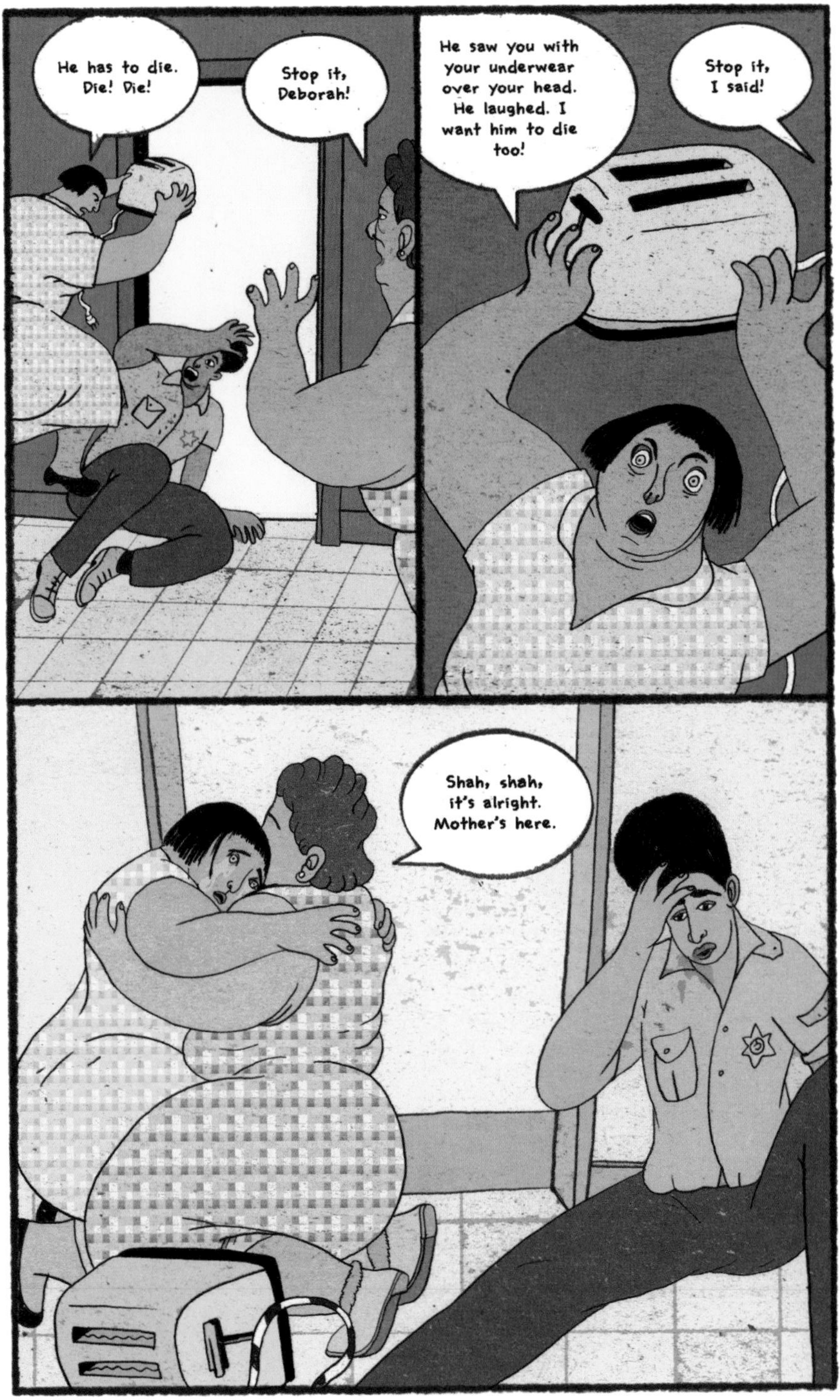
He has to die. Die! Die!
Stop it, Deborah!
He saw you with your underwear over your head. He laughed. I want him to die too!
Stop it, I said!
Shah, shah, it's alright. Mother's here.

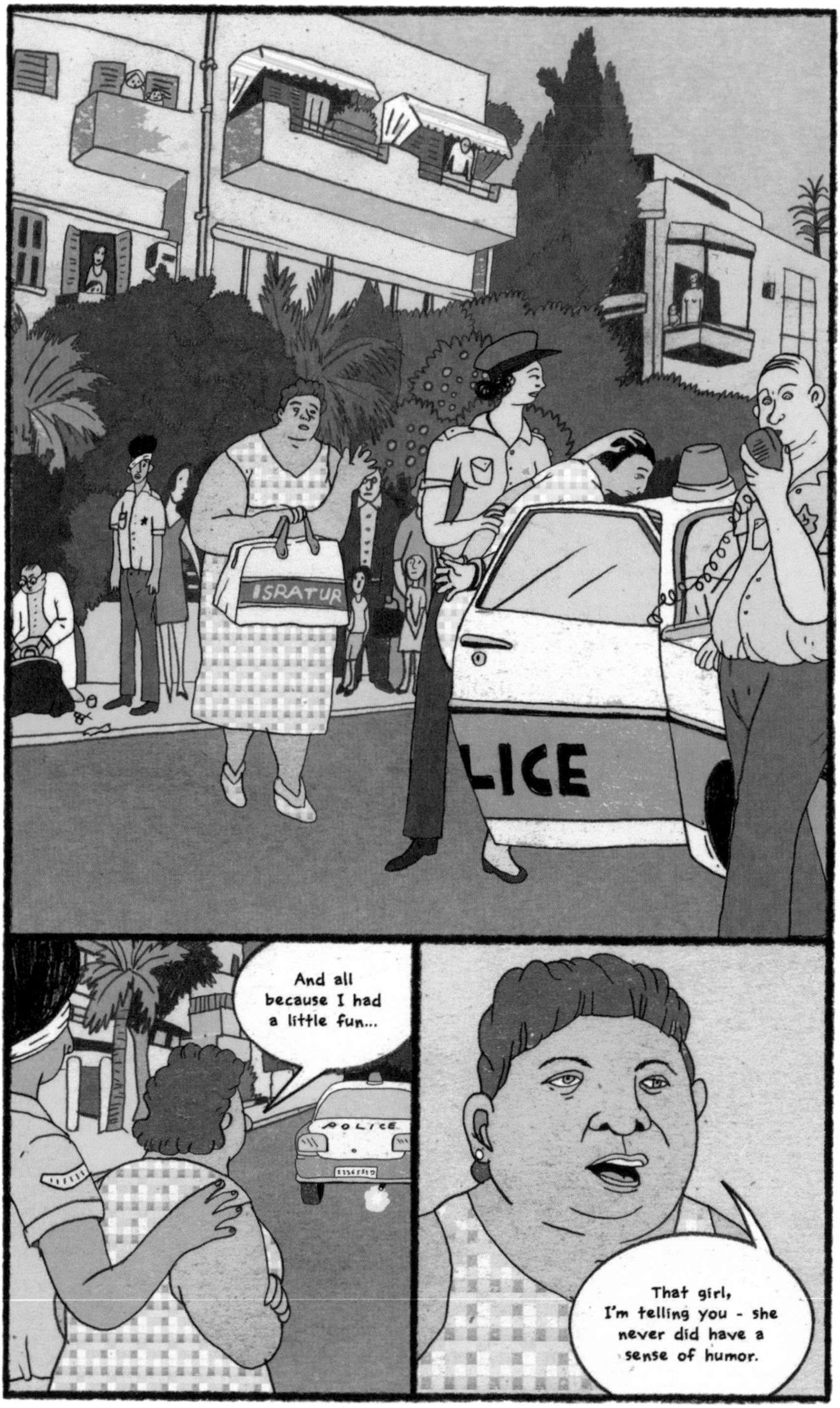
ISRATUR
LICE
And all because I had a little fun...
POLICE
That girl, I'm telling you - she never did have a sense of humor.

HOMECOMING

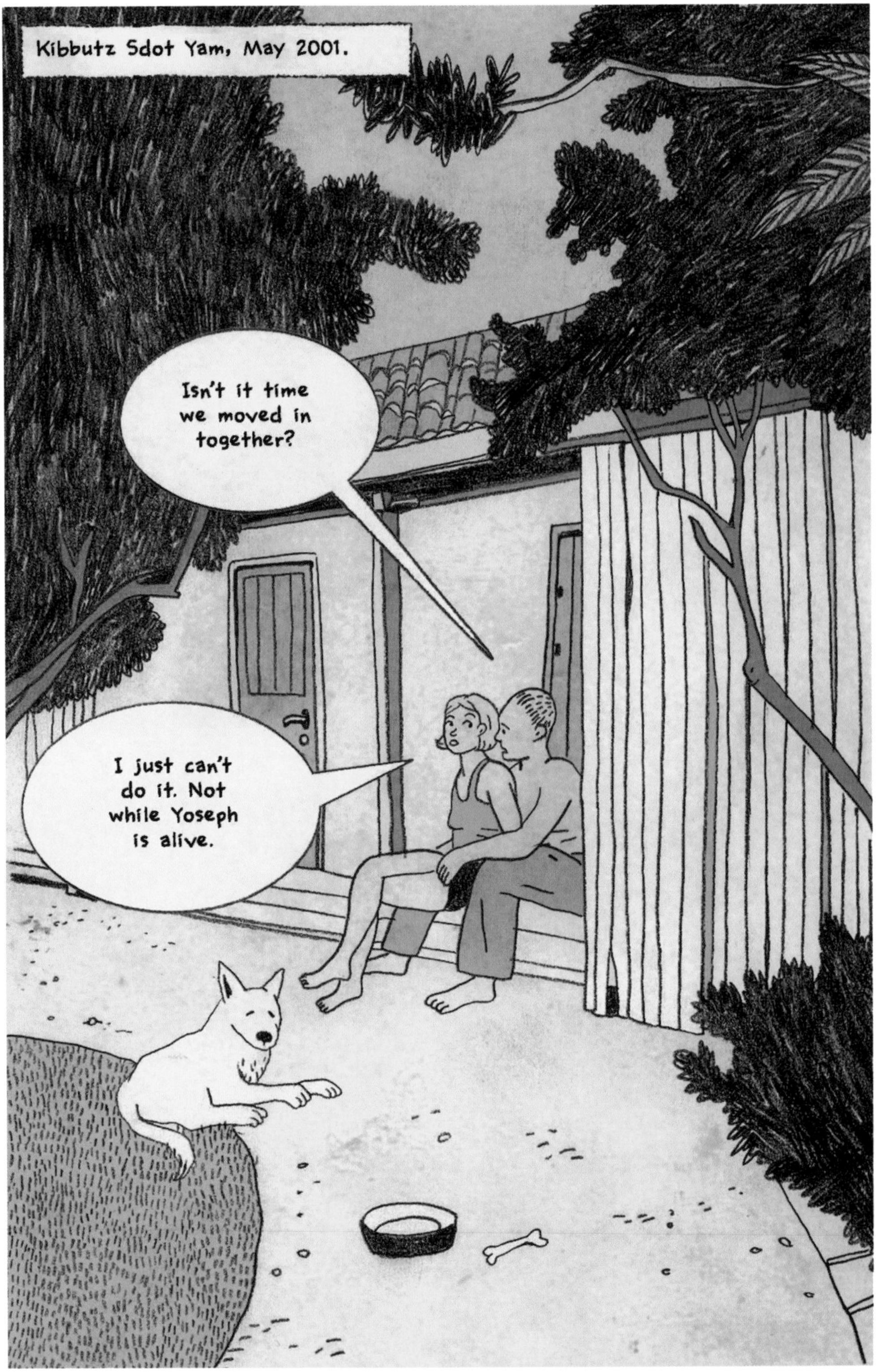
Kibbutz Sdot Yam, May 2001.
Isn't it time we moved in together?
I just can't do it. Not while Yoseph is alive.

Max had heard that answer a thousand times before, and it was starting to sound like an excuse.
Mali! Mali!

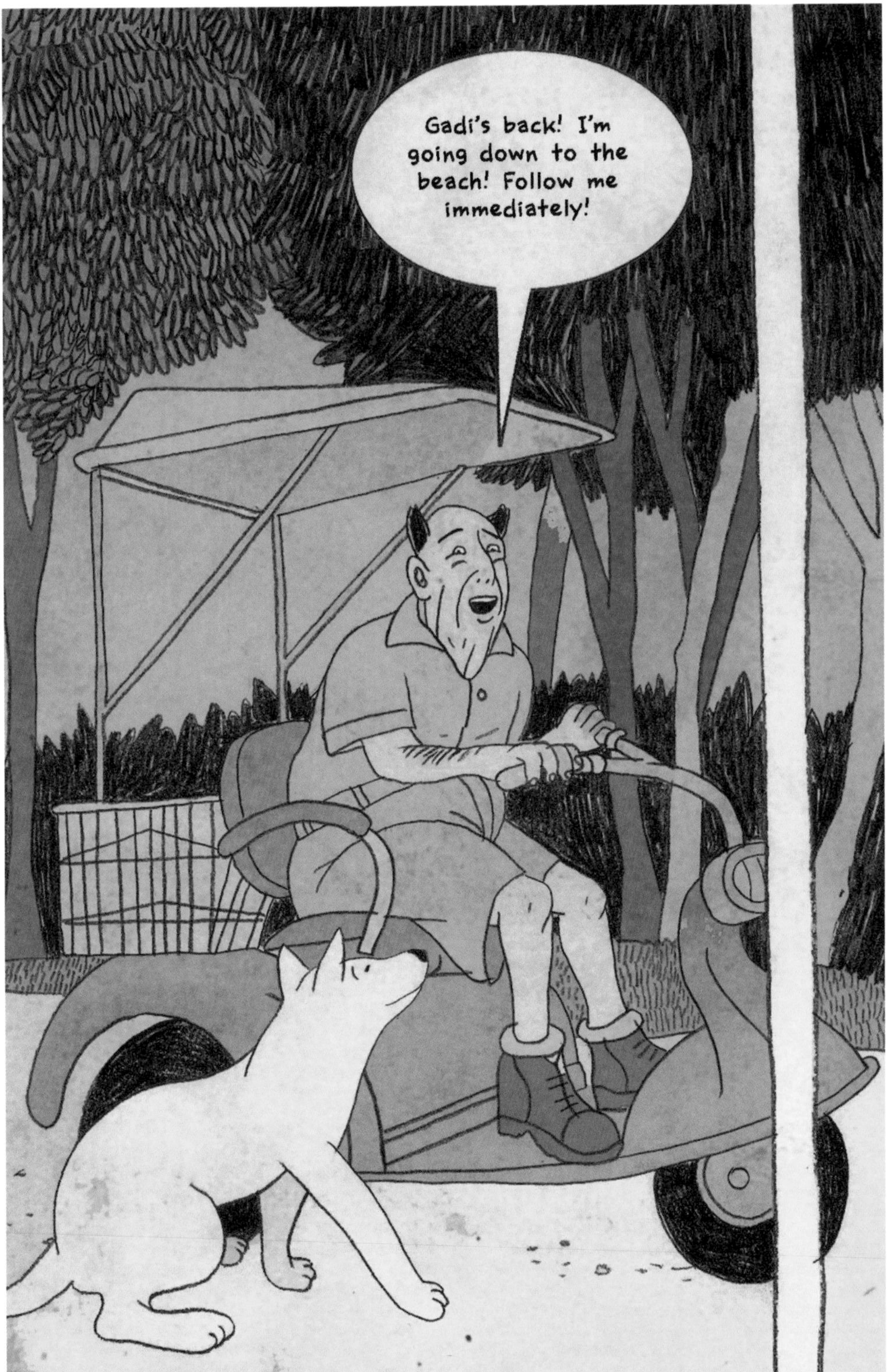
Gadi's back! I'm going down to the beach! Follow me immediately!

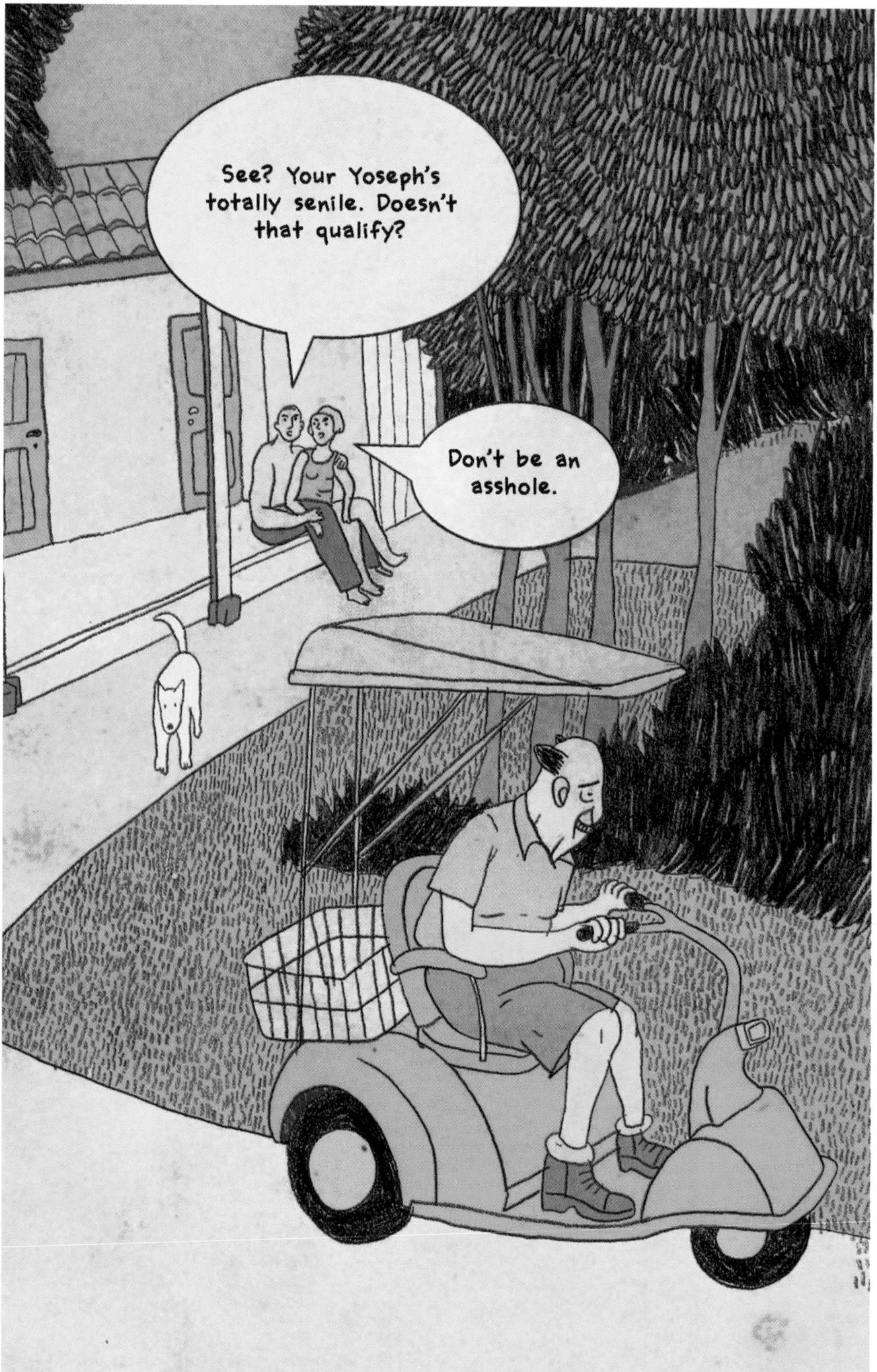
See? Your Yoseph's totally senile. Doesn't that qualify?
Don't be an asshole.

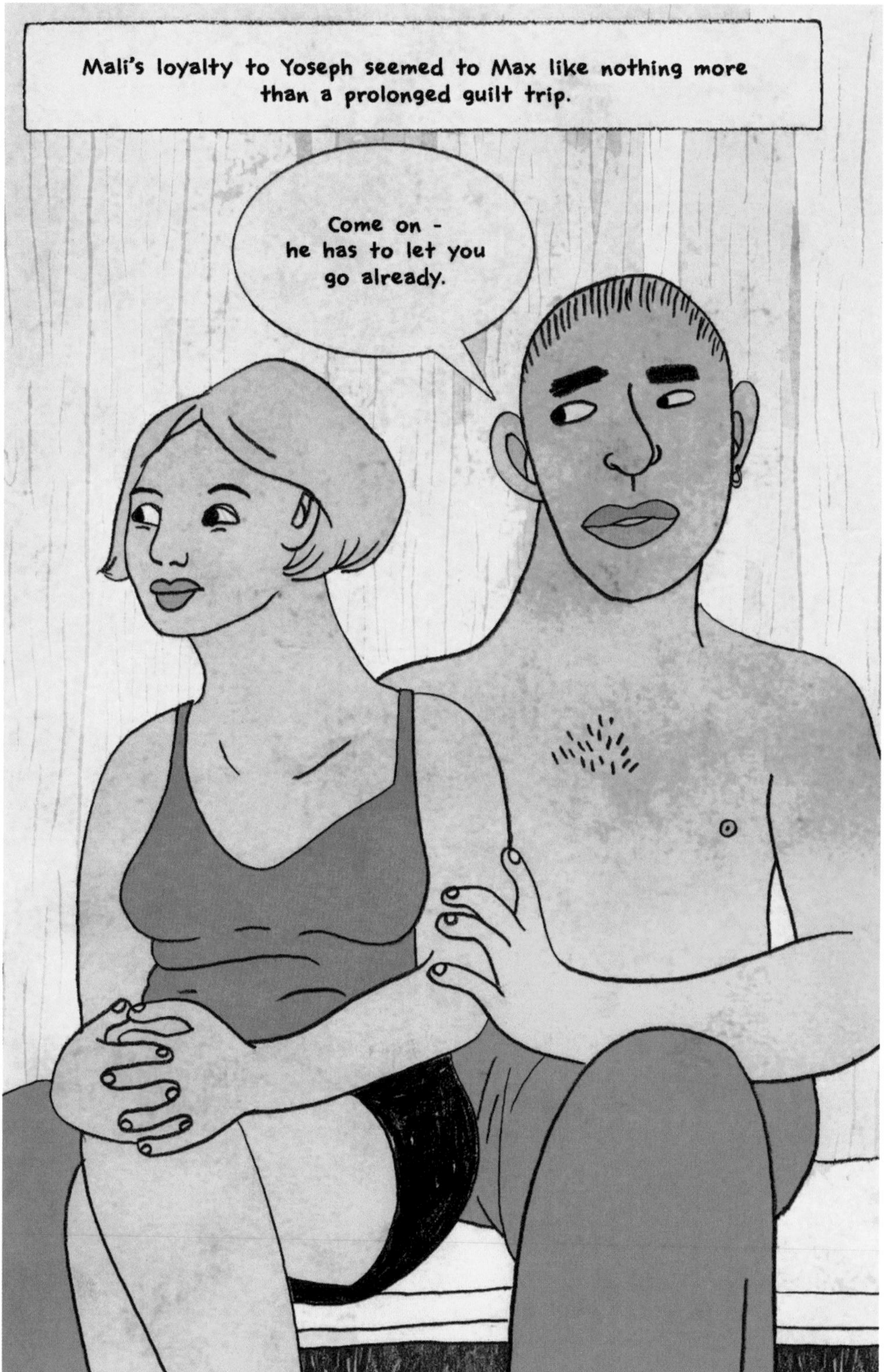
Mali's loyalty to Yoseph seemed to Max like nothing more than a prolonged guilt trip.
Come on - he has to let you go already.

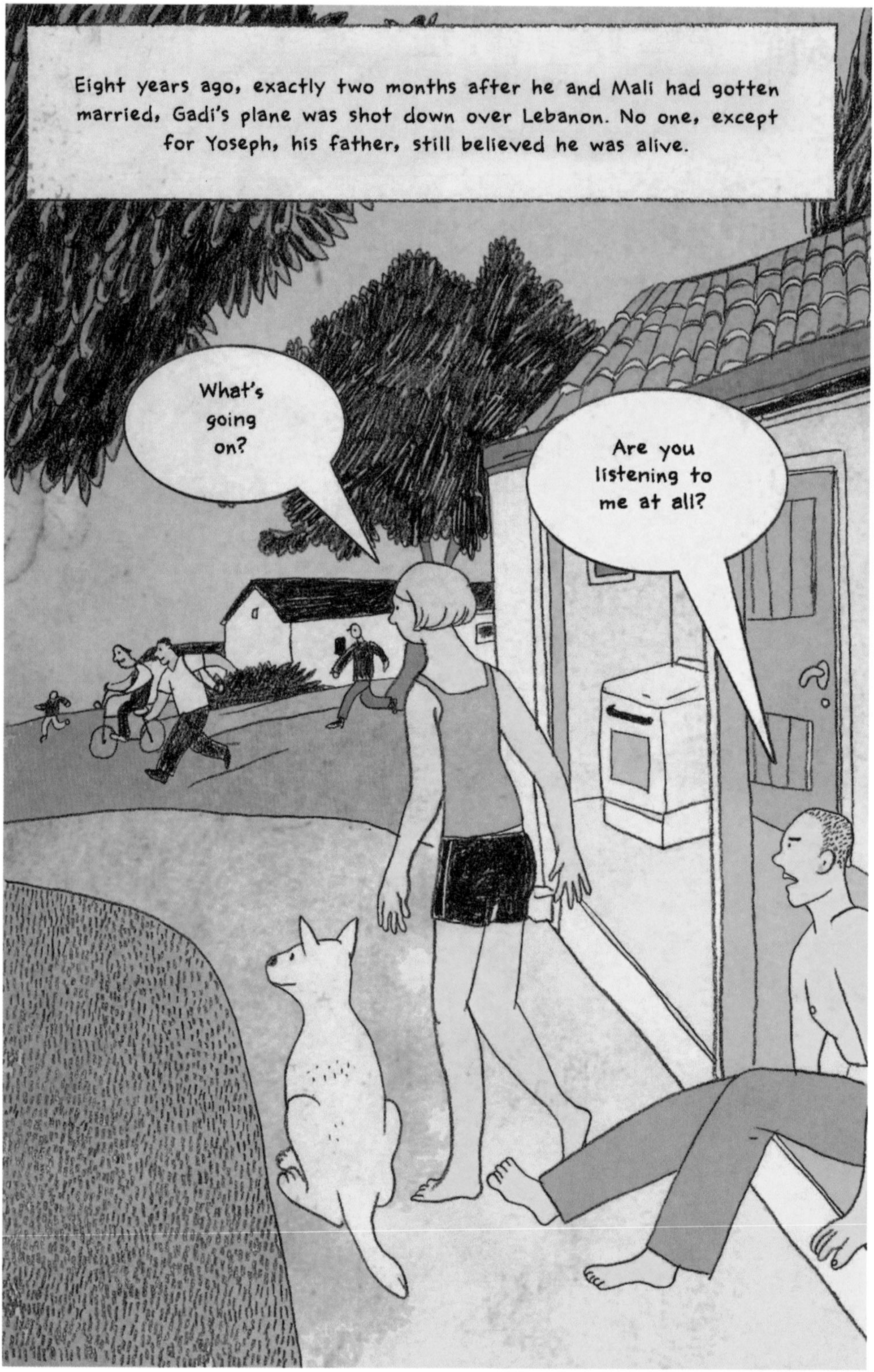

Eight years ago, exactly two months after he and Mali had gotten married, Gadi's plane was shot down over Lebanon. No one, except for Yoseph, his father, still believed he was alive.
What's going on?
Are you listening to me at all?

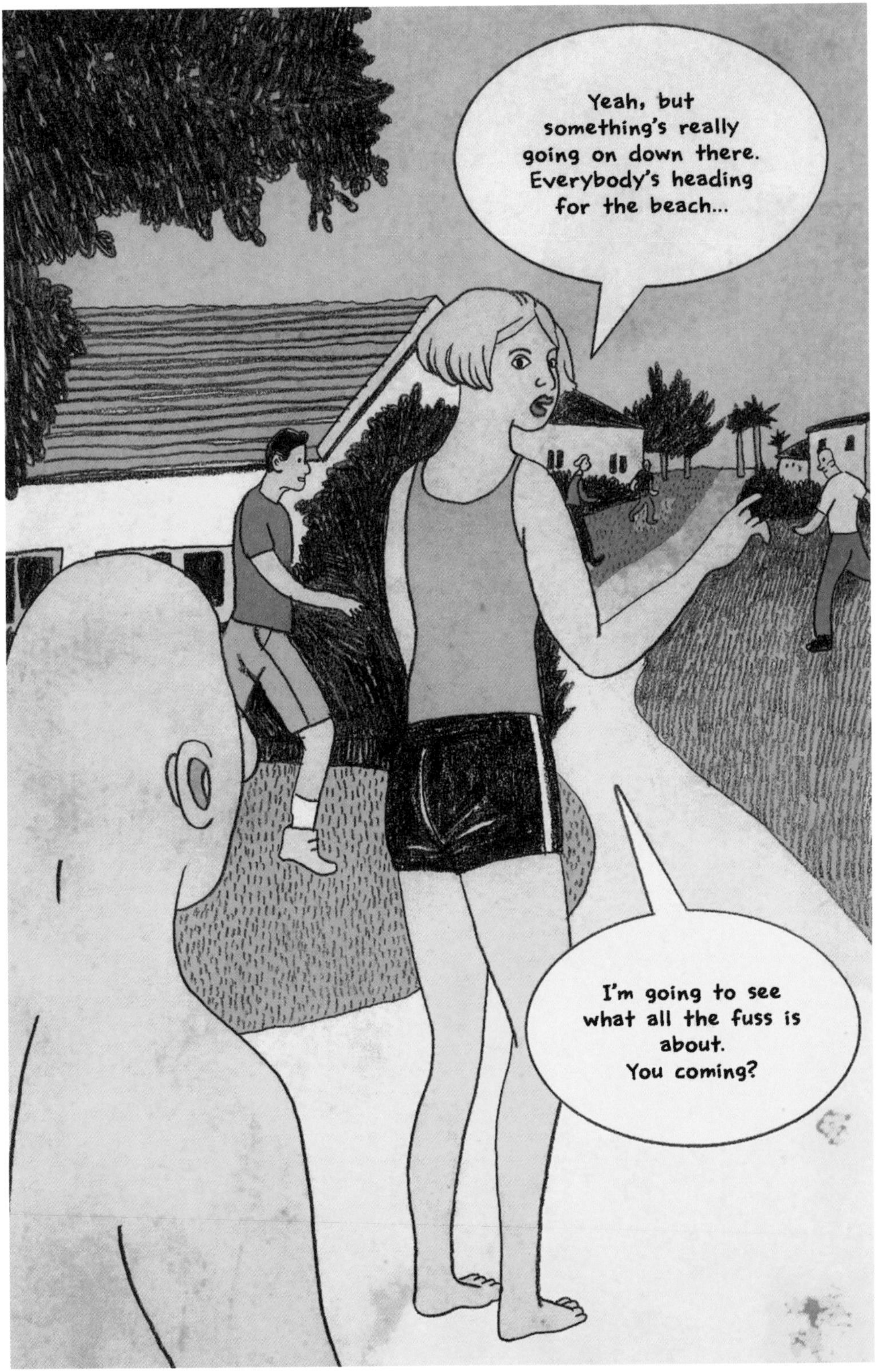
Yeah, but something's really going on down there. Everybody's heading for the beach...
I'm going to see what all the fuss is about. You coming?

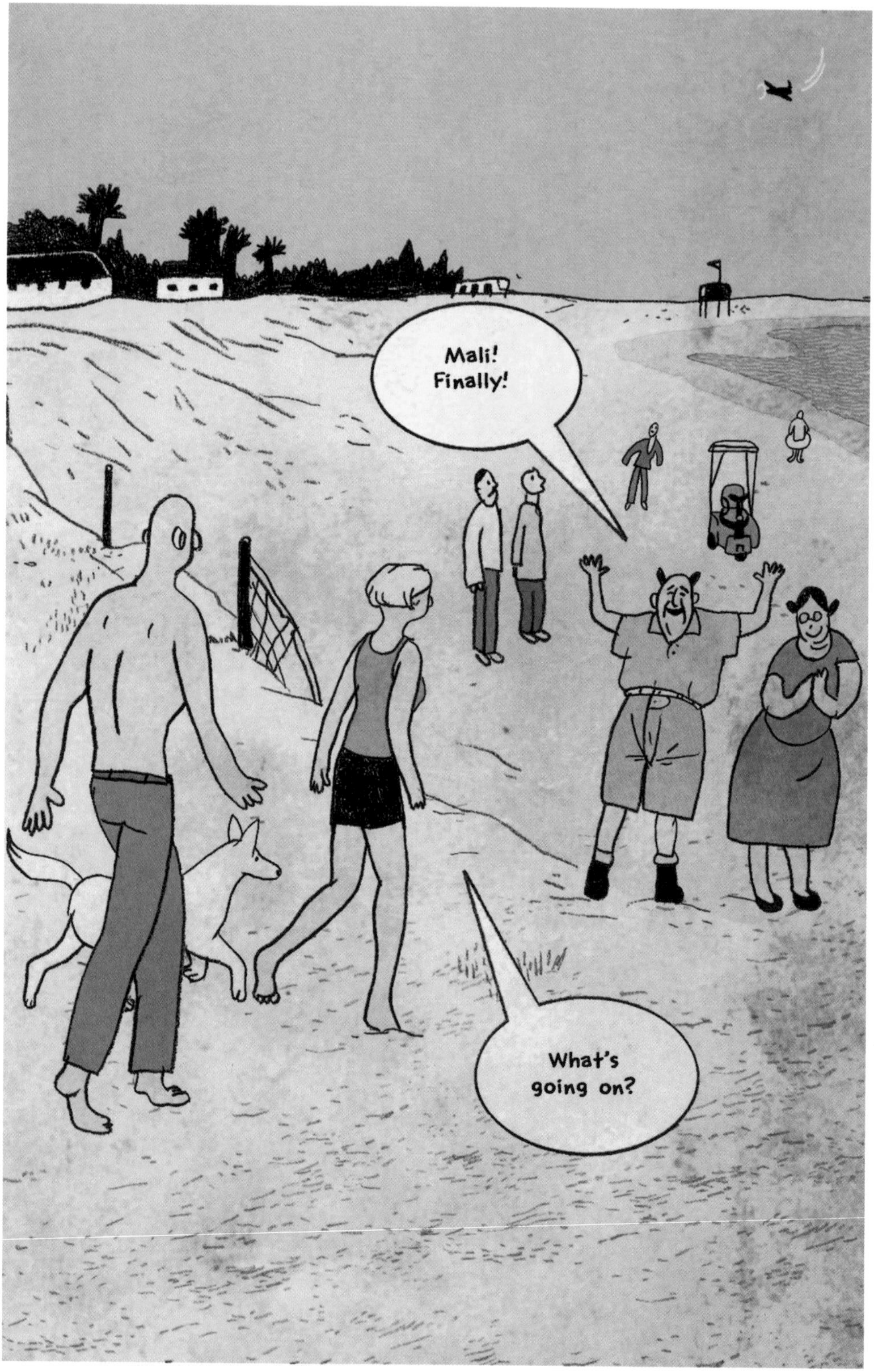
Mali!
Finally!
What's
going on?

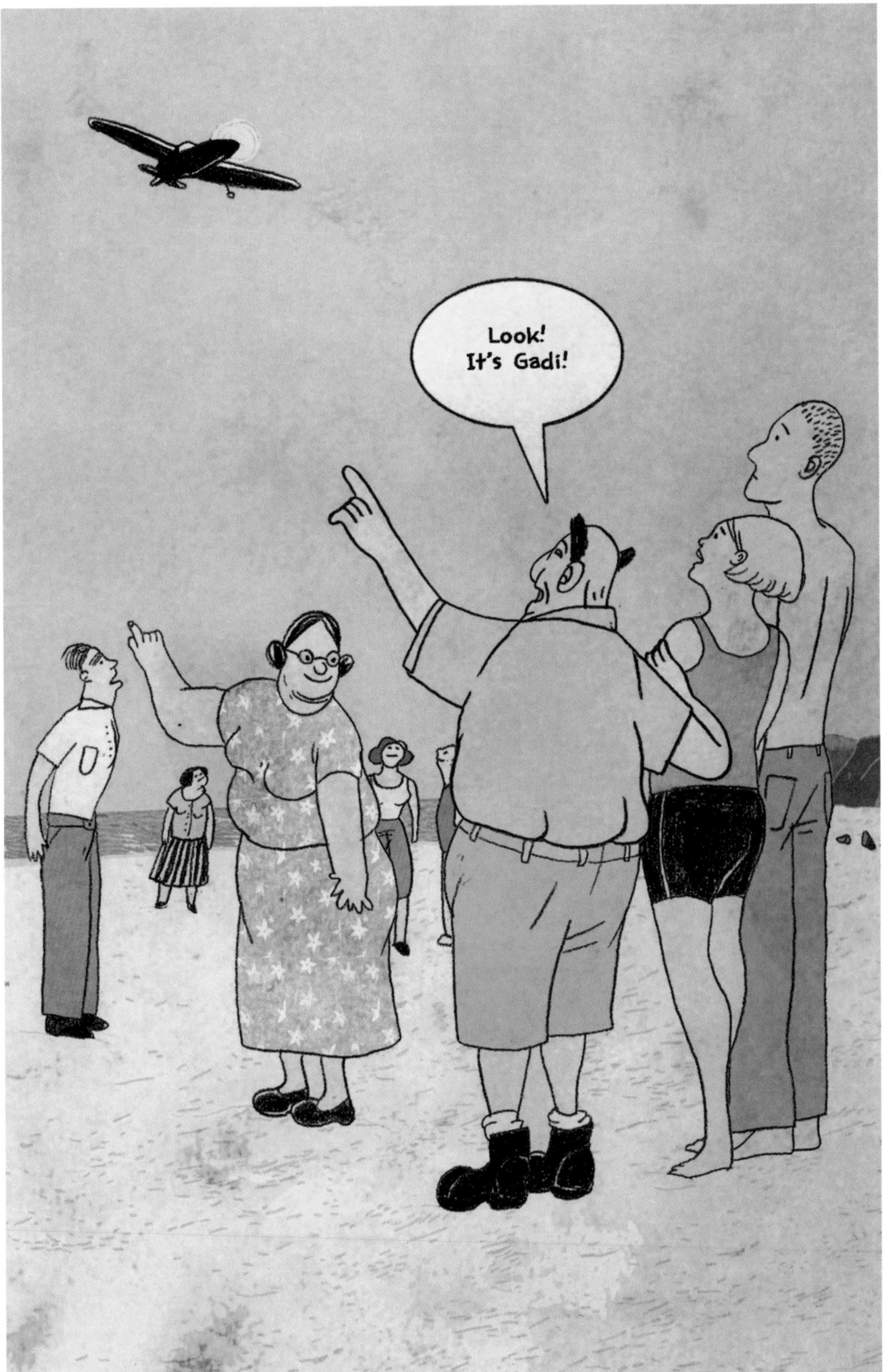
Look! It's Gadi!

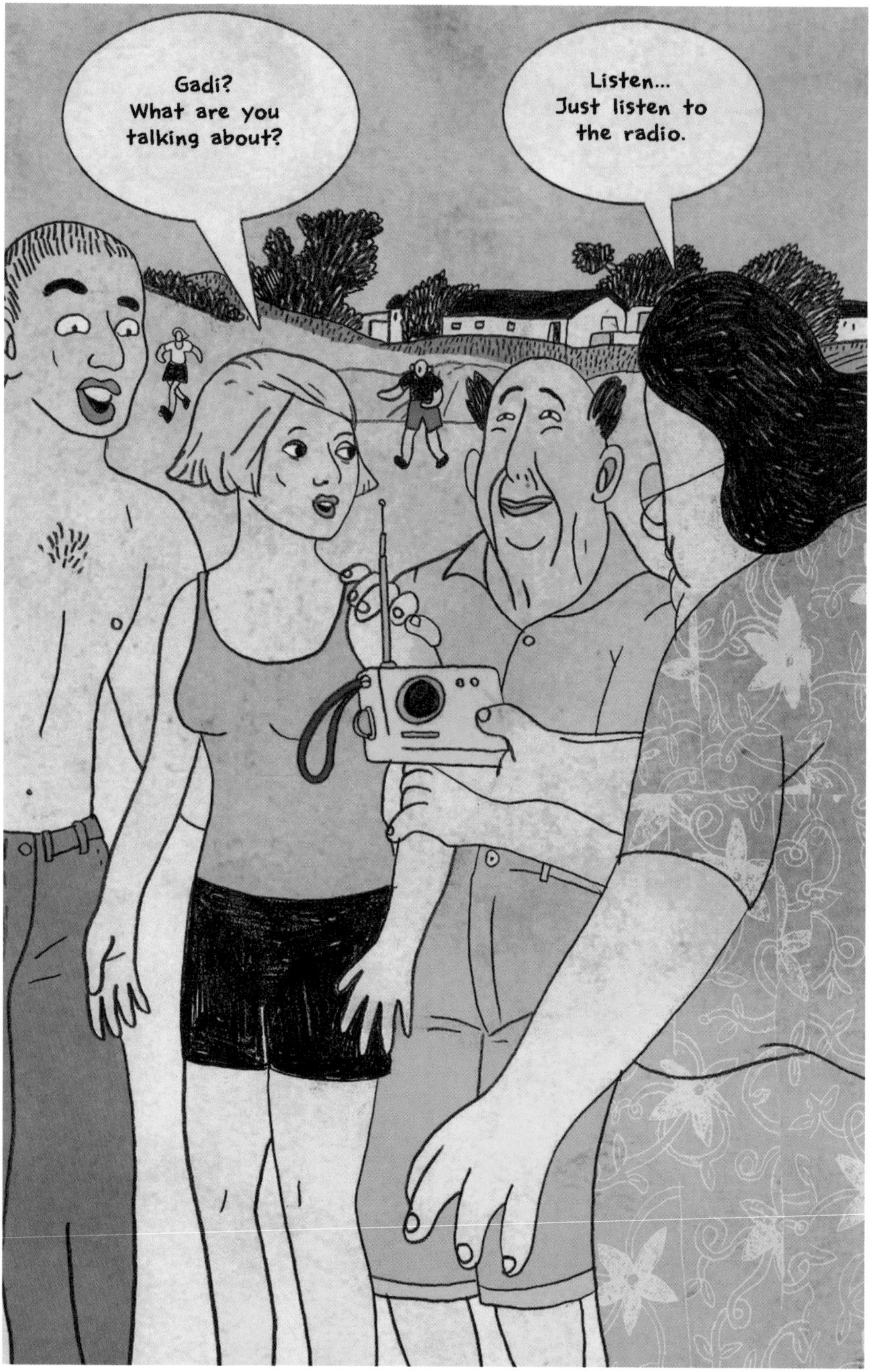
Gadi? What are you talking about?
Listen... Just listen to the radio.

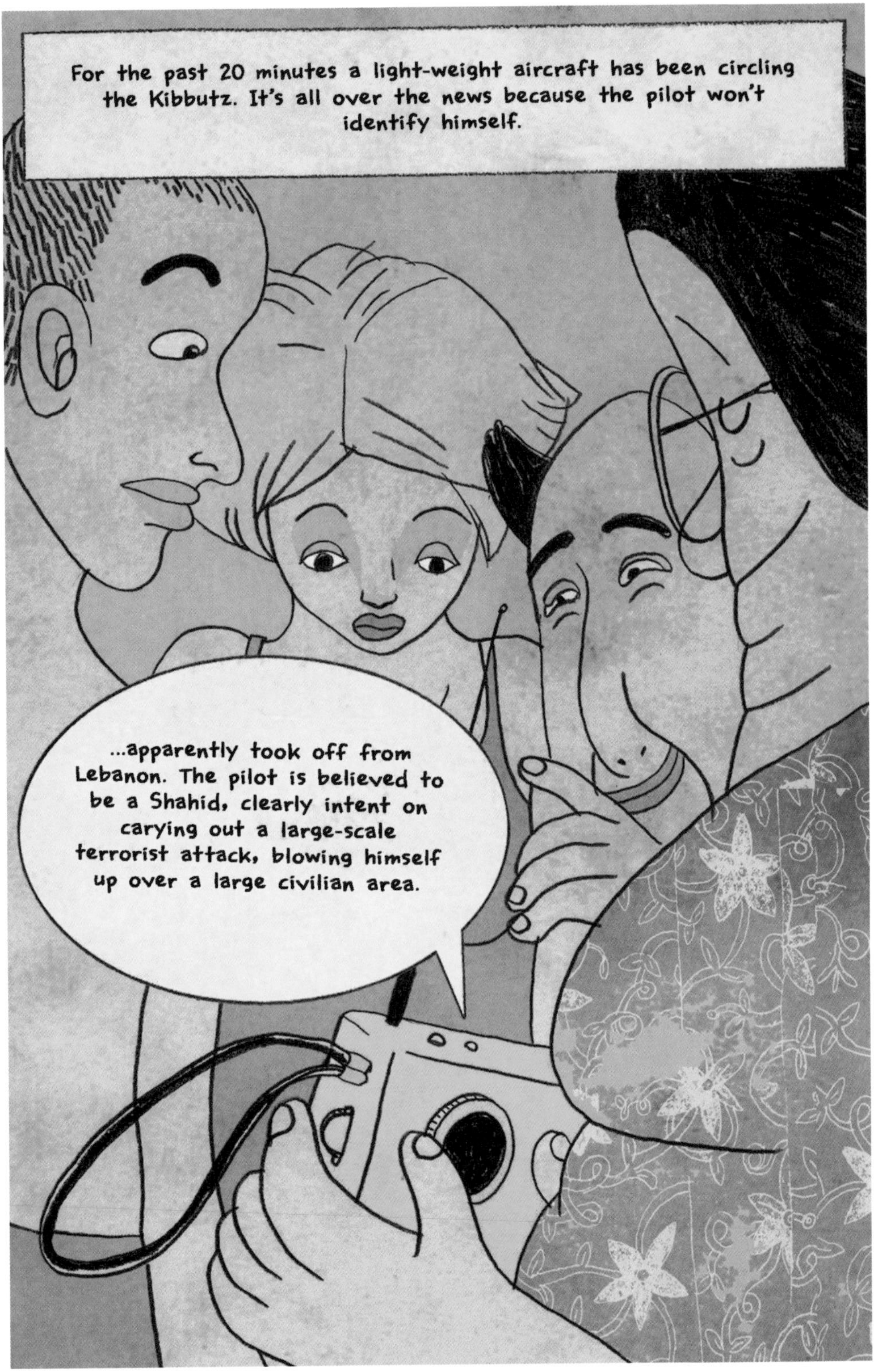
For the past 20 minutes a light-weight aircraft has been circling the Kibbutz. It's all over the news because the pilot won't identify himself.
...apparently took off from Lebanon. The pilot is believed to be a Shahid, clearly intent on carying out a large-scale terrorist attack, blowing himself up over a large civilian area.

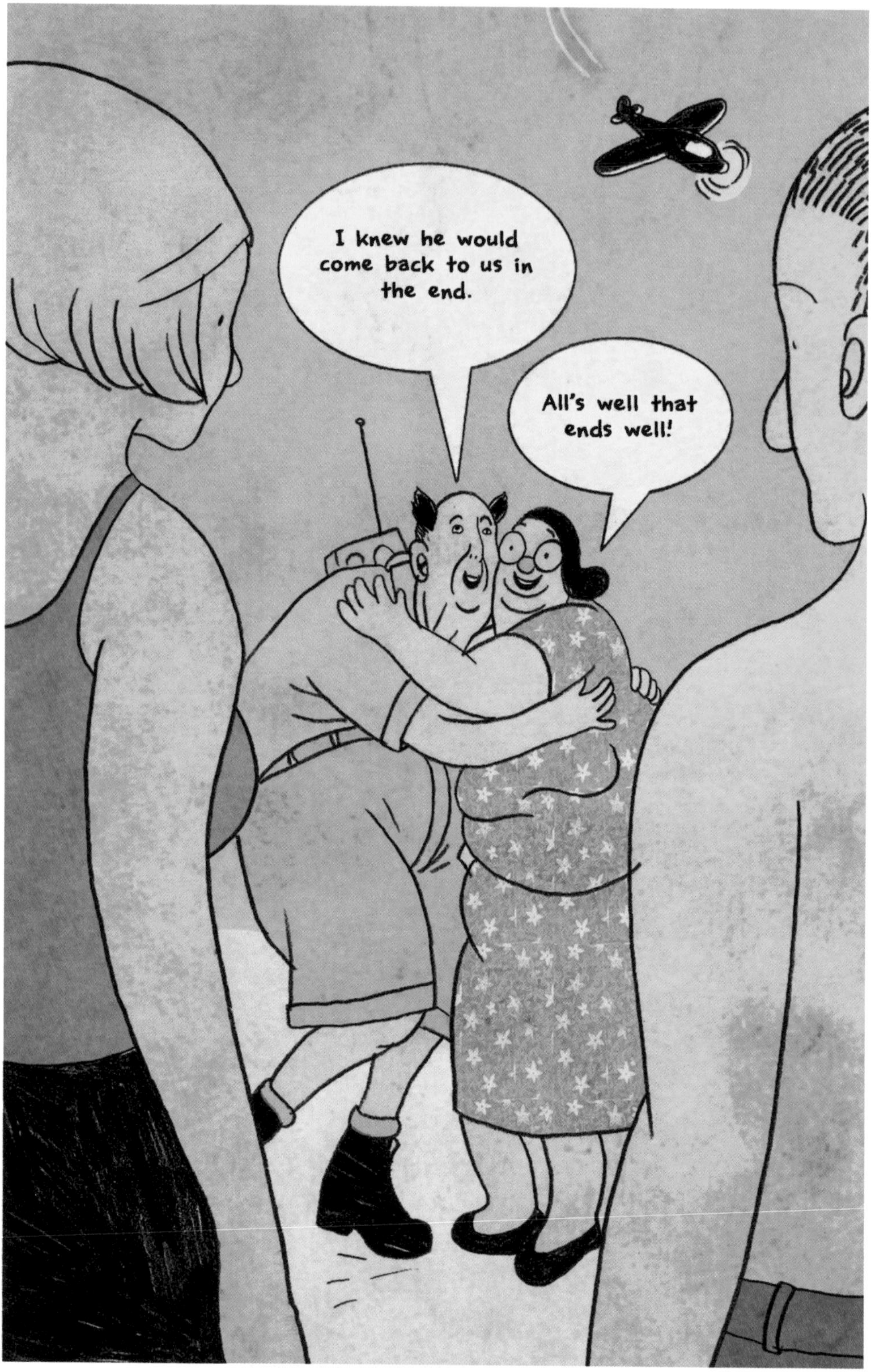
I knew he would come back to us in the end.
All's well that ends well!

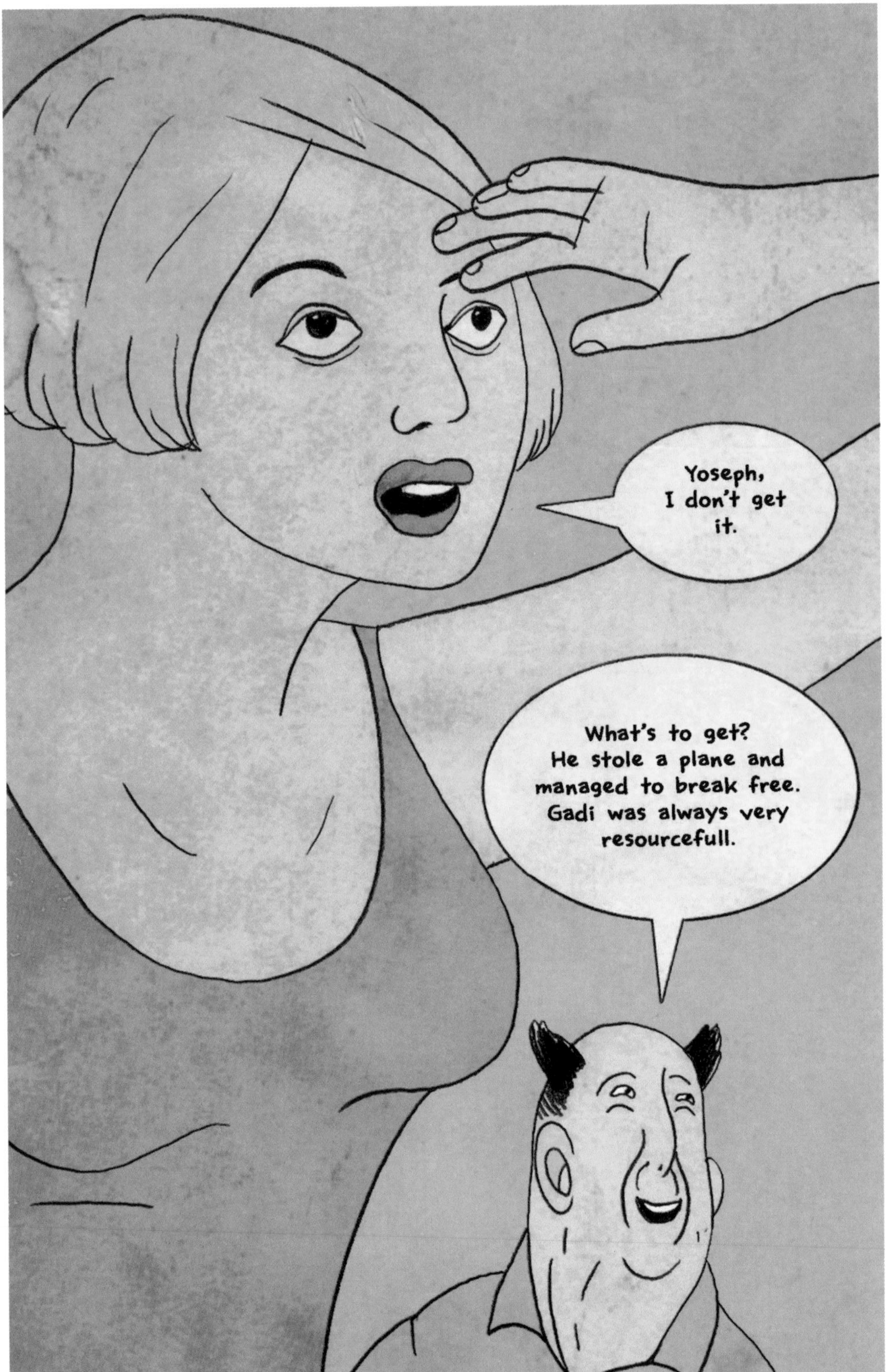
Yoseph, I don't get it.
What's to get? He stole a plane and managed to break free. Gadi was always very resourcefull.

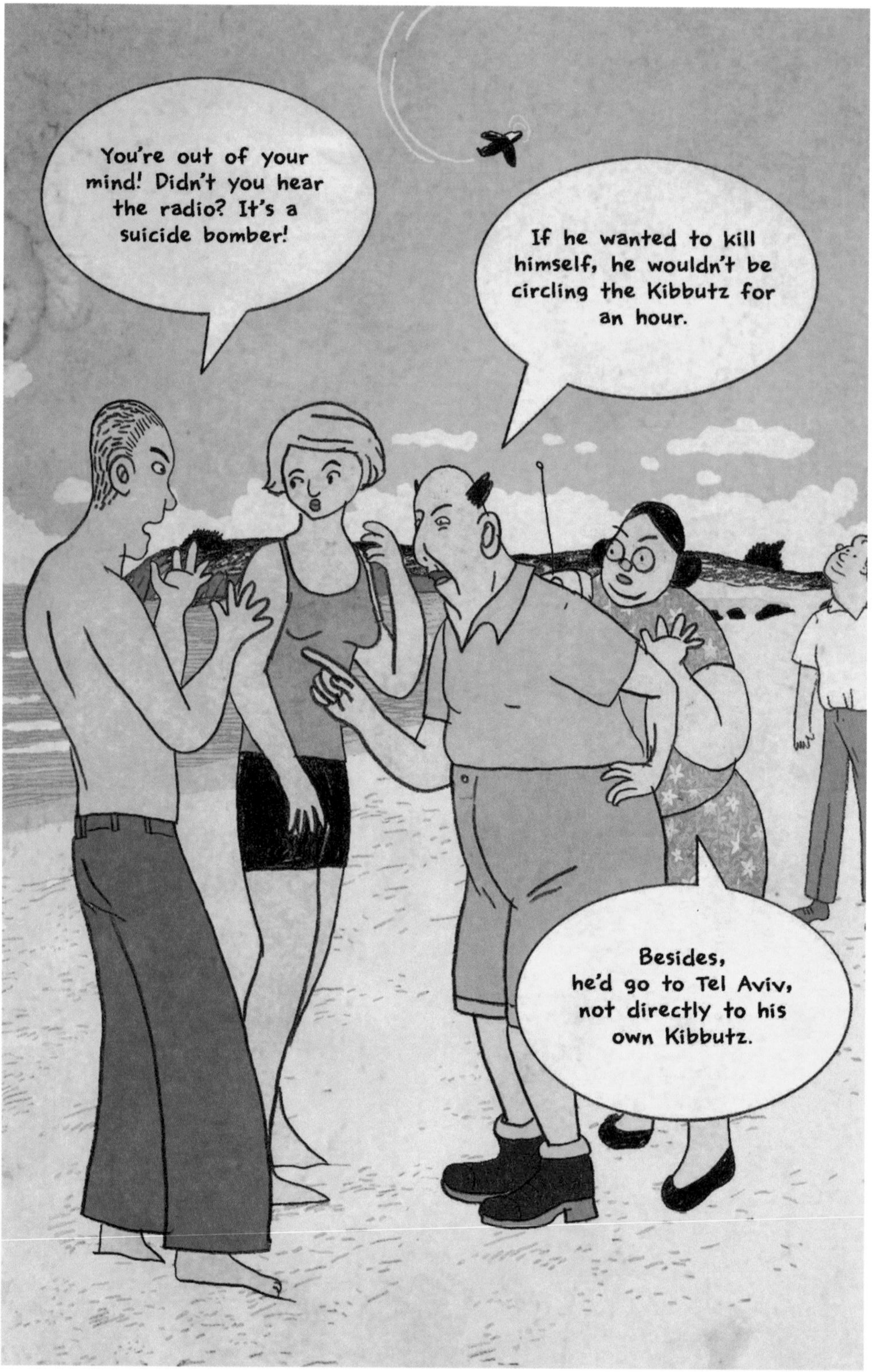
You're out of your mind! Didn't you hear the radio? It's a suicide bomber!
If he wanted to kill himself, he wouldn't be circling the Kibbutz for an hour.
Besides, he'd go to Tel Aviv, not directly to his own Kibbutz.

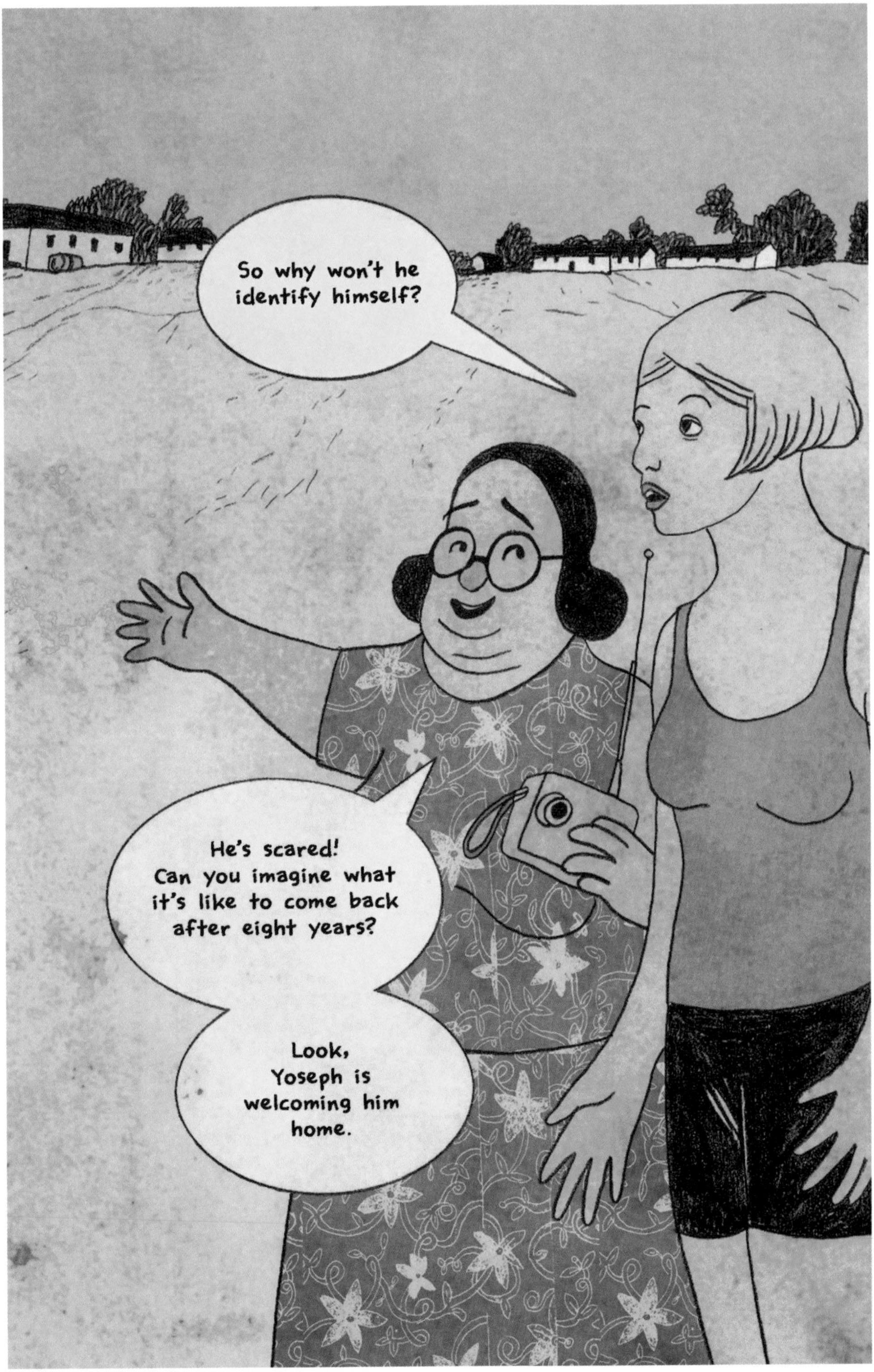
So why won't he identify himself?
He's scared! Can you imagine what it's like to come back after eight years?
Look, Yoseph is welcoming him home.

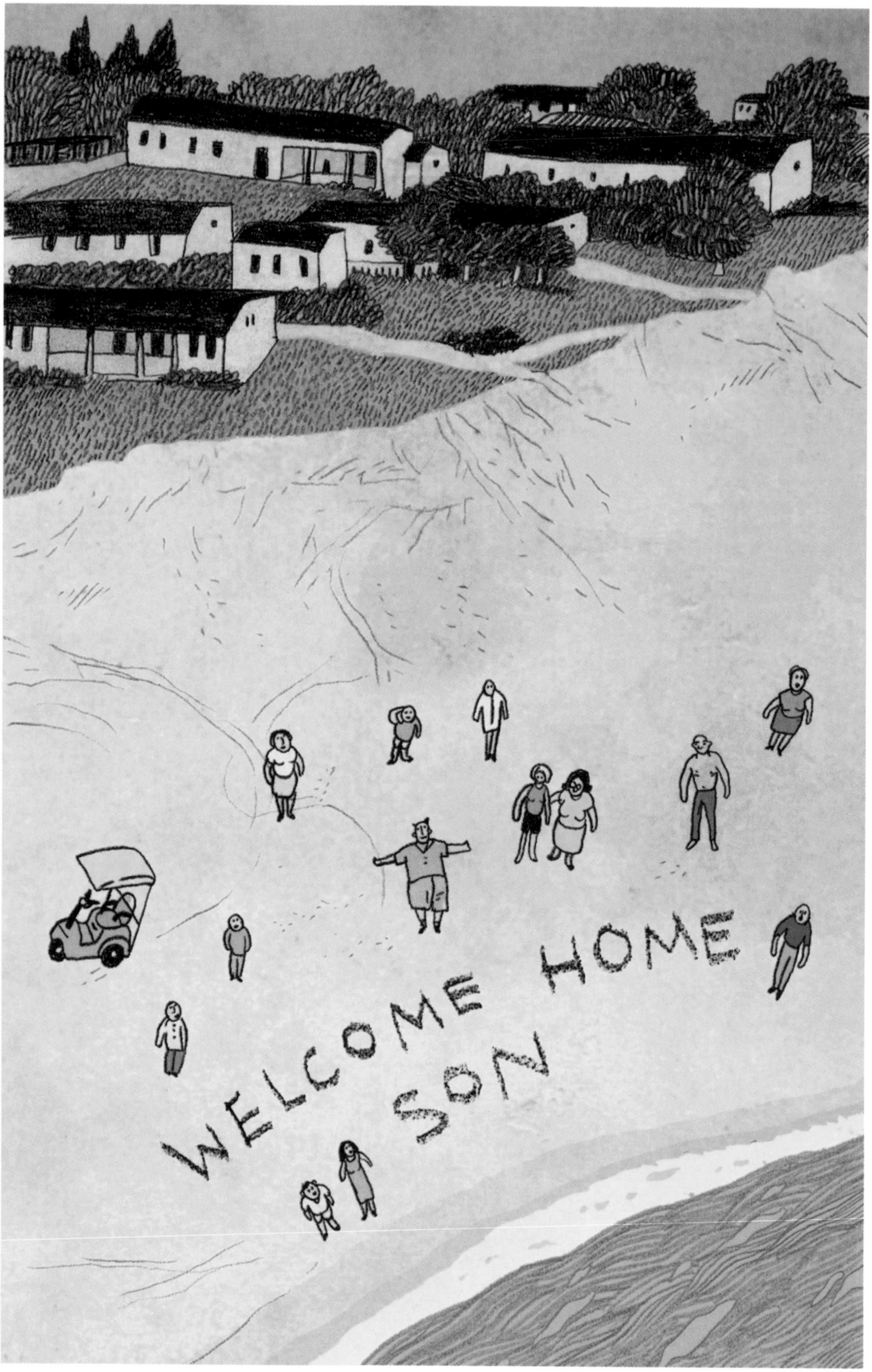
WELCOME HOME
SON

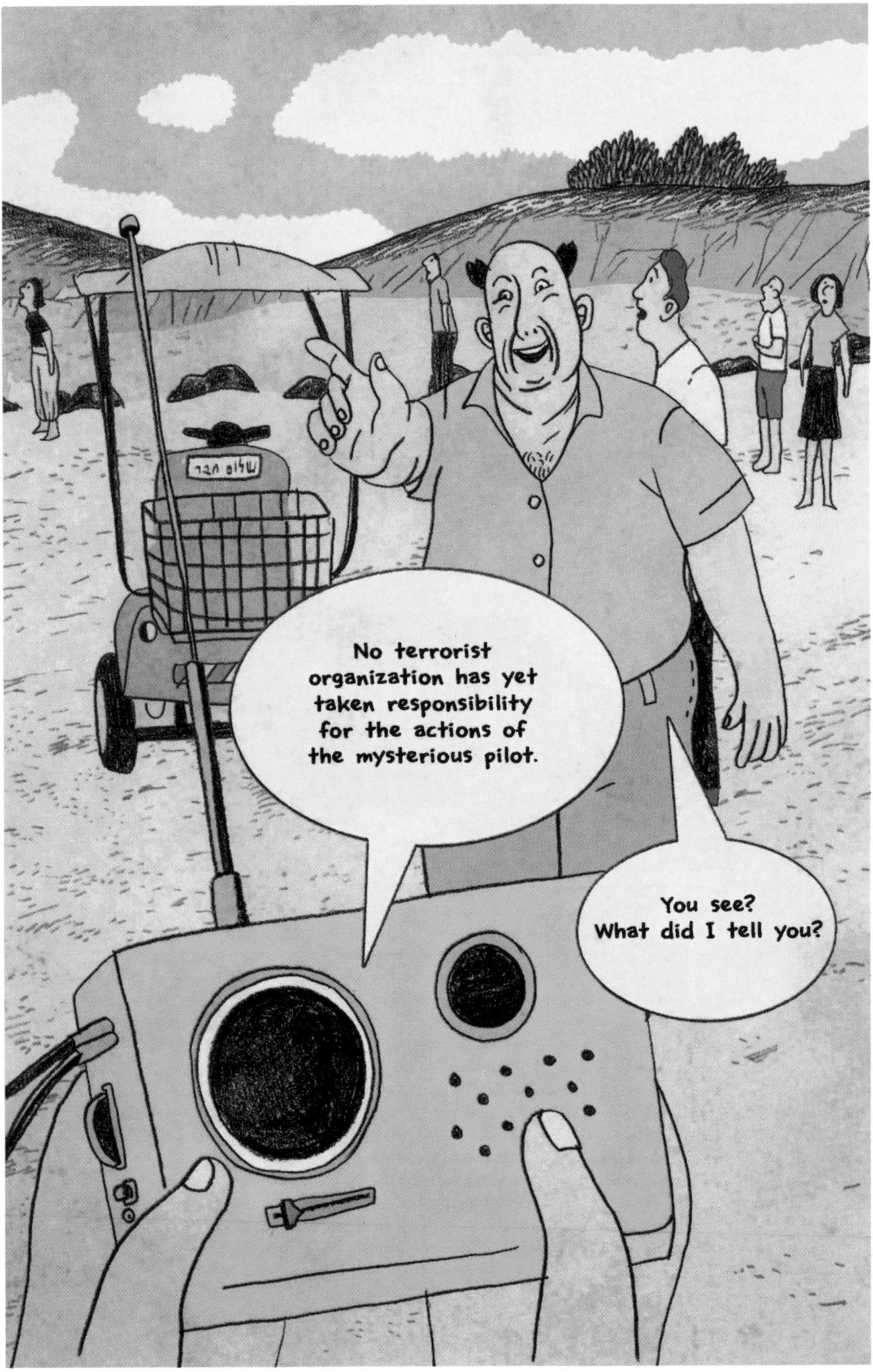
שלום חבר
No terrorist organization has yet taken responsibility for the actions of the mysterious pilot.
You see? What did I tell you?

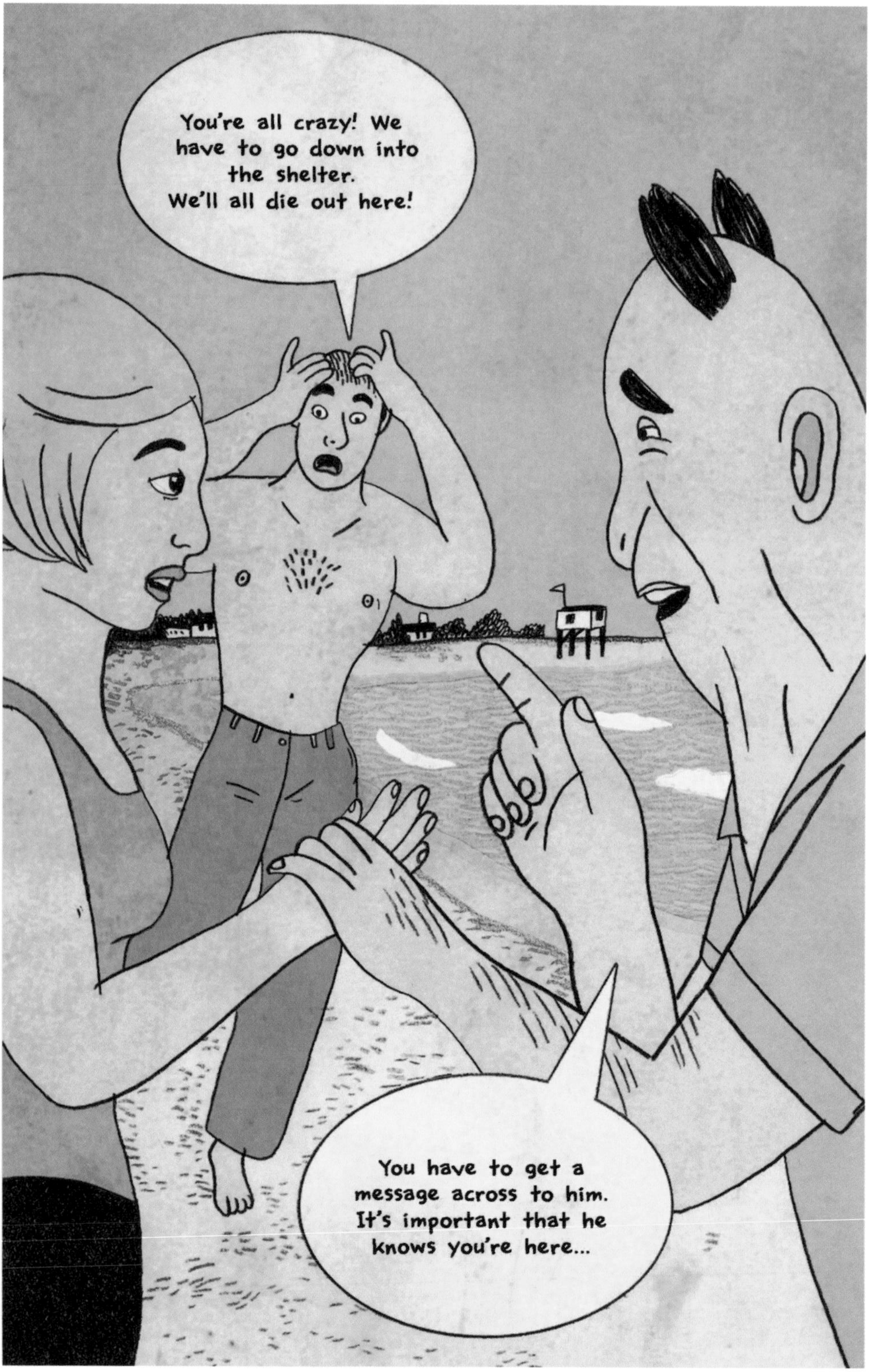
You're all crazy! We have to go down into the shelter. We'll all die out here!
You have to get a message across to him. It's important that he knows you're here...

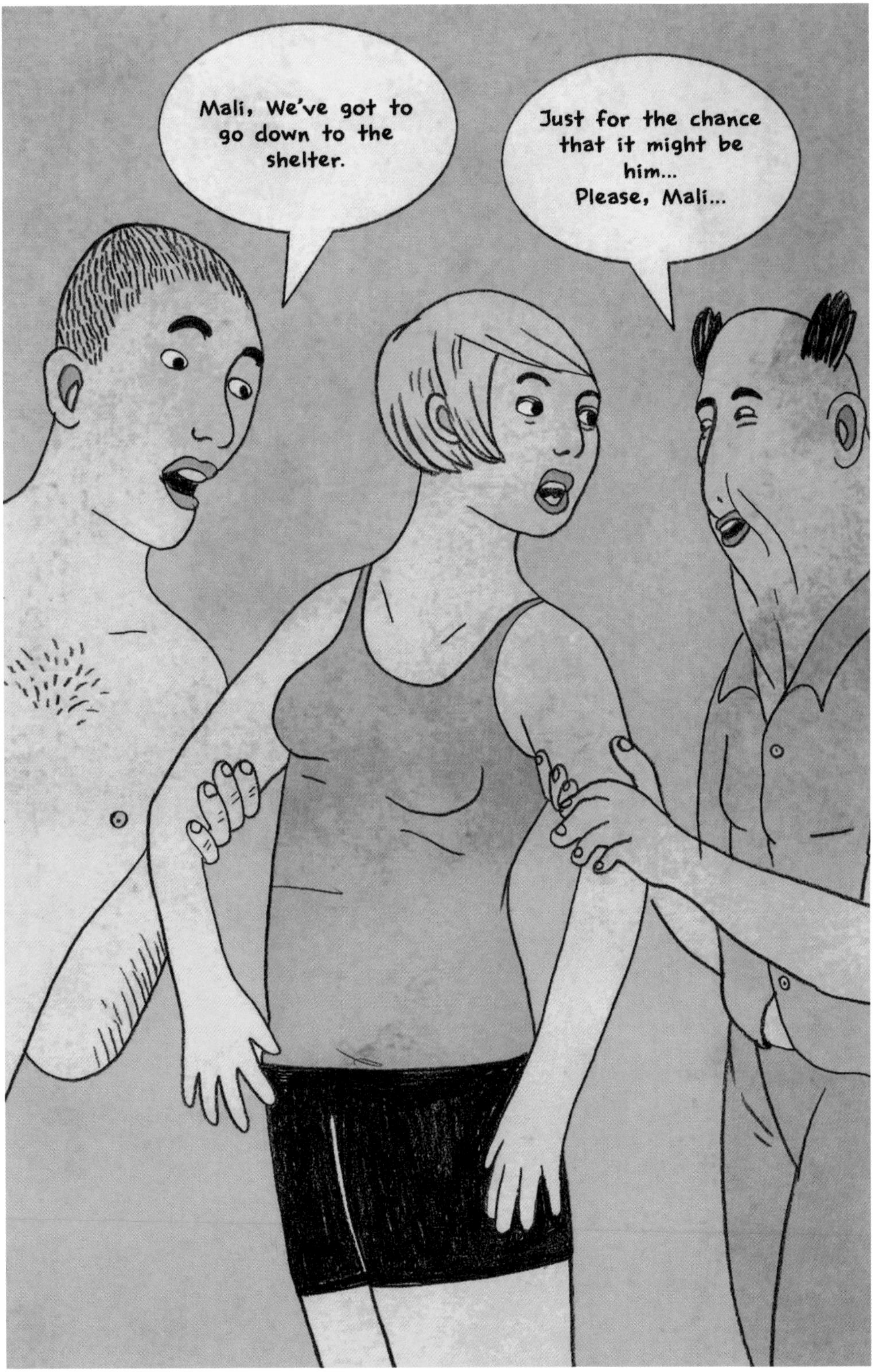
Mali, We've got to go down to the shelter.
Just for the chance that it might be him... Please, Mali...

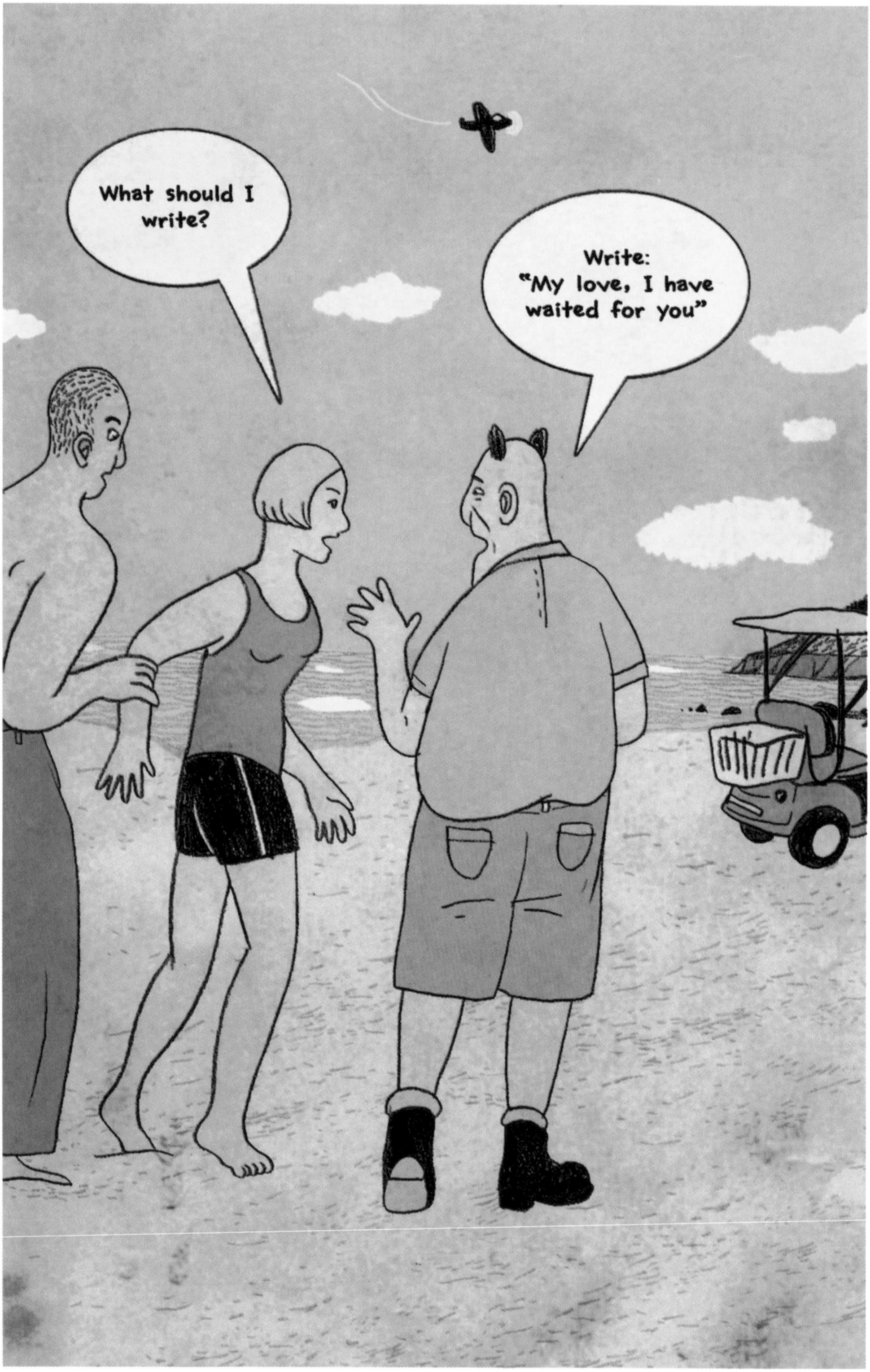
What should I write?
Write: "My love, I have waited for you"

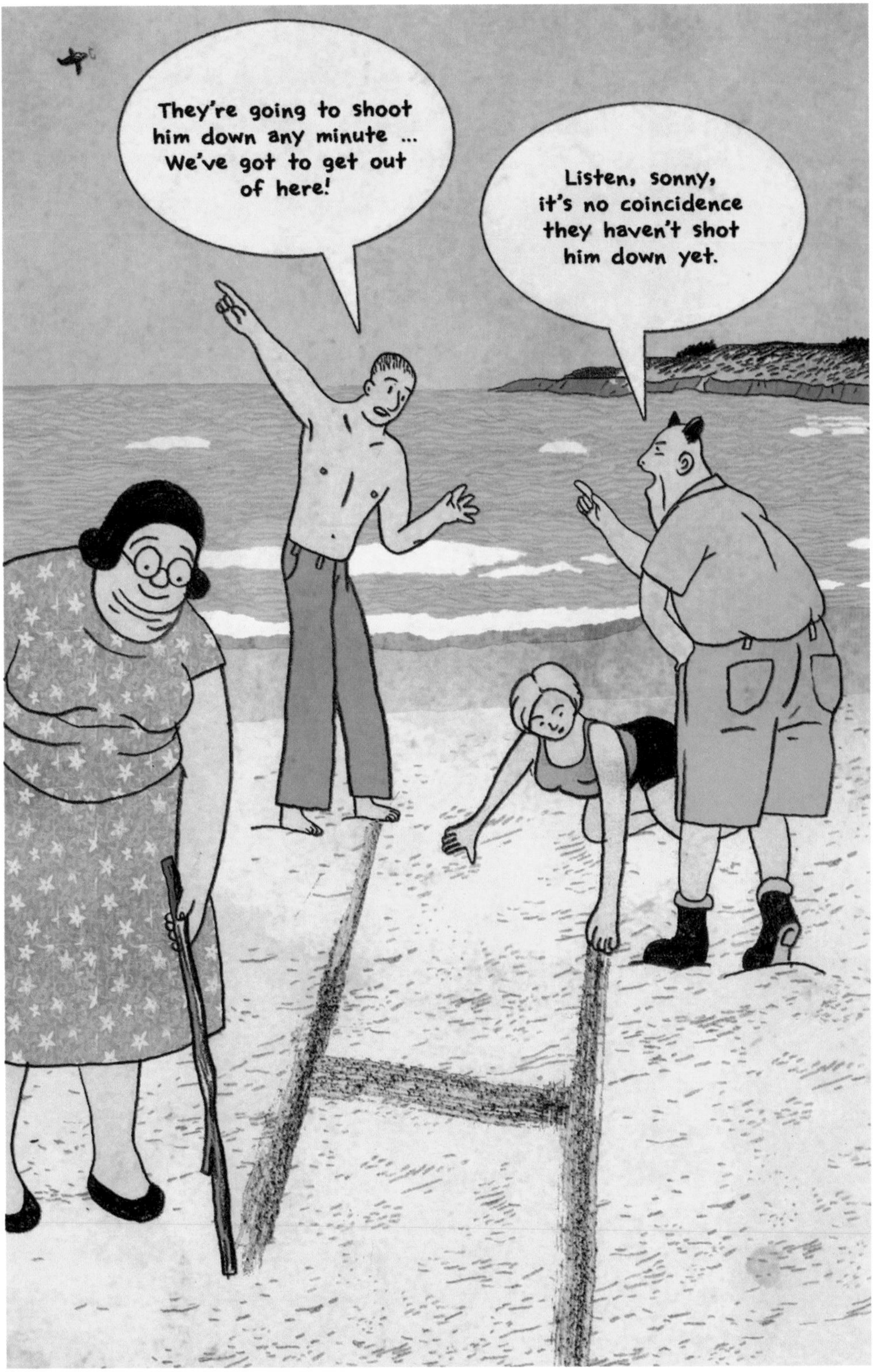
They're going to shoot him down any minute ... We've got to get out of here!
Listen, sonny, it's no coincidence they haven't shot him down yet.

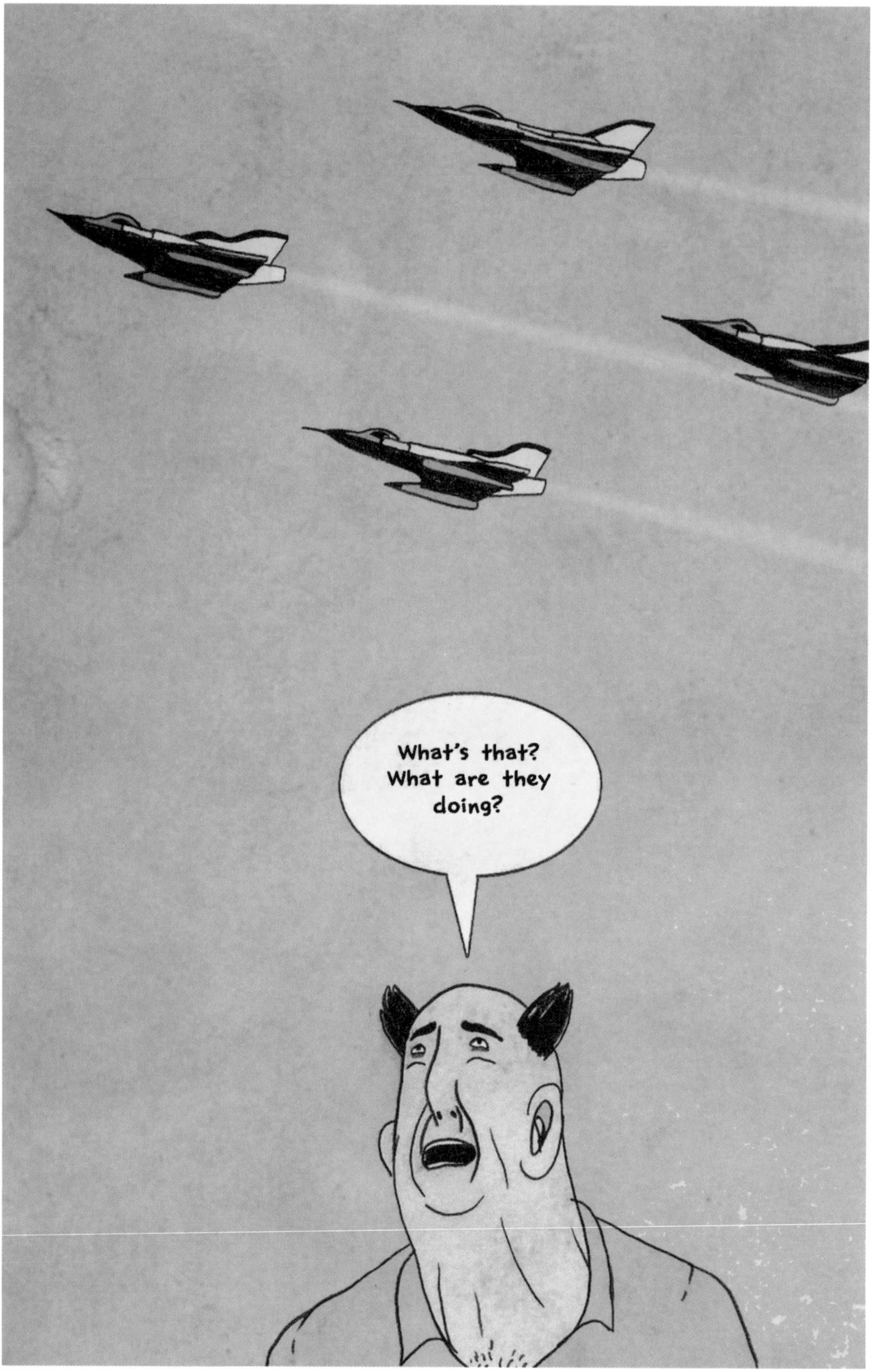
What's that? What are they doing?

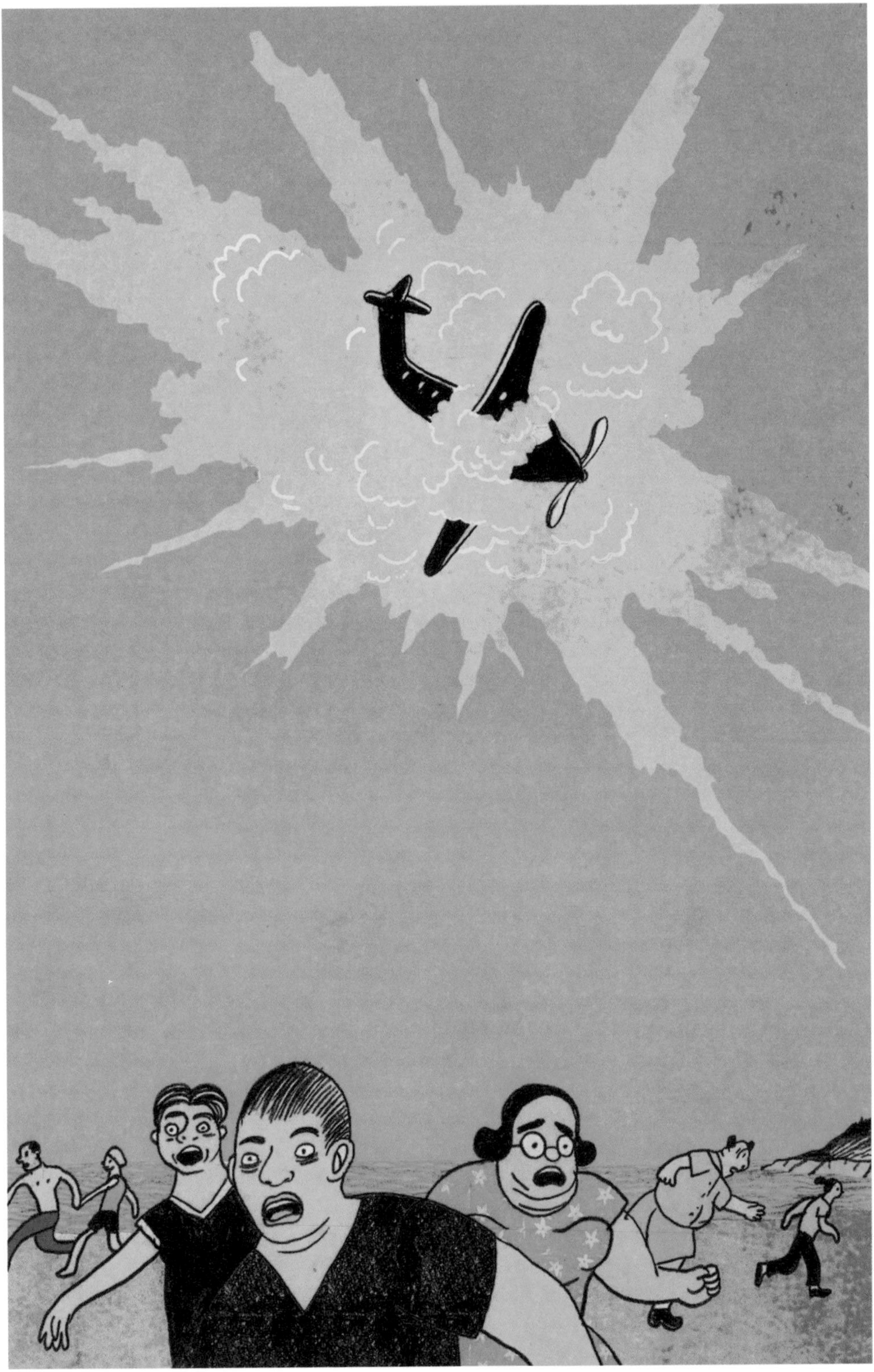

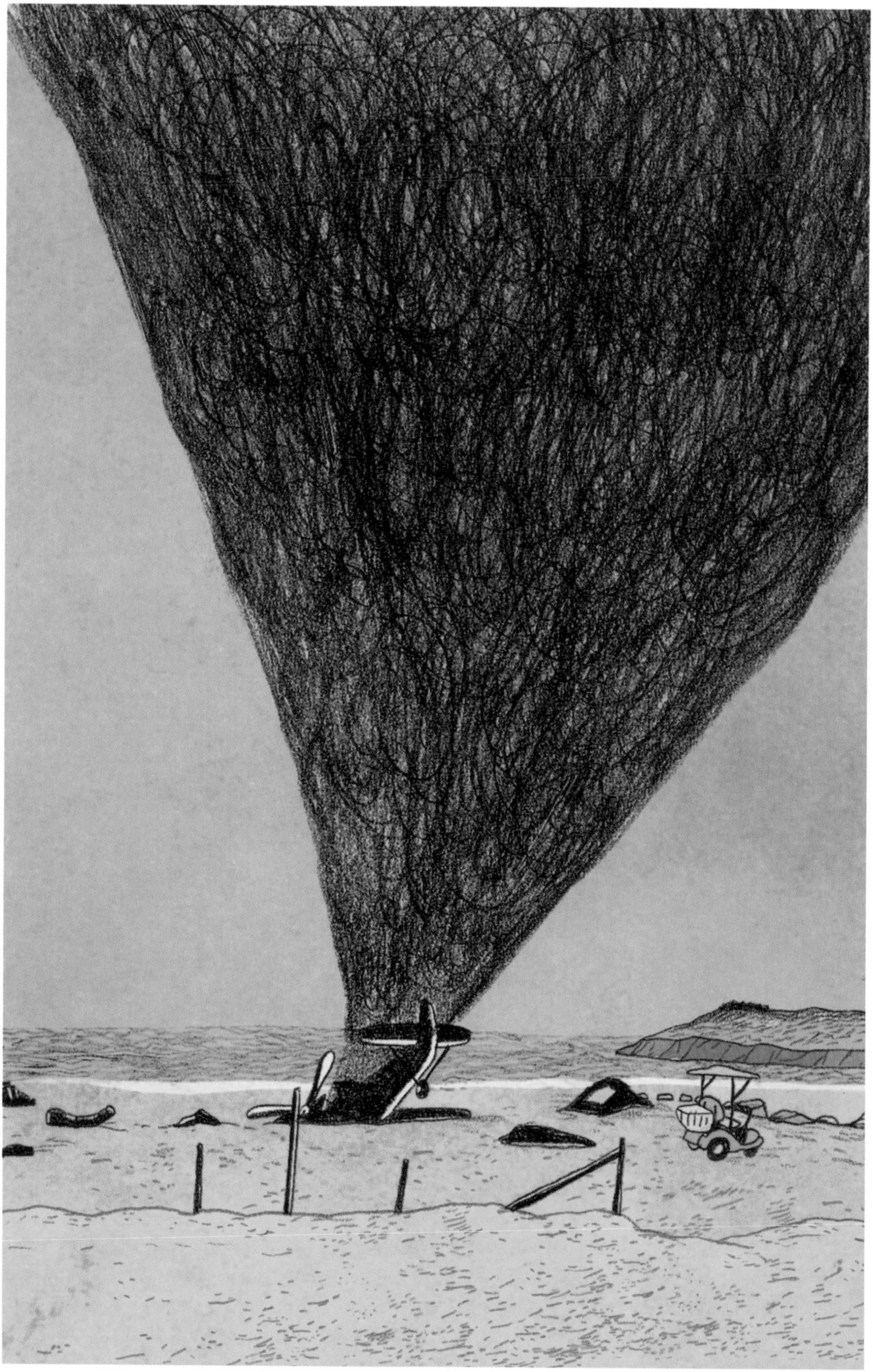

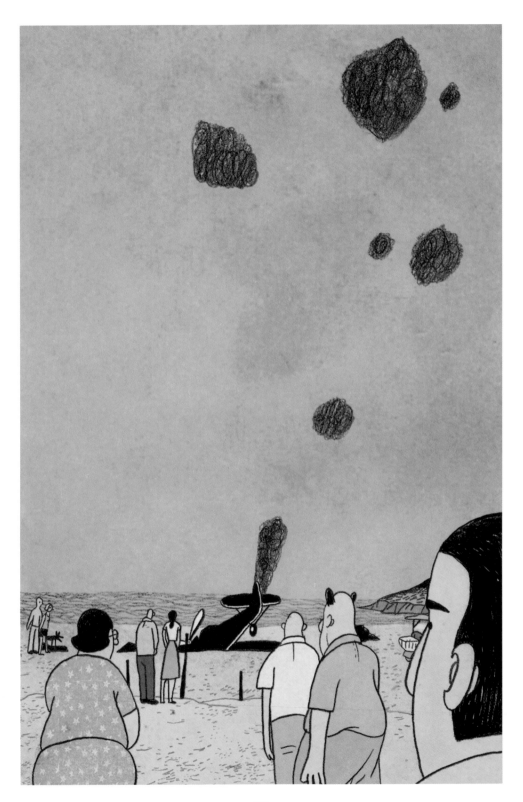

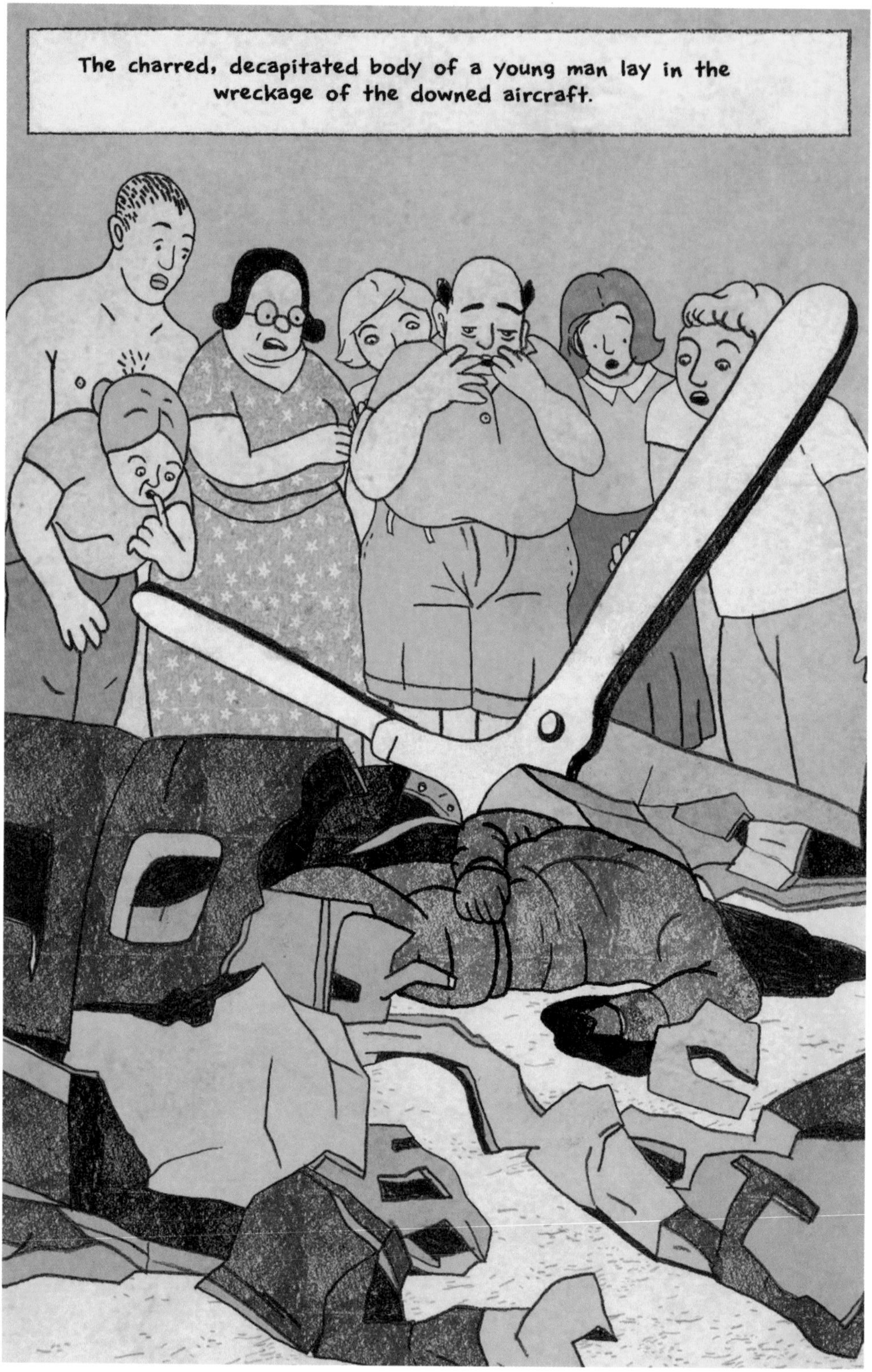
The charred, decapitated body of a young man lay in the wreckage of the downed aircraft.

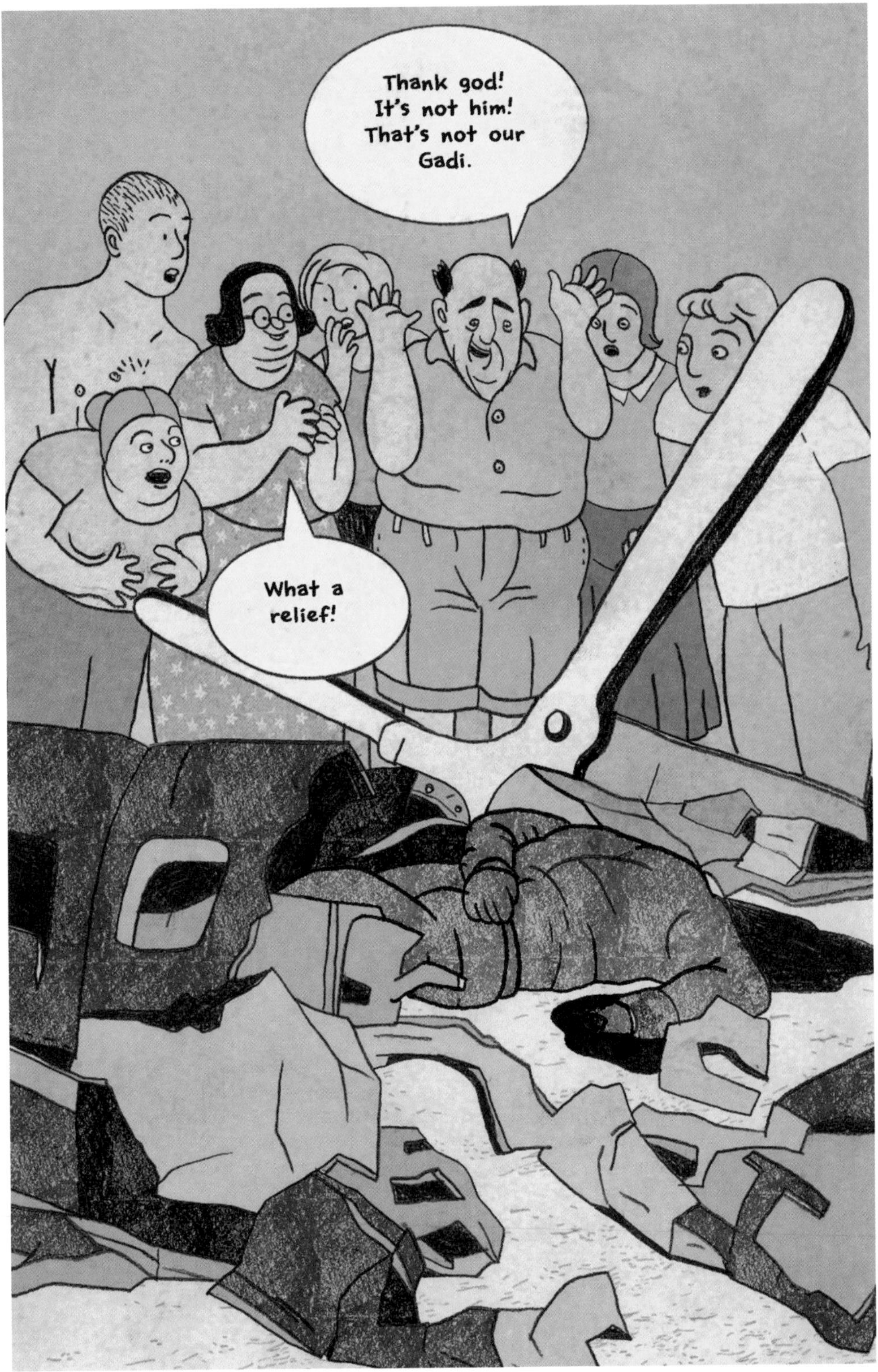
Thank god! It's not him! That's not our Gadi.
What a relief!

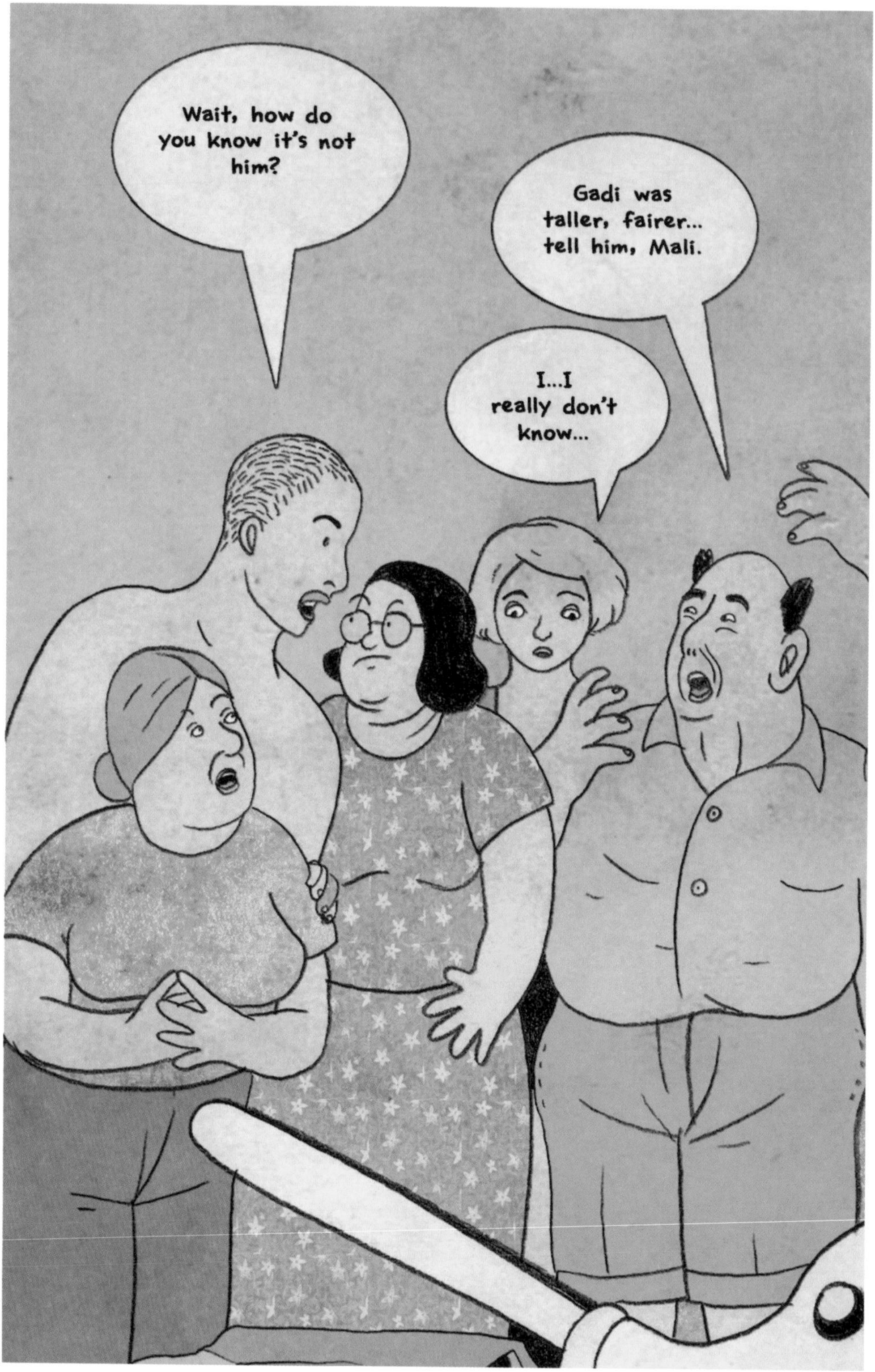
Wait, how do you know it's not him?
Gadi was taller, fairer... tell him, Mali.
I...I really don't know...

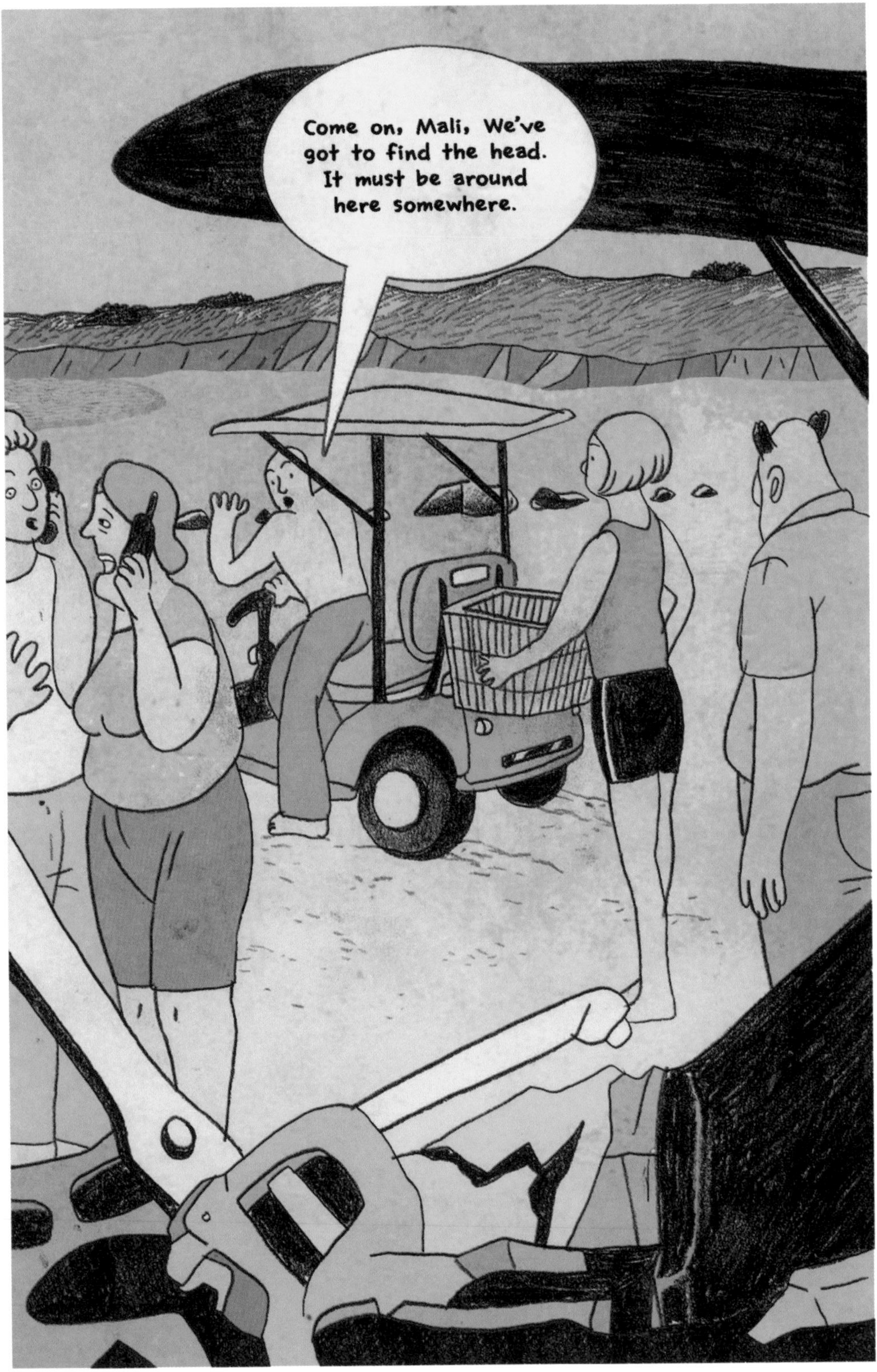
Come on, Mali, We've got to find the head. It must be around here somewhere.

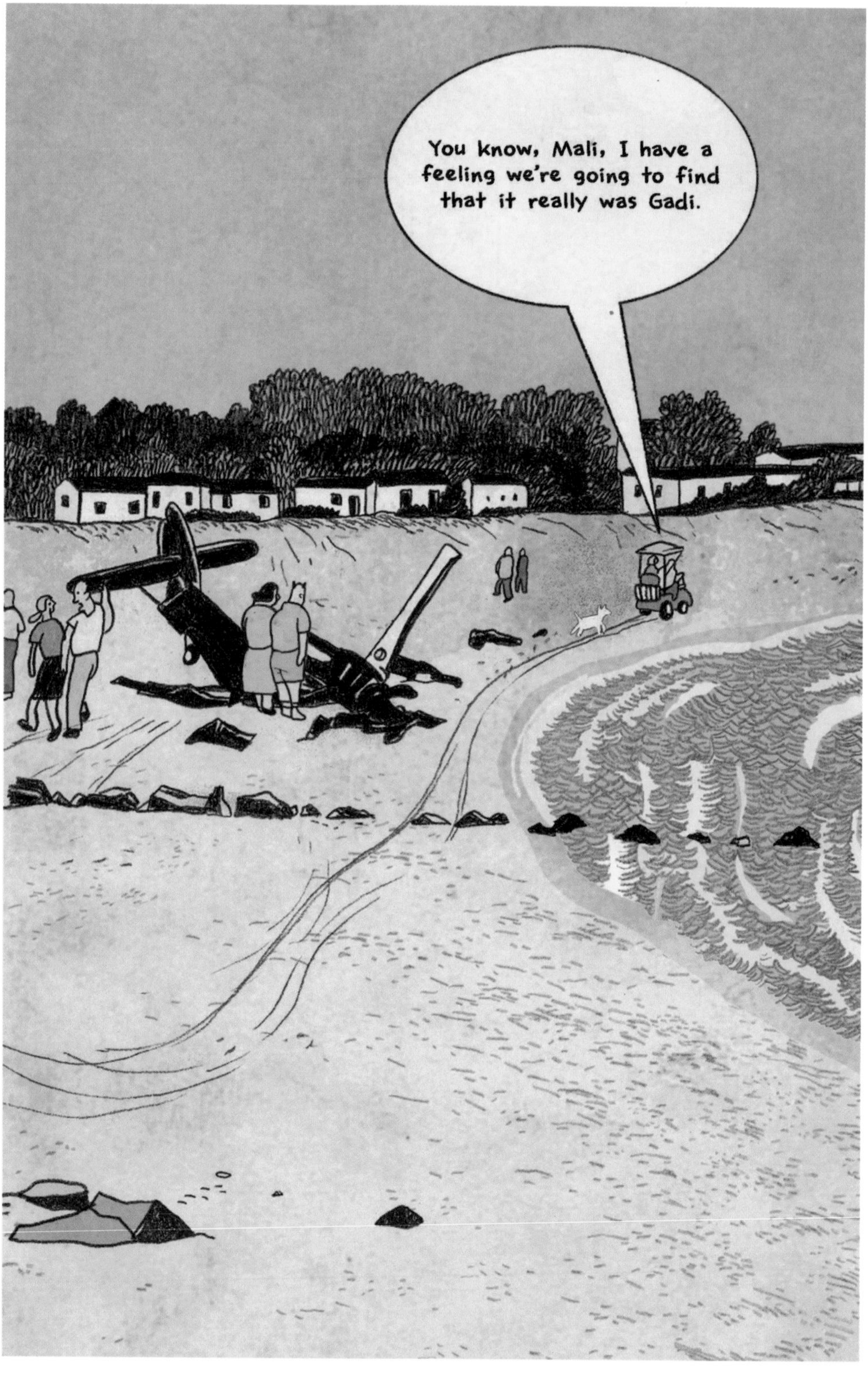
You know, Mali, I have a feeling we're going to find that it really was Gadi.

THE KING OF THE LILLIES

Louise Wagschul was in a quandary; Her daughter Lilly had
already turned 12, and was showing no signs of acrobatic
aptitude. They had been getting by so far, but the applause was
growing weaker with every show, and the other day
two men had walked off right before the double-back somersault. No
man had ever left her little show in the middle before.
"I'm getting older," Louise said to herself.
"Sooner or later my audience will abandon me. I think it's time for a
career transition."

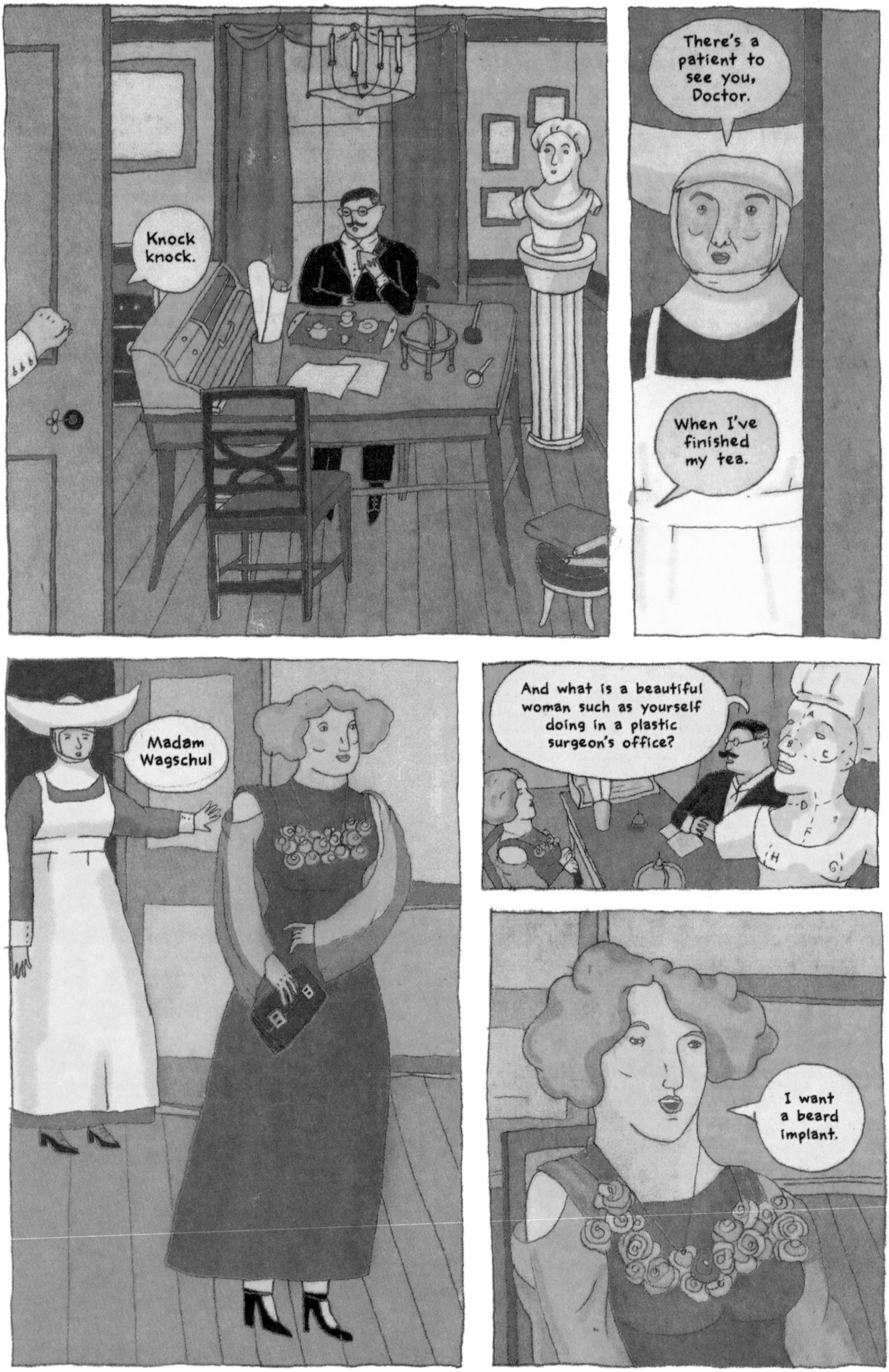
Knock knock.
There's a patient to see you, Doctor.
When I've finished my tea.
Madam Wagschul
And what is a beautiful woman such as yourself doing in a plastic surgeon's office?
I want a beard implant.

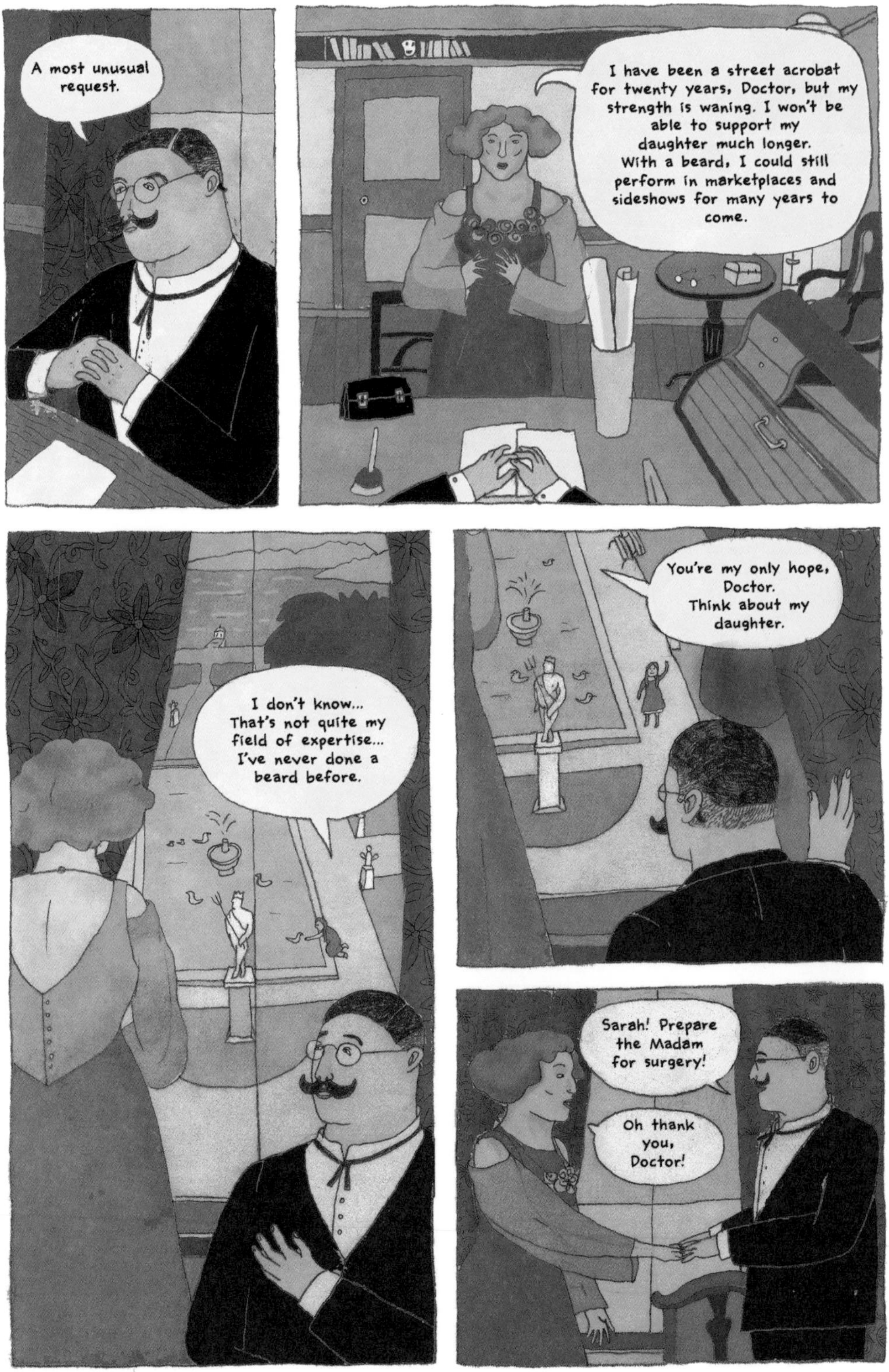
A most unusual request.
I have been a street acrobat for twenty years, Doctor, but my strength is waning. I won't be able to support my daughter much longer. With a beard, I could still perform in marketplaces and sideshows for many years to come.
I don't know... That's not quite my field of expertise... I've never done a beard before.
You're my only hope, Doctor. Think about my daughter.
Sarah! Prepare the Madam for surgery!
Oh thank you, Doctor!

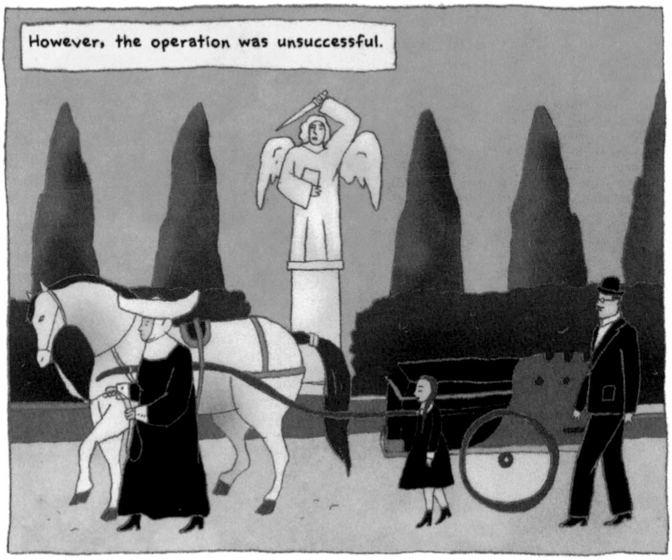
However, the operation was unsuccessful.

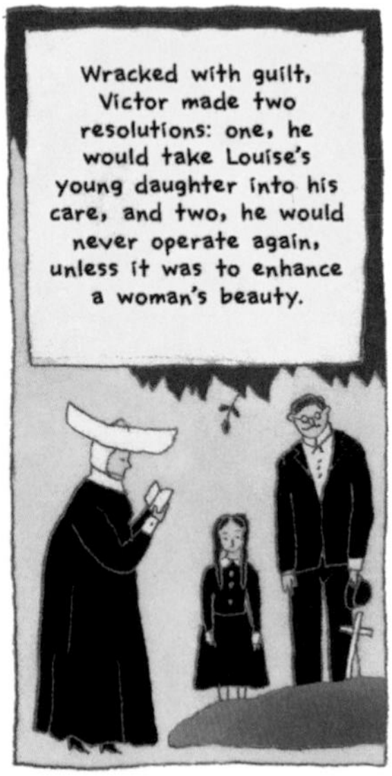
Wracked with guilt, Victor made two resolutions: one, he would take Louise's young daughter into his care, and two, he would never operate again, unless it was to enhance a woman's beauty.

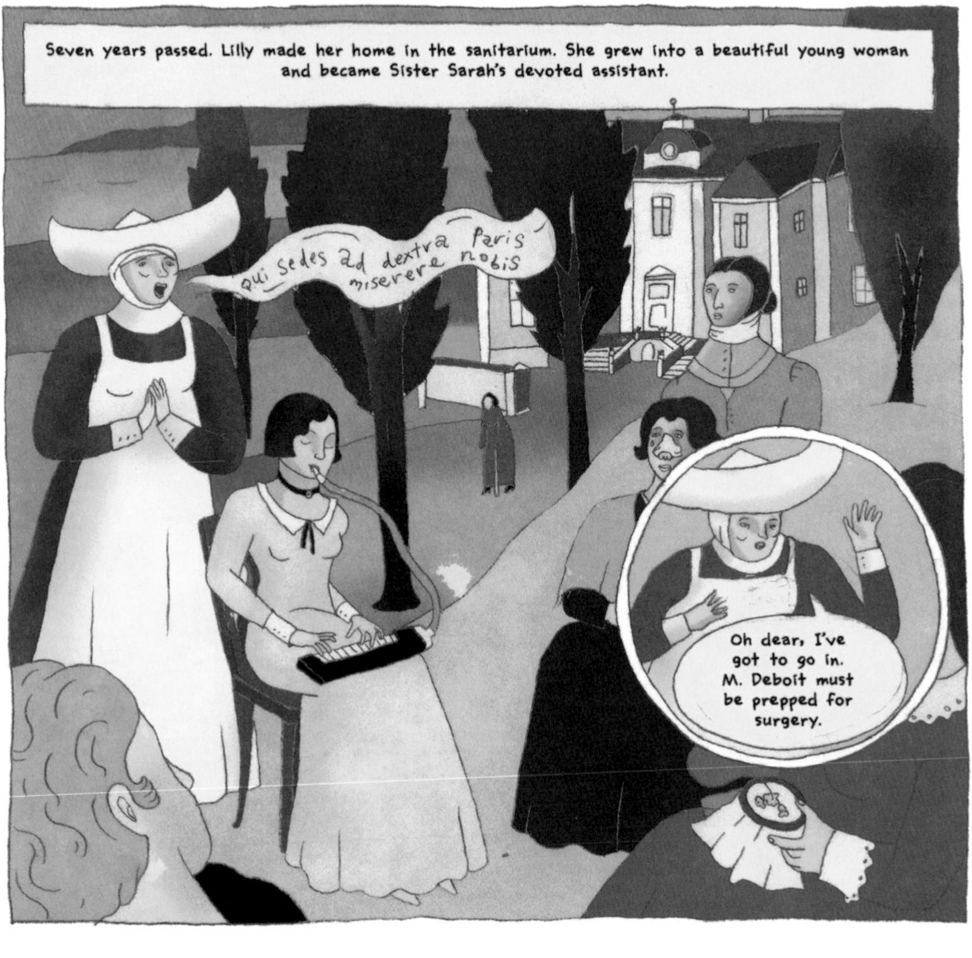
Seven years passed. Lilly made her home in the sanitarium. She grew into a beautiful young woman and became Sister Sarah's devoted assistant.
qui sedes ad dextra Paris miserere nobis
Oh dear, I've got to go in. M. Deboit must be prepped for surgery.

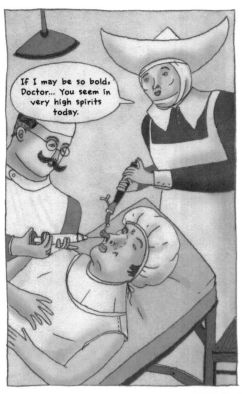

If I may be so bold, Doctor... You seem in very high spirits today.

You read me like a book, Sarah. I intend to propose to Lilly this evening.

Propose? Why, I had no idea... that you and she...

I have kept my feelings to myself all these years, waiting only for her to grow up.

And... does she know?

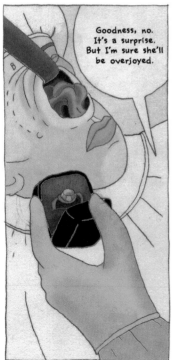

Goodness, no. It's a surprise. But I'm sure she'll be overjoyed.

The standard procedure, Sarah.

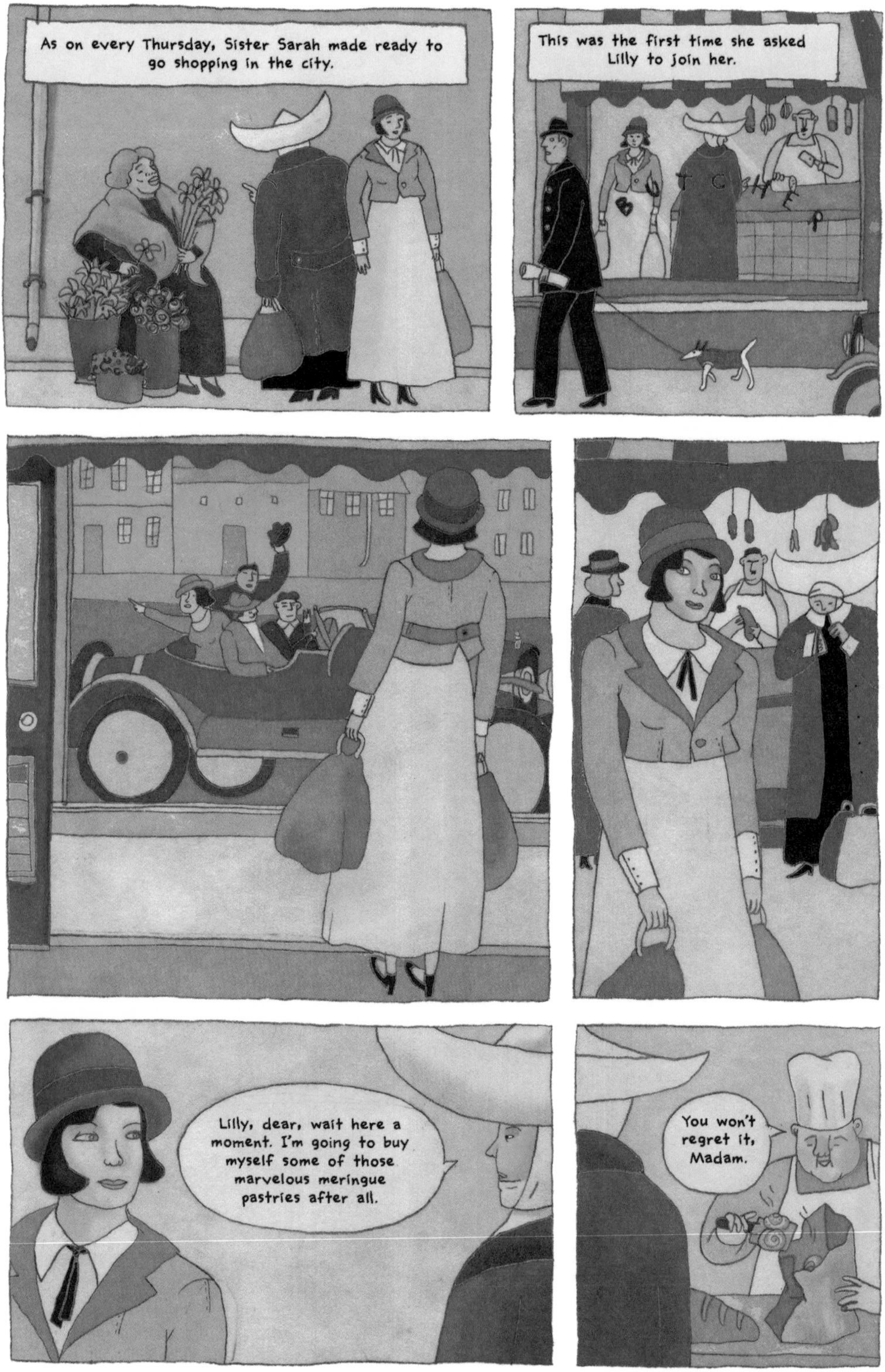
As on every Thursday, Sister Sarah made ready to go shopping in the city.
This was the first time she asked Lilly to join her.
Lilly, dear, wait here a moment. I'm going to buy myself some of those marvelous meringue pastries after all.
You won't regret it, Madam.

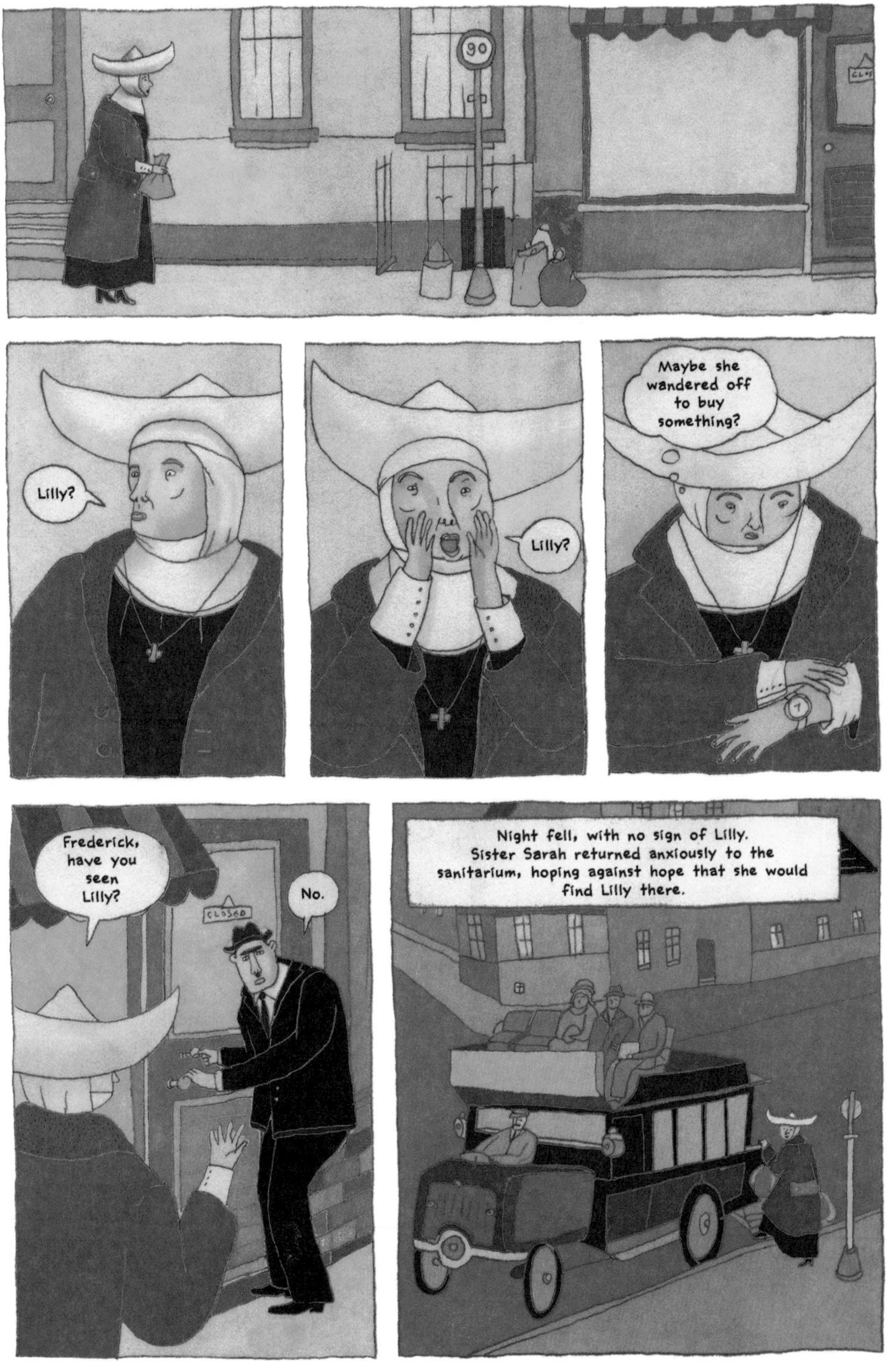
Lilly?
Lilly?
Maybe she wandered off to buy something?
Frederick, have you seen Lilly?
No.
CLOSED
Night fell, with no sign of Lilly. Sister Sarah returned anxiously to the sanitarium, hoping against hope that she would find Lilly there.

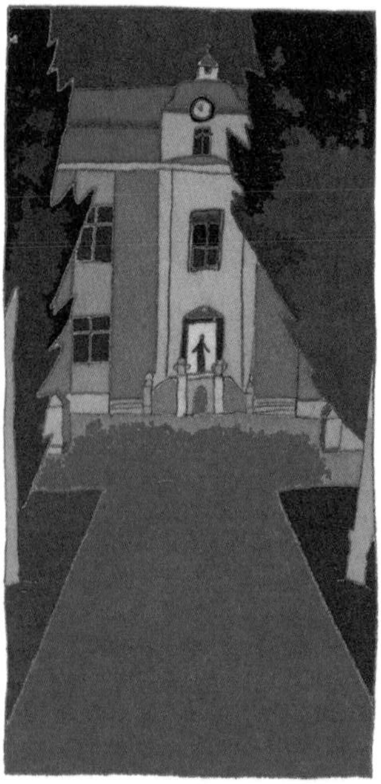

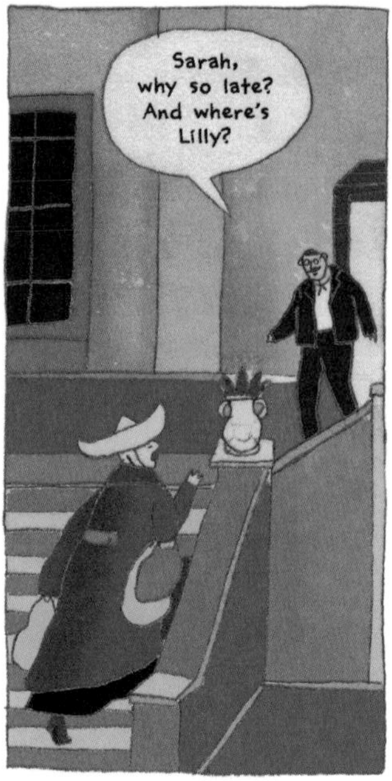
Sarah, why so late? And where's Lilly?

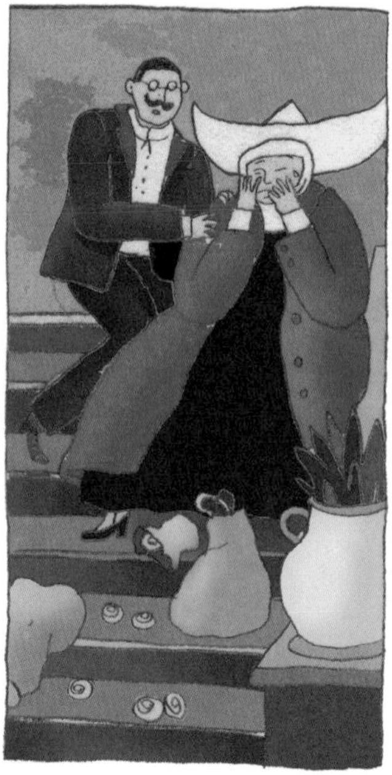

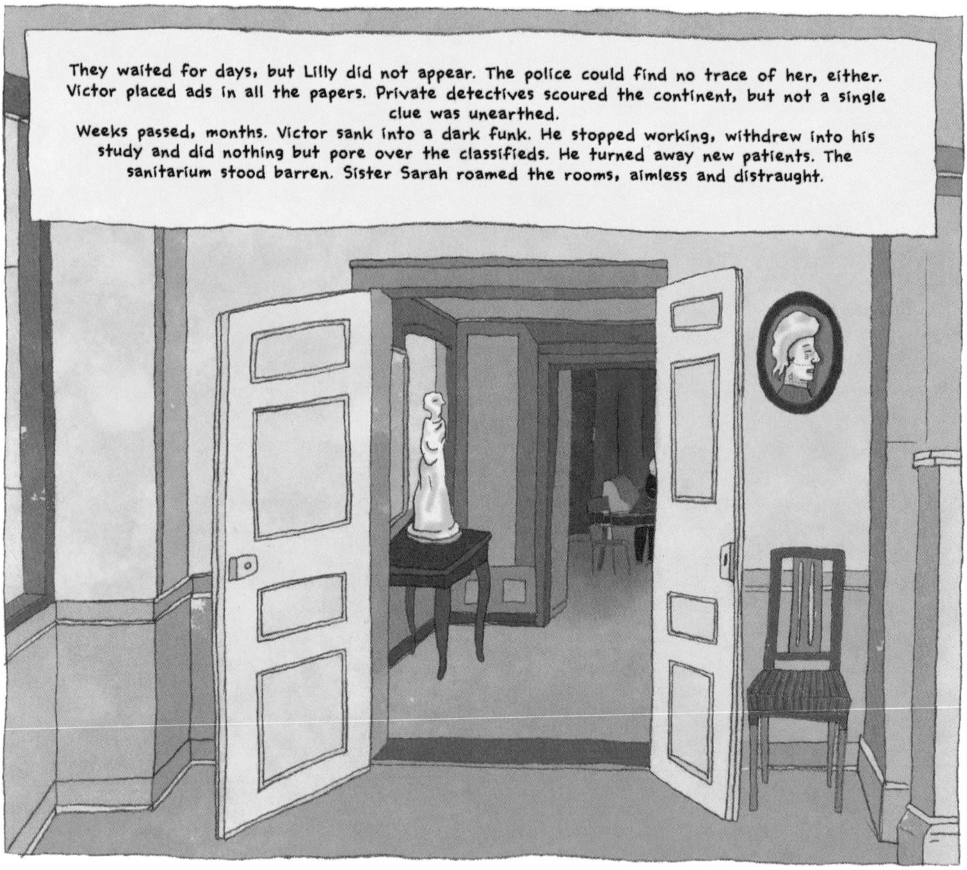
They waited for days, but Lilly did not appear. The police could find no trace of her, either. Victor placed ads in all the papers. Private detectives scoured the continent, but not a single clue was unearthed.
Weeks passed, months. Victor sank into a dark funk. He stopped working, withdrew into his study and did nothing but pore over the classifieds. He turned away new patients. The sanitarium stood barren. Sister Sarah roamed the rooms, aimless and distraught.

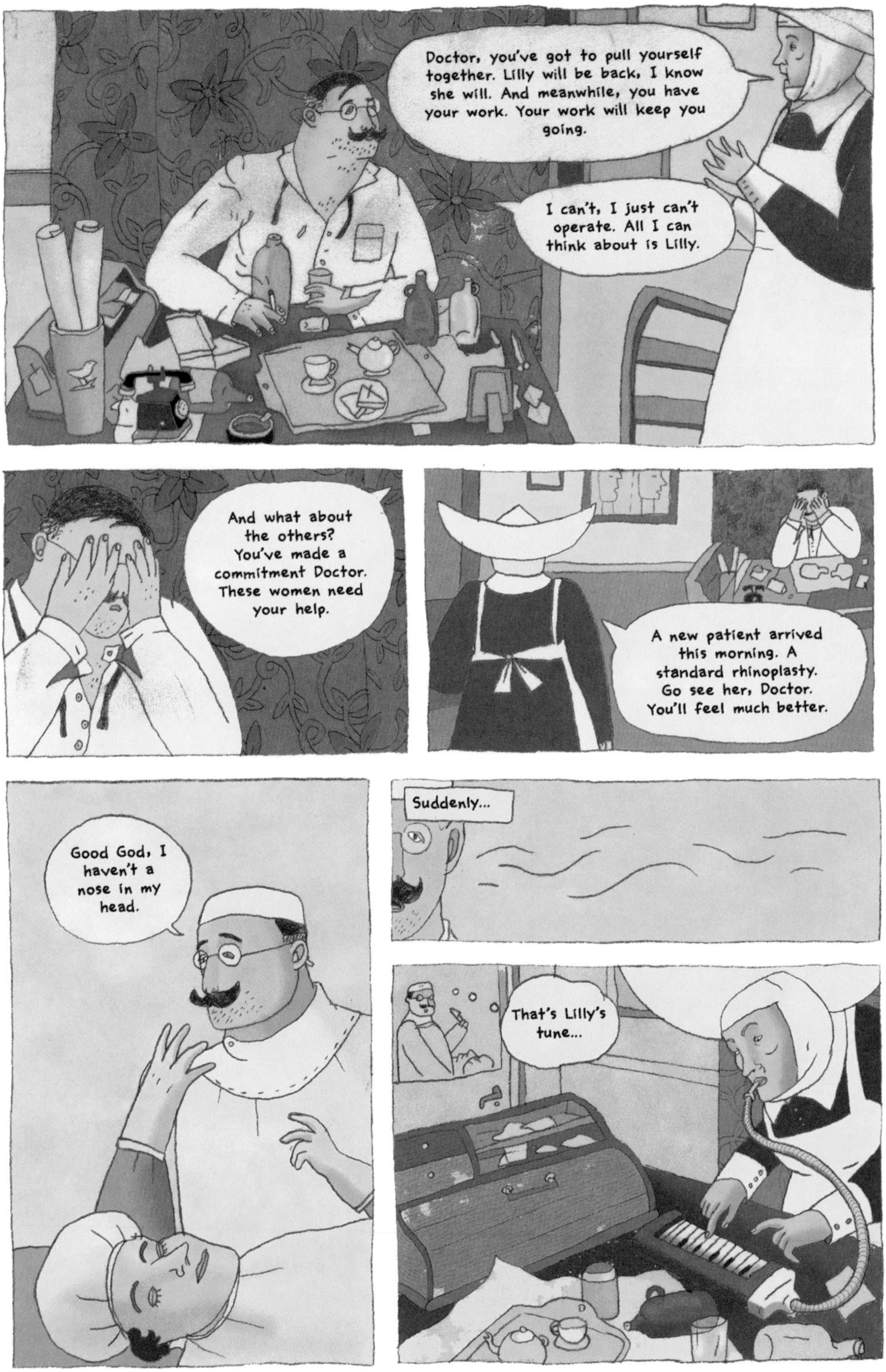
Doctor, you've got to pull yourself together. Lilly will be back, I know she will. And meanwhile, you have your work. Your work will keep you going.
I can't, I just can't operate. All I can think about is Lilly.
And what about the others? You've made a commitment Doctor. These women need your help.
A new patient arrived this morning. A standard rhinoplasty. Go see her, Doctor. You'll feel much better.
Good God, I haven't a nose in my head.
Suddenly...
That's Lilly's tune...

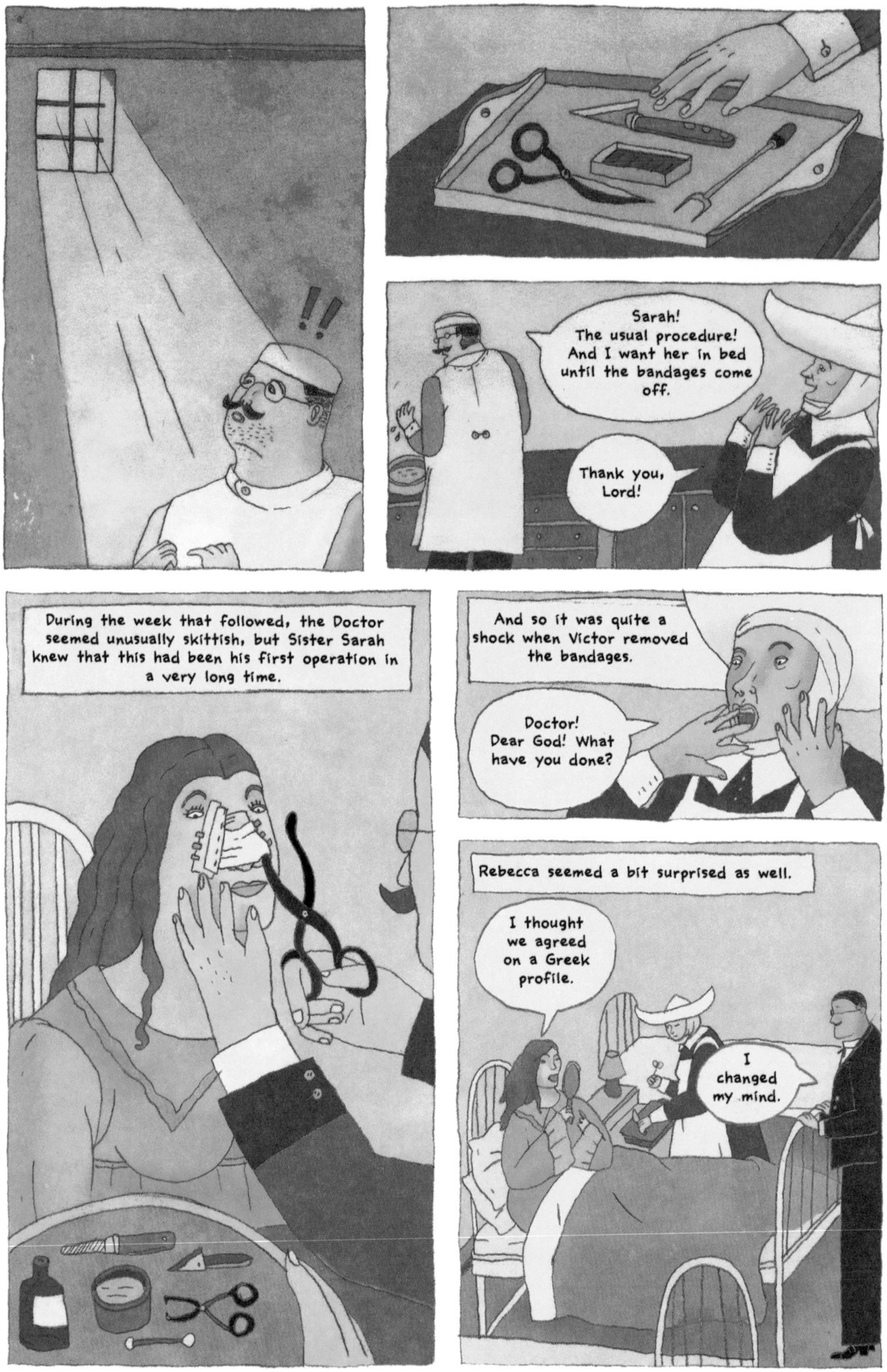
!!
Sarah!
The usual procedure!
And I want her in bed until the bandages come off.
Thank you, Lord!
During the week that followed, the Doctor seemed unusually skittish, but Sister Sarah knew that this had been his first operation in a very long time.
And so it was quite a shock when Victor removed the bandages.
Doctor!
Dear God! What have you done?
Rebecca seemed a bit surprised as well.
I thought we agreed on a Greek profile.
I changed my mind.

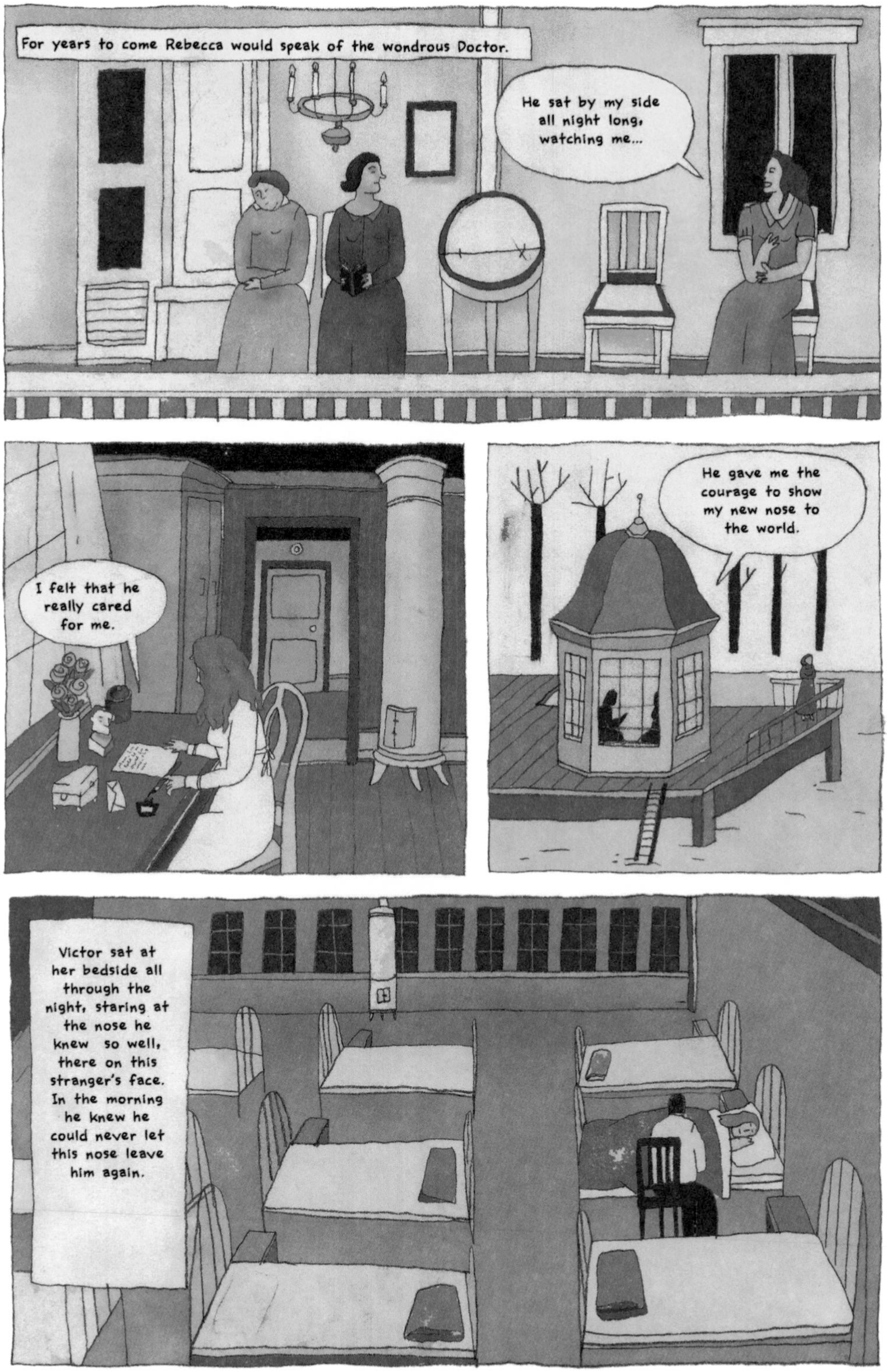
For years to come Rebecca would speak of the wondrous Doctor.
He sat by my side all night long, watching me...
I felt that he really cared for me.
He gave me the courage to show my new nose to the world.
Victor sat at her bedside all through the night, staring at the nose he knew so well, there on this stranger's face. In the morning he knew he could never let this nose leave him again.

Madam Snitt, the operation was a complete success. But I have a hunch that a slight eyelid tuck will bring out your exquisite nose more prominently.

I don't know... my fiance' is expecting me...

And don't worry about the money. It's all on the house.

Think about it, Rebecca. Wouldn't your fiance' be delighted if you were truly perfect?

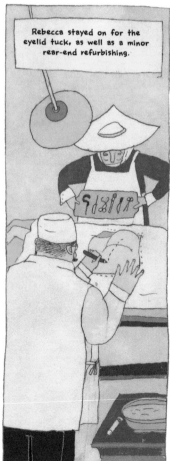

Rebecca stayed on for the eyelid tuck, as well as a minor rear-end refurbishing.

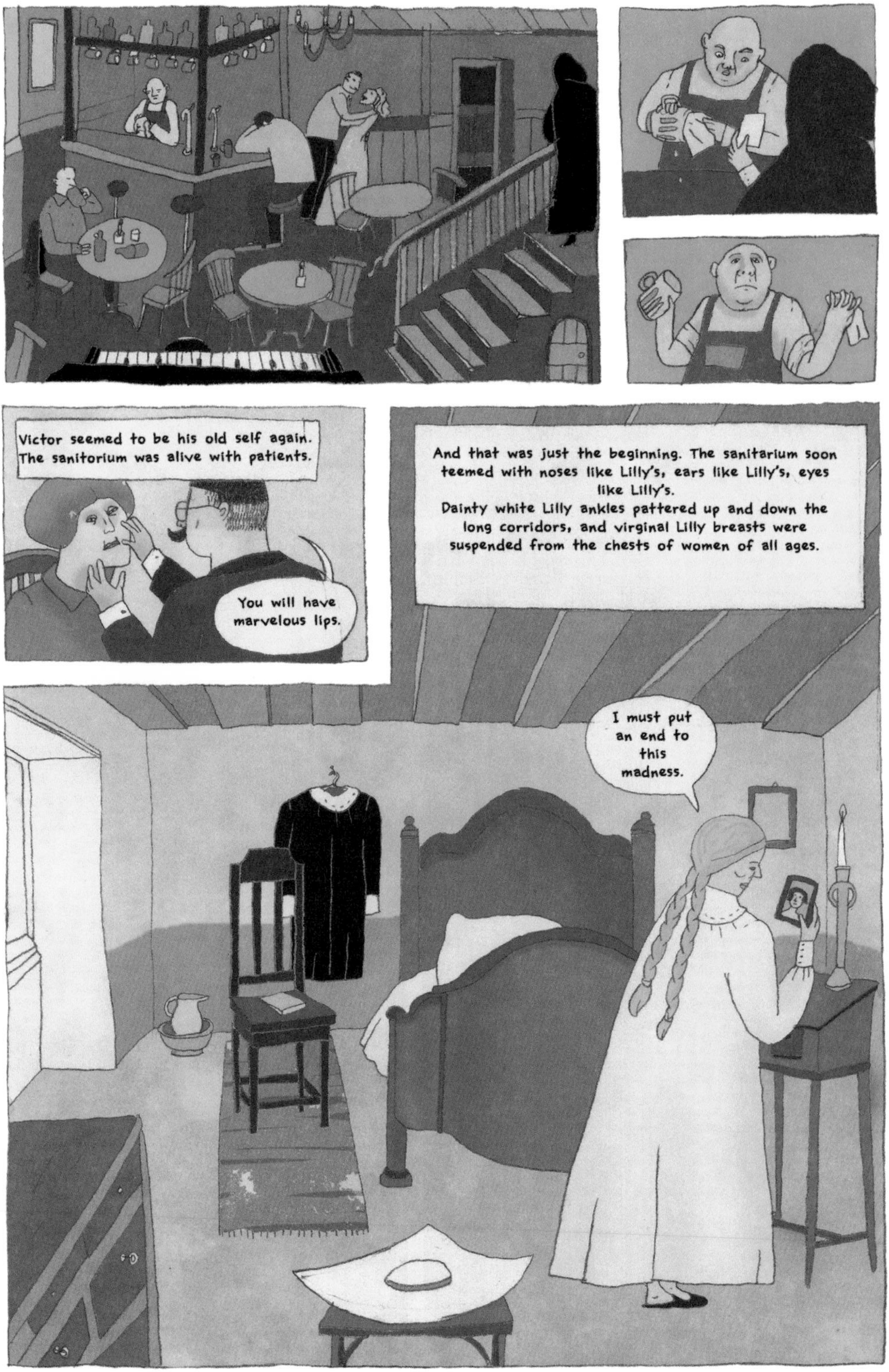

Victor seemed to be his old self again. The sanitorium was alive with patients.
You will have marvelous lips.
And that was just the beginning. The sanitarium soon teemed with noses like Lilly's, ears like Lilly's, eyes like Lilly's.
Dainty white Lilly ankles pattered up and down the long corridors, and virginal Lilly breasts were suspended from the chests of women of all ages.
I must put an end to this madness.

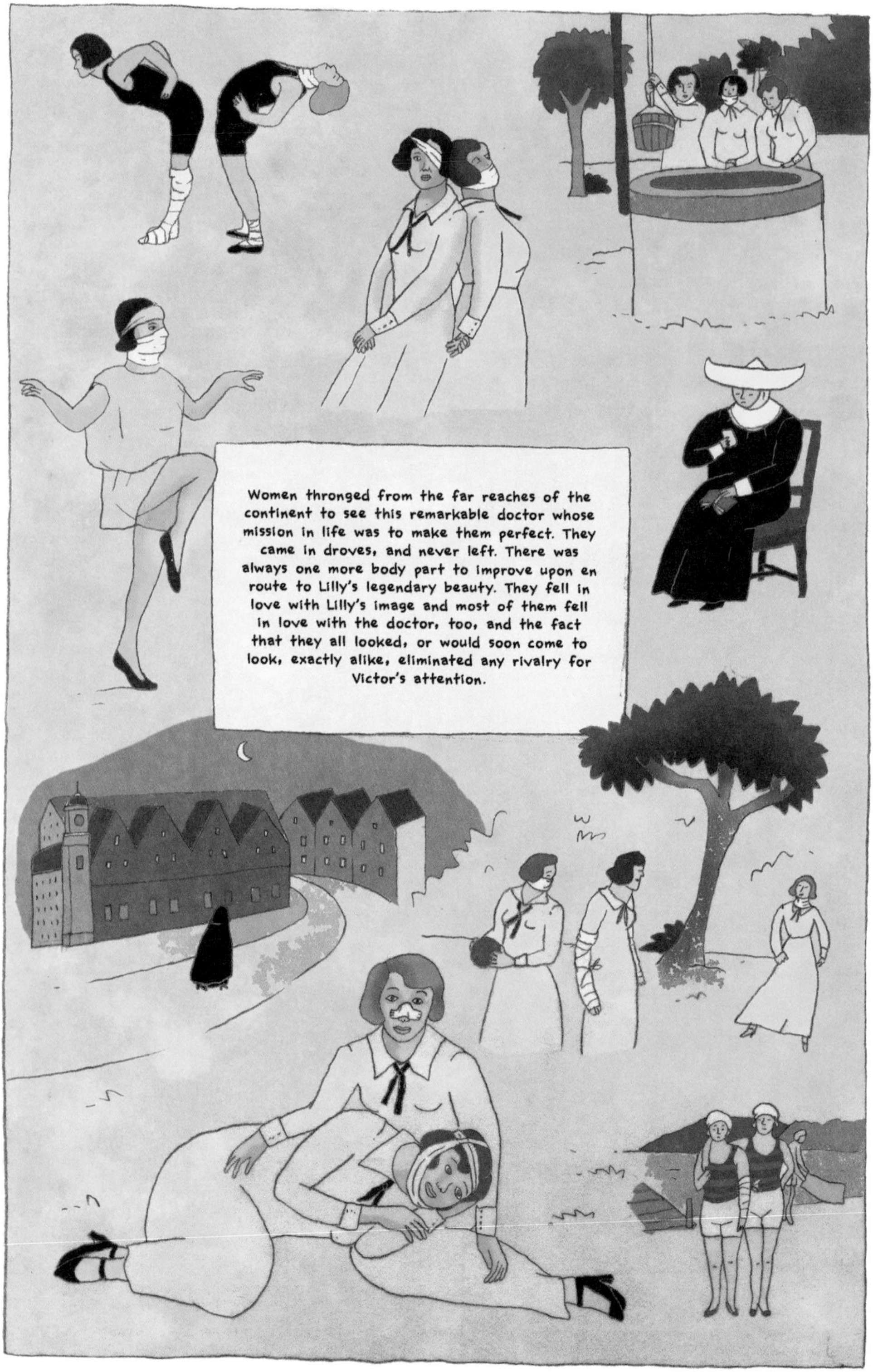
Women thronged from the far reaches of the continent to see this remarkable doctor whose mission in life was to make them perfect. They came in droves, and never left. There was always one more body part to improve upon en route to Lilly's legendary beauty. They fell in love with Lilly's image and most of them fell in love with the doctor, too, and the fact that they all looked, or would soon come to look, exactly alike, eliminated any rivalry for Victor's attention.

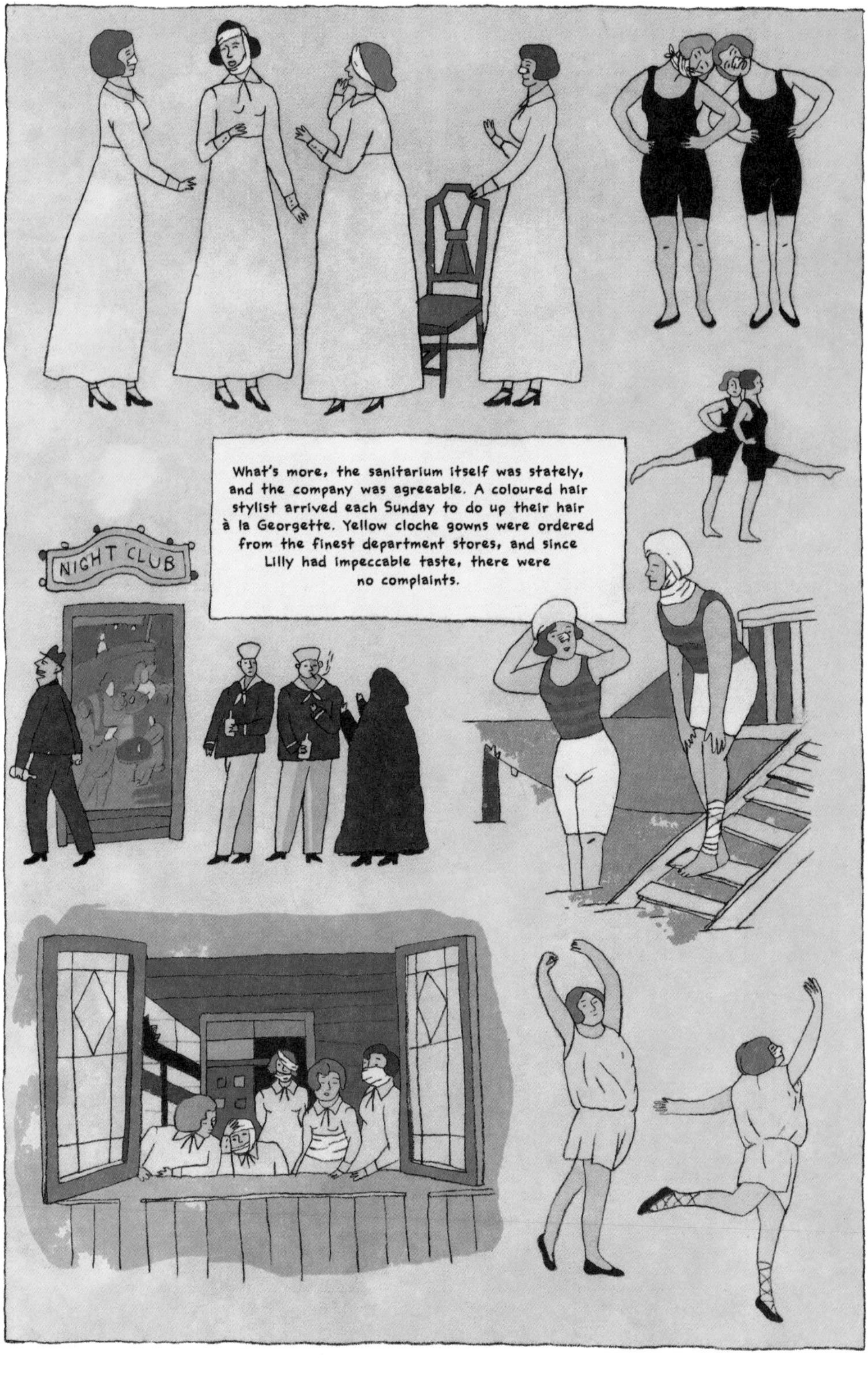
What's more, the sanitarium itself was stately, and the company was agreeable. A coloured hair stylist arrived each Sunday to do up their hair à la Georgette. Yellow cloche gowns were ordered from the finest department stores, and since Lilly had impeccable taste, there were no complaints.
NIGHT CLUB

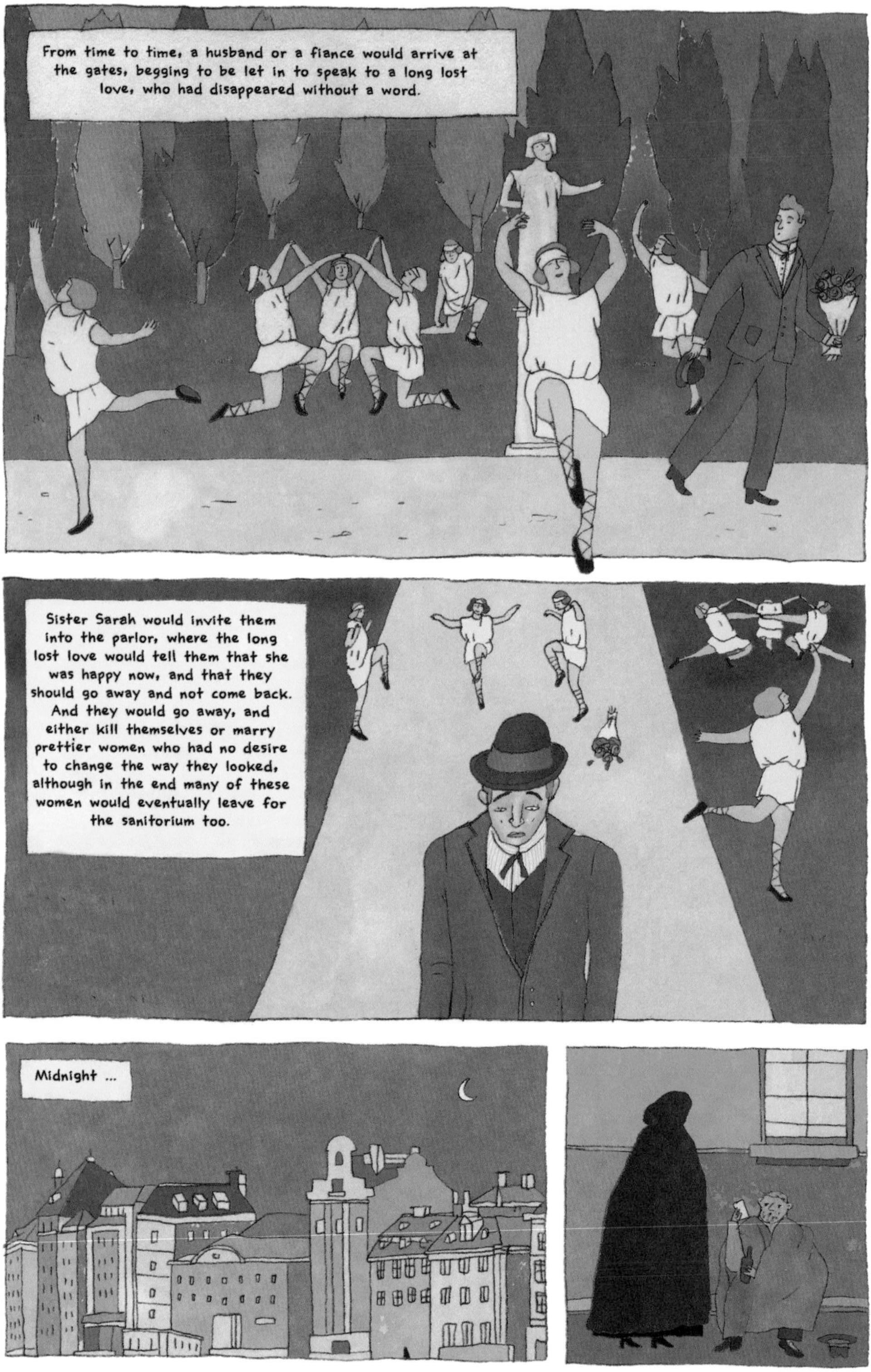

From time to time, a husband or a fiance would arrive at the gates, begging to be let in to speak to a long lost love, who had disappeared without a word.
Sister Sarah would invite them into the parlor, where the long lost love would tell them that she was happy now, and that they should go away and not come back. And they would go away, and either kill themselves or marry prettier women who had no desire to change the way they looked, although in the end many of these women would eventually leave for the sanitorium too.
Midnight ...

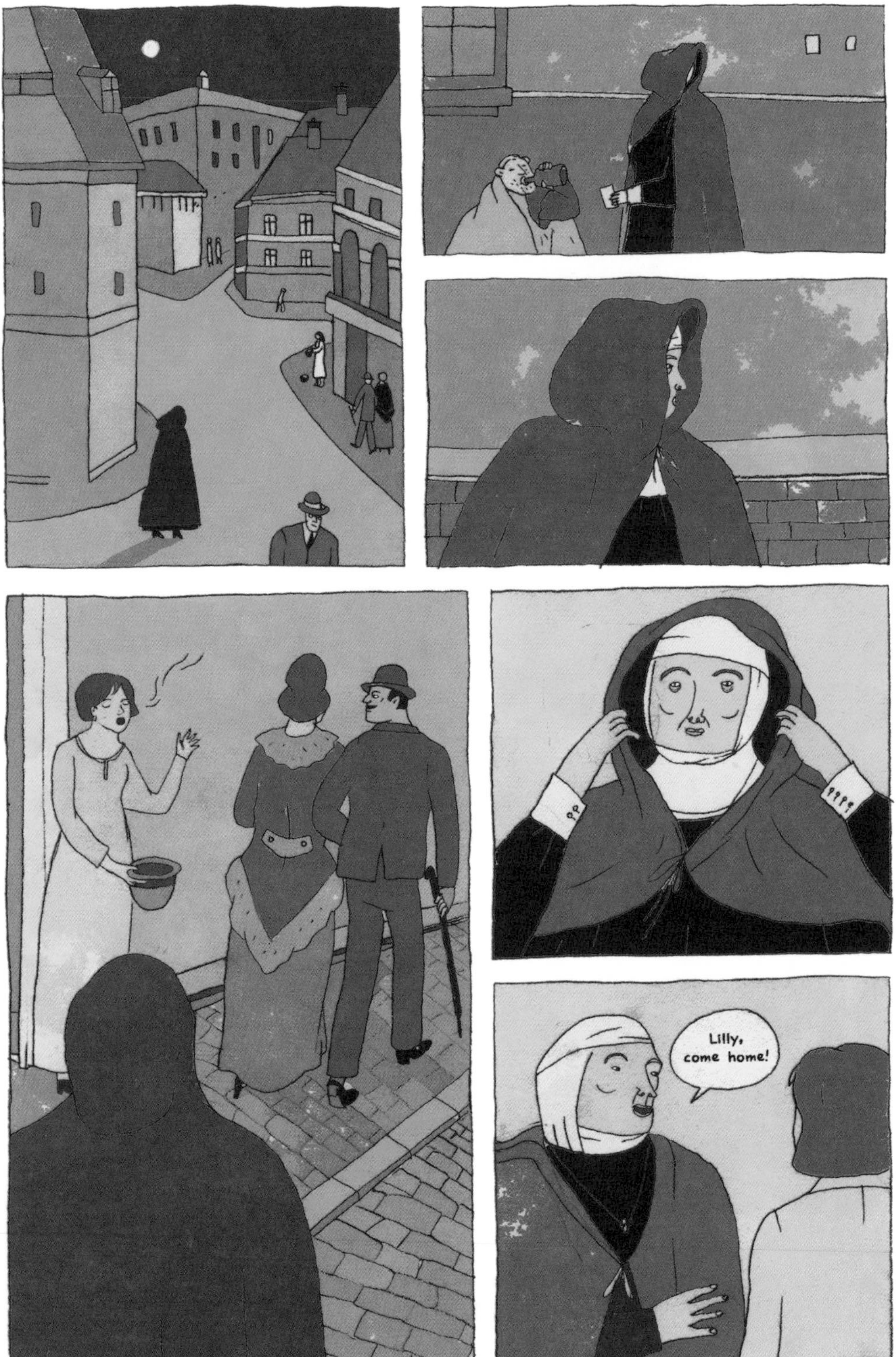
Lilly, come home!

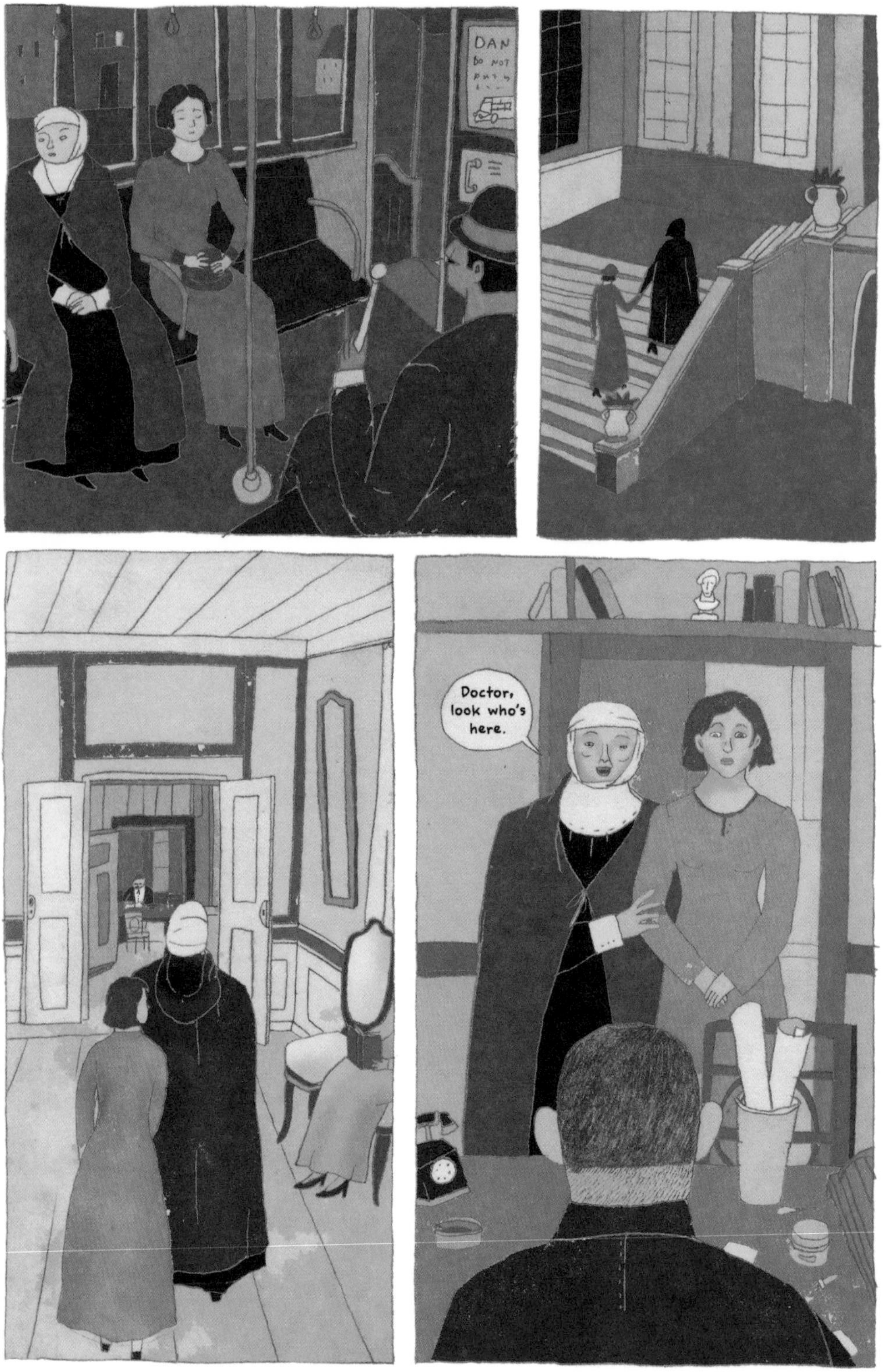
DAN
DO NOT
Doctor, look who's here.

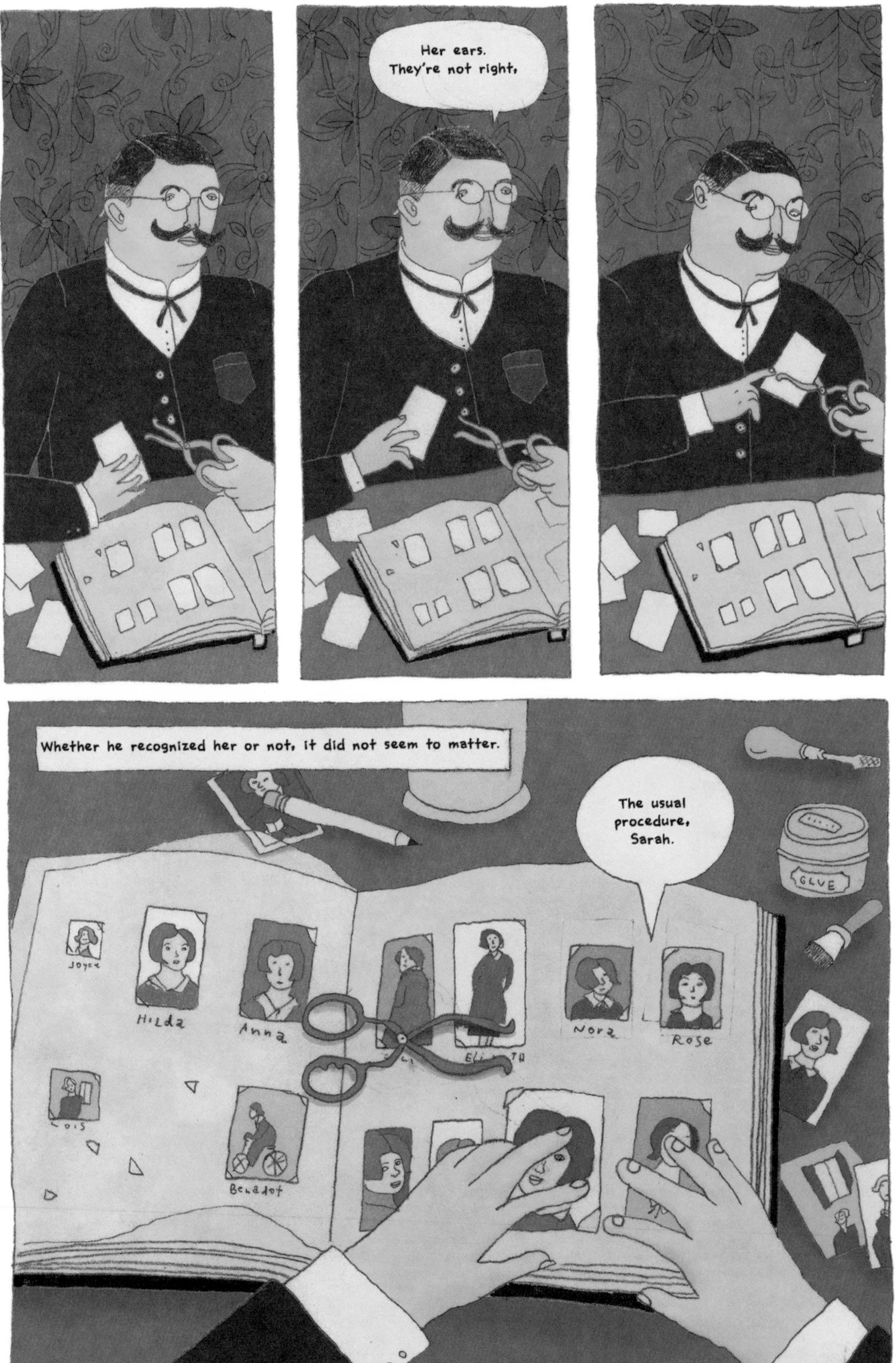
Her ears.
They're not right.
Whether he recognized her or not, it did not seem to matter.
The usual procedure, Sarah.
GLUE
Joyce
Hilda
Anna
Nora
Rose
Lois

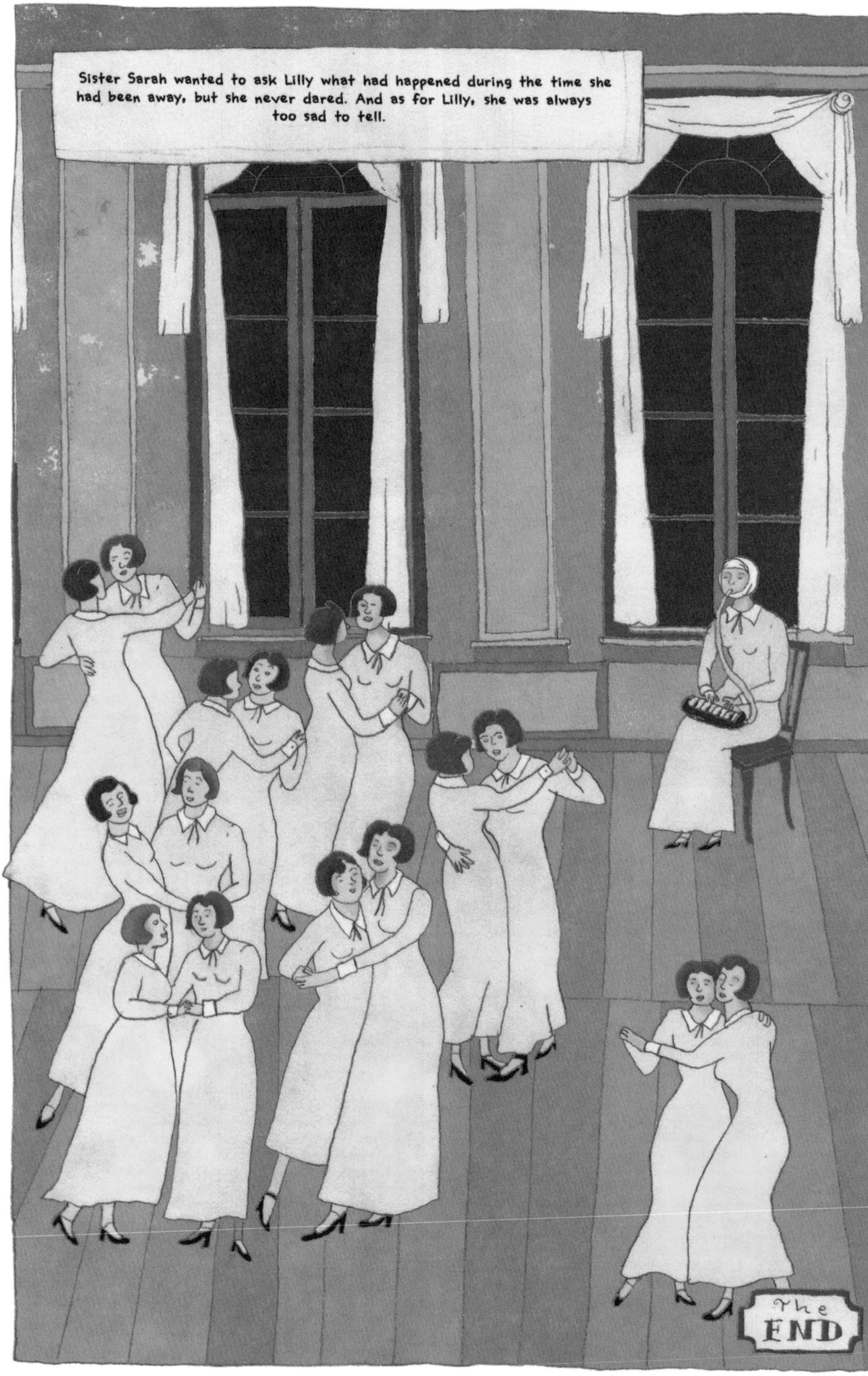
Sister Sarah wanted to ask Lilly what had happened during the time she had been away, but she never dared. And as for Lilly, she was always too sad to tell.
The END

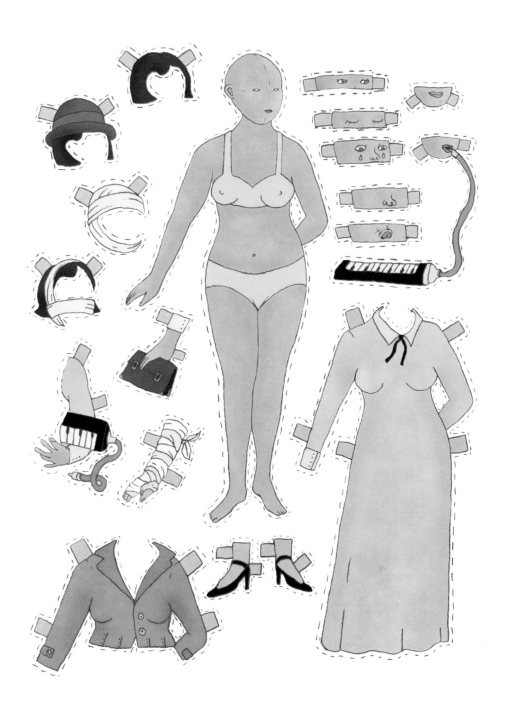

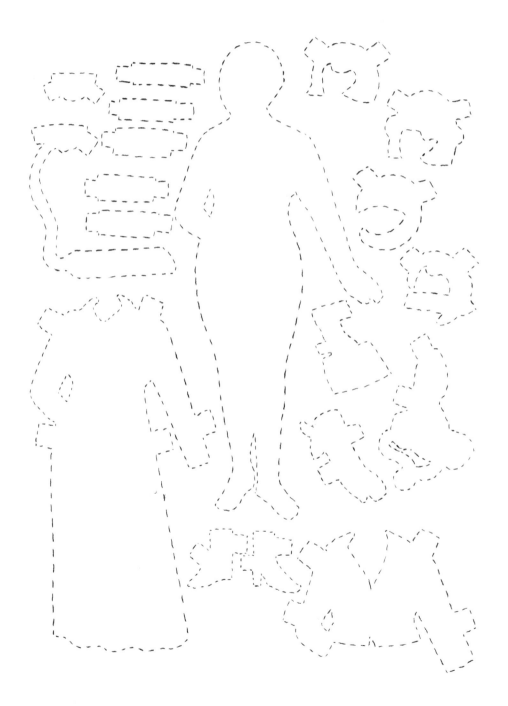

YOUR NUMBER ONE FAN

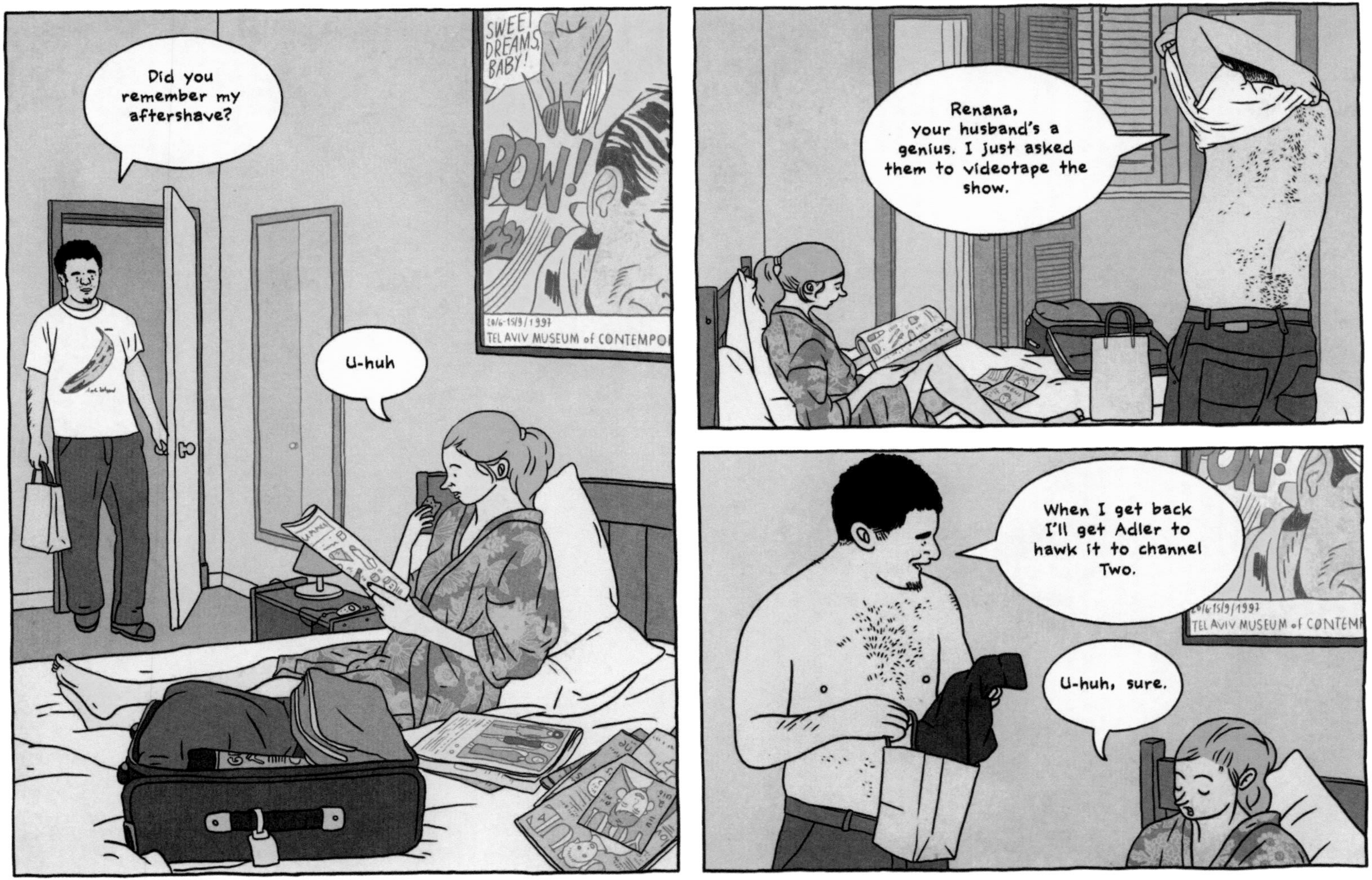
Did you remember my aftershave?
U-huh
SWEET DREAMS, BABY!
POW!
20/6-15/9/1997
TEL AVIV MUSEUM of CONTEMPO
Renana, your husband's a genius. I just asked them to videotape the show.
When I get back I'll get Adler to hawk it to channel Two.
U-huh, sure.

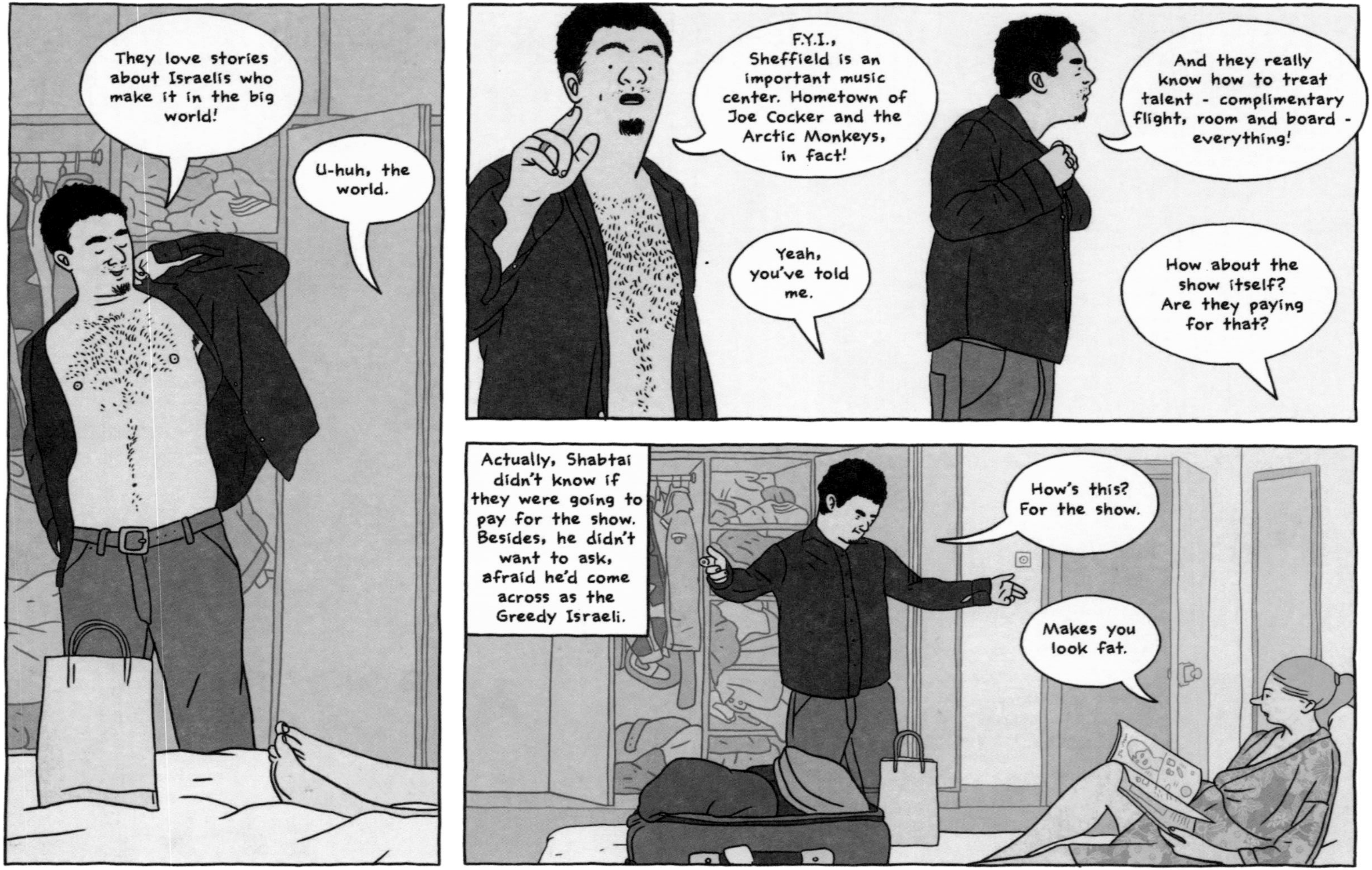
They love stories about Israelis who make it in the big world!
U-huh, the world.
F.Y.I., Sheffield is an important music center. Hometown of Joe Cocker and the Arctic Monkeys, in fact!
Yeah, you've told me.
And they really know how to treat talent - complimentary flight, room and board - everything!
How about the show itself? Are they paying for that?
Actually, Shabtai didn't know if they were going to pay for the show. Besides, he didn't want to ask, afraid he'd come across as the Greedy Israeli.
How's this? For the show.
Makes you look fat.

Two years ago, Shabtai took time off from copywriting at the ad agency to cut his own disc.

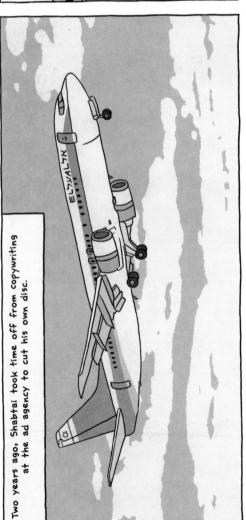

It was seriously better than the usual schlock released in Isreal, but sold hardly a hundred copies.

He sent his EP to some foreign agents he'd found on the net, but none of them called back, and Renana was really starting to bask in it. Then Jackie Seligman called.

And of course it wasn't aired - local DJ's are infamous for their provinciality, they can't stand anybody who challenges the market. Who needs them?

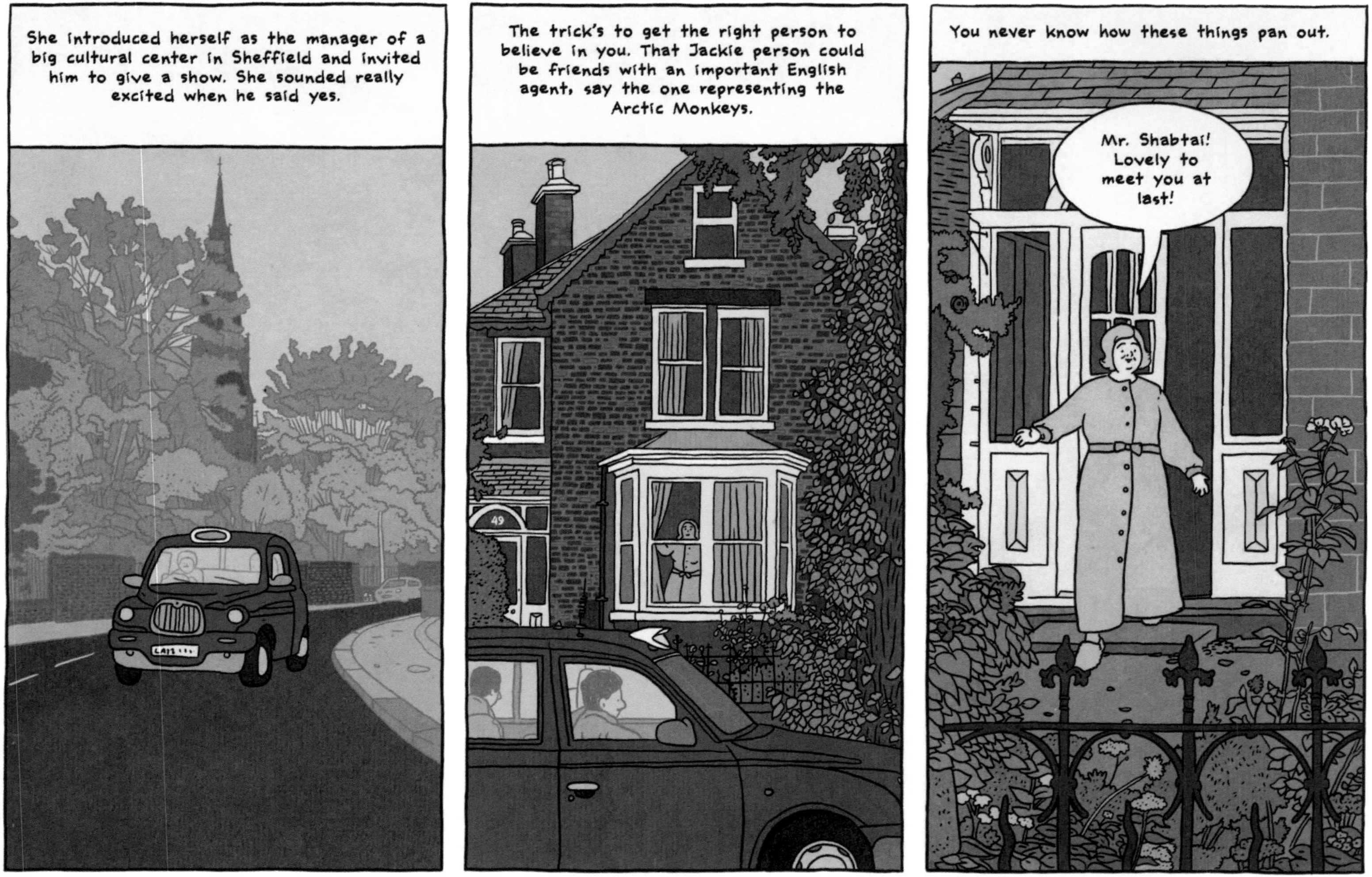
She introduced herself as the manager of a big cultural center in Sheffield and invited him to give a show. She sounded really excited when he said yes.
The trick's to get the right person to believe in you. That Jackie person could be friends with an important English agent, say the one representing the Arctic Monkeys.
49
You never know how these things pan out.
Mr. Shabtai! Lovely to meet you at last!

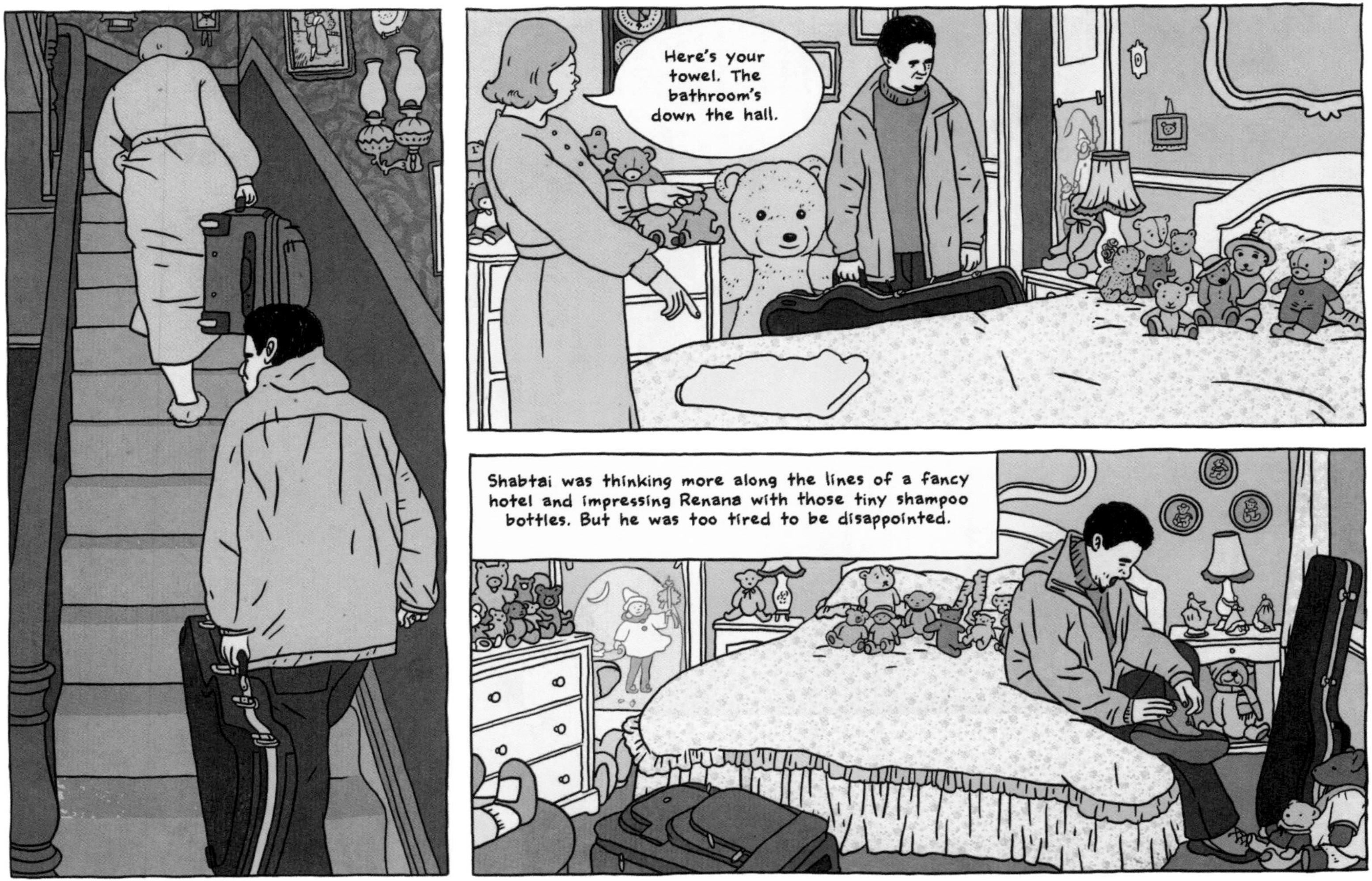
Here's your towel. The bathroom's down the hall.
Shabtai was thinking more along the lines of a fancy hotel and impressing Renana with those tiny shampoo bottles. But he was too tired to be disappointed.

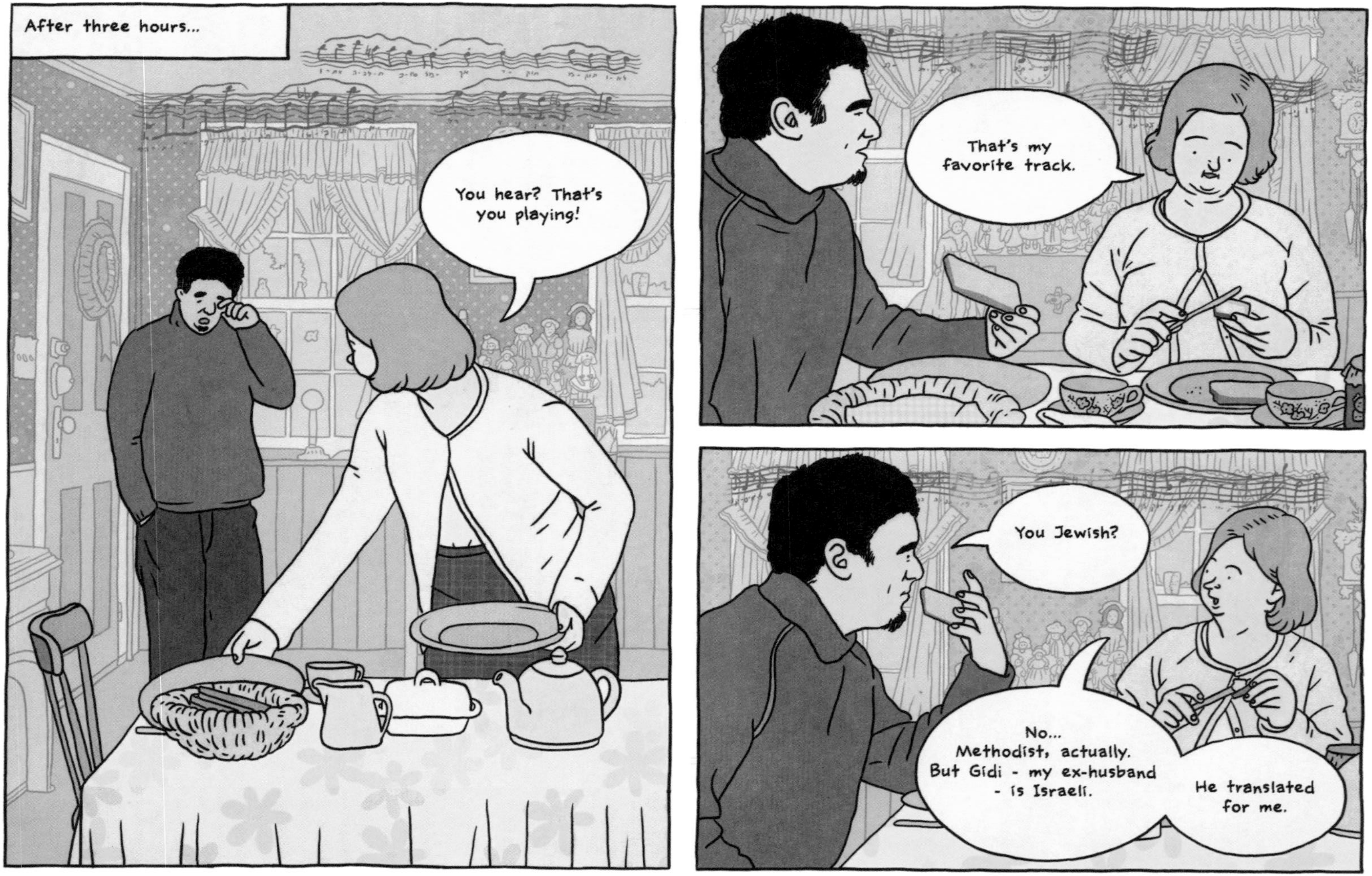
After three hours...
You hear? That's you playing!
That's my favorite track.
You Jewish?
No... Methodist, actually. But Gidi - my ex-husband - is Israeli.
He translated for me.

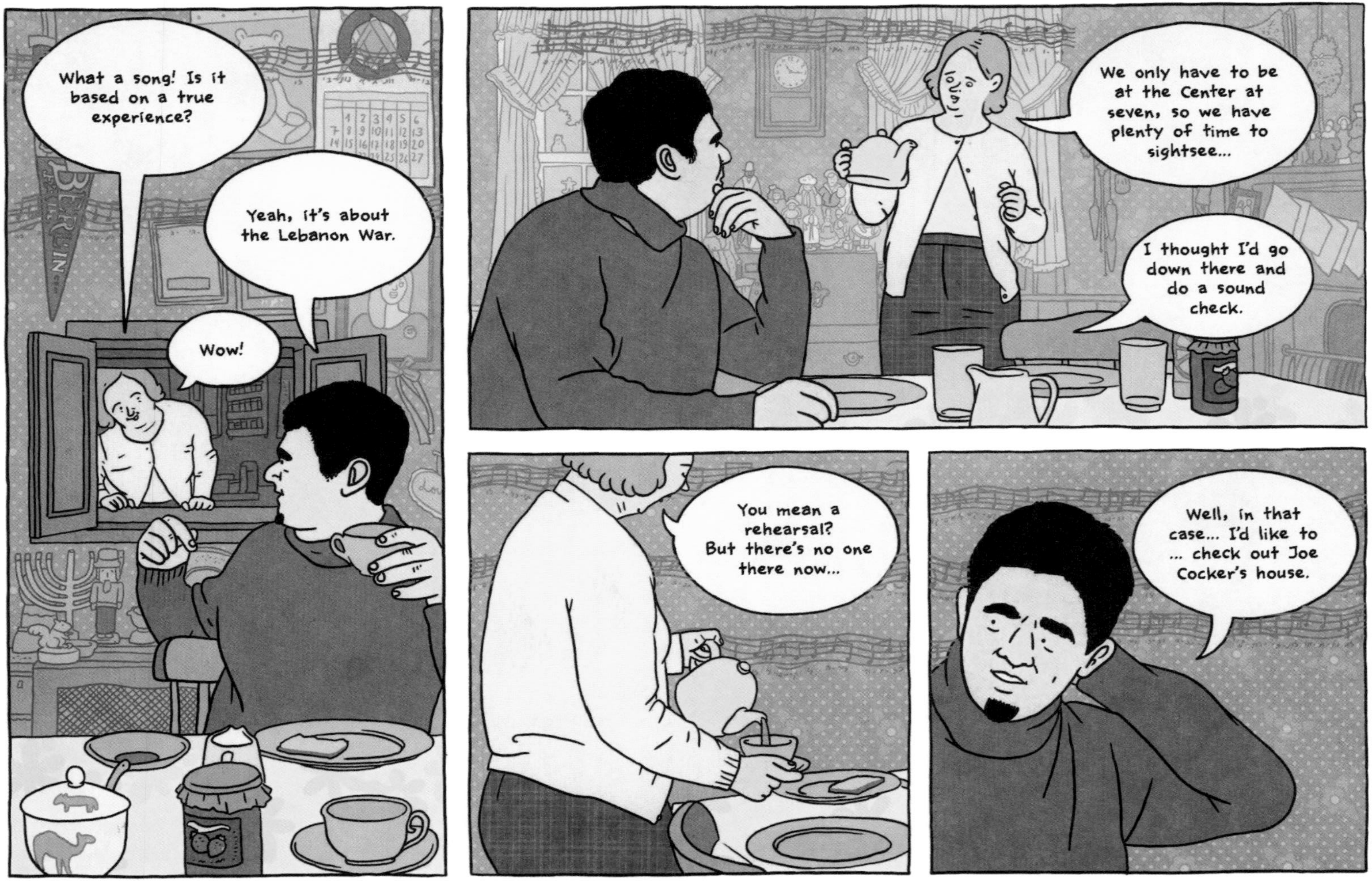
What a song! Is it based on a true experience?
Yeah, it's about the Lebanon War.
Wow!
BERLIN
We only have to be at the Center at seven, so we have plenty of time to sightsee...
I thought I'd go down there and do a sound check.
You mean a rehearsal? But there's no one there now...
Well, in that case... I'd like to ... check out Joe Cocker's house.

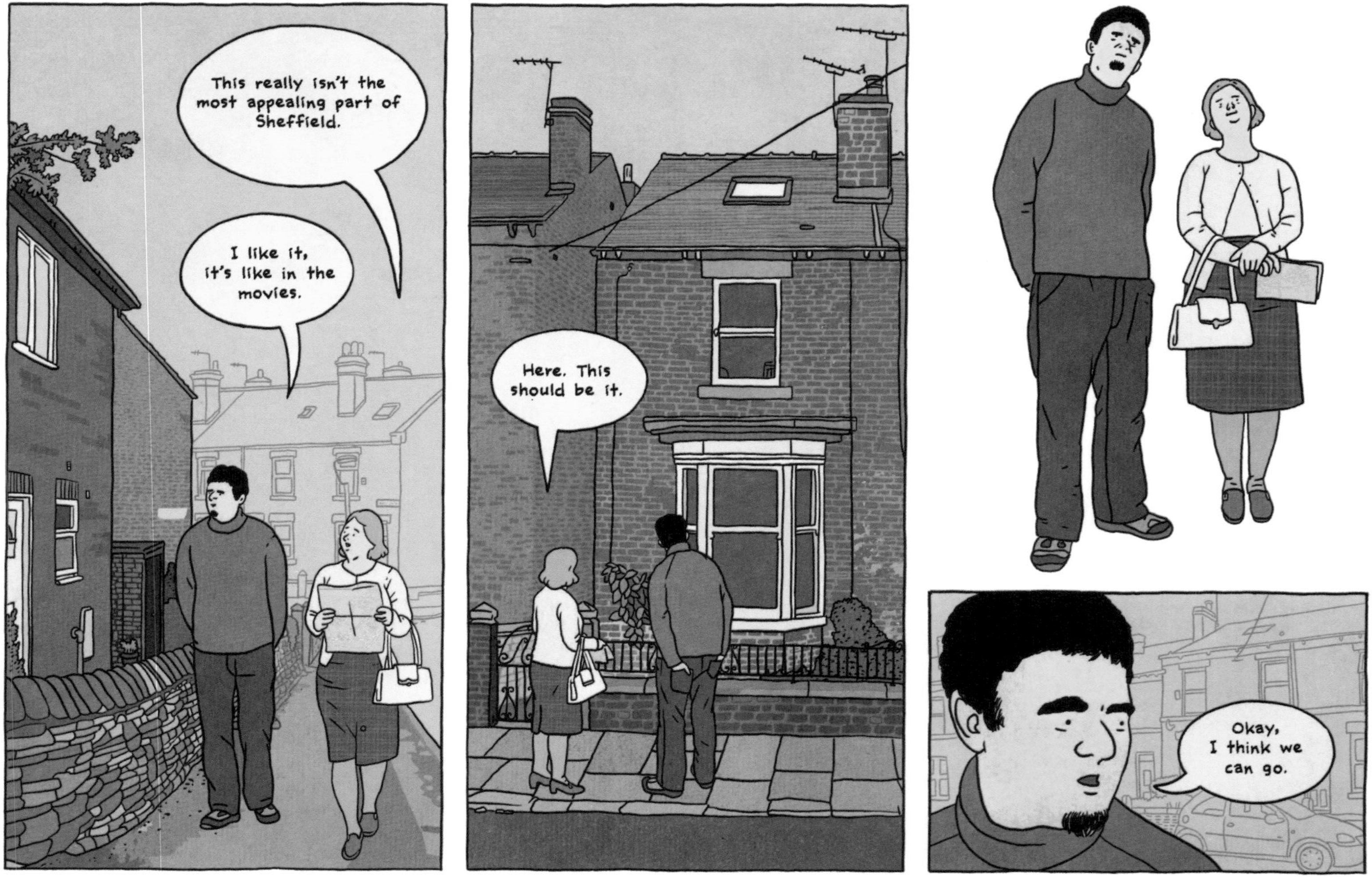
This really isn't the most appealing part of Sheffield.
I like it, it's like in the movies.
Here. This should be it.
Okay, I think we can go.

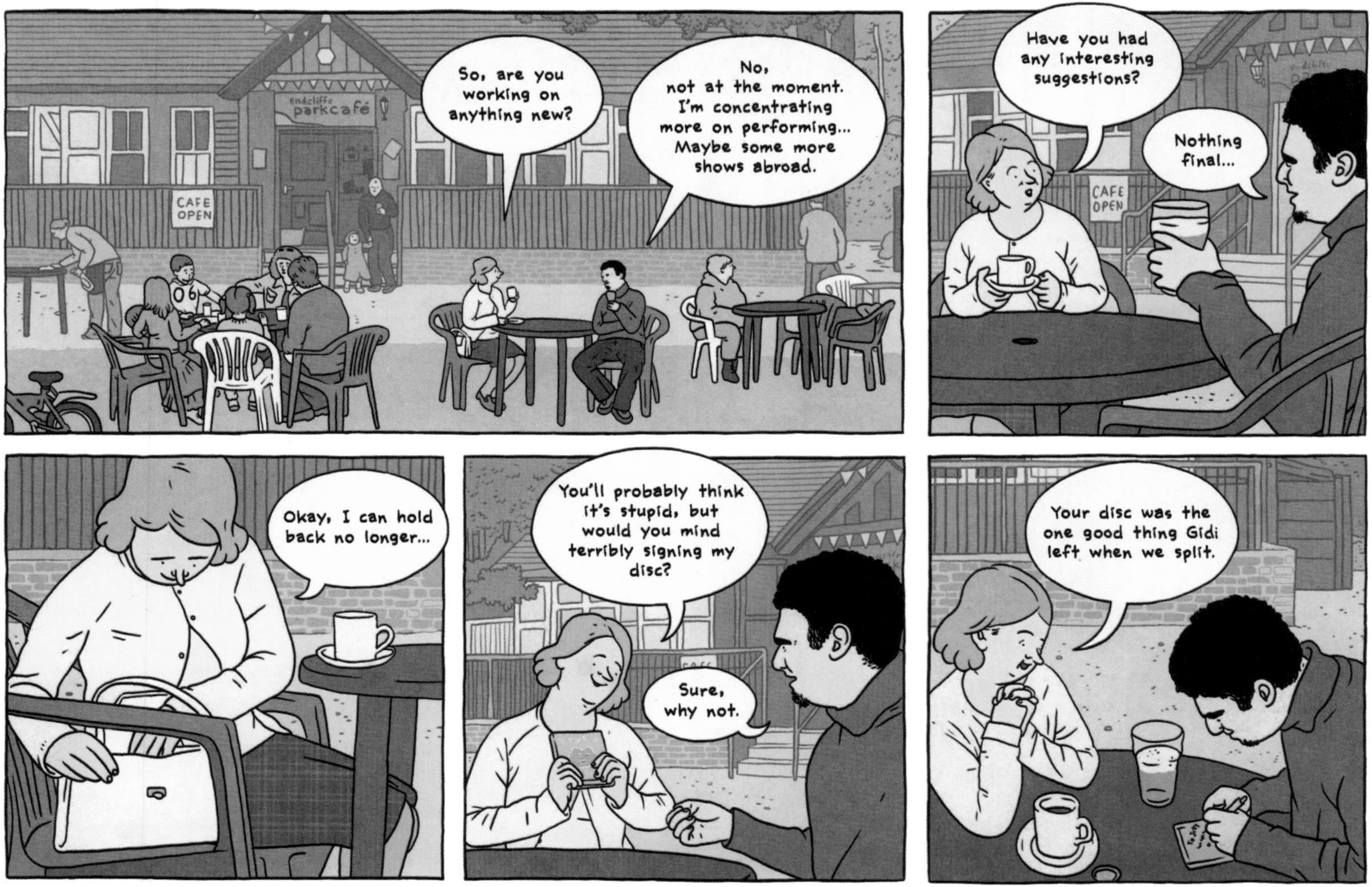
endcliffe parkcafé
CAFE OPEN
So, are you working on anything new?
No, not at the moment. I'm concentrating more on performing... Maybe some more shows abroad.
Have you had any interesting suggestions?
Nothing final...
Okay, I can hold back no longer...
You'll probably think it's stupid, but would you mind terribly signing my disc?
Sure, why not.
Your disc was the one good thing Gidi left when we split.

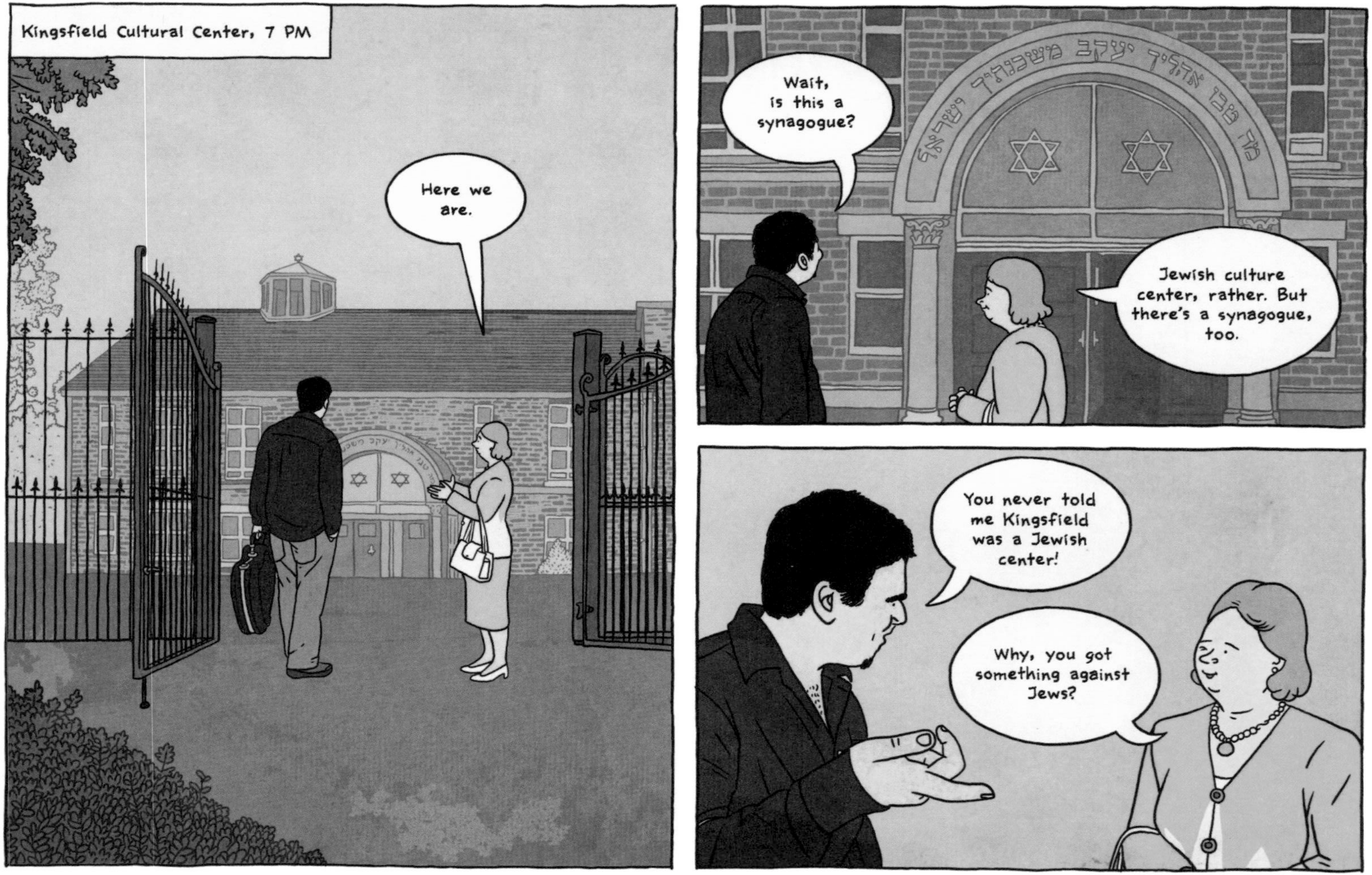
Kingsfield Cultural Center, 7 PM
Here we are.
Wait, is this a synagogue?
Jewish culture center, rather. But there's a synagogue, too.
You never told me Kingsfield was a Jewish center!
Why, you got something against Jews?

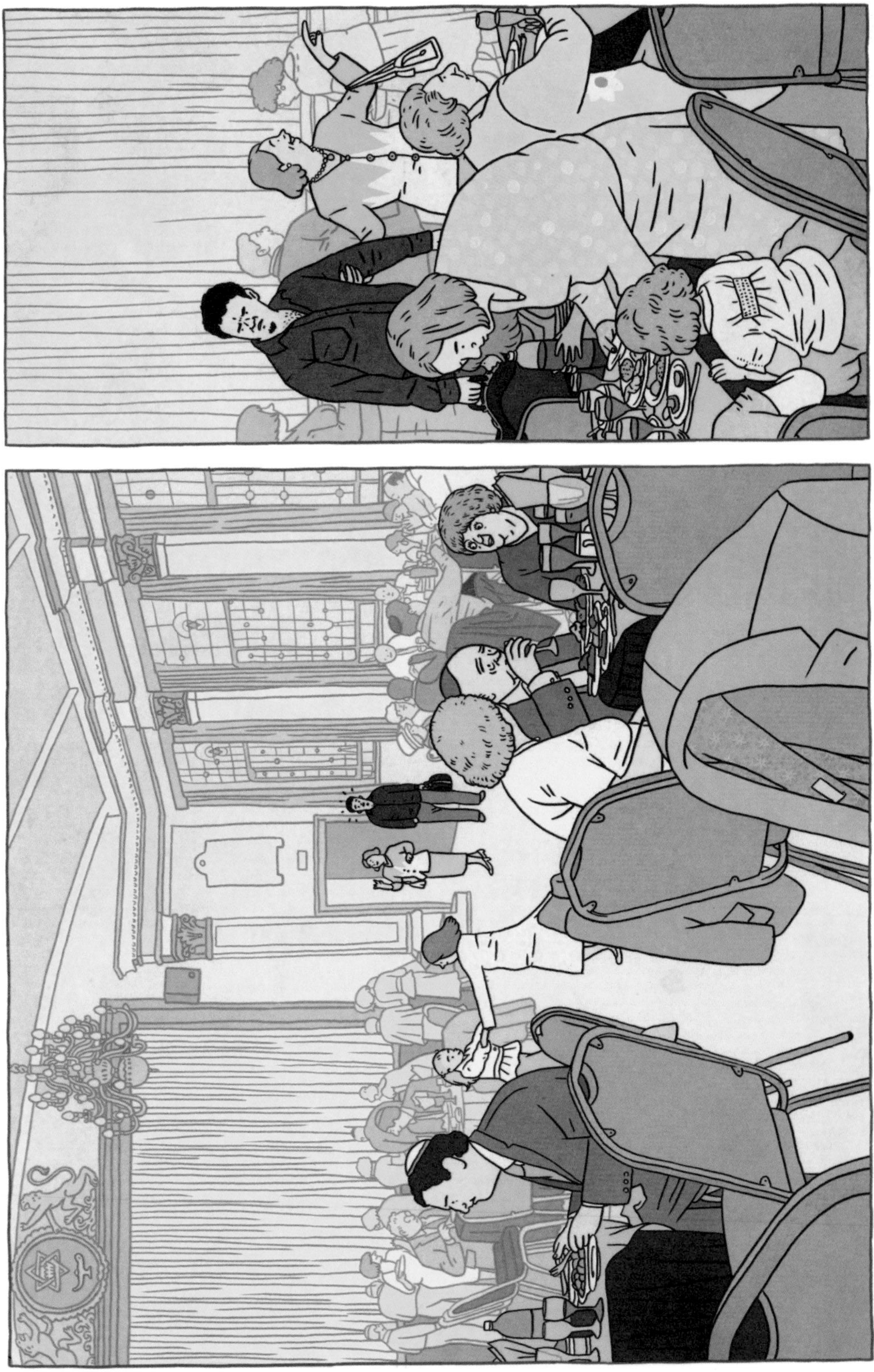

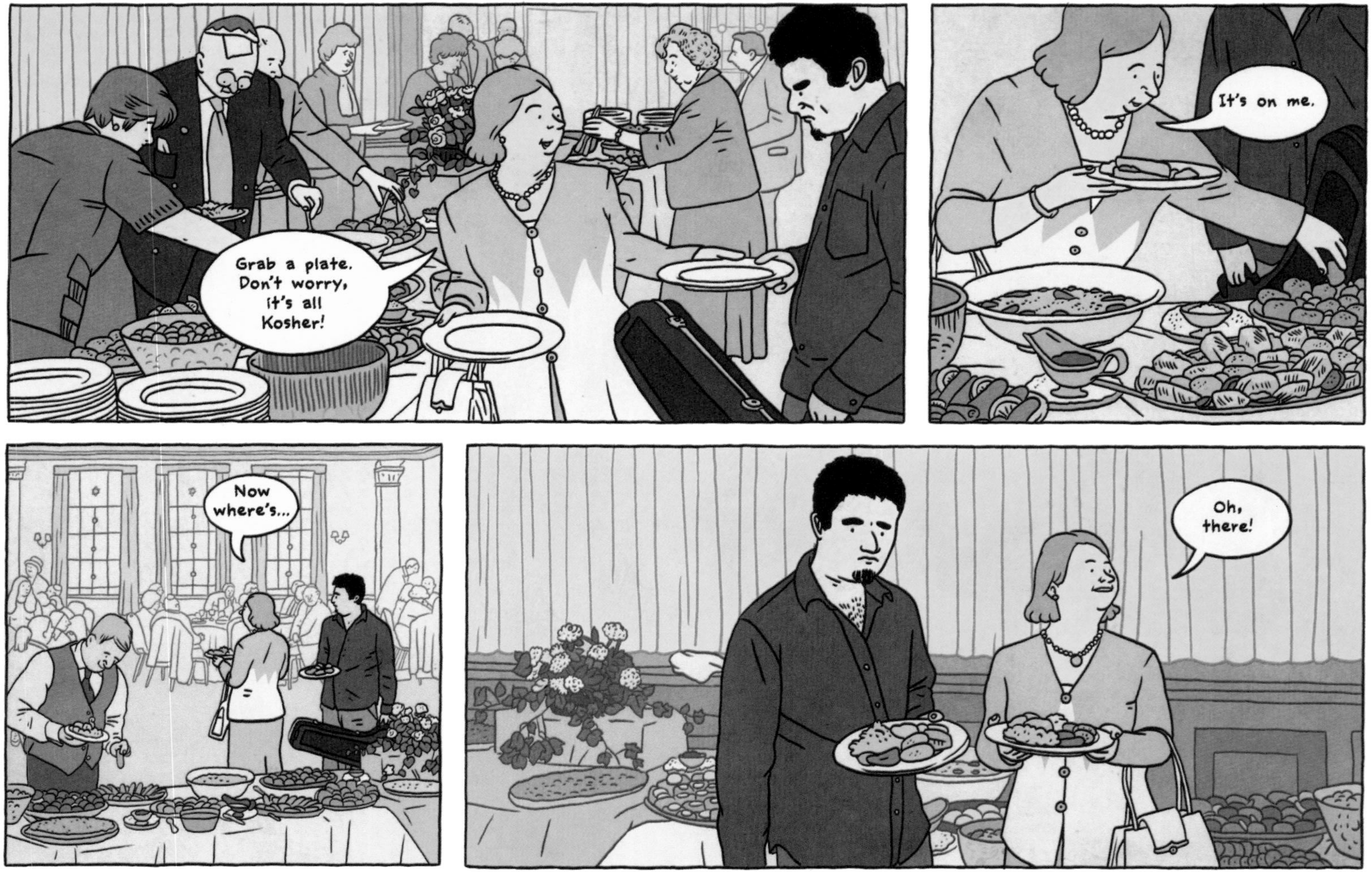
Grab a plate. Don't worry, it's all Kosher!
It's on me.
Now where's...
Oh, there!

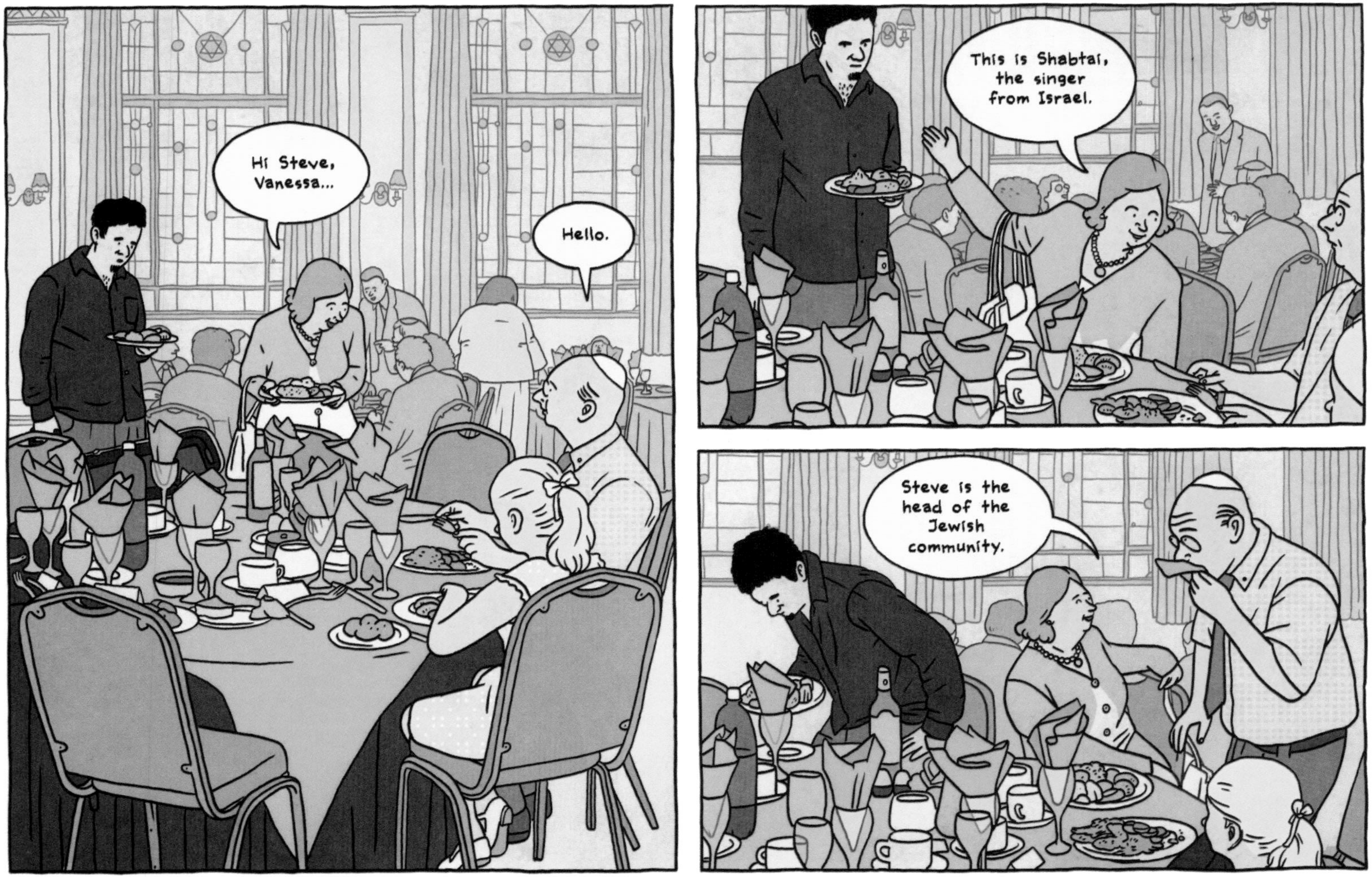
Hi Steve, Vanessa...
Hello.
This is Shabtai, the singer from Israel.
Steve is the head of the Jewish community.

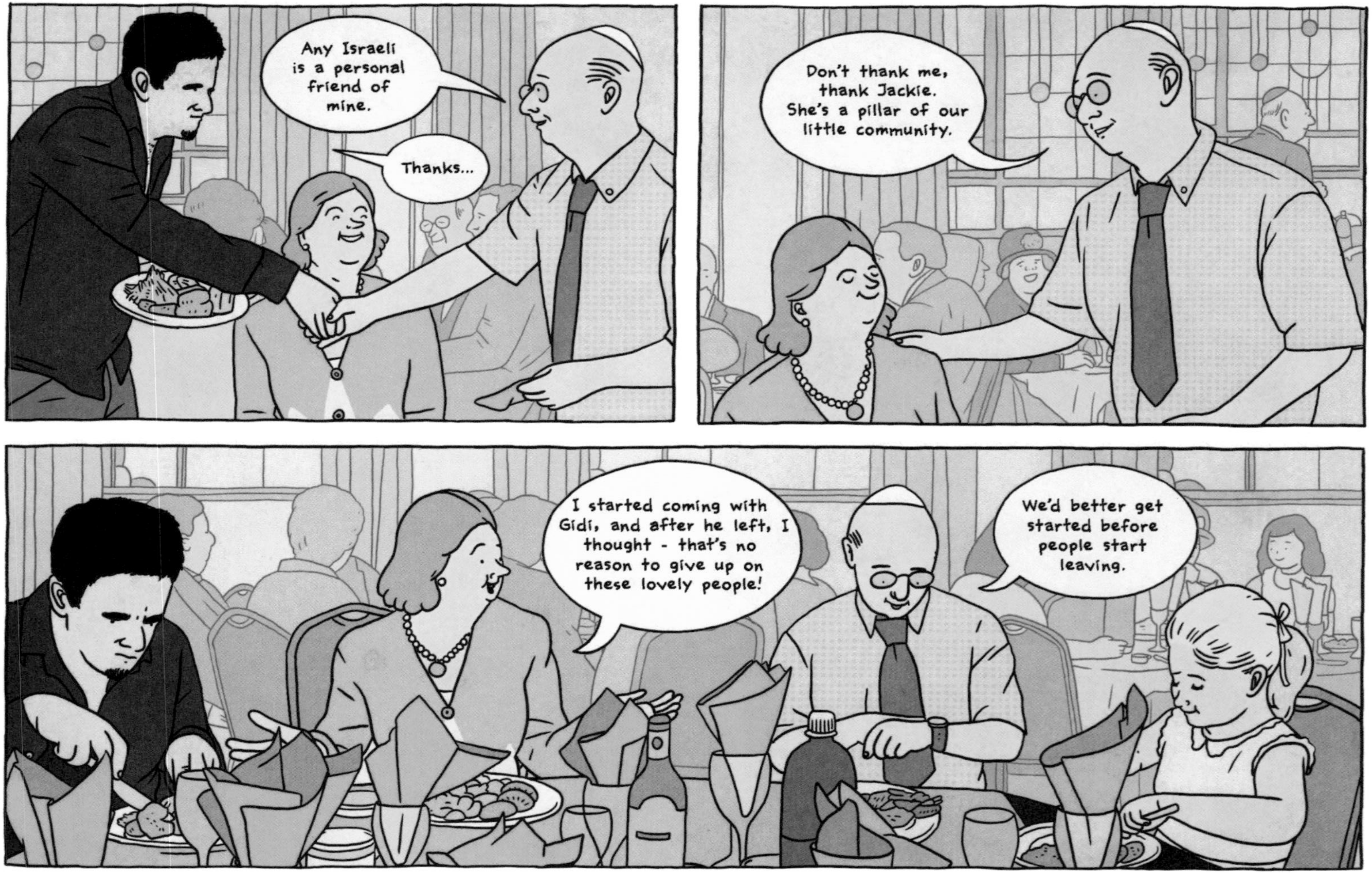
Any Israeli is a personal friend of mine.
Thanks...
Don't thank me, thank Jackie. She's a pillar of our little community.
I started coming with Gidi, and after he left, I thought - that's no reason to give up on these lovely people!
We'd better get started before people start leaving.

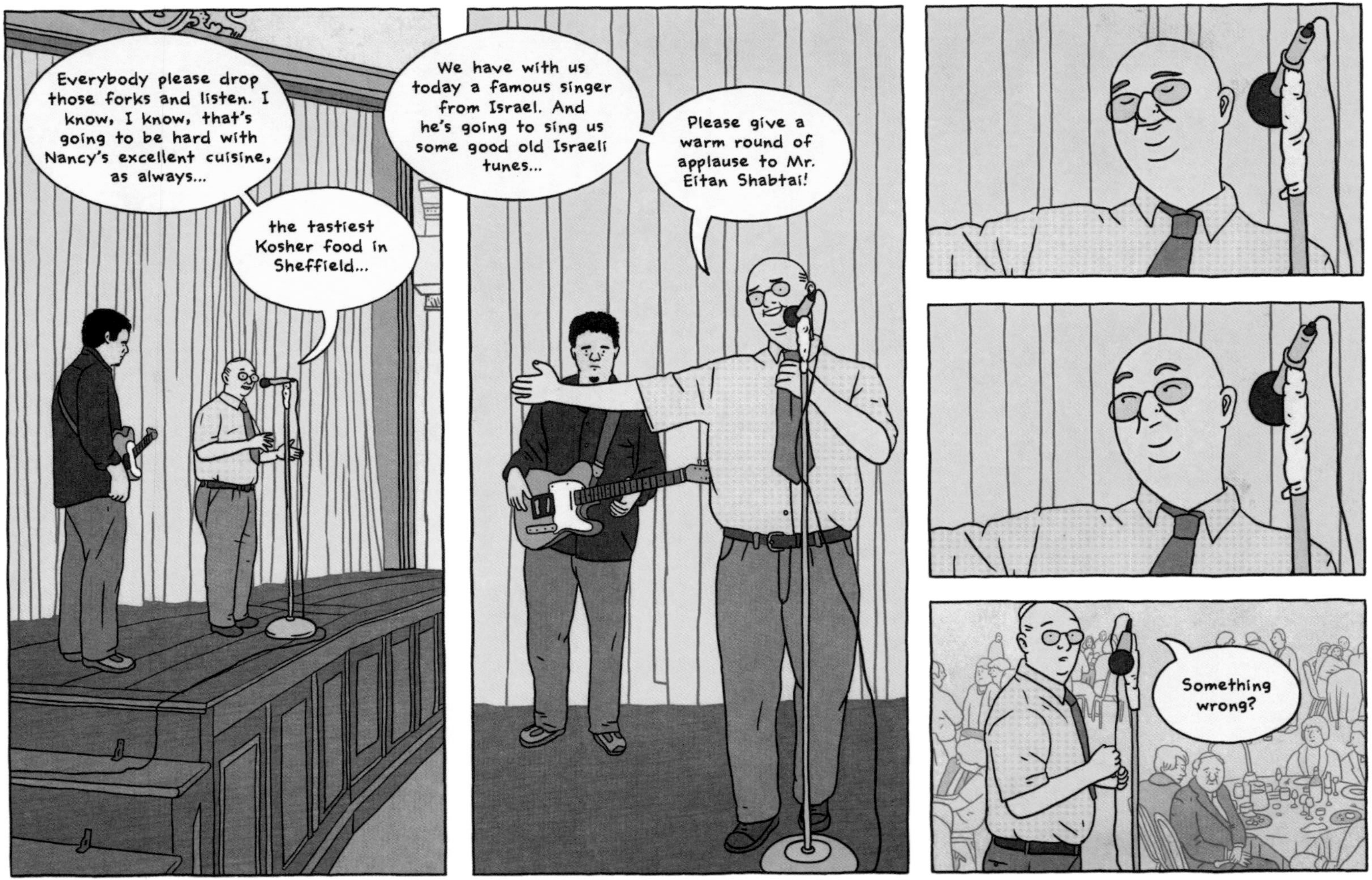

Everybody please drop those forks and listen. I know, I know, that's going to be hard with Nancy's excellent cuisine, as always...
the tastiest Kosher food in Sheffield...
We have with us today a famous singer from Israel. And he's going to sing us some good old Israeli tunes...
Please give a warm round of applause to Mr. Eitan Shabtai!
Something wrong?

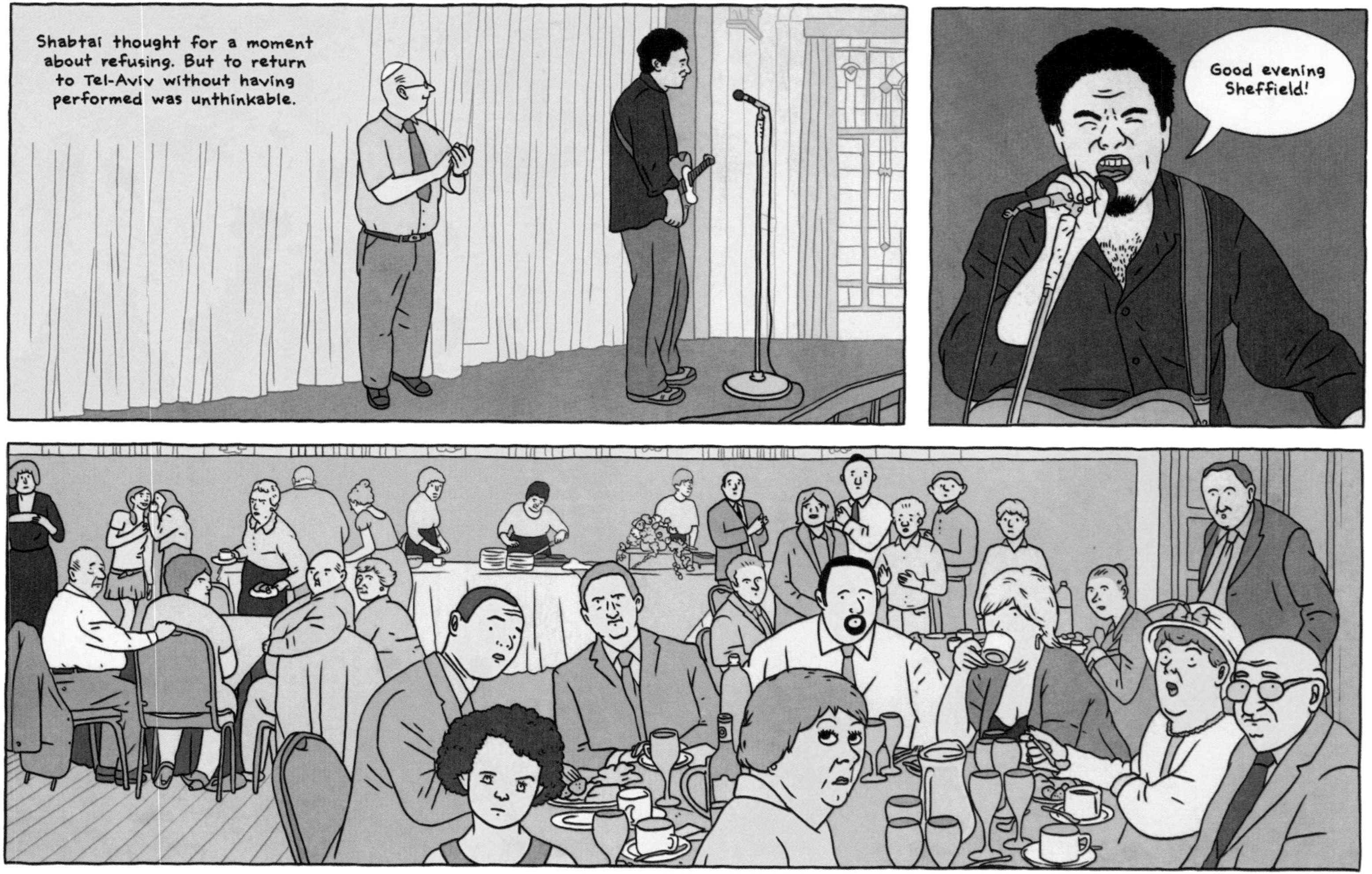
Shabtai thought for a moment about refusing. But to return to Tel-Aviv without having performed was unthinkable.
Good evening Sheffield!

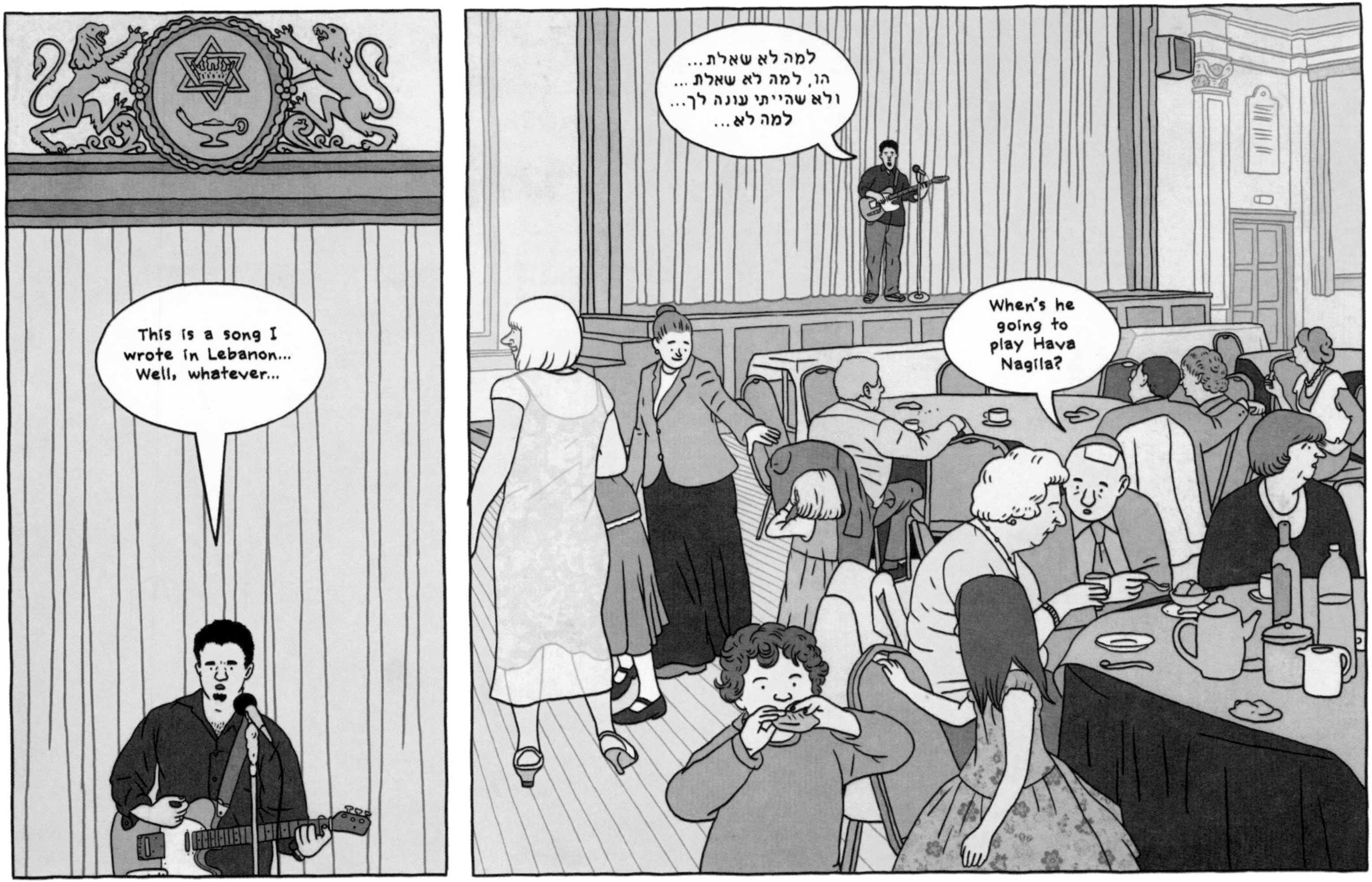
This is a song I wrote in Lebanon... Well, whatever...
למה לא שאלת...
הו, למה לא שאלת...
ולא שהייתי עונה לך...
למה לא...
When's he going to play Hava Nagila?

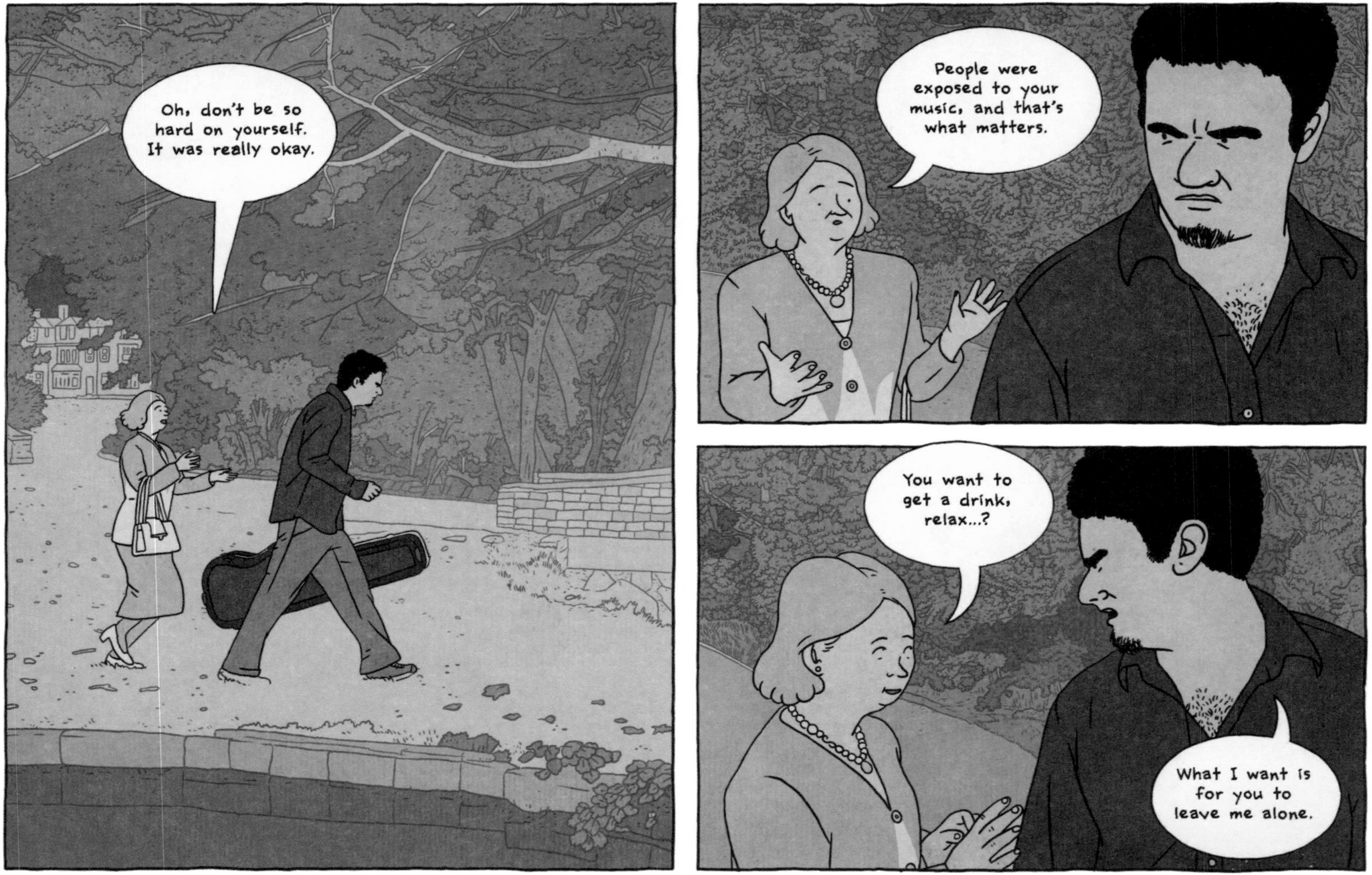
Oh, don't be so hard on yourself. It was really okay.
People were exposed to your music, and that's what matters.
You want to get a drink, relax...?
What I want is for you to leave me alone.

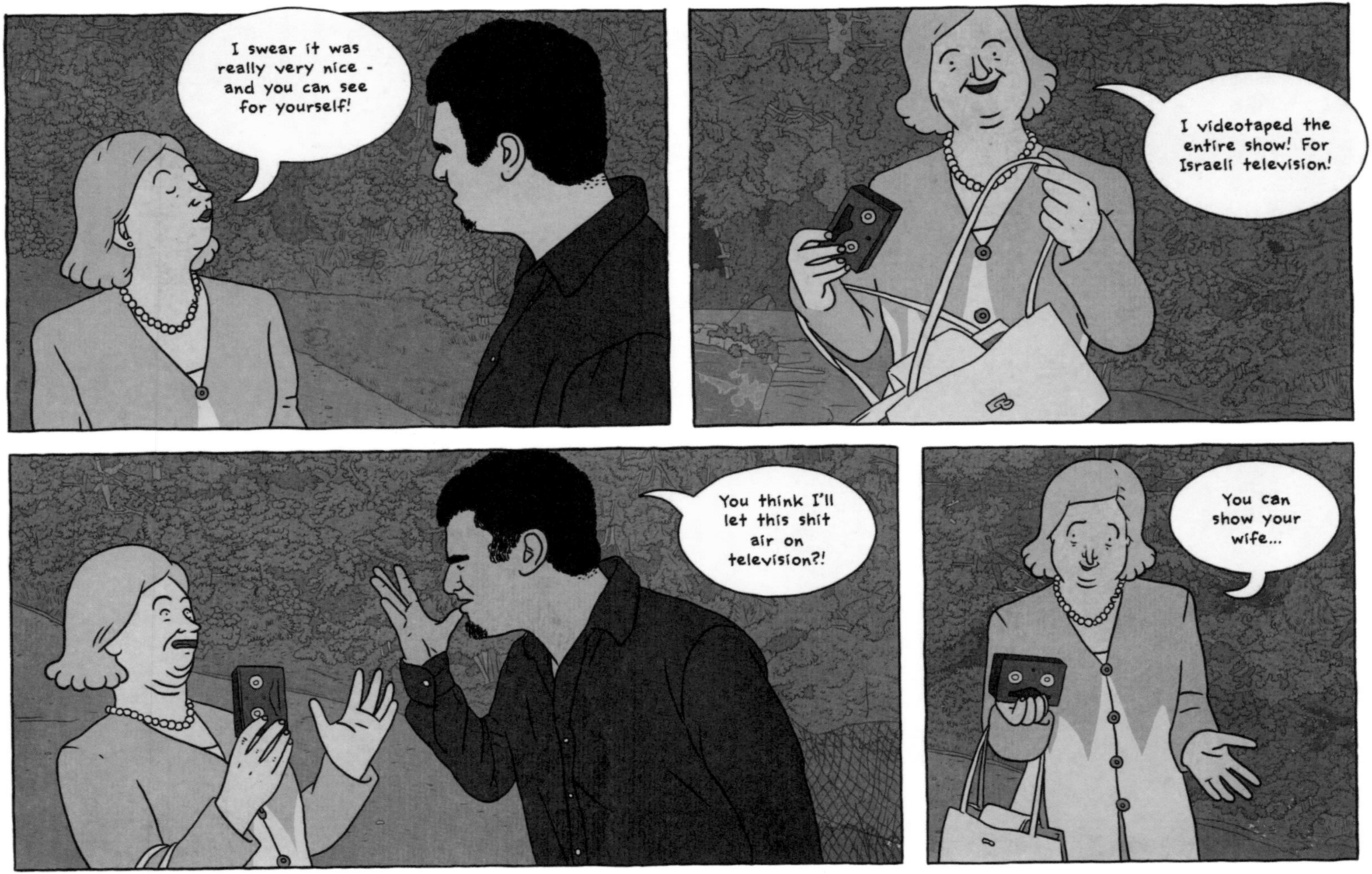
I swear it was really very nice - and you can see for yourself!
I videotaped the entire show! For Israeli television!
You think I'll let this shit air on television?!
You can show your wife...

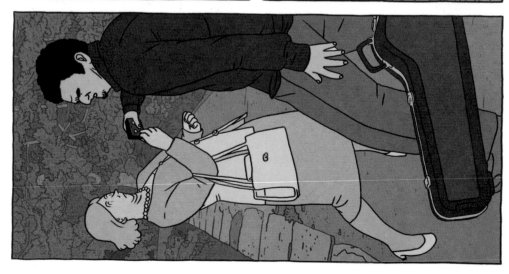

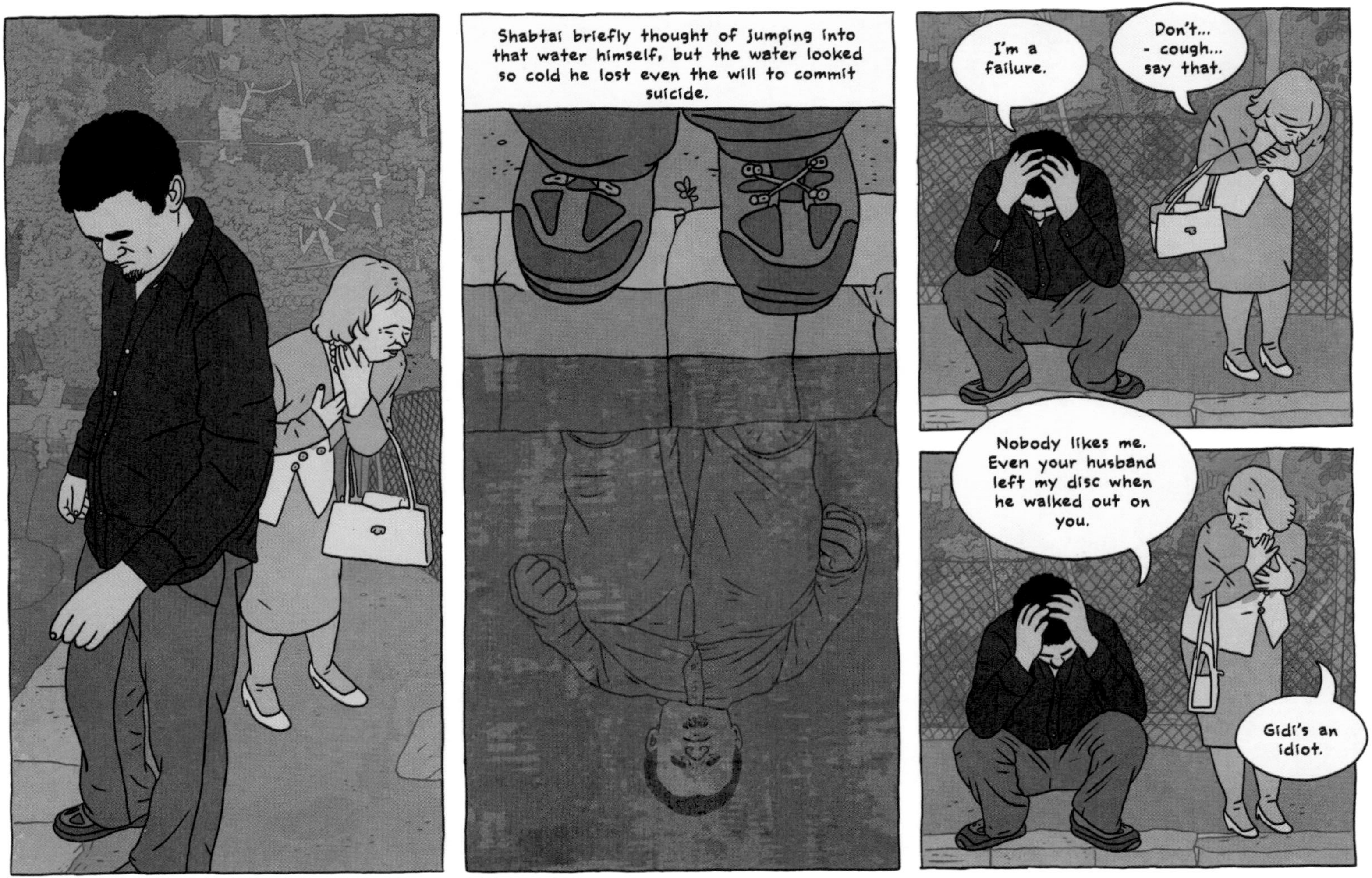

Shabtai briefly thought of jumping into that water himself, but the water looked so cold he lost even the will to commit suicide.
I'm a failure.
Don't... - cough... say that.
Nobody likes me. Even your husband left my disc when he walked out on you.
Gidi's an idiot.

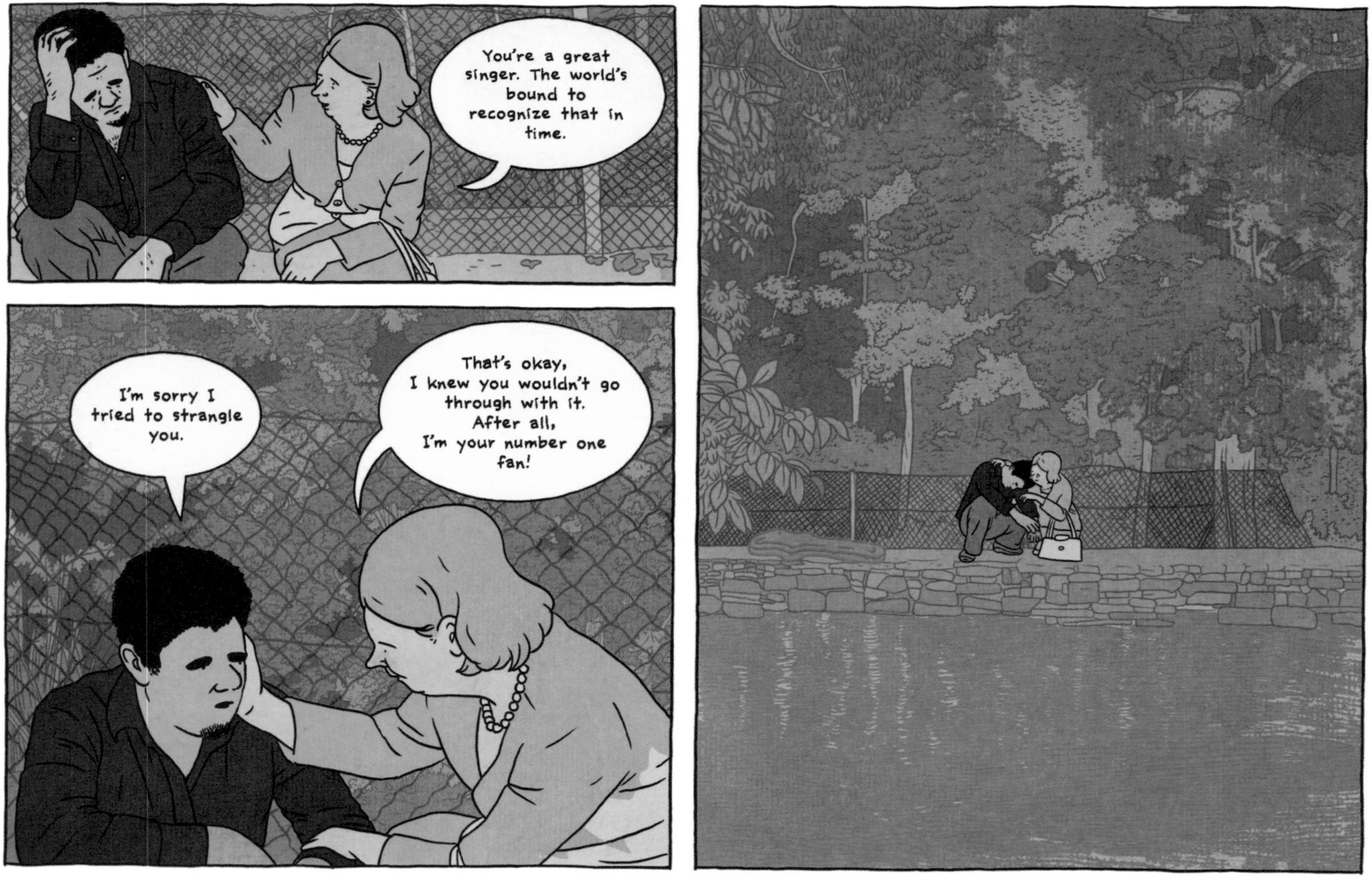
You're a great singer. The world's bound to recognize that in time.
I'm sorry I tried to strangle you.
That's okay, I knew you wouldn't go through with it. After all, I'm your number one fan!

Author's Note

The stories in the collection were written between 1998–2007. The oldest one is "King of the Lillies." At the time, I still believed that only in far away places and times—like Sweden of the early 20th century—could crazy stories happen.

"Bygone" was written a year afterwards—my first story set in Israel, but it was only in "Homecoming" (2002) that I was able to use what is unique to the Israeli reality, which led to "Jamilti" (2003) and later on to *Exit Wounds*.

It was a process of development, both artistic and personal, to realize that real life is bizarre and grotesque enough to base a story upon, and this insight/understanding affected the style of the drawings as well.

Most of the stories have some issue around old family photos. I have an obsession for family photos as objects as much as I have for families as a subject. The photograph focuses on a moment in life but hides a bigger issue, which is much the same as making a comic. Besides, it is really fun to draw from old photos.

All the stories (except "Jamilti," which first appeared in *Drawn & Quarterly* volume 5) were published originally by Actus independent Comics. I want to thank my colleagues and friends in the Actus collective—Yirmi Pinkus, Batia Kolton, Mira Friedmann and Itzik Rennert—for their support and help in creating these stories.